# COAL, WAR & LOVE

*A Novel*

## RUDEAN LEINAENG

ISBN: 978-1-54397-339-6 (paperback)
ISBN: 978-1-54397-340-2 (ebook)

Printed in the United States of America.
First printing edition 2019

This book is a work of fiction. With the exception of Albert Sidney Johnson, Sr. and wife Evelyn Ashton Johnson, their immediate family members, as well as certain historical figures and events, any references to real people, living or dead, or real places, are used fictitiously and are products of the author's imagination.

Title of Cover: Colored Man Is No Slacker
Creator: Renesch, E. G. (Edward George), born 1879, artist
Date Created/Published: Chicago, IL: [Publisher not identified], [1918]
Repository: Library of Congress Prints and Photographs Division, Washington, D.C. 20540 USA
http://hdl.loc.gov/loc.pnp/pp.print

Photos courtesy of Thomas Allen Harris and Harold Epps
Author's photo by Lyle Ashton Harris and Briscoe Savoy

Tulipbud Press
Bronx, New York
www.tulipbudpress.com
rudeanleinaeng@gmail.com

O, yes,

I say it plain,

America never was America to me,

And yet I swear this oath—

America will be!

From: "Let America be America Again"

*A Poem by Langston Hughes, 1935*


To my grandfather, Albert Sidney Johnson, Sr., the dreamer, who risked life and limb in the war to achieve the dream.

To my grandmother, Evelyn Ashton Johnson, the romantic, who held down the home front and saved the dream.

To my mother, Joella Alston Johnson, the encourager, who–through love, understanding, and acceptance–enhanced the dream.

And, to my father, Albert Sidney Johnson, Jr., the chronicler, who–through faith and perseverance–fulfilled the dream and loved to tell the tale.

# CONTENTS

# PART TWO ............................................................................... 159

# PART ONE

# CHAPTER 1

## *Albert – 1909*

⁓⁓⁓⁓

I awoke in a sweat at five that morning in one of the ship's small cabins. I had dreamt of Pa again–his angry, distorted face, demanding complete and unquestioned obedience, my eleven-year-old frame mirroring a measured defiance, and Ma's quivering lips, silently praying for peace between us. It was the day that Pa pulled me out of school, the day he trampled my dreams.

As I hurriedly dressed for the breakfast service, I tried to shake off the resentment I felt. After all, it had happened nearly twenty years ago. Three hours later, the ship docked in New York and I headed straight for the grim Harlem rooming house I called home. I was dead tired.

I had been in this city for nearly two years, coming from everywhere you can imagine, and had landed a waiter's job on the People's Nightline Steamer, which plied the Hudson River between New York and Albany carrying both passengers and freight. The pay wasn't much, and I had been laid off during January and February when the river froze over, but it was better than shoveling coal. Anyway, the tips and free meals made it well worth my while. To tell the truth, I was dispirited and tired. I was tired of roaming, tired of living at that dreadful Harlem rooming house, but most of all tired of being alone. Years ago, when I was working at a West Virginia coal mine, an older miner advised me to find a good woman to love. Well, I had traveled clear across this country, around the world in fact, but I still hadn't found her. And I had no idea of what she even looked like.

---

When I reached the rooming house, I went to fetch my uniform from Claudine, the landlady's youngest daughter, who had washed and pressed it. I knocked on her door and when she opened it, she threw me a come-hither look.

"Come on in, Al, and rest a bit."

"I don't have time, now. I just dropped by to pick up my uniform."

"What you always so busy at?" she asked, holding out the clean uniform with one hand and grabbing my sleeve with the other. "One would think you was a big shot or something."

I snatched the uniform, paid her fifteen cents, and scurried down the dimly lit hall to my room. "See you around, Claudine."

She sucked her teeth and slammed the door. Claudine was good-looking and shapely, but she was not the kind of woman I was interested in. So I kept my distance. To me, she spelled trouble, with a capital T.

After sleeping the day away and then eating a meal of collard greens, lima beans and ham hocks at Pete's, a local greasy spoon, I dropped by Bill's Place on Seventh Avenue, the tavern I usually frequented. I hadn't been there for a few weeks.

Bill, the proprietor, and several of the regulars greeted me as I approached the polished wooden bar. "Well if it ain't Mister Al Johnson," Bill shouted. "Where the dickens you been, man?"

"I've been to hell, and back again."

"Well, at least, the devil let you loose," one of the regulars said.

"Yeah. The man was too cool for hell!" another replied. We all laughed.

I pushed my way through the crowd and joined my friend Deek Williams at the bar. He was a sleeping car porter. We would sometimes meet for a drink at the Dockside Tavern in Albany, and I was surprised to see him here in Harlem.

"Yeah, I'm off tonight, but gotta catch a train at Grand Central in the morning."

"I work tomorrow, too. This is my first night off in well over a week."

We bought each other drinks and continued to shoot the breeze. As the night wore on the bar got more congested, and the noise became deafening, with each man trying to out talk, out drink, out lie, and out laugh the other.

About midnight, a fancy lady in a shiny blue dress and dangling rhinestone earrings worked her way up to the bar and stood beside me. Some of the men whistled and made flirty remarks as she passed them by.

Deek looked her over and whispered, "Maybe you'll get lucky tonight."

"Man, she ain't my type," I whispered back. He laughed.

The fancy lady flashed me a bright smile. So I treated her to a drink and we chatted for a while. She looked attractive in the soft glow of gaslight, but as she snuggled closer, I nearly gagged on the scent of her cheap perfume. I inched away.

She reared back and asked, "What's the matter, sweetie? Don't momma look good enough?"

"I have a lady at home."

"Maybe you'd best stay there with her or someone else will." After saying that, she moved on to a slick-looking fellow, who was eyeing her from the end of the bar.

I left the raucous tavern about two in the morning and quickly walked home through the dark streets of Harlem. As I passed by Doyle's Saloon, where the well-to-do and talented Negroes congregated, I heard the muted sounds of ragtime piano. In those days, Harlem had a mixed population of Jews, Italians, Irishmen, and colored folks. It was first opened to Negroes five or six years earlier by the colored real estate agent, Philip Payne, and as colored people moved up from the crowded tenements of Tenderloin and San Juan Hill in lower Manhattan, as well as from the Deep South, whites began moving out. Obviously, each group frequented its own saloons and speakeasies.

The following afternoon I climbed out of bed, reluctant to face another day. My tiny room, with its peeling pea-green walls and threadbare carpet–home to all manner of vermin–was ugly and uninviting. As I stretched out my stiff frame, the smell of stale bacon grease and cabbage from the nearby kitchen assaulted me, so I threw open the window and took a deep breath.

I needed to hurry. I was due at the pier at half past five, and the ferry would push off promptly at seven. It would be another long, tedious night.

The upriver trip went as expected and after the passengers disembarked in Albany early Saturday morning, I cleared the tables, ate breakfast, and took a nap until four. At six thirty that evening, the New York City-bound passengers began to board and the whole routine started again. I waited tables for the festive dinner crowd until ten when the dining room closed for the night.

At five o'clock Sunday morning, I stood alert at my station, waiting to greet the breakfast diners. We would dock in New York in two hours. Then I saw her. She was standing at the dining room entrance wearing a green satin gown with a matching shawl loosely draped about her shoulders. Her small hands were encased in spotless white gloves, gray pearls adorned her ears, and a black velvet ribbon encircled her neck. She was my dream come true with deep bronze skin, soft as down, almond-shaped eyes, pink-blushed lips, and high-boned cheeks. Accompanying her was an attractive, conservatively dressed, older woman, perhaps an aunt or a sister. I hurried over and escorted them to a small table in the corner and waited while they decided on their order. When she looked up, with her soft brown eyes, and fluttered her long eyelashes, I felt a disturbing tremor.

"Can I help you young ladies, this morning?"

"Yes, I'll have a cup of tea with toast," she said, smiling sweetly.

"How about you, Jennie?" she asked, glancing over at her older companion.

"I'll have the same and a fried egg as well. Evie, why don't you take an egg, too? My goodness, you eat just like a bird."

*Evie! Her name is Evie*, I thought, as I caught a whiff of her delicate passionflower perfume.

"No thanks, Jennie. I just want tea and toast this morning."

"Well, I certainly hope you don't waste away."

"My dear, let's not quarrel," she said, patting her companion's gloved hand.

"Jam and butter?" I asked, trying to recapture Evie's attention.

"Yes, that would be lovely."

I brought their order along with a dish of butter, an assortment of jams, a jug of hot milk, and a bowl of sugar. After I poured the tea, I had no excuse to remain at their table any longer. Besides, other patrons were trying to catch my attention.

"I hope you enjoy your breakfast," I said as I walked away. They smiled and nodded.

I waited on the other patrons, but I watched Evie. I watched as she buttered each slice of toast and spread it thick with jam. I watched as she cut each slice into four pieces and delicately bit into each one. I watched as she licked traces of jam off her lips and dabbed her mouth with the white cloth napkin. I watched as she put three cubes of sugar and a bit of milk into the flowered teacup, lifted it to her lips, and sipped the tea. When they had finished eating, they asked for the check. Evie opened her green satin purse and paid the bill, leaving me a whole dime for a tip. Jennie, on the other hand, threw me a withering look. She must have noticed me watching Evie.

A half an hour later the ship docked in New York. I was still attired in my white waiter's jacket when I left the dining room and raced to where the passengers were disembarking. There were Evie and Jennie, chatting merrily and lifting their long skirts as they descended the ship's ramp. I watched her and felt a deep stirring in my chest. It was as if my senses were awakening and my inner walls of indifference and dissatisfaction were crumbling. She skipped off the ramp and by chance dropped her green purse. When she bent down to retrieve it, she glanced over her shoulder and for a glorious second our eyes met. Then she smiled at me. Seeing this, the ever-vigilant Jennie clutched her arm and steered her away from the ship.

Gripping the ship's rail, I thought, *Could she be the one I've been searching for?*

I returned to the dining room, and while I cleared the tables, I recalled the places I had traveled, sights I had seen, and women I had been with since leaving Virginia over ten years ago. Evie was special, and I desperately wanted to get to know her. As I rode the trolley back to my room in Harlem, all I could think of was Evie eating hot buttered toast. Then a cold shiver ran down my spine.

*Oh Lord, what if I never see her again?*

# CHAPTER 2

## *Evie*

I was lost in thought as I quietly strolled across the sun-glistened Brooklyn Bridge with my sister Jennie at my side. It was early Sunday morning, and all was quiet, except for the horn blasts of a passing barge on the river below and the clip-clop of a horse-drawn carriage. I held my perfumed handkerchief against my nose to mask the smell of the horse droppings on the roadway. Besides Jennie and me, there were only two other pedestrians on the bridge.

As I walked along, I began to shiver in the early morning March chill—or was it the thought of the handsome stranger who made me tremble? When I first saw him, my heart started racing. When he looked at me, I blushed and hoped that my bronze complexion would hide it. When he asked for my order, I batted my eyelashes, flirting shamelessly. When he walked away and waited on the other diners, I watched him. I watched him from the corners of my eyes, even as he was watching me. When I finished my tea, I glanced at the pattern of leaves in the cup and my poor heart quivered. But then I felt Jennie's probing eyes on me, so I pushed the cup away.

Who is this handsome stranger disturbing my tranquility? How dare he break into my thoughts, uninvited? He's just a man, a man I don't even know. Yet, he watched me so intently.

I wondered what his name was, wondered all sorts of things about him. Then I tried to banish him from my thoughts, but his image kept reappearing.

*Evie*, I scolded myself, *this is no way for a respectable young lady to behave. This is not the way you were brought up.*

We stepped off the bridge walkway and crossed the street to wait for the trolley that would carry us home to the Weeksville section of Brooklyn.

"A penny for your thoughts," Jennie said.

"Oh Jennie, it feels good to be going home after the long, cold winter in Cohoes."

"Yes, I'm sure Mother and Father have sorely missed you."

"They've missed you, too!"

"I've been away for so many years. Weeksville hardly feels like home anymore."

"Don't say that. Mother and Father's home will always be your home."

"My life's in Cohoes now, and I'm happy you joined me up there."

In Cohoes, we lived with our cousin, Mattie, who was the first and only colored schoolteacher there, and we worked as seamstresses at the Peabody Collar Factory. Besides Mattie, I only knew a few people in Cohoes and spent most of my free time reading poetry, writing in my journal, and sewing outfits for Jennie and myself. I never told Jennie, but I was homesick for Mother and Father.

"I like it in Cohoes, too," I said, "especially working at Peabody's and earning my own money. But I still miss Weeksville. There are so many interesting lectures, meetings, and socials to attend and I especially enjoy the musical concerts."

At the mention of music, I playfully started humming the "Toreador Song" from the opera *Carmen* and I imagined I was standing before an orchestra. What a glorious sight! Brown, black, and yellow faces. Each man finely tuning his instrument and each one dressed in a black-tie tuxedo. I lifted my baton and began to conduct the orchestra only I could see.

Jennie pinched my arm. "Evie, restrain yourself. Have you gone mad?"

Startled, I shook the vision from my sight. "Sorry, sometimes, I do get carried away."

"Hey there, let her be!" a middle-aged white man called out. "I was enjoying the music."

He was standing several feet away, grinning and leaning against the lamp-post, also waiting for the trolley. When Jennie glared at him, he tipped his hat and smiled.

"I just can't abide riffraff," she said.

"Never mind him. He's a bit tipsy this morning."

She stepped off the curb and peered down the street. "When is this darn trolley ever going to come?"

She was impatient, and so was I. But I was impatient for spring flowers to bloom and eager to fall in love.

When we finally reached home, Mother and Father led us into the dining area where we enjoyed warm biscuits, dripping with butter, and hot tea.

"Are you going to church, Mother," I asked.

"We plan to attend the evening service, so we can spend more time with you girls."

"So how's life up there in Cohoes?" Father asked. This was the first time I had been away from home.

"It's nice but very quiet," I replied.

"And how have you been getting along, Jennie?"

"Just fine, Father. I'm used to the quiet life. By the way, Cousin Mattie sends her regards."

"Oh yes, how's she doing? Is she married yet?"

"No, she hasn't," Jennie said. "The school board would make her resign if she got married."

"That's an unfair rule," Mother remarked.

Father shrugged. "My dear, that's the way it is."

"It shouldn't be. Now, Jennie, tell us about the journey. I've always wanted to take a trip on the Nightline."

"Well, Albany is 160 miles away and it takes the boat twelve hours to get there."

"Oh my, that long!"

"Yes," I said, "but it's a comfortable trip, and the ship has a lovely dining room."

"With a snooping waiter who kept staring at Evie!" Father raised his eyebrows, but I feigned disbelief.

We continued to talk and catch up with each other's lives: Father's plumbing business, Mother's sewing circle, neighborhood gossip, and our work at the Peabody Collar Factory. After we had conversed a while, I put a record on the RCA Victor gramophone Father had bought last June when I graduated from high school. It was an extravagant gift. I started singing and prancing around to the music, imagining I was dancing with the handsome stranger, and this time Jennie couldn't object because no one else was there, except Mother and Father.

Right after dinner, Jennie and I went for a stroll in the park where we ran into Flo and Prudence, two of my best girlfriends. We hugged and kissed each other.

"Oh, Evie, how we missed you. Are you back for good?" Flo asked.

"No. Just for the day. We have to get back to work tomorrow."

"I wish I had a job, so I could earn my own money," Prudence said.

"Did you hear that Barbara Lee got engaged," Flo asked. "The wedding's this summer."

"How nice," Jennie remarked.

"And Dr. Martin's son, Jerry, is going to open a men's tailoring shop right here in Brooklyn." Prudence grinned. "He told me he's still sweet on you, Evie."

"Well, I wish him good luck with the shop."

"Say, how's Delores Brown?" Jennie asked. "I used to be good friends with her elder sister, Maybelle."

"Delores? That wild one!" Flo shook her head. "We really don't know about her. Her parents sent her away to relatives in South Carolina and quite frankly I think she's... in a family way."

Prudence waved her hand at Flo. "Hush your mouth girl. You don't know that for sure."

Jennie raised an eyebrow. "Hmmm, what a pity. Who's the daddy?"

"Let's pray she's not expecting," I said. "Her life would be ruined."

When we finally returned home at four that afternoon we found Father and Mother in the parlor. Father was seated in his armchair and in a somber mood.

"I hope you girls are going to spend the night."

"We shouldn't have stayed out so long," I whispered to Jennie.

"I'm sorry, Father," I said, "we have to leave by five thirty this afternoon to catch the seven o'clock ferry to Albany."

"But you just got here."

"I know, but we're due back at work at eight tomorrow morning."

"Evie, there's no need for you to work. You can stay home and help your mother around the house. And Jennie, if you find a job around here, then both of you can live at home. In my country, all the family lives together."

"But Father, I like working," I replied.

"The only employment we could get down here is domestic work," Jennie said, "and Irish women have taken most of those jobs. Our work at Peabody's is better and pays more."

He shrugged, sighed deeply, and after a moment spoke again. "Evie, I wish you had followed your English teacher's advice and attended Hampton Normal after high school. Then, you could've gotten a good teaching job here in Weeksville."

"Those jobs are also scarce, Father."

Jennie smirked. "Well at least Evie could have gotten a respectable husband at Hampton, and with her good looks and breeding, a well-to-do one."

Father hissed. "That's not the point of college, Jennie."

I had thought about going to college, but I didn't want to cause my parents additional expense. They were both in their mid-sixties and needed to save for the day when Father retired from his plumbing business.

"Now, now," Mother said, "we've had such a lovely day. Let's not quarrel."

I dashed across the room and knelt beside Father, taking his rough hand in mine. It smelled of pipe tobacco. "Don't fret, dear. I promise we'll come back next Sunday."

He nodded and gently squeezed my hand.

Jennie and I rushed back to Pier 41, desperate to make the seven o'clock Nightline departure. After boarding, we climbed up to the ship's gallery on the third deck and stretched out in the deck chairs. I gazed through the gallery's enormous windows, and beheld the night sky, with stars as bright as diamonds, and for a moment, I imagined myself dancing along the Milky Way. As I drifted off to sleep, an unspoken question haunted my dreams: would I see the handsome stranger again? I awoke with a start when Jennie tapped my shoulder, saying we should retire to our second-class stateroom.

Early the next morning, we went to the dining room. As we entered, I saw him in a spotless white coat with a small tea towel draped on his arm, taking an order from a plump elderly woman, who was accompanied by a thin man about the same age. The handsome waiter was quite tall, light brown skin, clean shaven, and from what I could see had straight white teeth. His dark wavy hair was neatly combed back from his remarkable face.

Finally, he looked up, spotted us, and rushed over. "Good morning, ladies. Did you have a pleasant stay in New York?"

"Yes, we certainly did," Jennie said.

After he escorted us to a table, I ordered my usual breakfast: tea and toast.

Jennie pointed her finger at me. "Evie, you'd best have an egg, too."

I didn't want to cause a fuss, so I agreed to the egg. He brought our order, poured the tea and left. The dining room was busy that morning and I feared he wouldn't have time to chat.

We had nearly finished breakfast when he approached the table and asked, "Was everything all right?"

"Yes, everything was delicious," I said. "Even the egg I didn't want."

He laughed with his eyes and turned to Jennie. "Ma'am, I don't mean to be forward, but I was wondering if you would allow me to introduce myself?" An uncomfortable silence hovered over the table in the otherwise noisy dining room and I held my breath waiting to see how Jennie would respond.

"Whatever for, young man?"

"I'd like to give you and the young lady my personal service. Many of my prominent customers enjoy being greeted by name."

He inclined his head toward an elegantly dressed white gentleman, who was seated a few tables away, and the gentleman nodded in return.

"Alright then, go ahead," Jennie said.

"My name is Albert Sidney Johnson, formerly of Lexington, Virginia. I was raised there, and my parents live there. After I left Lexington, I worked as a sailor on a merchant ship and then served in the United States Navy and traveled to nearly every country in the world. At present, I reside in Harlem." He waited.

"Humph . . . I'm Mrs. Jennie Powell and this is my younger sister, Miss Evelyn Ashton. Our family home is in Brooklyn, but we're employed in Cohoes, New York, right outside of Troy."

He bowed. "How do you do, Mrs. Powell and Miss Ashton? I'm very pleased to meet you." And then he took his leave.

After he was out of earshot, Jennie turned to me. "Well, I never heard of such a thing! He has a lot of nerve." I was quiet and tried to hide my delight.

As soon as the boat docked that morning, Jennie and I ran to catch the trolley to the Peabody Collar Factory in Cohoes. I spent the whole day sewing men's detachable collars, but even the hum of hundreds of sewing machines couldn't drown out my thoughts of Albert Sidney Johnson, the handsome waiter.

During the next two weekends, I saw him again as the Nightline steamed back and forth between Albany and New York, and we managed to chat each time he served us. I left the dining area for a few minutes one morning and when I returned, Jennie said that Albert had told her he would like to court me if I wasn't spoken for.

"Whatever did you tell him, Jennie?"

"I told him he would have to come to Brooklyn and ask Father's permission. Father will put him straight and end all this nonsense! Evie, I know you can't possibly be interested in the likes of him. He's just a common waiter."

*Albert is coming to Brooklyn.* I bit my lip, trying to hide my excitement.

Usually, I followed Jennie's advice on such matters since she was older and wiser, but this was different. Somehow, I couldn't think of Albert as "just a common waiter."

"Is he really going to come?" I asked.

"He said he'd be there next Sunday at noon," she replied, pulling her face into a scowl.

The next week dragged by as I anxiously awaited his visit. I saw him again early Sunday morning as we sailed to New York, and he reminded Jennie that he would call on Father later that day.

When we reached home, the family gathered in the kitchen for a light repast of boiled eggs, ham, and cinnamon scones. We had nearly finished our meal when Jennie announced the news of Albert's impending visit.

"Jennie, what do know about this gentleman?" Father asked.

"The man's an itinerant waiter who thinks way too much of himself."

Shaking his head, Father scowled. "Then why the heck did you invite him?"

"I want you to tell him that it's no use. That Evie's way too good for him."

"What do you have to say, Evie?" Father asked, his eyes searching mine.

"It's up to you, Father." However, in my secret heart, I prayed that Father would give him a chance.

Mother glanced around, spreading her sweet smile among us. "You say he's coming for lunch today?"

"Yes. He'll be here around twelve," Jennie said.

"Well, there's always enough food for another guest."

A few minutes after noon, the much-anticipated visitor arrived.

# CHAPTER 3

## *Albert*

～᠑ ᠑～

I finished my shift on the Nightline about eight that morning and rushed home to Harlem where I shaved, bathed, and dressed. On my way out, I stopped to check my appearance in the full-length hall mirror.

"You lookin' mighty dapper this morning, Mr. J. Where might you be off to?" Claudine asked as she stepped into the hall sporting a bright red robe.

"Good morning, Claudine. I'm off to Brooklyn to meet some friends."

"She must be mighty pretty to get you up and about this early."

Waving goodbye, I set off on my long journey. I almost got cold feet walking through the tree-lined streets of Brooklyn on my way to meet Evie's parents.

*What have I got to offer this beautiful, young woman? She's cultured and well educated. I'm neither. What makes me think she would accept my offer of court-ship and that her father would even agree?*

I had worked deep underground in dangerous coal mines, fought off thieves in foreign ports, and served on a battleship off the coast of Cuba, but I can't remember being this nervous.

At exactly 12:15 p.m. I knocked on Evie's door. Her sister Jennie answered and greeted me with pressed together lips. "Good afternoon, Mr. Johnson."

"Good to see you again, Mrs. Powell."

"Please call me Miss Ashton. That's what I go by around here."

I thought it strange, but I wanted to get on her good side, so I asked no questions. Miss Jennie Ashton seemed to feel I wasn't good enough for her baby sister and I didn't blame her. Maybe, I wasn't.

Jennie showed me into the parlor and after she introduced me to her parents, I took a seat on the sofa and Mr. Ashton sat down in his armchair.

"Sir, thank you for allowing me the privilege of visiting your home today."

"You're welcome, Albert. By the way, Jennie tells me you work on the Nightline. I hear it's a fine steamship."

"That it is, sir. I wait tables in the dining room."

"How do you like it?"

"It's good for now, but I hope to get something better soon."

Mr. Ashton was a sturdily built man, about sixty, with a rich coffee-brown complexion that complimented his short silver-grey hair. He appeared reserved and spoke with a slight accent that I couldn't quite place. His wife was the opposite. She was a cordial, middle-aged woman with very fair skin, high cheekbones, and long red hair, which flowed down her back to her waist. Frankly, I couldn't tell whether she was white or colored.

While Mr. Ashton fiddled with his unlit pipe, I quickly glanced around the room taking note of its elegant furnishings: a colorful needlepoint tapestry hanging above the sofa; a fine seascape painting mounted on the opposite wall; silver-framed photographs of family members displayed on a lace-covered table; a lavish assortment of crocheted white doilies adorning nearly every surface; a whatnot with shelves of polished stones, seashells, and ornamental vases standing in the corner; and an exotic African wall mask keeping watch over it all. Although I yearned to have a lovely home like this someday and hoped that Evie would be the one to share it with me, I couldn't help but wonder if I could give Evie the life she deserved.

We continued to exchange pleasantries, but as the afternoon wore on I became aware that Mr. Ashton was sizing me up even before I had a chance to state my case, and I was more than a bit uncomfortable. After a short while, Mrs. Ashton called us in for lunch, a mouthwatering repast of roast pork, steamed rice with gravy, garden peas and carrots, and hot buttermilk biscuits. It was then I remembered I hadn't eaten since the night before.

After lunch, while the ladies cleared the table, Mr. Ashton and I retired to the parlor, each carrying a cup of hot tea. I told him about growing up in Virginia, toiling in a coal mine, working as a sailor on a merchant ship, and my stint in the Navy. Then he began to recount his life, and the more we talked, the more we discovered how much we had in common. We had both been seamen for several years and had traveled to ports far and wide.

At last, he revealed that he was from the island nation of Madagascar in the southern Indian Ocean.

"Madagascar! It's not every day I meet someone from Madagascar," I said.

"How true. I've been longing to meet some of my fellow countrymen since I arrived in America but have only come across a few."

"Sir, when I was a seaman, our ship docked at a port on Madagascar's West Coast. The place stuck in my mind because I couldn't tell if the natives there were Asian or African or a mixture. There were many French sailors and soldiers parading about the wharf, too."

"Could it have been the port of Mahajanga?"

"Umm . . . I believe it was."

"I'll be darned!" he said, his eyes lighting up. "The people of my island are of mixed Asian, East African and Arab ancestry. The central highlanders and East Coast tribes appear more Asian, but the West Coast people look more African. For centuries the bloody French had been trying to get a foothold in Madagascar but were held in check by the British, the major power in the region."

Wringing his hands, he sighed bitterly. "In 1884, the British betrayed us. The French invaded the island and took the capital, Antananarivo. Two years later, my country became a French colony. I had left the island by that time."

Next, he began to describe the turbulent history of Madagascar and how he came to leave his family and home. It was as if a floodgate had suddenly opened and long-suppressed memories poured out like water.

Even as I listened to his captivating tale, I wondered if we would ever get around to talking about Evie.

# CHAPTER 4

# *James Soemba Ashton, The Madagascan*

**M**y father's people lived on the West Coast of Madagascar, not far from the sea. Some were fishermen, like my father. Some were boat makers, and others were farmers. The powerful Merina tribe inhabited the East Coast and the Central Highlands but ruled the entire island. The Merina were known as the rice-eating people, although all the Malagasy ate and loved rice.

Before I was born, the queen of the Merina tribe, Ranavalona, ordered the missionary schools to close and all missionaries to leave the island. She also made the practice of Christianity a crime punishable by death or enslavement.

According to my father, who had been a teacher at the London Missionary Society School in our village, the Queen hated Christians and feared that her people were turning away from the customs of their ancestors. When I turned seven, the villagers rebuilt the schoolroom hut, and my father began teaching the children to read and write the scriptures in Malagasy and English.

Our West Coast village was a great distance from the Merina stronghold, Antananarivo, and was separated from it by fast-flowing rivers and high mountains, so the Queen didn't find out about the school for many years. Besides, the Queen had bigger fish to fry. Her army was busy raiding villages all over the island, taking captives and selling them as slaves to French and Arab traders in exchange for arms.

One afternoon when I was about sixteen, a convert ran into the schoolroom and gasped that the Queen's soldiers were approaching the village looking for Christians. The blood drained from my father's face, but he immediately regained his composure and told the students to go home and act calmly.

"If anyone asks you if you are a Christian or know any Christians, say to them, 'But sir, what is a Christian?'"

"Father," I said, "should they lie?"

"They are only children," he replied. "They're too young to be martyrs." Looking up toward heaven, he whispered, "Good Lord, forgive me."

As the students left the schoolroom, with anxiety etched on their faces, he blessed each one. "Do not be afraid, my child. May the God of Heaven protect you!"

He went to the side of the room where the communion flatbread was stored in a basket. Removing a large handful, he wrapped it in a banana leaf and placed it, along with a drinking gourd, in his cloth pouch.

Handing me the pouch, he said, "Run quickly, my son, to Uncle Bako's village, and hide there. It's a half day's journey and this bread will sustain you on the way."

"Father, please let me stay."

"Soemba, you are my oldest child, and they will be looking to punish you for my disobedience to the Queen. After the soldiers have left the area, make your way to the seaport at Mahajanga and find a British ship there. Tell the Captain you're a London Missionary Society student." Then he prayed for my safety and went to tell my mother, Domohina, to take the younger children back to her father's village, down the coast. She would be safe there.

I had never disobeyed my father before, but that day I hid in a grove of trees not far from the village. I heard the marching feet of the soldiers and the cries and screams of the villagers but could not see what was happening. Later that night, I crept into the home of a village elder. He told me that when the soldiers arrived, they first questioned the school-age children, but the children pretended they knew nothing. Then they dragged my father from the schoolroom to the village meeting place, where the terrified villagers had gathered, and they questioned him. He proclaimed he was a Christian but would not implicate anyone else. They pushed him to the ground, kicked and beat him, and finally made him drink the poison from the tangena tree. And he died. Seemingly satisfied that they had punished the guilty, the soldiers demanded food and, after eating, departed the village.

I also planned to leave the village that night, but the elder insisted that I stay with him and rest a while, for the forest, full of evil spirits and snakes, was a dangerous place at night. Grief stricken, I tearfully asked the elder if my father was killed because the ancestors were angry with him.

"No, my child, even though he was a Christian, he always showed deep respect for the *razana*, our ancestral spirits, and our tribal traditions. Now rest and sleep."

He hid me in his wife's kitchen hut, and I dreamed of my father, convulsing from the poison but silently praying. Suddenly, I felt a hand on my shoulder and jumped up in fright.

"It's time to go, my son," the elder whispered. "It's the hour before cockcrow."

As I was leaving, I asked about my father's body. He said it was laid out in the schoolroom, but it was too dangerous to go there now. He assured me that the villagers would bury him later that day, and when it was safe, my father's brother and my mother could come and give my father a proper burial.

I moved quickly through the forest toward Uncle Bako's village, stopping briefly at dawn near a tree to eat the flatbread my father had given me. I was thirsty, so I climbed the tree, lowered the gourd through a hole in the top and scooped up fresh water from inside the trunk.

When I reached my uncle's village that afternoon, he gave me food and a mat and led me to a secluded cave where I immediately fell asleep. Three days later, my uncle guided someone to my hiding place. He was the oldest son of my mother's brother.

"Have courage, Soemba," he said. "Your mother is safe in our village. She sent you this message: 'Goodbye my son and go safely. I release you. And even if we do not meet again in this life, I will carry you always in my heart.'"

*Never to meet my mother again!* An enormous sense of loss overtook me, and I began to weep.

After hiding for a week, I decided to make my way up the West Coast to the Mahajanga seaport. Before I left, Uncle Bako warned me to be careful and not to tell anyone I was a Christian because the Queen had spies, even on the West Coast. He gave me his *lamba* cloth to wrap myself and food and water to carry and said when I ran out, I should approach any nearby village and ask for hospitality.

I followed the lonely footpaths along the forest edge, stopping now and then at remote villages, where I was given refuge. Each night I would wrap myself up in Uncle Bako's *lamba*, take shelter under a spreading tree, and fall asleep reciting the Twenty-Third Psalm. One night as I lay down, a swarm of insects, greedy for their evening meal, bit me all over my face. Then I saw a red owl perched on a high branch and trembled with fright because we Malagasy believed that this bird was an evil sign.

"Yea, though I walk through the valley of the shadow of death," I whimpered, "I will fear no evil for thou art with me." When I awoke the next morning and found that the evil bird had flown away, I gave thanks to the Lord.

A few days later, exhausted and bedraggled, I finally reached my seaport destination and found a British ship about to set sail. The sailors said that they had docked in Mahajanga to get fresh food and water which they had just finished uploading.

Captain Ashton, the ship's skipper, stood on the bridge and roared with laughter when I told him I was a London Missionary Society student. "You'll find no frigging missionaries aboard this ship." The first mate who was standing nearby cackled.

"Please Captain, have mercy on me. You're my last hope of escape." Then I broke down and told him the whole story.

"So Queenie is after you, boy. I hear she's mean as a snake and tough as flint. By the way, who did you say directed you to this ship?"

"The spirit of my dead father showed me the way, sir, and God of Heaven protected me."

He scratched his red beard and looked nervous. "You Malagasy. Always talking about spirits of the dead."

"But the *razana* are very important. They look after us."

"Well, there's nothing I can do for you, boy. Try another ship!"

I plodded back toward the gangway. My father had told me to find a British ship and this was the only one I saw flying British colors. I was desperate and thought about stowing away, but the first mate was following me. Then I heard the Captain call him back.

When he reached the bridge and spoke to the Captain, he yelled, "Missionary!"

I stopped.

"Missionary boy!" he called again, running toward me.

"What is it, sir? I've done nothing wrong!"

"Captain Ashton wants to see you, right away."

I hesitated, getting ready to flee, but he grabbed my arm and dragged me back to the bridge. I was terrified they were going to turn me over to the Queen for a ransom.

"Don't look so fearful, Missionary boy," the Captain said. "I've decided to give you a try as my cabin boy."

I fell at the Captain's feet. "Oh, thank you, thank you, sir."

"Mate, show this lad where to bunk down and then show him the ropes. But first, make sure he has a good wash-up. He stinks!"

"Step lively lad," the first mate said. "Captain don't allow no dead weight on this ship."

As the ship weighed anchor and set sail, I began to realize that I was beyond the reach of the Queen. I had followed my father's instructions and was safe at last. Now I was entering the world beyond, a vast unimaginable place. I was excited but also frightened.

During the next few years, I waited on Captain Ashton hand and foot, learned to tie the ropes and scramble up the rigging to trim the sails. When Captain found out I could read and write, he made good use of those skills, too. After serving four years as a cabin boy, I became an ordinary seaman, and finally, after a long while, the captain promoted me to the ship's boatswain, in charge of the deck crew and the rigging. Often, during night watch, when the crew was fast asleep and all was quiet, I would look out into the immense darkness, where sea met the sky, and catch sight of my father and me in his fishing boat, casting nets into the deep blue waters.

Then I'd remember that terrible day the queen's soldiers came for him. He could have run away, but then they would have killed someone else in his place. I prayed that Mother has woven a sacred shroud to wrap his body and that Uncle has removed him from his temporary grave and reburied him in our ancestral tomb so that his spirit can rest in peace. For years I sorely grieved because I had not been there to bury my father.

I never returned to my country or saw my dear mother or my family again. One day, in the mid-1870s, our ship docked in Cape Town, after having been at sea for a long stretch. I was a young man in my twenties, raring to get drunk and have a good time. When I went ashore, I was directed to a rough and ready black shebeen in District Six, on the slopes of Devil's Peak. Upon entering the tavern, I ordered a drink, and as I looked around, I spotted a bronzed complexioned man, who was sitting alone at a small wooden table. Strangely enough, he resembled my people at home.

We started talking and drinking home brew, and when I told him I was from Madagascar, his bloodshot eyes snapped open. "You, a Malagasy man? I'm the son of Adian Kibanga van Madagascar. My father was taken from the island as a boy by the Dutch East India Company and held captive for many years in Cape Town. When the British kicked out the Dutch, my father was sold to a farmer, and in 1834, a few months after I was born, my father and my mother were set free, along with all the enslaved people in the colony."

Then my friend told me about the hardships and daily humiliations he and others still faced in the British Cape Town Colony of Southern Africa.

*What a cruel world*, I thought.

I wanted to embrace this brother in exile and I suddenly realized how lonely I had been all these years. This man was family, the family I would never see again.

"Son of Adian Kibanga, you are Malagasy, too!" I said, slapping my hand on the rickety table.

He threw back his wooly head, laughed riotously, stood me to a drink, and hung on my every word, as I told him all about home . . . Madagascar.

# CHAPTER 5

## *Albert*

M esmerized by this man's story, I could taste the sea-salty wind on my tongue and feel the deep well of loneliness he must have experienced those years away from home.

Mr. Ashton shook his head as if waking from a dream. "Sorry, Albert, for rattling on so. I can't imagine what came over me. Even my good wife hasn't heard the unsavory details of my former life and my lovely daughters know precious little about it."

"Well sir, it's an amazing tale and I'm proud you shared it with me. Did you meet Mrs. Ashton here in New York?"

"Yes, but first I found a job as a plumber's helper on Long Island and learned the craft. After a few years, I started attending the Methodist Church and met my wife there. Her flaming red hair fascinated me. She was the most beautiful creature I had ever seen."

Two hours had passed, and finally, we got around to talking about Evie. He said that she was the jewel of his heart and that he loved her dearly. He told me she had several suitors the summer after she graduated from high school but turned them all down, and when summer ended she left home to live with her sister in Cohoes.

Then he looked me straight in the eye. "Now tell me what I can do for you, young man."

I cleared my throat, hoping to speak the magical words that would bring about a favorable response.

"Mr. Ashton, I'm very fond of your daughter even though I've only known her for a short while, and I've come to ask for your permission to court her. I wish to assure you, sir, that my intentions are entirely honorable and that my purpose is marriage. I don't own any property, but I have a job and have accumulated some savings that can get us started, if and when we decide to marry.

"Another thing sir, I'm about ten years older than Miss Evie. Some may find that objectionable, but on the other hand, I'm old enough to know what I want. I realize she's way too good for me, but I promise to do my utmost to care for her and make her happy if she'll have me."

"Well, young man, I suppose that's all anyone can ask," Mr. Ashton said.

I had spoken from the heart. And there was nothing left to say. As he sat there, quietly reflecting, I glanced at the mantel clock. Time was running out; I had to leave within the next half hour to get back to the Nightline and that would be cutting it close.

Finally, he spoke. "My daughter graduated from High School and nearly went to college. How much education do you have, Albert?"

"Only four years, sir, but I've been learning on my own ever since I left school."

*This will probably kill my chances*, I thought.

"Four years? A colored man without an education has little prospects for making a decent living."

"I know that, sir."

He scratched his head. "And what skills do you possess?"

"Well, I'm an experienced cook and waiter. I've worked as a coal miner, railroad porter, and handyman, and I was a boiler man in the Navy. I guess that's about it."

"Hmm, you've certainly been around."

28

He rose from his easy chair, pulled on his pipe, walked to the front window, and looked out.

I glanced at my watch. Time was flying, but I dared not rush him.

"Albert, I like you. I like the way you carry yourself, and I'm sure you'll make some woman a fine husband, but not Evie."

My heart sank.

"Evie's use to the finer things in life and with your lack of education, I don't think you'll be able to provide for her. She needs a man on her same social and educational level. I'm not getting any younger, and I'd like to see her settled–but with the right person. I'm sorry, son."

*Was Pa's decision about my schooling going to rob me for the rest of my life?*

"I understand, sir. You just want what's best for your daughter." I stood up, trying to hide my disappointment. "I'd best be getting back to the ship now."

As I followed him to the front door, he called Mrs. Ashton and Evie into the hall.

"Albert's leaving, and I doubt he'll be back."

A pained expression crossed Evie's face as she took my hand in hers and bid me farewell. I thanked Mrs. Ashton for the lovely meal, shook hands with Mr. Ashton, and stepped out into a dismal world, a world where there was no possibility of ever having Evie.

The next week crawled by like a tortoise climbing uphill. The Nightline continued to sail up and down the Hudson, and I continued to wait on the patrons with a forced, cheery demeanor.

"Good evening, sir."

"It's a pleasure to see you again, ma'am."

However, on the inside, I was in utter turmoil. I'd finally found the woman of my dreams, the woman I could love, but almost immediately I had lost her.

When Evie and Jennie came to the dining room that Monday morning as the ship sailed toward Albany, I asked another waiter to serve their table. I couldn't bear to face them and see the smirk on Jennie's face.

After they had finished their breakfast and left, the waiter handed me a small envelope. "I think the lovely young lady left this for you. I found it under her seat while I was clearing the table."

*Oh my God, a note from Evie.*

I stashed it in my pocket, and when I left the ship later that morning, I sat on the pier, and read it.

*My Dear Albert,*

> *I am distressed that Father will not allow you to keep company with me. I was so hoping he would approve of our courtship. Of course, Jennie is dead set against it, but Mother seems sympathetic.*

> *I will be in Brooklyn next Sunday and was wondering if you could meet me after church. There's a small park on Bergen Street, about half a mile north of Weeksville, where we could sit and chat for a while without being seen. I plan to arrive there at half past twelve and will wait for you until one.*

*Yours truly,*

*Evelyn*

My heart raced wildly as I perused her letter, but my head told me that she just wanted to say a proper goodbye.

On Sunday morning, I entered the park at eleven and took a seat on a bench. Time crawled by as I waited. And when she hadn't arrived by one, I became anxious.

*Is she still coming? Has she changed her mind?*

By quarter to two, I had given up hope and was about to leave, but five minutes later, she came racing into the park, her wide pink hat flapping about her face and her long purple skirt flowing in the breeze.

"Oh, my goodness, I'm so sorry. We got out of church late because the guest preacher went on and on. Then I had to sneak away from my family and practically run the entire way here."

"I'm delighted you made it."

She plopped down on the bench. "Can't stay long. They'll be looking for me at dinnertime."

Adjusting her purple skirt, she moved closer. "I just want to tell you I wish things could have been different for us. I wish we could have gotten to know each other."

"I would have liked that very much."

For a short while, I sat there gazing at her, breathing in her nearness, my eyes spellbound by her wistful, yet lovely countenance. She leaned toward me, resting her head on my shoulder, and I had an overwhelming desire to wrap her in my arms.

Finally, she tapped my hand, "Albert, I must go, now. They'll be worried."

"Can we meet again sometime?"

"I don't know. If Father ever found out . . . I don't want to hurt him."

Her lovely fragrance swirled about my head as I walked her to the edge of the park. I wanted to accompany her home, but she was afraid that someone might see us. So I stood there and watched her as she hurried away. I stood there and watched her until all I could see was a tiny figure, a blur of pink and purple.

# CHAPTER 6

## *Evie*

❦

"Evie, where in the world have you been?" Jennie asked. "We've waited dinner for you!"

"Sorry. I went for a walk."

Jennie arched her eyebrows. "A long walk!"

"Are you all right, dear?" Mother asked.

"I suppose so."

Father pursed his lips. "Well, you don't sound okay. You're not mooning over that fellow, are you?"

I looked away and shrugged. Mother and I fetched the serving bowls and passed them around the table. But I had no appetite.

"You need to eat," Jennie said. "We have to catch the ferry this evening and you'll be hungry later."

Then she turned toward Father. "She's just disappointed about that no-good waiter."

"Jennie, leave her be!" Father said. "Is that true, Evie?"

"Yes, yes, it is."

I excused myself and ran upstairs to my bedroom. I needed to get away from everyone, especially Jennie. After a few minutes, Mother came in and sat down beside me on the bed.

"Dear, your Father just wants what's best for you."

I sighed. "I know, Mother."

Jennie breezed in. "Evie, don't bother yourself about him. He's too poor, too old, and too ignorant for you. Besides, he has nothing except a menial job. You're a lady and you deserve a much better man."

"I think Albert's a special person," I said, "and I wish you had given us a chance."

"A chance for what? If you married him, you'd be scrubbing floors all your life."

"That's enough of that, Jennie," Mother said.

Ignoring Mother's reprimand, Jennie walked toward me. "Now that he's out of the way, a respectable young man of substance can court you. You could marry a pastor or a teacher or a prosperous businessman."

I stood up and faced her. "I'm not interested in those so-called respectable young men you keep going on about. Al's exciting, and I like him. I wanted you to like him, too."

"You're talking nonsense, girl. Father did the right thing. You could have messed up your future with that no-good tramp!"

"Jennie, please stop it," Mother said.

For the first time in my life, I yelled at my older sister. "Like you did Jennie?"

"How dare you?" she said.

Then she slapped me, and I collapsed on the bed. Looking aghast, Mother jumped up and ordered Jennie to apologize, but she stormed from the room.

Father rushed in. "What the hell's going on here?"

"Jennie slapped Evie," Mother said, as she encircled me in her arms.

Father gasped. "Don't worry Evie, I'm going to give her a good piece of my mind." And he rushed downstairs to confront her.

That night Jennie and I didn't utter a word to each other as we sailed back to Albany, and to her consternation, I refused to respond to her overtures the next day. When she apologized again on Tuesday, I decided to forgive her, but

I knew that things could never be the same between the two of us. I would no longer be the compliant younger sister.

After my estrangement from Jennie, I felt a strong desire to seek solace in Al's arms. *We could meet in a public place again, so as not to sully my reputation. But to what purpose? Our romance can only end in heartbreak for us both.*

# CHAPTER 7

## *Albert*

$\sim\!\!9\ \ 6\!\!\sim$

The night following my rendezvous with Evie, I stood at the ship's rail gazing at the sky. It was way past midnight, and all was quiet. A sliver of moonlight lit the night as I searched in vain for the Orion, the heavenly constellation the sailors pointed out when I was a youth on a merchant ship. In those days, I believed it was my lucky omen, but right now my luck had run out. As I studied the heavens, Evie's face appeared in the mist and I felt the pain of loss even more deeply. I longed to see her again, but I knew it was impossible.

*Maybe I should quit this town and make a fresh start somewhere else.*

Two and a half weeks later, I received an astonishing letter. It had gone to the Nightline's head office and then to the ship's purser, who delivered it to me. As I glanced at the return address and saw it was from Mr. Ashton, my hands began to sweat.

*I hope to God he didn't find out about my secret meeting with Evie.*

When I finished the morning shift, I rushed into the galley, where Cook and his helpers were cleaning up, and tore open the letter. Mr. Ashton asked that I drop by his home as soon as possible. He said he would explain everything then. Borrowing a pen and paper from Cook, I dashed off a note telling him I would be there on Sunday.

Jennie answered the door that afternoon and greeted me with a grimace. "What are you doing here?"

"Your father asked me to come around."

I waited on the porch while she went and called him.

"Oh yes, Albert. Glad you could make it. Do come in."

When we were seated in the parlor, he smiled and said, "Did you know you caused a ruckus in my household?"

I bit my lip nervously. "How's that, sir?"

"Never mind. I guess you're wondering why I called you back after our last chat."

"Yes, I certainly am."

He opened his mouth as if to speak and then closed it. All sorts of dreadful thoughts were racing through my mind.

"Albert, I simply want to know . . ." He shifted in his chair and cleared his throat. "Are you're still interested in courting Evie?"

His question knocked me for a loop and it took me a second or two to recover.

"Yes, sir. I very much want to court her!"

"Let me explain. A week after I sent you away, Jennie and Evie quarreled. I'd never seen Evie stand up to her sister before, so I knew she was serious. Then I realized I'd taken Jennie's opinion of you as gospel and hadn't considered Evie's feelings. I was troubled by their argument, so I talked the situation over with my wife. She has a lot of what our people call 'mother wit' and I value her opinion.

"She said, 'Dear, if he has enough motivation and love, he'll move heaven and earth to support his wife just like you did. Remember, you possessed few worldly goods when I agreed to marry you. I didn't know your background and what to expect from you as a husband. I asked myself: Who is this African that wants to marry me? Who are his people? What are his customs? How will he treat me? Fortunately, I listened to my heart, and it turned out quite all right.'

"Well, after hearing that, I questioned Evie about her feelings for you and cautioned her about your limited earning power. It was then I decided to let her follow her heart and see where it leads her. After all, isn't that what courtships are for?"

"Yes, sir."

"So that settles it. You have my permission to court my lovely daughter. I'm trusting you to do the right thing."

When he announced the news to the family over lunch, Mrs. Ashton smiled, Jennie scowled, and Evie beamed, but I jumped clear over the moon.

Over the next three months, Evie and I spent every Sunday together, strolling about the streets and parks of Brooklyn, or sitting in the Ashton's lovely garden, laughing and chatting. We also sent notes to each other, sharing our hopes and dreams. Jennie was our constant chaperon and to tell the truth, she got on my nerves. One day, she cornered me in the garden while Evie stepped into the house to fetch some lemonade.

"I pray this courtship comes to nothing. You know you're not good enough for my sister. She's had much better suitors than you, refined young men with money and education. Why don't you just go away and leave her be!"

I tried to explain that I adored Evie and thought she cared for me and our courtship was a time to explore our feelings for one another, but she stormed away into the kitchen, slamming the back door. I was angry, but I held my temper for the sake of Evie.

# CHAPTER 8

## *Evie*

I was thrilled that Father had agreed to let Al come a-courting. I liked his demeanor, the way he spoke, and his fine manners, but I dared not tell that to Jennie.

"I don't understand why Father changed his mind about that no count drifter," Jennie said one evening, as we rode the trolley home from the Peabody Collar Factory. "You deserve someone better!"

"Jennie, nothing is settled yet. I promise to get to know him before I decide."

"It's a waste of your time." She glanced out the trolley window and then turned toward me. "Evie, I'm only looking out for your good."

I nodded.

Al would come to see me at my parents' home on Sundays when Jennie and I traveled down from Albany. One day, we decided to visit the Brooklyn Museum and Jennie tagged along. As we strolled around the landscape gallery, my eye was drawn to a fine watercolor depicting a small English cottage awash in sunlight and surrounded by a sea of brilliant flowers. I asked Al if he liked it.

"It's colorful, but aren't the flowers too big?"

Jennie rolled her eyes. "It's the perspective, Albert. By the way, how often do you visit museums?"

"Seldom. I'm working most of the time."

"Do you ever attend concerts? Evie loves music and the finer things of life."

"I'll try to take her when I can."

"Jennie, please!" I said.

"I'm only telling the truth."

"Miss Jennie, I like music and art, too. I'm a lucky guy to have found a cultured young lady, like Evie. Thanks for giving us a chance to enjoy this museum together."

Frowning, Jennie stalked away. Poor Al just shook his head.

Once we returned home, we entered the garden. Al and I settled in the double swing underneath the grape harbor where the fragrance of lilacs and early spring roses permeated the air. Taking a seat nearby, Jennie folded her arms, pinched her lips and watched us.

I excused myself and ran into the house. "Mother, how can Al and I get to know each other with Jennie swallowing every word?"

Mother opened the back door and called her inside.

Then we swung back and forth, laughing with joyous abandon, just like children. Finally, he took my hand in his and kissed it when he thought no one was watching and I felt the thrill of his touch right down to my toes. I stroked his smooth cheek but stopped when I spotted Mother standing at the kitchen window.

After Al left for the ferry, I went to help Mother wash the dinner dishes. We were putting away the silverware when Jennie stomped in. "Don't blame me if your darling daughter gets into trouble."

Mother shook her head and sighed.

The following Sunday, Al and I visited a charming park near Weeksville. We took a seat on a bench and huddled together to make room for Jennie. To our surprise, she walked past us and sat down a good distance away. I imagined she was getting bored with our company.

Then Al began to tell me about his travels at sea—the outlandish people he had met and the strange places he had visited. I'm sure he embellished those tales, but I didn't mind. He told me about a country where the women were confined to their tents and compounds and not allowed to go out, not even to shop in the market.

I giggled. "I hope you don't plan to shut me away if we ever got married."

"Of course not. You'd never stand for it."

He also recounted the stories he had heard as a boy from Cousin Sister, the family housekeeper, heartbreaking stories of slavery, loss, and hard times. When he spoke of her husband being crushed to death in a mill during slavery and her two young boys being sold away, I nearly wept.

But what fascinated me most was Al's description of the rituals practiced by my father's people in Madagascar, especially their close relationship with the ancestors, the *razana*, and their custom of digging up and rewrapping the bones of relatives—things Father had never told us about.

Then he said he wanted to hear about my life. I protested saying it had been unexciting, even dull, but he insisted that he was interested in everything about me.

"I was born in Brooklyn, the youngest of three children. Mother said that she carried me around on a pillow for the first six months because I was so small. When I was a child, Brooklyn was a rural area with many small farms and plenty of churches. Father was the head of our family and we respected and loved him. The saddest moment of my life was when my brother died. I was seven at the time. He was twelve."

"What happened to him, Evie?"

"Father said it was pneumonia. I thought my parents would never get over it, especially Father. I overheard him tell Mother that it might have been a curse from the old country."

Al gently stroked my hand, and I was quiet for a moment.

"After my brother passed and Jennie went to a high school in Troy, I was the only one left at home. Mother taught me how to speak, dress, sew and keep house, in other words, how to become a refined young lady."

We stood up and strolled the park's garden paths, observing the colorful flowers and shrubs.

"Tell me about your high school days," Al said.

"I loved high school, especially my English classes. My teachers encouraged me to write stories and poems, and in my senior year, I won a contest for a story I had written. The prize was a book, a wonderful novel by Miss Pauline Hopkins, a colored woman. Imagine that, a colored woman writer!"

He opened his eyes wide. "First time I've ever heard of a colored woman writing a book."

"It's true. Miss Hopkins' book, *Contending Forces*, depicts colored women who are virtuous, spirited, and clever, and colored men who are intelligent and industrious."

"It's about time someone has written a book like that. I'm sick to death of the press vilifying colored people and describing us as 'coons' and 'darkies'." He took my hand in his, as we continued to walk.

"Oh, I almost forgot to tell you about our garden parties. On Saturday mornings, Mother and I would often bake pastries and invite my girlfriends over for afternoon tea, and I'd read their tea leaves. I had a reputation for knowing certain things and they were always asking for my advice."

"Reading tea leaves? I don't believe in that superstitious stuff." Then he laughed as if it were a joke.

"Believe it or not, my predictions usually came true. Mother said that I was born with a veil and that's why I have second sight."

"Well then, Miss Evie, tell me what you predict for us."

"It doesn't work that way. I can't just dream up a prediction. Most times I don't see the whole, but pieces of a larger puzzle that must be put together."

He laughed again, this time under his breath. "I see."

But I knew he didn't, and I became angry and hurt.

I stopped and faced him. "How dare you laugh at me?"

"Evie, I didn't mean to . . ."

"It's getting late. I'm going home." Walking briskly, I called Jennie and we left the park, while Al stood there and watched, open-mouthed.

Two days later, I received a note saying that he was sorry for poking fun at me and if it was all right, he would apologize in person on Sunday. When he arrived, carrying a box of Belgium chocolates, I decided to give him a second chance, but I wanted him to respect my predictions and abilities.

"Think back to your past, Albert. Wasn't there someone who had a sense of what was about to happen? Someone in touch with the spirits?"

"Hmm." He rubbed his chin and nodded. "Yes, now that you mention it, Cousin Sister. She took care of my brothers and me when we were little, and she would tell me things that often came true. In fact, she predicted that one day I'd meet someone wonderful, just like you, Evie."

He seemed strong yet vulnerable, and I liked that. But still, I didn't dare tell him about my guardian spirit who from time to time advised me. A woman must have some secrets of her own.

I was falling for Albert, but I wanted to know more about him, so I asked, "Tell me about growing up in Lexington."

He took out his pocket watch and fiddled with it. "To tell the truth, there's not much to say."

# CHAPTER 9

## *Albert*

～❧ ❧～

**W**hen I called on Evie the following Sunday, I decided to come clean about my early life. It wasn't a pretty picture. We were sitting on the couch, Jennie was across the hall in the dining room, and Mr. and Mrs. Ashton had gone out to visit friends.

"I didn't have the opportunity to attend high school like you did." I looked down at the parlor floor. "I didn't even finish grade school. Right after Cousin Sister left for California, Pa took me out of school to keep house and take care of Timmy, my baby brother, because Ma was working as a house-keeper at Washington College. But my younger brothers–Grant, Ulysses, and Richard–were allowed to continue their education. At the time, I was just eleven and madly in love with Miss Mary, my fourth-grade teacher, who had assured me that if I studied hard, I could be somebody someday."

"My goodness. Just eleven!"

"I hated Pa because of it. I didn't want to grow up to be a worn-out field hand or a tenant farmer."

Covering her mouth, she gasped. "Couldn't you reason with him?"

I shook my head. *Evie comes from a caring family, so different than mine. I don't want to burden her with the gruesome details of my short-lived rebellion against Pa.*

"After I left school, I read the Bible to my mother every evening, and that helped my reading a lot. Miss Mary sent over a storybook that I studied until

I knew every word. At fourteen, I left home to work in a West Virginia coal mine and returned to Lexington after three years. A few months later, I left the South for good and became a sailor on a merchant ship. From then on, the world became my classroom."

She squeezed my hand tenderly. "You speak so well. You sound as if you finished high school or even college."

"Well, there was a seaman on the merchant ship everyone called the Professor, who taught me elegant ways of expressing myself. He also taught me a great deal about the world, the people in it, and how to read the stars like a map. I didn't know how he acquired all his knowledge or why he was just a sailor. Some said that years ago he had killed a man in a fight and had to run away to sea.

"So later, when I joined the Navy, I listened to the officers and emulated those who spoke well. By this time, reading had become an ingrained habit that helped me pass the lonely hours at sea. It was then I vowed that if I ever had a son, I would give him a good education, and even send him to college."

Evie beamed as she leaned toward me. "I'm sure you will."

I gazed at her, beautifully attired in a yellow linen suit, and then looked around her elegant parlor. It was a far cry from the dreary Harlem boarding house where I lived.

*Jennie is right about one thing. Evie is used to the finer things in life.*

I stood up, walked across the room, and studied the African mask peering down at me from the wall.

"I love her dearly," I whispered to the mask, "but will I be able to give her what she desires, or even what she needs?"

# CHAPTER 10

## *Evie*

O ne Sunday Al arrived early so we could attend Bethel Tabernacle AME Church on Schenectady Avenue. After the service, we shook the pastor's hand and left the sanctuary, but Prudence waved me back into the vestibule, while Jennie and Al waited outside.

"When's that fellow going to pop the question?" she whispered.

"I don't know. Hope it's soon."

She peeked at him through the open church door. "He sure is tall and handsome."

When we reached home, Al and I stepped into the parlor, and Jennie went to set the dinner table.

"I meant to tell you that these needle crafts are beautiful," he said as he ambled about the room. "Did you make them?"

"Most of them. I like doing needlepoint and sewing. Since I was fifteen I've been making all my clothes."

"You must be an excellent seamstress. Say, I could use a new suit."

I laughed. "I don't sew men's clothes."

"What about the Peabody collars?"

"That's my employment."

"I mean, how do you like working there?"

"Oh, it's quite alright. I've been there for nearly a year. They claim it's the largest detachable collar factory in the country. When I first arrived, the white seamstresses threw me nasty looks and made me feel uncomfortable. But by now some have gotten used to me, even if they're not friendly, while others still seem to dislike me. I just ignore them and do my best work."

"Don't you get tired of their bigoted attitudes?"

"Sometimes."

"Well, if we get married, you won't have to put up with them anymore."

"But I like my job. I like earning my own money, besides I've been helping Jennie with her family obligations."

"Oh?"

"Dear me. I shouldn't have said that. It's a secret."

"Miss Jennie seems to have a few secrets. Anyway, we'll discuss your job another time."

A minute later, Mother called us to lunch, and I was glad to change the subject. After we had eaten, I asked Al to tell me more about his life and travels. I knew I might never go to any of the far-flung places he had visited, but I enjoyed seeing them through his eyes.

"After I was honorably discharged from the Navy in 1904, I went home and spent a month with my family in Virginia. I wanted to see Ma and Farfar, my grandfather, who was a carpenter. I was close to him, but Pa and I didn't get along.

"Then I decided to see America. Traveled and worked clear across the country from East to West, going wherever the road took me. Went everywhere except the Deep South." Al next described the sights he has seen in San Francisco, a hilly city that was slightly more tolerant than the rest of the country and said that he had almost settled down there.

"I was looking for a place where a man like me could make a decent life but found the same prejudices everywhere, any differences were just a matter of degree. Spent three years looking for that good place, where I could live and breathe free. I finally realized that that place, if it existed at all, had to be inside me. Then I drifted back East."

After courting me for over three months, Al proposed. "Evie, I want to marry you. I've loved you from the first time I laid eyes on you, and these past few months have proved the rightness of it. I can't promise you a bed of roses, but I pledge to do everything in my power to make you happy and comfortable. Take your time. Think about it and then decide if you want to share your life with me."

He kissed my hand and took his leave.

Despite what Jennie thought, I had fallen deeply in love with him. He didn't have much money, but he made me feel like a queen. Nevertheless, nagging questions haunted me. *Will we be happy? Will he find a good job? What kind of life will we have?*

I sought advice from my guardian spirit, but she was elusive. That night I had a dream: Al and I were skipping through sunny fields of wildflowers, laughing happily, but then, in the far distance, an ominous cloud appeared. Hard as I tried, I couldn't foretell what that cloud might mean.

# CHAPTER 11

## *Albert*

B y the end of June 1909, I knew that Evie was the woman I wanted to spend the rest of my life with, so I asked for her hand in marriage. She agreed, but I had to get permission from her father. I approached Mr. Ashton warily since our courtship had been rather short.

"Al, I was expecting this. You and Evie seem so much in love. I'll help you find a place in Weeksville. Or you can live here with us."

"Sir, I was thinking about moving to Albany. There are good factory jobs up there and it's less expensive than New York City."

"So far away? Does Evie know about this?"

"Yes, sir. I've discussed it with her."

He sighed. "Okay. I guess you two know what you're doing."

Then I explained we would only marry after I had landed a new job and rented an apartment. Suddenly he pulled me into a corner and whispered that there was something he needed to tell me about Evie. Just then, Mrs. Ashton called us to the dining room, and all through lunch, I wondered what it could possibly be. After eating, Mr. Ashton and I ambled to the front porch and sat down in the rocking chairs.

He cleared his throat. "Al, I've noticed how you enjoy good food."

"I certainly do. In fact, I'm a pretty good cook."

"Well, my daughter, Evie, has many fine talents. Unfortunately, cooking isn't one of them. Her mother tried to teach her, but the lessons didn't stick.

She doesn't like to cook. Never did. To tell the truth, except for cakes and puddings, her cooking is barely edible. I thought it best to tell you."

I breathed a deep sigh of relief. "Mr. Ashton, I love your daughter and when I marry her, it will be for better or worse, and that includes her cooking."

He chuckled. Then I followed him to the dining room where the women were clearing the table.

"Mother," he said, addressing Mrs. Ashton, "Albert has asked for Evie's hand in marriage and I've agreed."

Evie ran over and kissed his cheek. "Thank you, Father."

Jennie turned to him. "I hope you won't live to regret this."

"I've made my decision and you'll abide by it!" he said.

She nodded.

"Jennie," Mrs. Ashton said, "can't you be happy for your sister?" She stretched her arms toward me. "Welcome to the family, Albert."

From that day on, I never got much sleep. Whenever the boat docked in Albany, I pounded the pavements looking for work and a place to live, but to no avail. Then I would wait tables on the ferry most of the night. I didn't mind working on the Nightline, but it was no job for a married man since you had to work nearly every night. I actually enjoyed talking to some of the patrons, especially one New York State legislator, who frequently took the ferry and ate in the dining room. His name was Senator William Carey. Somehow, he took a liking to me and would always ask how I was doing. One evening, as I brought his dinner, I mentioned that I was looking for a job in Albany.

"Can you cook, Al?"

"Yes sir, I'm an excellent cook."

"Well, my brother is the head chef at the Capitol's restaurant. Go and see him and tell him I sent you."

Two days later, when I finished my shift, I changed into a clean white shirt, navy slacks, and gray jacket, and went to see Senator Carey's brother.

When I arrived, he told me that the assistant cook's job was already taken, but I should try the maintenance department and ask for Irish. They were looking for an experienced boiler man or stoker.

There it was again. It seemed like coal was pursuing me. I had tasted and breathed its dust in a West Virginia mine, and I had shoveled tons of it into a Navy battleship boiler. I had had enough of working with coal, but the thought of marrying Evie prompted me to inquire about the job. I descended the stairs to the basement and spotted Irish, the maintenance supervisor, a redheaded young fellow of medium build. After introducing myself, I asked about the job. He looked skeptical, but when I mentioned Senator Carey's name, he nodded and showed me into his small office, and then into the adjoining boiler room. It was a big steam furnace, heating the Capitol in winter and furnishing hot water all year round. He asked what I knew about steam boilers, explaining they had trouble with it last winter and had gotten complaints from the legislators when there wasn't enough heat. I walked over to the boiler's controls and started telling him how to keep it operating properly and about my experience as a stoker in the Navy after the Spanish-American War. By the time I finished, the Irishman looked relieved and told me to report for work in September, the day after Labor Day. It was July, and September was nearly two months away.

My official title was to be the janitor, but it was understood that I would be responsible for keeping the steam boiler operating. We quibbled over the salary and finally agreed on an amount that was somewhat more than I was currently earning. I filled out the employment form, handed it to Irish, left the office, and walked back to the ship. I was a little dubious about this job offer and kept looking for factory work, which paid even more. I couldn't shake the feeling that he'd rather give this position to another Irishman or at least to another white man.

During the following days, I also searched for a decent apartment. Even though I hadn't started the new job yet, I figured I had enough savings to pay the first three months' rent, and I still had my waiter's job on the Nightline. I trudged from place to place, following every lead, looking for a flat to rent. Several owners turned me away saying they had just rented the apartment, although the 'for rent' signs were still in the windows. One of them told me he doesn't rent to coloreds and I should look for a place down by the waterfront. I'd seen those shacks, and there was no way I'd take my Evie down there.

I'd been looking for about two weeks when I saw another 'for rent' sign. The blue frame house on First Street had alleys on both sides, and from what I could see, an unkempt garden in the back. It was an upstairs apartment in a two-family house. The owner, Mrs. Abigail Jones, an elderly white widow, lived downstairs. At first, she treated me coldly and said she had promised the apartment to someone else. It was the same old story again.

"But the sign is still in the window, ma'am. Do you mind if I see it? Just in case the other family doesn't take it?"

Reluctantly, she let me in and led me upstairs. When I told her that I worked at the Capitol building (a slight exaggeration), she warmed up and showed me around the nice-sized apartment, which surprisingly had an indoor water closet and bathtub, but no electricity. The flat smelled musty and seemed as if it had not been occupied for some time. There were cobwebs in every corner, and it was sorely in need of a cleaning, a paint job, and minor repairs. One of the doors was coming off the hinge, and a few of the windows were jammed shut. I approached the kitchen sink and turned on the faucet. Clean water gushed out.

"See you have running water, ma'am."

"Oh, yes. My late sister lived up here with her grown son and had the plumbing and the fixings put in three years ago. Said she was too old to use an outer house and was entitled to some indoor conveniences. Shortly after that, she passed away."

"And her son?"

"My nephew? Moved down to New York City after his ma died. I get a letter from him once in a while and a card on my birthday."

From her conversation, I gathered that a few other people had looked at the apartment but hadn't rented it. I explained to Mrs. Jones that I was getting married soon and needed the place for my new wife.

"Young man, what did you say your name was again?"

"Albert Johnson, ma'am. My wife to be is Evelyn Ashton from Brooklyn."

"Well, Albert," she said, "if I rent you this apartment . . . that is, if the other folks don't take it, I'll allow no loud parties up there."

"Mrs. Jones, my wife's a very refined young lady and doesn't go in for that sort of thing. Besides, we don't know anyone in Albany."

She looked reassured and led me into a spacious front room, which contained small tables, a sofa, and two armchairs, covered with dusty sheets.

"This furniture belonged to my sister," she said, as she patted the sofa lovingly, "but I don't have room for it in my place. I plan to sell it before the new tenants move in."

"I imagine you miss her very much."

"That I do, and my nephew, too. We were all very close. Never had children of my own, you see."

"Mrs. Jones, would you mind if I painted this place and did some repairs if you decide to rent it to me? That is, if the other folks don't take it."

Her eyes lit up. "Oh no, I wouldn't mind in the least."

"Well, thanks for showing me around. I'll be in touch," I said as I made to leave.

"Wait, Albert, I'm not sure about those other folks. Did you say you would paint and fix it up? I'll even reduce the rent a dollar or so."

"Okay, it's a deal."

We haggled back and forth on the rent and finally agreed on twelve dollars a month. I signed the lease for the rundown apartment, paid the rent for the remainder of July and for August, and spent the next couple of weeks washing the windows and floors, repairing the door, and painting the rooms. I even persuaded two of my Nightline shipmates to help me during their off hours. When it was finished, I gave up my boarding house room in Harlem and moved my belongings to Albany.

Mrs. Jones told me about a used furniture shop where I purchased a double bed, a dresser, and a round kitchen table with four chairs. From Mrs. Jones, I bought the parlor furniture she had inherited from her late sister, which was in good condition: a dark green upholstered couch, two green armchairs, two wooden lamp tables, and a slightly worn green and yellow flowered rug. I also purchased a brand-new feather mattress for the bed, several lanterns, and a few kitchen items. The die was cast. I had spent a good part of my savings fixing up the apartment, and I really needed to start that new job soon.

Evie and I began planning for our small wedding. It was the beginning of August and I didn't know if we should wait until I started the new job or to go ahead and get married that month. We decided not to wait. I still had my waiter's job, which I would keep right up to the day before the wedding.

A few weeks before I was due to report to the new job, I dropped by the Capitol to check with Irish, the supervisor. He seemed surprised to see me. Fumbling his words, he admitted that he had given the job to someone else, a young man named Kevin Walsh. I could have strangled him, but I held my temper.

"Didn't you tell me I had the job?"

"I think I told you to come back after Labor Day and we'd see about it."

"No! You said I had it because I had good experience."

"Well, I'm sorry," Irish said, scowling, "Kevin has more!"

Kevin, who was standing a few feet away, nodded in agreement. "That's right, boy. What the heck you know about boilers?"

I grabbed Kevin by the collar, "Who are you calling, 'boy'?"

"Al, he didn't mean anything," Irish yelled.

I let him go and he scrambled away. I had to get out of there before I did something I'd really be sorry for.

"Hey, wait a minute," Irish said as I walked toward the door. "Being there was a misunderstanding, how'd you like to be Kevin's assistant? Of course, the pay would be less, but you could work your way up."

"No thanks. I'll keep on looking."

I stomped out of Irish's office, nearly blinded by anger. As I ascended the stairs, I overheard Kevin say, "What an uppity nigger."

Looking neither left nor right, I trekked down the streets of Albany, and when I reached the dock, I sat on a log and tried to think. Evie and I were due to get married in thirteen days, the last Saturday in August. *Should we postpone the wedding?*

A short while later, I made tracks for our apartment and wrote two letters: one to Evie, explaining our predicament, and the other to Mr. Ashton. On my way back to the Nightline, I stopped at the post office and mailed Evie's letter. I would hand deliver Mr. Ashton's to Weeksville on Tuesday, as soon as the ferry arrived in New York. I was in a terrible mood that evening, but I still had to smile and chat with the dining room patrons.

On Thursday morning, shortly after the boat docked again in New York, a surprise visitor dropped by the dining room as I was clearing the tables. It was Mr. Ashton. We went outside on the deck. I was sure he would suggest delaying the wedding until I found a better job.

"Albert, I appreciate your writing me about your work situation. That must have been a terrible disappointment for you."

"Yes sir, it was. Seems like you can't trust anybody these days."

"Well, I think you two should go ahead with the wedding. You still have this waiter's job."

"But we would only be able to see each other one night a week and the three days the boat docks in Albany."

"If you and Evie really want to be together, you will have to adjust your expectations and make good use of the time you have. Some men work on the railroad and leave their wives behind for weeks at a time. Others go off to war and their poor wives remain alone for years. Al, you're a colored man in America. Nothing is ever going to be easy!"

"Amen to that, sir. I'll run over to Cousin Mattie's when I get back to Albany and see what Evie wants to do."

# CHAPTER 12

## *Albert*

❦

On the last Saturday of August 1909, Evelyn Ashton was joined in holy wedlock to Albert Sidney Johnson in the chapel of All Saints Cathedral on Capitol Hill in Albany, and I was the happiest man in the world. Evie, wearing a simple but elegant white silk dress with a matching hat and holding a small bouquet of lilies, never looked lovelier. Two of my fellow waiters were my best men and Jennie and Cousin Mattie stood up for Evie.

Following a brief wedding ceremony, a luncheon was held in our honor at the church hall. Cook, a good friend and a chef on the Nightline, brought over a delicious repast, including a white wedding cake decorated with tiny yellow and pink roses, and my best men furnished five bottles of champagne for the toast. Altogether, there were twenty guests, including the wedding party, Reverend Phillips and his wife, and Mr. and Mrs. Ashton, who had sailed from New York on the Nightline. The only ones missing were Ma and Pa. I imagine they couldn't afford to travel all the way up from Virginia.

After the festivities, and after family and friends had said goodbye, I took Evie by the hand and we strolled to a nearby photography shop to have our wedding portrait taken. Then I escorted my bride to our apartment on First Street and carried her across the threshold. Suddenly, we felt awkward. We had never been alone together before. Evie had lived a sheltered life, and as much as I desired to crush her in my arms and make love to her right away, I knew I'd have to take the time to overcome her shyness and get to know her first.

# CHAPTER 13

## *Evie*

When Al carried me over the threshold, I was happy beyond my wildest expectations. I was wife to a handsome and wonderful man who cherished me. When he led me into the parlor and held my face between his hands, the thrill of his touch ran down my spine, my knees nearly buckled, and I trembled with excitement. *Alone together at last!*

"Anything wrong, darling?"

"Oh, nothing. It was a lovely wedding wasn't it?"

"Yes, and you're my beautiful bride."

I looked deeply into his eyes, burning with brown intensity. He smiled and kissed me. Wrapped in his arms, I breathed in his manly scent and tasted his salt-tangy lips. His hands, workman-rough but tender, caressed my shoulders, meandered down my back, and lingered on my hips. It was a lovely feeling and I longed to stay in his strong arms forever. Again, I shivered, aroused by his touch, but not knowing what to expect next.

After some time, I broke away and went to change out of my wedding dress. When I returned to the parlor, wearing an exquisite peach silk dressing gown, he gasped and once more enfolded me in his arms. Breathing heavily, he crushed my body into his, as I rested my head on his broad chest. Several minutes later, he loosened his grip and pointed at two glasses of champagne on the lamp table.

"I know you don't usually drink, darling, but this is a toast to our future."

I giggled. "But, I don't want to get tipsy on our wedding night."

He laughed. "Honey, just take a sip."

Gazing into each other's eyes, we raised our glasses. "To my beautiful bride, my dream come true. May we always be as much in love as we are today."

As dusk approached, he led me into the bedroom, closed the makeshift curtains, and went to change into his pajamas. I removed my dressing gown, and garbed in a silk nightdress, I slipped between the sheets. Then I noticed a vase of lovely yellow roses on the bed stand.

*How sweet of him.*

A few minutes later as we lay facing each other in our soft, feathery bed, he whispered, "I've been waiting for you all my life. Now you're finally mine." He reached for me and my heart began to pound. With his lips pressed against mine, he slowly began caressing my tingling body while I quivered with anticipation.

"Are you afraid, Evie? I promise not to hurt you," he murmured.

I kissed him back, touching his tongue with mine. "I know that, darling. I'll never be afraid with you to guide me."

At that moment, I realized how much I desired him. I wanted to please him. And I wanted him to make passionate love to me. I threw my arms around my husband and pulled him closer. And that night we became one.

# CHAPTER 14

## *Albert*

E vie and I spent that weekend getting to know and explore each other in ways we couldn't have done before. On Monday afternoon, I reluctantly tore myself from her arms and left for the Nightline. The ship returned to Albany on Wednesday morning and when I reached home, she told me how much she missed me while I was away. Later that afternoon, as I was departing for the ship again, she mentioned that Peabody had given her a week's unpaid leave and she was due back to work on Friday.

"You didn't quit your job?"

"I thought I'd continue working for a while. We could use the money."

"I don't want you to work," I said, biting my lip to hide my dismay. "It's too much. I witnessed the toll that working had on Ma years ago. It took all the life out of her. I don't want you to go through that."

I knew she was upset, but I had to leave for the pier right away, or else I'd lose a day's pay. As the ship glided down the Hudson that evening, I worried about Evie. *This is one thing I must insist on. She's got to quit that job.*

After sailing from New York City on Thursday, the Nightline reached Albany early the next morning, and I raced home from the pier with great trepidation. *Will Evie be there? Or has she gone back to work?*

As I opened the apartment door, the smell of sizzling bacon hit me, and I breathed a sigh of relief. When we sat down for breakfast, Evie said that she had gone to Peabody's and told her supervisor she wouldn't be coming back.

I was happy as a lark, but I could sense her disappointment. However, her mood seemed to brighten a few days later when our landlady, Mrs. Jones, invited her over for tea, sweet biscuits, and neighborhood gossip.

Two weeks after the wedding there was a burst of excitement in our apartment. Evie's large hope chest, filled to the brim with linens and fabrics, had arrived from Brooklyn, along with her Singer sewing machine and several boxes of books, china, and silverware. She seemed delighted to have her favorite possessions around her and immediately began fixing up our new home. She said that she adored the new apartment, especially its spaciousness, but teased that it looked like a hospital because all the rooms were painted white. Before long, blue and yellow flowered drapes embellished the bedroom, a blue quilted comforter covered the bed, and red-and-white-checkered curtains enlivened the kitchen. In the parlor, light green, leaf-patterned draperies beautified the windows, and white crocheted doilies adorned the sofa and chairs. Because of Evie, our apartment became my sanctuary on First Street, but I couldn't spend much time there because of my work on the Nightline.

# CHAPTER 15

## *Albert*

❧ ❧ ❧

During my days off, I kept looking for work, but most of what I found were low paying porter-like jobs. It seemed that all the factories, mills and industrial plants in Troy and Schenectady were closed to colored men, and I wondered if I had made a mistake dragging Evie into all of this. She was used to the finer things of life, and I was worried about providing for her. One morning as I was leaving the Nightline after my shift, I was shocked to see a familiar face ascending the ramp and wondered what the hell he was doing here.

"Hello, Al, thought I might find you at the docks. How's it going?"

"What do you want?" I wasn't in the mood for idle chatter.

He stuffed his hands into his pants pockets. "I was wondering if you were still interested in tending the boiler?"

"Humph, what happened to Kevin Walsh?"

Irish explained that Kevin had mishandled the finicky steam boiler and that the building had been without hot water for nearly a week. He said that he was getting all kinds of flak from the legislators and from the chef at the Capitol's restaurant, so he decided to look me up.

"Are you still interested?" he asked again.

*If it weren't for Evie, I'd tell him to shove it.*

"Only if it's a permanent job and at the same salary we negotiated. But I'll need an assistant who I could train to tend the boiler when I'm off."

He agreed, and we went over to the Capitol's personnel office to fill out the paperwork that affirmed my starting date, working days and hours, and salary. That same evening, I informed the Nightline's restaurant manager that I would be leaving at the end of the week, but I wouldn't say a word to Evie until I started the new position.

I had been working at the Capitol for nearly a month, when Irish hired Tom Tuttle, a young colored man, to assist with the boiler operations. The work was both exhausting and dirty, but it was a steady job with a schedule that allowed me to spend every evening and most of the weekend with my wife, and that was its saving grace.

One Saturday afternoon, I eased down into my favorite chair to read the newspaper. Evie, looking lovely as usual, fetched my slippers and began plumping the pillow behind my head. To my delight, she had even cooked an edible lunch–not great, but not bad either–and I wondered what I had done to deserve all this attention. We had been chatting for a while when Evie brought up the subject of Jennie, saying that her sister thought the world of me. I doubted this because Jennie had never liked me. Then Evie remarked that we needed to furnish one of the spare bedrooms because someone might want to stay over.

*I hope to God it isn't Jennie.*

The thought horrified me, so I played dumb, thinking of a hundred reasons why her sister shouldn't move in here.

"Evie, we're just getting on our feet. We don't have money for an extra bed."

"I understand that, dear."

She thumbed through the *Ladies Home Journal*; I buried my head in the newspaper, hoping that the matter was settled.

"Albert, can I tell you a secret?"

*What now?*

"Go ahead."

"First, promise never to mention what I'm going to tell you to another living soul, especially Mother and Father."

"Okay, my lips are sealed." I playfully clasped my hand over my mouth.

She was quiet for a moment. I waited and then resumed reading the newspaper.

"Aren't you even curious, dear?"

"Yes, but I'm sure you'll tell me when you're ready."

Another minute passed.

"Albert, what I want to tell you is that . . . that Jennie has a son, a nine-year-old son, named James."

I dropped the paper and stared at Evie. "Jennie, a son?"

"Yes dear, remember I told you she attended the Upstate Academy in Troy."

"Yeah."

"She was quite young and impressionable when she went off to school."

"I'm listening."

"Well, after graduation about ten years ago, she eloped with a young man, a no count, ne'er-do-well, who left her in the lurch when things got rough."

"Go on."

Evie sighed. "After he left, Jennie found that she was with child and had nowhere to go. She hadn't told Mother and Father about the marriage, so she felt she couldn't tell them about the baby either. Then she confided in Cousin Mattie and Cousin Mattie took her in. James was born and when he was six months old, she boarded him out with a family in Cousin Mattie's neighborhood and Jennie went to work at the Peabody Collar Factory."

"You mean she boarded out her child with strangers?"

"Yes dear, what else could she do? She had to work. But she went to see him whenever she could."

I shook my head and muttered, "That poor kid."

"Don't be so hard on her Albert. Anyone can make a mistake and choose the wrong person. I'm so happy I chose you."

"Let me get this straight. Jennie never told her parents about any of this. They don't know they have a nine-year-old grandson who's living with some people in Troy, and the boy doesn't know his grandparents. Is that right?"

"Yes, dear. That's why it's a secret."

"Damn it, Evie, I know what a secret is!"

Evie pursed her lips. "You don't need to curse, Albert."

I looked at my wife, almost disbelieving what she had told me. Prim and proper Jennie had a secret child–a nine-year-old boy of dubious origins. I wrinkled my brow and shook my head again. Evie cleared her throat. I was sure she was about to drop the other shoe, so I steeled myself.

"Jennie asked if James could come and live with us and attend school in Albany. I'm certain he wouldn't be any trouble."

I was speechless.

"I told Jennie I'd have to ask you, being that you're the head of our family." She rubbed her delicate hands together and smoothed out her stylish skirt.

"Why can't he live with his mother and Cousin Mattie?"

"Well dear, Jennie says he needs a man in his life, a man he can look up to. And you'd be a good influence on him."

"You don't say!"

"Besides, Jennie works all day at the factory, and the boy would be left alone."

"Evie, we've just gotten married. I don't want the responsibility of raising a child."

"But what if I become with child?"

"Well, that would be different, I'd be raising my own child. I'm just getting settled into the new job and we don't need another mouth to feed."

"Albert," she said, seemingly on the verge of tears, "I don't think he eats that much. I'll tell Jennie she has to help pay for his upkeep."

"I'm not about to starve any child living with us, and I don't want Jennie's money!" I slammed my fist on the lamp table. "What's more, he's a growing boy. He'll need clothes and other things."

"I know you wouldn't starve him. But remember that we're indebted to Jennie for chaperoning us during our courtship."

I grumbled, trying to think of a way out of this. *Yes, we have an obligation to Jennie, but raising her child . . . it's too big a price to pay.*

"Why doesn't she tell your parents about him? It doesn't seem fair to deprive them of their only grandson. He could even live with them."

"I agree, but that has to be Jennie's decision."

"Evie, you're helping her deceive your parents, and now you want me to deceive them, too. I simply won't do it!"

"All right, dear." Evie twisted her lace handkerchief around her fingers. "I'll tell them that when they come for dinner tomorrow."

"Tomorrow? Darn it! I was looking forward to a restful day."

I snatched up the newspaper and pretended to read. It was then I realized that Evie, my cotton-soft Evie, had a will as strong as steel.

The next day at noon, the boy arrived carrying a small cardboard suitcase in one hand and a worn baseball mitt in the other. His conniving mother, Jennie, accompanied him. When Evie opened the door, James ran up and hugged her. I was several feet away, observing the scene. Then Evie brought James over and introduced us.

"Pleased to meet ya, Uncle Albert."

"It's nice meeting you, son."

He extended his small hand, and I shook it. Suddenly, he reached up and hugged my waist. When I glanced at the tattered cardboard suitcase with the baseball mitt perched on top, the totality of his belongings, I sensed a desperate yearning in his little frame. My heart reached out to him, but my head posed a question: *Would I be able to support this boy once Evie and I have children of our own?*

# CHAPTER 16

## *Evie*

I was a lucky woman. At nineteen, I was mistress of my own household and wife to a wonderful man, whom I loved. The only drawback was that Albert had to work so hard to earn a living and even then, he wasn't earning enough to provide the luxuries to which I was accustomed. Nevertheless, I was grateful to have a spacious apartment to decorate. Although this neighborhood was pleasant, I wished we lived closer to Manhattan or Brooklyn. Albany could be rather dull. The only thing that kept me amused, after I finished my household chores, was window shopping at the downtown department stores or browsing through the books in the Pruyn Library on North Pearl Street. I also enjoyed going to Mrs. Jones's apartment for tea and cake twice a week, and sometimes I'd have her up to mine. She seemed amazed at the way I was fixing up the flat and said she had never seen it look lovelier.

First Street was on the border of Arbor Hill, a residential area where the streets were lined with elm and chestnut trees. Unlike Weeksville where all our neighbors were colored, our neighbors in Arbor Hill were Irish, Dutch, Polish and German. We were the only colored family on the block and people barely spoke to us. I had been living in Arbor Hill for about two months when the woman next door greeted me as I was passing her house on my way downtown.

"Halo, Miss," she called out in a German accent.

Surprised, I looked up and spotted her on the porch.

"How your mistress this morning?" she asked.

"My mistress?"

"Yes, Mrs. Jones. You clean her house, don't you?"

"No. She's my landlady." *How dare this foreign woman assume I'm a maid? She doesn't even know me.*

"You live there?" she asked, pointing to Mrs. Jones's house.

"Yes, my husband and I live in the upstairs apartment."

"Oh, sorry. I thought you was her maid. But, then again, I wondered why you dressed so smartly."

"I'm Mrs. Johnson. Who might you be?" I smiled warily.

"I'm Mrs. Schmidt."

"Nice meeting you, Mrs. Schmidt. By the way, I'm looking for a maid, too. Let me know if you hear of one."

Mrs. Schmidt's mouth fell open, but she recovered quickly. "I surely will."

Without even saying goodbye, she rushed into her hallway and shut the door. Frankly, it was wishful thinking about hiring a maid. Al and I had to count every penny to make ends meet. Despite this, Al had generously bought a bed for James and allowed him to move in with us. We were just getting used to him being around the house.

One morning in mid-November, I went downtown to shop for Christmas gifts, but everything was way too expensive. Christmas had always been a jolly time in Weeksville and I was disappointed when Al declared that we couldn't afford to buy gifts that year. But it wouldn't have been Christmas without presents, so I took the household money and bought a yard of blue plaid flannel for a vest, a fine piece of burgundy silk for a cravat, and a few cotton remnants at the dry goods store. I would make the gifts myself. The next afternoon, I pulled out my sewing basket and got started. The blue vest would be for Al and the burgundy cravat for Father.

I was sewing in the dining room when I heard the front door open. It was James, returning from school.

"Hello, Auntie," he called from the hall.

"Hello, dear. Have a nice day at school?"

"Yes, very nice."

When I looked up, he was standing at the dining room door. I beckoned him over and he sat down beside me on the sewing bench.

"Auntie, how long can I stay with you and Uncle?"

"Dear, this is your home now."

"It is?" He flashed a bright smile.

"Are you happy living here?"

"Yes, Auntie. I like it and I really like my new school. My classmates and I play baseball nearly every day."

"Well, Uncle and I are delighted to have you."

He looked up at me. "Auntie, I wish you were my mother."

"Don't say that, James. Your mother loves you very much."

"Yes, Auntie."

"Now go and change your school clothes so you can wear them again tomorrow. I hope you didn't get them dirty."

"They're still clean, Auntie."

"By the bye, the stoves are low on coal. Can you fetch some from the cellar?"

"I'll remove the ashes and take them down, too."

"That's a good boy. But first, change your clothes."

I reached out and squeezed his shoulder. *James is such a big help around the house. I hope he'll grow closer to his mother.*

I glanced at the wall clock; it was nearly four in the afternoon. I needed to hurry so I ran into the bedroom and laid out my dress, petticoats, unmentionables, and shoes. After washing up, I slipped on my undergarments, buffed my nails, and rubbed a spot of cold cream into my face and hands. If I wasn't careful, my hands would become rough from housework and that simply wouldn't do. Next, I combed my hair, applied a little rouge, dabbed lavender toilet water behind my ears, and slipped on my dress. Taking a lingering glance in the mirror, I decided I was ready to welcome my husband home.

Al arrived about six that evening, grimy and exhausted from feeding the monstrous boiler. After he bathed and dressed, he donned his smoking jacket and we all ate supper together in the kitchen. Then Al and I retired to the parlor and sat down in the gentleman's and lady's armchairs that flanked the round lamp table, while James went to finish his homework.

"My, my, Mrs. Johnson, you certainly look ravishing tonight."

"Do I, really? Thank you, dear."

*His approval makes all my efforts worthwhile.*

"How was your day today?" he asked.

"Fine. I've been working on Christmas gifts."

"Now, Evie, we can't afford to give presents this year. We're just getting on our feet."

"Sweetheart, I'm only making a few things with the material I have in my hope chest: a pink and white flowered dress for mother, yellow and blue aprons for Jennie and Cousin Mattie, and a silk cravat for Father." I didn't dare tell Al I'd spent most of the grocery money to buy fabric.

"What about James?"

"I'm knitting him a brown and white muffler set."

"Shouldn't we get him a toy? I saw a stereoscope viewer with baseball view-cards for forty cents in the hobby shop. You know how he loves baseball. Anyway, I won't have any spare money 'til month's end, so we'll see about it then."

"Oh, I almost forgot about your parents."

"Don't worry, I'll write them a letter and put fifty cents in it."

"Do you think I'll ever get to meet them?"

"Maybe, if they visit Albany, but I'm not taking you to Jim Crow land!"

*I'd never been south, but could Lexington be that bad?*

Then I began to consider the folly of using the grocery money to buy fabric. *Will we run out of food? I could go into the pin money Mother gave me, but I want to save that. I'd better talk to Al.*

"Dear, can you leave me a dollar tomorrow morning? I have to pick up something."

"Did you go through the household money already?"

I crossed my fingers. "No, but I still need a dollar, or two."

Al slowly withdrew two dollars from his beat-up wallet and said, "Evie, we're on a tight budget. We still have to eat the rest of this month! And remember there are three of us now."

I pouted. "Maybe I should have kept my job."

"And who would cook and clean and take care of James?" Sighing deeply, he stared at his open hands. "Evie, I'm doing the best that I can."

"I know you are, dear."

I went into the kitchen and added two dollars to the one already in the cookie jar, praying that the money would carry us until month's end, and hoping I would still be able to buy my favorite chocolates.

When I returned to the parlor, Al was engrossed in the newspaper. Now and then, he would pause and tell me about an article he was reading. "Here's something about a new breakfast cereal, Grape-nuts. Some rascal called them 'Gripe-nuts' and said they tasted like a bowl of hay."

He laughed out loud.

"We should really try some, dear. It's supposed to be healthy."

"No thanks! I'll stick with eggs, bacon, and hot buttered biscuits."

He continued to leaf through the paper. "Here's another: Henry Ford is selling his new Model T horseless carriage for nine hundred and fifty dollars."

"That's a lot of money."

"When he first opened his factory, he said he wanted to make cars for the masses. Well, at nine hundred and fifty bucks, he has a long way to go."

"Do you think we'll ever be able to afford one?"

"If you stop buying chocolate."

He laughed again. Just then James skipped into the parlor to say goodnight.

When Al finished the paper, I snuggled up on his lap. Encircled by his strong arms, I looked into his eyes. "Sweetheart, it seems that something marvelous is being invented every day. New breakfast foods. Horseless carriages. Electricity. Telephones. Even flying machines!"

"All these things are fine and dandy, Evie, and I welcome them, but what I really wish is that someone would find a way, or even invent a machine, to end the bigotry and prejudice against our people."

"But Al, it's the sunrise of the century: a time for peace, a time for prosperity, and a time for progress. The world is changing, it's changing so fast that I think we must have a share in it. Lord knows it just has to get better for colored people in this country."

He kissed my forehead. "I hope so, Evie. I hope and pray so."

# CHAPTER 17

## *Evie*

A few days later, I put on my brown tweed suit with a matching cape and traveled downtown to window shop at W.M. Whitney's, one of Albany's finest department stores. The weather was brisk, yet sunny, the air was fresh, and I enjoyed being outdoors. As I gazed at the red-suited Santa and his green-costumed elves in the dazzling Christmas display, I thought: *Thank heavens window shopping is free.*

I entered the crowded store and was cautiously inspecting the latest Paris fashions when a tall, well-dressed white woman approached. At first, I thought she might be a saleswoman but then realized she looked far too elegant for that.

"Good morning, Miss. I like your outfit. Did you buy it here?"

"No. I made it myself."

*I can't afford to buy anything at Whitney's.*

She took a step toward me, trying to get a closer look. "It's very lovely!"

I thanked her and turned away.

"Excuse me, do you sew for other people, I'd really love to have an outfit made."

"I just sew for myself and my sister."

"I don't mean to be pushy, but my husband recently brought me a fine piece of blue wool from London, so I need a good seamstress. From what I can see, my dear, you have a smart sense of fashion and your workmanship appears excellent."

*This woman claims she's not pushy.*

"Oh my, I nearly forgot to introduce myself. I'm Mrs. Vincent Foster of State Street."

I told her my name and we exchanged pleasantries. Mrs. Foster was an attractive, middle-aged, woman with grey-streaked, brown hair.

"Mrs. Foster, I'd like to oblige you, but I don't think my husband would approve."

"Then we won't tell him. It'll be our little secret," she said, with a clandestine wink. "And I'll make it well worth your while."

I hesitated for a moment but then decided to take on the job. *If I earn extra money, we can have a nicer Christmas. And Al won't be any the wiser.*

Then Mrs. Foster described the style she wanted and gave me her address. "Can you drop by tomorrow to take my measurements and pick up the fabric?"

"That'll be fine."

"How much do you charge?"

"Twenty dollars."

"Twenty? Alright, see you tomorrow."

I had no idea if this was a high or low price, but when she looked shocked I knew it was on the high side. I was glad. I didn't want to sell my talents cheaply.

I was excited about the whole adventure but would have to keep it secret from Al. The next day I got up early and by ten, I was riding the trolley to Mrs. Foster's house on upper State Street. From the outside, the large brick house appeared to be a mansion and I wondered if I should have asked for twenty-five dollars instead of twenty. I rang the doorbell and the Negro maid answered.

"Good morning, I'm here to see Mrs. Foster."

"Are you selling something?"

"No. Tell her Mrs. Johnson is here."

"I'll call her."

Mrs. Foster came to the door. "Oh yes, the dressmaker. What is your name again?"

"Mrs. Johnson."

She looked a bit perturbed. I think she was expecting to call me by my first name.

"Come right in," she said.

She showed me into the library, a lovely room with a yellow and lavender brocade settee and four matching armchairs, lavender and purple silk draperies, and an exquisite oriental rug. My eyes were drawn to a wall lined with oak bookcases, filled to the brim with volumes of all types and descriptions. I took a closer look and realized I was acquainted with several of the works, especially the poetry books. When Mrs. Foster saw me examining the titles, she bragged that many of the books were first editions and I could only imagine what they cost. I thought that someday I'd like to have beautiful possessions such as those.

A few minutes later, Mrs. Foster walked over to her antique desk and inspected the two sketches I brought. "These are so beautiful–I can't decide– and so very fashionable, too." She laughed. "Did you steal them from Paris?"

"I'm glad you like them. While you're making up your mind, let me take your measurements."

After she settled on one of the designs, she sent her maid, Flossie, to fetch the fabric. It was a bright blue, lightweight wool. I placed it in my carry bag and prepared to leave.

"Mrs. Johnson, can you pick up the lining material at the dry goods store? I'd like to get this outfit made as soon as possible."

"I'll buy it today. The suit should be ready in a week's time. Can you drop by my home next Friday morning at ten for a fitting?" I handed her a calling card with my particulars.

*If she comes to my place, it'll save me time.*

"Umm, you live on First Street in Arbor Hill," she said, glancing at the card. "That's not far from that 18th century Ten Broeck Mansion. I know just where it is. See you next week."

As soon as Al left the next morning, I got right to work on the new project. The high-quality fabric was beautiful. Working quickly, I cut a pattern from old newspapers and then cut out the material. It was already Friday and I couldn't sew on the weekend since Al would be home most of the time. I worked all day Monday and Tuesday and by Wednesday, at three in the afternoon, I had finished Mrs. Foster's suit, all except the hem of her skirt. On Thursday, I cleaned the house until it was spotless. The next morning about ten, I heard Mrs. Foster's Ford motorcar pull up in front of the house and ran to look out the window. A few neighbors had popped out of their houses to inspect the newfangled machine. Mrs. Foster's driver, a young man dressed in a jacket, knickerbockers, knee-high stocking, and a flat cap knocked on the outside door.

"Good morning. Is this Mrs. Johnson's place?" he asked in a thick Irish brogue.

"I'm Mrs. Johnson."

"Oh! Mrs. Foster's here to see you." He walked back to the motorcar and helped her out.

As Mrs. Foster and I walked up the stairs to my apartment, Mrs. Jones called out, "Is everything alright, Mrs. Johnson?"

"Everything's fine. I'll talk to you later."

She was being nosy, and I hoped she wouldn't tell Al about my guest with the motorcar. I showed Mrs. Foster into the parlor and invited her to have a seat.

"Oh, Mrs. Johnson, what a charming little place you have. And what lovely embroidery. Do you live here with your husband?"

"Yes, he's at work now."

She picked up the wedding picture on the lace covered lamp table. "What a handsome young man! Have you been married long?"

"About four months."

"Newlyweds. How sweet. If you don't mind me asking, what does Mr. Johnson do?"

"He's an engineer."

I don't know why I said that, but he could have been an engineer, instead of a stoker, if he had gone to college and if America wasn't so prejudiced.

Her eyes widened in surprise. "Really."

"Now let's see how this suit fits you." After she tried it on, I pinned up the hem and agreed to deliver it on Tuesday.

At ten o'clock on Tuesday, I knocked on Mrs. Foster's door and couldn't believe my ears when her maid, Flossie, asked me to go around the back. I was incensed and wanted to leave, but I also wanted to collect my wages. Fuming, I marched down the garden path, entered the kitchen, and handed Mrs. Foster the cloth bag containing her outfit. She was sitting at the kitchen table, leisurely sipping her coffee and asked me to join her. I declined, telling her I was in a hurry.

"Hope you don't mind coming in the back way. No sense in your traipsing all through the house."

"Mrs. Foster, would you like to try on the suit again?"

"Yes, just to make sure."

There had been a half a yard of fabric left over, so I sewed her a narrow-brimmed bonnet. After the way she treated me that morning, I was sorry I'd done that.

Flossie showed me into the library while Mrs. Foster went to her bedroom. She soon appeared wearing the suit and hat and said that they fitted perfectly. The softly tailored outfit consisted of a long tunic jacket, usually worn with fox furs by those who could afford them, and an ankle-length slightly flared skirt. Women's fashions were moving away from tightly fitted waists and long, wide, skirts that swept the floor.

"Mrs. Johnson, this suit is simply divine, and I love the little hat. I'll wear it when I'm cruising in my motor car."

When the telephone rang, Mrs. Foster's maid called her to the phone. Then the young woman entered the library and sat down next to me. "You does beautiful work, ma'am. How long you been sewing?"

"I started when I was thirteen. Simple things at first. Later, I learned to sew and design my own clothes. My name is Evelyn, Evelyn Johnson."

"Mine is Flossie, ma'am, Flossie Mae Brown."

"Pleased to meet you, Flossie. How do you like working for Mrs. Foster?"

"She alright, except the hours is too long. Never get much time off. Only Thursday afternoons."

I threw Flossie Mae a sympathetic look.

"She always say she's progressive and that her granny was an abolitionist," Flossie said. "One day I asked her what that word progressive mean. She say it mean you are tolerant and generous. I say to myself I wish she would be generous with my time off."

I laughed.

"I see Flossie is amusing you," Mrs. Foster said, as she sailed into the room. Flossie immediately stood up.

"She's been telling me a funny story. Mrs. Foster, I really have to go. I have another stop to make."

"Alright, how much do I owe you?"

"Twenty dollars plus two dollars for the lining and sundries."

She looked in her purse and said she only had tens and fives.

"Can I give you two tens? You can drop by tomorrow for the rest."

"I'm busy tomorrow. If you give me twenty-five dollars, I'll get change and mail you the balance."

Flossie was watching us until Mrs. Foster ordered her to go and finish her work.

"Alright. Here are two tens and a five. You owe me three. I'll look for it in tomorrow's mail."

As I descended the front stairs, Mrs. Foster called out, "Goodbye, Mrs. Johnson, and thanks for the hat."

I rode the trolley downtown and splurged a dollar-fifty of my new wealth on a box of Belgian chocolates and a bottle of Essence of Roses toilet water.

*How dare she act as if I was going to keep her change?*

To soothe my nerves, I discreetly slipped a piece of the chocolate into my mouth and let it melt on my tongue. Immediately, I felt a calming, pleasurable sensation. Just then, a distinguished looking, well dressed Negro gentleman, with slightly graying hair, approached.

He doffed his brown derby. "Good afternoon, Miss. I believe we are acquainted, aren't we?"

"We most certainly are not!" I said, and I rushed off down the street, leaving him with a puzzled expression on his face.

Moments later I realized I had smiled as I savored the chocolate and the poor man thought I was smiling at him. I hoped he didn't think I was crazy or what's worse, flirtatious! I continued Christmas shopping and bought a fountain pen and a bottle of ink for Al and a bag of peppermints and a baseball for James. Then I went to the post office, where I purchased a two-cent stamp and mailed three crisp one-dollar bills to Mrs. Foster. I had sixteen dollars and ninety cents left, which I would hide in my lingerie drawer. This money, along with the twenty dollars Mother had placed in my hope chest, would be my umbrella on a rainy day.

By the time I reached home, it was nearly 2:30. I would have to hurry to get dinner cooked and prepare myself for Al's arrival. I tried to start a fire in the cook-stove and was about to give up when James came in from school.

"I see you're home early."

"Yes, Auntie. Baseball practice was canceled today."

"Well, try to get this darn fire going. I need to cook."

He removed the morning ashes, added more coal and started the fire. Meanwhile, I cut up the potatoes and put them on to boil. In another pot, I added a chicken and water and placed it on the stove too. James stood there watching me, so I enlisted his help. "Please cut up these carrots and throw them in the chicken pot."

"Should I cut up an onion, too? Uncle says it gives chicken a good flavor."

"Yes. And when you finish that, rush to the grocery store and buy two cans of sweet peas."

I went into the bedroom, assembled my clothes for the evening, and began dressing. This cooking business was getting on my nerves. When James returned, he said that the chicken was boiling and asked if he should put it on a cooler part of the stove.

"No, don't bother," I called out. "It needs to cook fast. Just mash the potatoes."

"What should I use, Auntie?"

Returning to the kitchen, I took out a bottle of milk, a slab of butter, and the potato masher and placed them on the counter. "Use a little salt and pepper too. And warm the peas in a small pot."

Later that evening, when we sat down for dinner, I noticed that James was chewing the mashed potatoes and I warned him to eat properly.

"Sorry, Auntie."

"It's so full of lumps, Evie. The boy has to chew it."

"It's his own fault. He didn't mash it smoothly enough."

"James mashed the potatoes?"

"Yes, I was teaching him to cook."

"And this rubbery chicken. Did he cook this, too?"

"No. I cooked that myself."

"Well, at least the canned peas taste good."

*That's because I added butter and sugar to them.*

After eating the lumpy potatoes, rubbery chicken, and sugary sweet peas, Al got up from the table. "Well, if you're going to teach young James to cook, Evie, it's high time you learned yourself." And he strode out the room.

As I sat there eyeing the remnants of the ruined dinner and the dirty dishes, I became furious. After what I had been through that day, I was in no mood to be insulted by my husband. So I took a deep breath and ate another piece of chocolate.

# CHAPTER 18

## *Evie*

❧ ❧

We usually attended Israel AME church on Sundays, but on this particular Sunday, Al announced that he had other plans. "I'm going to give you a cooking lesson."

"What about church?"

"I'm sure the Lord will forgive our absence."

"Will He?"

"Even the Good Lord appreciates a finely cooked meal."

"Al, don't be blasphemous!"

"It's true. Why do you think those church sisters cook so well? They make a mean mess of greens and fried chicken."

He chuckled and hugged me.

I went into James's room and found him already dressed for Sunday school. After seeing him off, I returned to the kitchen.

"Okay. What do you have in mind?"

"We're going to make beef stew and string beans."

"String beans?"

It was the beginning of winter and I hadn't seen any in the market.

"Yeah, Deek Williams, the railroad porter, brought a crate of them up from the south. He carried a sack over to my job yesterday, and I put them in the icebox when I got home."

Al assembled all the ingredients on the small counter next to the sink and explained the process as if I was a child. I smiled and nodded. I was disappointed that we were not attending church that morning. I enjoyed the service. Besides, it was one of the few places in Albany I could show off my handsome husband.

"Evie, while I cut the meat, can you peel the potatoes?"

I glanced at the eight large white potatoes he had placed on the counter. *Why so many? It looks like we're feeding an army. Oh, I forgot–James has to eat, too.*

I picked up the sharp knife and started peeling. By the time I finished, the large potatoes had become the size of an egg. I cut each in half and asked what I should do next.

"Evie, you left too much potato on the peel. No wonder you go through a whole sack of them so quickly."

He took up the peels and re-peeled them trying to recover the wasted potato meat. While Al was busy with the potatoes, I glanced around our kitchen. Strangely enough, it was my favorite room. I liked the way the white walls showed up the red and white checkered curtains and the green and red linoleum floor. I would often sit here in the mornings, the sun streaming through the windows, and read the newspaper and eat breakfast. Then Al interrupted my musings.

"Now Evie, I want you to take these onions and cut them up small."

I concentrated this time and began cutting up an onion.

Al winced when he saw what I was doing. "You're not going to put that onion skin into my stew, are you? Try peeling it first. Let me show you." He took the paring knife, cut off a thin slice of onion at the root, loosened the skin and pulled it off in one piece.

"I usually remove the skin after cutting them," I said. "It's easier that way."

"But then you've got to pick out the skin from the pieces."

"I suppose so."

I continued peeling and cutting up the onions with no further comments from the gallery. By then, Al had cut up the beef and chopped the vegetables. He waited until I finished with the onions and showed me how to season, flour and brown the meat.

*That's a lot of work and I might even burn myself.*

"Can't we just boil the meat?"

"Browning brings out the flavor. Besides, boiling will make it tough. Better to simmer it slowly."

After the beef was browned, he added onions, potatoes, carrots, garlic, parsley, and sage. Then and only then, he poured in just enough water to cover everything. "We'll add salt and pepper later when the meat's nearly done."

When the stew began to boil, he moved the pot to the cooler part of the stove, covered it, and let it simmer. I was getting bored but didn't dare show it.

"Al, do we have to stand here all afternoon and watch the stew?"

"No, but we need to check it often. The hotness of this stove varies, and I don't want it to burn. Now let's make the string beans."

*Well, at least I know how to cook those. I'll show him I'm not a complete fool in the kitchen.*

While I strung, cut and rinsed the beans, Al took a ham hock from the icebox and quartered it.

"Let these hocks simmer, then throw in the string beans. Be careful not to burn yourself."

After half an hour, I added the string beans to the pot and went to get the salt–besides sugar it was the only seasoning I used.

"Hold on sweetheart, taste the water first. The hocks give it a salty flavor."

"What about sugar? I usually add a little to my vegetables."

"That's because you add too much salt," he said, raising his voice.

"You don't have to yell!"

"Sorry dear. I don't mean to be impatient, but you don't add sugar to vegetables. Those stewed tomatoes you make are sweet as candy."

I puffed out my jaws.

"Don't fret, Evie. Your stewed tomatoes are delicious. Only cut the sugar in half. Another thing, dear, taste as you go."

"But if I taste as I go, I'll get full and won't be able to eat my dinner."

"Just put a tiny amount on your tongue to see what it needs."

"This is so complicated, I wonder if I can remember it all. Besides, I detest cooking. You knew that when you married me."

Placing my hand on my hip, I looked up and frowned.

"Evie, we all have to do things we don't like in this life. At work, I shovel hundreds of pounds of coal and ash every day. I need my nourishment, or I won't have the strength to do my job. I can't live on tea and toast like you do. Now if you want me to stop by a tavern to get a hearty dinner before I come home each night, I'll do that."

I was riled up, but my guardian spirit warned me: *Be careful of what you say. That which is spoken, cannot be undone.*

"Please, dear, come straight home. I'll try to fix you a decent meal, as best I can."

"That's all I ask. It doesn't have to be fancy. I want you to also have time to do your needlework, your poetry and the other things you enjoy."

Al and I finished cooking the dinner together. He watched the pots while I set the kitchen table with my best china and good silverware, wedding gifts from my parents. When everything was ready, I called James in for dinner and dished up the food. He and Al ate like ravenous lions, smacking their lips after every bite. I, of course, ate like a lady.

"That's a mighty fine meal you prepared Mrs. Johnson," Al said, as he pushed back from the table, patting his stomach.

"Thank you kindly, Mr. Johnson."

He reached over and took my hand. James beamed. We were happy again, but the best part was that there was enough food left over for the next two days.

From then on, Al and I rose early on Sundays and prepared dinner together before going to church. James helped, too, by chopping the vegetables. At church, I prayed that someday we could afford to hire a cook and a washerwoman.

## CHAPTER 19

# *Albert – 1910*

In June, when Evie was heavy with our first child, I received a letter from Timmy, my youngest brother, saying that my grandfather, Farfar, was very ill and had called for me. Farfar, whose real name was Olaf Johnson, was Pa's father. He was a white carpenter who had emigrated from Sweden to the American south before the Civil War. For the past few years, he had been living with my parents who took him in when he got too old and sick to live alone. I was torn between going to see him and staying with Evie, but she urged me to go and asked Jennie to come over. After obtaining a three-day leave from work, I told Jennie to send a telegram to Pa's job at the Virginia Military Institute if the baby came early.

Then I went into the hall closet, pulled out the toolbox, and counted the money I had been saving since the first of the year. Eleven dollars and fifty cents plus small change. Ten dollars of this was for Evie's doctor bill, so I couldn't touch that. That left me with a dollar-fifty. I was about to give up on the idea of traveling south when I thought of my friend, Deek Williams. Early the next morning I stopped by the railyard and found him just about to board his train. He lent me his porter's rail pass, which took care of my carfare, but I still needed a few more dollars.

When I reached home, I put the doctor's money in an envelope and handed it to Evie. It seemed to me that ten dollars was a lot of money for delivering a baby, but I wanted to make sure Evie and the child would be all right. To my amazement, she said that she already had the doctor's fee and that I should use the money in the tool chest to travel. I couldn't imagine how Evie had gotten her hands on ten dollars, but I didn't ask. They say, "Never look a gift horse in the mouth."

The following morning, I boarded the train for Washington, D.C. As I rode along on the first leg of my journey, I thought about my brother Timmy. He was the only one of my four brothers who still lived in Lexington. I couldn't believe he was a grown man of twenty-two who had graduated from the Lexington Academy High School for Coloreds and had recently completed a teacher training program at the West Virginia Normal College. At least, he got a chance to get an education and I was proud of him.

Some time back, Timmy wrote that Farfar had sold his carpentry business and the big house and had moved into the cottage he had built for my late grandma, Ma Marie. It was the south. She was colored, and they were never married. He had made a new entrance for the cottage that faced the back road and had fenced in the surrounding land so that Pa and Timmy could visit whenever they pleased.

Later, Timmy wrote and described what happened when Farfar became frail and came to live with Ma and Pa. He said that Pa was worried about how the white folks in town would react when they learned that Farfar was living in a colored household. One Friday morning Farfar sent a note to Sheriff Gomer. In the past, Farfar had done several favors for him, and they were on good terms. The next day when the sheriff came riding into the colored neighborhood on his big reddish-brown bay, Farfar was waiting on the porch. The sheriff took a seat beside him. Timmy, who had been working in the garden, sat down on the front steps and listened to their conversation.

"Sheriff Gomer, you know I been feeling poorly these past few weeks. These kind folks, Emma and George, have agreed to let me stay with them for a little while so Emma can nurse me back to health. I called you here to get your advice 'cause I don't want no trouble from the law or the folks in town about this arrangement."

"Well, Mr. Johnson, I suppose it's alright being that you're sick. You just a houseguest and it ain't permanent. You know it's against the law for colored and white to live together."

"It ain't permanent. I still got my cottage in town."

"I really don't see a problem with that," the sheriff said, "and if anyone questions you, tell them to come and see me."

I changed trains in Washington, D.C., the nation's capital, and the curtain of segregation fell–saying you are just a nigger. On the southbound train, I was forced to sit in the dusty, hot car, reserved for coloreds. The nearly empty car had an odor of urine, probably coming from the waste bucket behind the curtain in the rear. After an hour or so, a colored porter entered the car and began picking up the trash and sweeping the aisle. He was a tall, fair-skinned gentleman with slightly graying hair.

When he spotted me, he nodded. "How you doing, sir?"

"Fair to middling. I'm surprised the railroad has assigned a porter to clean up this car."

"Well, I try to tidy up in here whenever I can. The price of the ticket is the same. So why shouldn't our folks have a clean car, too?"

I stood up and extended my hand. "Al Johnson, from Albany."

"Eugene Watkins, from Baltimore."

"You know what, Mr. Watkins, I once read an article about a young Creole from New Orleans, named Homer Plessey, who fought against Jim Crow trains. Even took it to the Supreme Court."

"My Lord. Never heard of such a thing!" He glanced over his shoulder and whispered, "What the heck happened?"

"The court let us down. Said it was okay to segregate coloreds from whites as long as they were given equal accommodations."

"Sir, that's got to be a joke," he said in a louder voice. "Whoever heard of colored people being given equal anything by whites?"

I had to laugh, in spite of myself.

After Watkins left, I settled down and ate the hard-boiled egg sandwiches I had brought with me. Then I took out my flask and drank some water.

"Hey boy, there's no drinking on this train."

I looked up and saw a pot-bellied conductor standing in the aisle. He was sweating profusely and smelled sour.

"Even water?"

"You sure that's water, boy?"

I poured a little into my cupped hand, and he smelled it. "Alright, go ahead and drink. I just don't want no drunk Negroes cutting up on my train."

In an instant, I was thrust back to where I was many years ago and I tasted the bitter gall of resentment and anger as it filled my gut and rose up to my mouth. My jaw and chest muscles constricted, and my hands tightened into a fist. But my face wore the mask of placid submission, the same mask that had been perfected by generations of enslaved and free black people. He stood there watching me and seemed to want to chat. I just wanted to be left the hell alone.

"Where you from, boy?"

"Albany, sir."

"You doesn't sound like a Georgia boy."

"Albany, the capital of New York State."

"Oh, no wonder, I got me a Yankee! Well, I'd best tell you how things are done down here."

"No need sir, I was raised in Lexington."

As he continued to talk and bombard me with "boy this" and "boy that," I remembered Pa teaching me how to survive as a black man in the south. At the same time, I imagined my strong brown hands around this conductor's fat white neck, squeezing until his eyes popped out. Then I smiled and relaxed.

"Say, what do you do up there in Al-ba-any?"

"I'm a laborer."

He snorted loudly. "If that don't beat all! You done traveled all that way up north to do the same job you could've done in Virginia."

"I suppose so."

"Well, I'd best be moving on. You all have a nice visit now and stay out of trouble."

"Yes, sir," I said, nearly choking on the words. *Good riddance, cracker. I will play the role of subservient Negro, so I can get back to my wife and unborn child in one piece.*

Yes, I was home again and knew I had done the right thing leaving Virginia thirteen years ago. Come to think of it, if I hadn't left Virginia, I would have never met Evie. How lucky I was to have found her. Despite the hardship of making a living to support my growing family, I was happy. Sometimes when I was at work, shoveling coal, I'd think, I can't do it another day – the exhaustion, the grime, the fumes, the boredom. Then I'd go home to Evie and know that I'd do anything, endure any hardship, to keep her, and the next day I'd be back tending the coal again. *My God, how I love that woman.*

At the next station, a pretty, dark-skinned young woman with a mouthful of sparkling white teeth, and wearing a bright yellow frock and bandanna, boarded the train. She was lugging a tattered, plaid suitcase and was followed by four children. The oldest one, a cute little girl about eight, was struggling to carry a big straw basket while the three smaller tykes each dragged a bundle wrapped in cloth. Jumping up, I took the suitcase and basket and placed them under a nearby seat. Then I took the younger children's bundles and put them on an overhead rack.

Before returning to my seat, I removed a clean white handkerchief from my pocket and gave it to the oldest girl who promptly wiped the snotty noses of her three siblings. Her mother seemed embarrassed and offered to wash it and mail it back to me when she reached her destination in North Carolina, but I told her to keep it.

An hour or so later I was dozing when I felt a light touch on my arm. *Oh no, it can't be that fool conductor again. Next, he'll be saying it's against the law to sleep on the train.*

But it was the little girl handing me a small package wrapped in newspaper. Inside I found a juicy fried chicken breast, resting on two slices of buttered country bread.

"Sir, my Ma done send this for you."

As I stared at this unexpected treat, my mouth began to water. Then I turned and faced the woman. "Ma'am, you sure you have enough for the children?"

"Yes sir, we have a-plenty." She smiled and gave each child a bread-wrapped wing.

Thus relieved, I tore into the delicious feast and fell back to sleep.

As I stepped off the train in Lexington, I found Timmy waiting for me in Pa's wagon. We embraced and while we were driving home, he informed me that he had recently landed a teaching position at the Colored Graded School in town, that Grant, the brother next to me in age, was running a turkey farm in the Midwest, and that Ma had retired at last from her housekeeping job at Washington College. I began to feel uneasy as we drove up the steep hill to the family home. Pa and I hadn't seen eye to eye since he took me out of school many years ago. The last time I visited, he asked how I was earning a living and seemed disappointed when he learned that I had been doing menial work. What the hell did he expect?

When the wagon pulled up in front of the house, I could hardly recognize the place. Pa had spruced it up, adding a two-room wing and a large front porch. Timmy said that they even had running water inside, which was practically unheard of in the colored part of town. Just then, Ma opened the screen door, dashed down the stairs, and hugged me with tears in her eyes. Pa ambled over from the back of the yard and shook my hand.

After greeting everyone, I tiptoed into Farfar's room. He was lying in bed, propped up on pillows and covered by a light quilt even though it was a warm June day. He recognized me right off although he hadn't seen me in six years. When I showed him Evie's photo, he managed a smile, mouthing the word "beautiful." He tried to talk but was too weak, so I did the talking. I settled all the old things that stood between us–resentments and secrets concerning Ma Marie and slavery. I told him that I would never forget him. I reminisced about the day he confessed that he was my real grandpa and said to call him Farfar, which means grandfather in Swedish. I was just seven years old. On that day, he gave me a shiny new coin that I treasured and kept in my pocket for a long time.

By the time I finished talking, tears were gently running down his face and I also wept. He squeezed my hand and closed those tired old eyes. Then, a tall man in his forties with a bushy beard entered the room. He looked familiar, but I couldn't quite place him.

"He's gone," I murmured.

"The old man's crossed over."

"He's crossed many rivers and the Atlantic, too."

"It's a blessing you got here in time. Al, don't you recognize me?"

"Uncle . . . Uncle Nate?"

"Yes, I arrived late last night."

We hugged, and Uncle Nate called Ma, Pa, and Timmy into the room. The five of us linked arms and prayed for the soul of Olaf Johnson, who was born Olaf Johansson many years ago in Sweden. Uncle Nate was Farfar's youngest son and Pa's baby brother. Because of a racist incident in Lexington when he was twenty, he was forced to flee north and he had made a new life in Philadelphia.

As was the custom in the south, folks came in droves, bringing food and offering condolences. Relatives, church members, old friends, and even my grade school teacher, Miss Mary, older but still elegant, was among the mourners. My boyhood friends, many of whom had become tenant farmers, dropped by, too—looking tired and used up, and I wondered if I seemed as worn out as they did. After a while, we stepped out on the back porch to share a bottle of moonshine. They told me about their lives in Virginia and asked me about life up North. They said they worked hard tenant farming for the planters but seldom saw a cent of profit at the end of the year and were afraid to ask for an accounting. I told them that things were better in the North, but—truth be told—it wasn't that great there either.

On Saturday, three days after he passed away, a funeral service was held for Farfar in the colored church, after which, his body was buried in the white cemetery with only Farfar's lawyer, who had made the arrangements, three of his white friends, and the immediate family standing by. Early Sunday morning, I said goodbye to my folks and Uncle Nate, promising to stay in touch. On our way to the train station, Pa handed me an envelope saying it was from Farfar. He explained that when Farfar sold his business and property some years ago, he gave some of the proceeds to Pa to extend the house and pay for Timmy's school fees. The rest he put away for Uncle Nate and me. I carefully deposited the envelope in my pocket, not wanting to open it until I reached home. The money, no matter how little, would come in handy to pay for all the things Evie would need for the new baby, including a crib.

The small station was abuzz with folks going north. Pretending to be friendly, Sheriff Gomer went around asking people where they were headed.

"Howdy, Sally Mae. Where you be off to?"

"Good day, Sheriff. I'm a-going to visit my ailing cousin up the tracks a bit."

"You be sure and come back soon, you hear?"

"Yes sir, I certainly will."

And so it went. There were a dozen or so families, all going to visit relatives. The funny thing was that many of them had several suitcases. It looked to me like they might be taking most of their belongings. The sheriff looked over their luggage, pushed back his hat, and scratched his head. I could see he was puzzled.

After a while, he approached me. "So you came for Mr. Johnson's funeral. He was a damn good carpenter and a fine man. Did you know him long?"

"Yes sir, I've been knowing him since I was knee-high to a grasshopper. Pa says he was near ninety when he died." *He knows well and good that I'm Mr. Johnson's grandson.*

The Sheriff and I chatted a bit, and then he tried to pump me for information. "Say, what you make of all these folks taking a trip?"

"Well, sir, I imagine now's as good a time as any. It's before the picking season and the Fourth of July holiday is next week."

The sheriff nodded. "Talking about the Fourth, what you think about the heavyweight championship fight coming up in Reno?"

"You mean the Jim Jeffries-Jack Johnson fight?"

"Yeah, what else, boy? That arrogant Johnson's finally going to get his comeuppance. The Boilermaker's going to wipe that sneering smile off his ugly, black mug. I would bet my whole salary on Jim Jeffries, but there's no takers because everybody knows that Jeffries gonna take back the championship. Why he can kill a man with one blow! I wish I could be there in Reno to see that trash-talking Negro when he hits the canvas!"

The sheriff threw back his head and laughed.

"To tell the truth, I haven't been paying much attention to the fight."

"What in tarnation you been doing? This is the fight of the century."

"Well, my wife's having her first baby in a few weeks and I've been worried about her and the child."

Sheriff stared at me as if I was soft-headed. "Is that all you been bothered about? Damn, women birth babies every day, some right in the fields."

Of course, I knew all about the fight. Read about it in the newspapers. Heard from my friend, Deek Williams, that colored folks have been betting on Jack Johnson like crazy, but I wasn't going to argue with the Sheriff about who would win. Let them settle that in the ring. Just then, the train pulled into the station. The Sheriff left the platform and walked to the hitching post to untie his horse. I suppose I should have been grateful to this man for allowing Farfar to live peaceably with his family for the past couple of years, but somehow my heart wasn't in it. There was too much bad blood between his people and mine.

I boarded the train along with the other passengers, who were traveling north for one reason or another. No one had any idea that this tiny stream of colored folks would in six years turn into a mighty river of humanity forsaking the warmth of the Southland for the cold of the North. Deprived of the ballot in the land of our birth, we would vote with our feet, walking, or riding anything moving. We would claim our dignity in a new land.

On the long ride home, I wondered what I would tell Evie about the trip. *Evie is a dreamer. She sees the world through the lens of what she would like it to be. She will ask if things have improved in the South and I will have to tell her no. Hell no! Black folks are still being cheated, disrespected, beaten and lynched. Never thought it was possible, but things down South have gotten worse. What was once custom—enforced by violence—has become law. These customs have clamped a heavy yoke on our people and the law we once hoped would protect us has turned dead set against us.*

When I finally arrived home on Monday, Evie welcomed me with a hug, a kiss, and a deep sigh of relief. Yes, she was heavy with child, but to me, no one ever looked lovelier. After eating breakfast, I stole into the water closet to open Farfar's envelope, and when I counted the contents, my knees buckled, and I had to sit down on the commode. There were five hundred dollars there, more money than I had ever seen in my life! Trembling, I hid the envelope in the bottom drawer of the toolbox. I didn't dare tell Evie the extent of our windfall; she would have found a way to spend it. I just said that Farfar had left us enough for a crib, and some other necessities.

On Monday, July 4, 1910, a week after I returned from Virginia, Jack Johnson, the heavyweight champion of the world, defended his title against the former champion, Jim Jeffries, the great white hope. Crowds gathered in cities and towns across the country to hear blow-by-blow accounts of the match that were relayed by telegraph from Reno, Nevada and announced over megaphones. They called it the "fight of the century" but the gist of the matter was that Jack Johnson beat the crap out of Jim Jeffries, knocking him out in the 15th and final round.

I was curious as to the backlash from the fight, so for next two days, I read all the newspapers I could find. Reports flooded in from across the country: Uvalda, Georgia; Houston, Texas; Washington, DC; Mounds, Illinois; Shreveport, Louisiana; and New York City. Celebrating Negroes held spontaneous parades and even prayer meetings in the streets. Whites, looking to rewrite history, attempted to lynch hapless blacks. Negroes emboldened by Johnson's victory, clashed with angry whites. All in all, twenty-three blacks and two whites died, and a slew of other folks were injured. In other words, all hell broke loose across America.

# CHAPTER 20

## *Evie*

I woke up one morning, about a month after Al's return from Virginia, and found that my sheets and nightdress were soaking wet. Struggling out of bed, I changed my gown, grabbed a sheet of paper from the dresser, and lumbered into James's room.

"James, wake up."

"Morning, Auntie," he said, rubbing the sleep from his eyes.

"Hurry and get dressed. I need you to run to the grocery store and call Cousin Mattie on their telephone."

"Did she get a phone, Auntie?"

"No, you're going to call the store near her in Cohoes. They'll get the message to her. Do you know how to use the phone?"

"Yes, Auntie. Uncle showed me the other day. I pick up the horn and say, 'Hello Central' and a voice in the box will ask what number I want."

"Excellent! Also, call Doctor Franklin. Both numbers are on this paper. Tell Cousin Mattie that she should come right away and tell the doctor that my water broke this morning. Can you remember all that?"

"Yes, Auntie, but what water do you mean?"

"Never you mind. Just remember the messages!"

When he had dressed, I handed him ten cents for the phone calls and he placed the folded paper in his pocket.

"Should I run to the Capitol to get Uncle?" he called as he bounded down the stairs.

"No, not yet."

Shortly after he left, I heard a soft rap on the apartment door.

"Who is it?"

"It's me, Mrs. Jones."

"Oh, do come in." I waddled out of the bedroom into the hall and found Mrs. Jones waiting there.

"How are you feeling, dear? James said your water broke."

"My heavens. Did he tell the whole neighborhood?"

"No, just me."

"I'm sorry. I'm just a little anxious."

"I thought I'd come up and see if you needed anything."

"I was trying to change the wet bed linen."

Mrs. Jones followed me into the bedroom and changed the sheets. Then, we went into the kitchen where she prepared tea and buttered toast. About fifteen minutes later, an out-of-breath James ran in.

"I left the message for Cousin Mattie with her grocer, and he said he'd send a boy to her house right away."

"Good."

"And Dr. Franklin said to call him back when the tractions come every four to five minutes."

Mrs. Jones laughed. "You must mean contractions."

"Oh, what's a contraction, Auntie?"

I rolled my eyes and sighed.

"Evie, mind if I explain it to him?" Mrs. Jones asked.

"Go right ahead."

"Sit down, James." She poured him a cup of tea and gave him a piece of toast. "Well, when a baby is about to be born, a lady's tummy muscles pull and push together to push it out. It's called a contraction."

"Like a muscle cramp?"

"Yes, just like a muscle cramp."

"I had a muscle cramp in my leg once when I was playing baseball. It really hurt."

"I'm sure it did, dear," Mrs. Jones said.

I shuffled back to bed, while Mrs. Jones rinsed out the dishes. Cousin Mattie, who was on summer vacation, rushed in before eleven. She stayed beside me the whole day, holding my hand, timing the contractions, massaging my tummy, wiping the perspiration from my brow, and encouraging me throughout the long and difficult labor. Doctor Edmond Franklin arrived at six, meeting Albert at the downstairs door as they both walked in, and he delivered my baby boy about nine that evening. We named him Albert Sidney Johnson, Jr., but we would always call him Little Al. Cousin Mattie washed off the newborn child and placed him in my arms. I was exhausted, but when I saw the bushy-haired, big-eyed, flat nosed bundle of joy that was my son and felt him sucking on my breast, I felt a surge of indescribable joy. Counting his fingers and toes and finding them all present, I thanked the Lord and drifted off to sleep.

When I awoke I asked for a hand mirror and what I saw was ghastly. I simply couldn't let Al see me like that, so I told Cousin Mattie to ask him to sleep in with James until I looked presentable.

"Evie, you're being unreasonable," he said, standing outside the bedroom door. "You'll always be beautiful to me."

"Al, if you really love me, you'll follow my wishes!"

"Darn it, Evie, I've never heard of such a thing."

"Please, Al. Oh my, I'm beginning to feel faint."

"Okay, okay," he said, and he stomped down the hall.

As I lay in bed, I heard Cousin Mattie advising him to be patient, explaining that some women are in a delicate state after giving birth. When he returned from work the following evening, he approached the bedroom but didn't enter.

"How're you feeling, Evie?"

"Hello, dear. I'm mending nicely."

"I miss you, sweetheart."

"I miss you, too, dear."

Cousin Mattie stayed with us for two weeks to help with Little Al. He was just two days old when she wrapped him in a light blue baby blanket, carried him into the parlor, and placed him in his father's arms.

I could hear Al's voice through the partly open door.

"James, come over here and meet Little Al. Now listen closely and try to understand what I'm about to say. It goes for both of you."

"I'm listening, Uncle."

"I expect you and Little Al to grow up to be responsible and accomplished young men, and I intend to help. I promise not to handicap you the way my Pa did me. I promise I'll encourage you to get a good education, and even go to college! I promise to remind you that you can be all you want to be. I won't hide the fact of cruel prejudice in this country, but I won't ever take away your dream or destroy your hope!"

"I understand, Uncle."

Then Al addressed the tiny baby. "Little Al, this fine young lad, James, is your cousin who will teach you many things, especially how to play baseball."

James giggled. "But Uncle, he's got to get older first."

I was so touched by what I heard that my eyes filled with tears. *This is a fine, fine man that I married.*

Ten days later, like a moth turned butterfly, I emerged from my cocoon and fluttered new wings. Bathed in the afterglow of the setting sun, I flew into the parlor and joined my husband there. He seemed delighted to see his lovely wife again.

My prayers about having a cook had been answered several weeks before the baby was born. At the time, I was heavy and cumbersome, so Al took over most of the cooking and said he would do it until I got back on my feet. Each Sunday morning, he would prepare a big pot of stew–chicken, beef or pork–with potatoes and vegetables, and we would eat it until it ran out, usually by Thursday. Then we would have to put up with my cooking until the next Sunday. Even after I regained my strength, my husband continued to cook most of our meals.

# CHAPTER 21

## *Evie – 1912*

Little Al was a fat little tyke of two, always laughing, grabbing things, and running away. He was a nice-looking child except for his nose, which was too flat and too wide. I attempted to train it by pinching it every chance I got, but it didn't help. When his father noticed this, he became annoyed.

"Evie, you can train horses but not noses. This boy has the nose God gave him."

My son shared a room with his cousin James and despite the sizable gap in age, they got along well. It seemed that Little Al listened to James more than he did to me, his own mother. Each night before he went to sleep, I would tell him a story and sing a song. He liked that, and I was enjoying being a mother.

My husband tried his best to provide for the family. Soon after Little Al was born, Al began painting houses and flats on weekends to earn extra income. I was glad about the additional money, but I worried that he was working too hard. When I expressed my concerns, he said he wanted to save for the boy's education. One Saturday morning during breakfast, Al announced that he was going to take James with him on a job.

"Gee, I'd really like that, Uncle."

"James is just a boy. He could fall off the ladder."

"Evie, he's about the same age I was when I had to take care of a whole household."

"That was twenty years ago. Times are different now."

"Wake up, Evie. Things are not that different, and for colored people, they may even be worse. This boy's got to learn a range of skills to survive, and I could use his help."

"I hope you're not going to put Little Al to work, too."

"Don't be ridiculous. He's only a tot." Al rolled his eyes, gulped down his tea, and went to fetch his paintbrushes and bucket from the hall. James and I followed him.

"Auntie, I want to help Uncle."

"Oh well, go ahead then!"

"We'll be home about four, Evie, and we'll be hungry," Al said as they walked out the door.


One day in early September, Al received a letter from Grant, his brother who lived in the Midwest. The letter said that Grant was traveling east on business and would like to come and see us later that month. When Al came home from work, we discussed the upcoming visit over dinner.

"I'm delighted that I'll finally get to meet your brother."

"I'm looking forward to seeing him, too," Al said, scratching his chin.

I removed the dinner plates and poured two cups of tea. "Grant mentioned that he's part owner of a thriving turkey farm. That's quite an accomplishment."

"Yes, it is. Grant and my other brothers were allowed to continue their education when Pa snatched me out of school. They had a better chance than I did."

*I hope I didn't say the wrong thing. I don't want Al to think I'm comparing him to his brother.*

Grant arrived on a Monday afternoon after having taken the train up from New York City. Smiling and blazing with confidence, he took us by storm and I was surprised by how handsome he was and how closely he resembled his big brother. Little Al took to him right away and James seemed amazed by the wild tales he told about Midwest America. That evening, when Al returned from work, the two brothers joked and talked until midnight, reminiscing about their childhood and catching up with all that was happening in their lives.

After Al left the next morning, I cooked Grant a hearty breakfast.

"Miss Evie, that was delicious," he said, wiping his mouth with a napkin.

"Have some more ham and eggs, Grant."

"Can't eat another thing. Well, maybe just one more cinnamon scone. They melt in your mouth."

I smiled.

"I wish I could have brought you one of our plump turkeys from the farm."

"That would have been nice. I've never roasted a turkey before."

"I can't believe that."

"It's true. Al does most of the cooking."

"I'll be darned. Well, come to think of it, he cooked most of our meals when we were boys. Ma went out to work every day."

We continued to chat about his life while I washed the dishes. Grant was nearly thirty and I was surprised he wasn't married yet.

"Are you seeing anyone special, Grant?"

"No, I'm too busy running the farm, but when I do find a nice lady, I'll make sure she likes to cook."

"Oh dear, I'm afraid I've disappointed you."

"Not at all. You're charming and beautiful, Miss Evie, and Al's lucky to have found you. Say, I've never visited Albany before. Will you have time to show me the town this afternoon?"

"Surely, but we'll have to take Little Al with us."

"Does James want to come, too?"

"He'll be busy practicing baseball after school."

About one o'clock, Grant and I, with Little Al in hand, set out for downtown Albany. We walked around the Hudson River pier and caught sight of two grand steamships, the Berkshire and the Morse. We visited the historic St. Peter's Church, explored quaint shops on North Pearl Street, and rode up Broadway in a horse-drawn carriage. By then, Little Al was fast asleep on my lap. We were still seated in the carriage when we glanced up State Street and beheld an awesome sight–the Capitol building, gleaming white in the afternoon sun.

On our way home, we dropped by the Broadway Café for a bite to eat and were ushered to a small table. Grant ordered a glass of milk for Little Al, two cups of tea for us, and an extravagant platter of cold meats, cheeses, and sandwiches.

"Well, Miss Evie, I enjoyed that tour. You certainly know your way around Albany."

"I enjoyed it, too. Al and I seldom get a chance to spend an afternoon out."

"Why not?"

"He works so hard that he just wants to rest on the weekend."

"And he also cooks?"

"Yes, on Sunday mornings, but I help."

Grant sipped his tea. "Wow. He's a good man and he's got himself a fine-looking woman."

I blushed.

"So what do you do for fun, Miss Evie?"

"I like reading, and even reciting poetry. I love to sew, and I've designed outfits for a few society women. They all said I did excellent work."

"Does Al know?"

"I'm afraid he wouldn't approve."

Grant laughed quietly. "Not only are you charming, but you're talented, too."

By the time we reached home, Al was already there, peevish and cross. That night, after I retired, I heard Al arguing with his brother in the parlor but couldn't make out what they were saying. The next morning at breakfast Grant said that he would be leaving that very afternoon.

"This afternoon? I thought you were going to stay for at least a few days."

"Al thought it best for me to leave. He didn't take kindly to me keeping you out half the day."

"Oh, my goodness. I'm sorry."

"Don't bother yourself. If I had a wife sweet as you, I'd keep her under lock and key, too. Besides, I had a first-rate tour of Albany."

I couldn't believe that Al was jealous of his own brother, so I confronted him that evening when he returned from work. He claimed that he was angry with Grant because Grant had ridiculed me, saying that a woman who couldn't cook was of no use to him. I don't know what Grant really said, but I thought that this time my husband had gone too far.

A few weeks after Grant's departure another letter arrived. It was from Mrs. Vanderpool, a leading member of Albany's colored community, and a congregant of Israel AME church.

*October 12, 1912*

*Dear Mrs. Johnson,*

*I was delighted by your charming poetry recitation last month at the church's cultural program. This type of activity is very important for the upliftment of the race, especially our young people who have few outlets for enrichment. I particularly enjoyed your tender interpretation of Longfellow's "The Slave's Dream."*

*Now, this is the reason for my note. Some dear friends of mine will be gathering for afternoon tea at my residence on the last Saturday of October at 3:00 p.m. I would be delighted if you could attend and grace this gathering with a poetry reading. One or two poems of your choice would be fine.*

*Very truly yours,*

*Mrs. Agnes Vanderpool*

I was thrilled by this invitation and shared the news with Al as we sat in the parlor.

"Are you thinking of attending?"

"It sounds like a lovely afternoon."

"I didn't know you were interested in that sort of thing."

"I used to hold tea parties for my friends in Brooklyn."

He snickered. "But this time you won't be reading tea leaves."

I sat up stiffly. "They want me to recite a poem."

"Evie, Mrs. Vanderpool and her set are the upper crust of Albany's colored society. Will you be comfortable with them?"

"Why not? I'm not trying to join their group. I'm merely attending a tea party."

"Some of those women can be pretty snobby just because their husbands own a business or have a five-dollar job. I don't want to see you slighted."

"Is that what this is all about? Your job?"

"Not at all."

"Al, are you forbidding me to go?"

"I would think you'd be too busy for tea parties."

I folded my needlepoint and placed it on the lamp table. "That's just the point, dear. I'd like to get out of the house once in a while. Besides, you're seldom home."

"Now Evie, you know I'm working."

"I know. But sometimes I feel like a bird in a gilded cage, locked up and admired."

"So you want to fly the coop, is that it?"

"If you feel that way, I'll tell her I can't attend!" *Why does he always have to spoil things? And look at the way he treated his own brother.*

Sighing, I rose up from the chair. "I'm going to bed."

He groaned. "Listen here, Evie . . ."

Before he could say another word, I dashed from the room.

# CHAPTER 22

## *Evie*

The next evening after dinner, we retired to the parlor and I began to read my poetry book. Al leafed through the newspaper.

A few minutes later, he cleared his throat. "Evie, if you really want to attend this tea business, go ahead. I don't want to keep you a prisoner here."

I continued to read without looking up.

"And if you can't find a babysitter, I'll come home early that Saturday. James and I should be able to take care of one little two-year-old."

I glanced at him. "I'll need a dress."

"But you already own a closetful."

"I'll need a new dress for my performance. I don't want to look shabby." *I must dress elegantly; otherwise, I'll never fit in.*

"Alright. Buy the material, but don't go overboard. I'm not one of those well-to-do business owners."

I smiled. "Whatever you say, dear."

The afternoon of the tea party, I donned my new pink and burgundy dress, a pink-feathered hat, and the pearl earrings and necklace Mother had given me for my eighteenth birthday and took the trolley for the short ride to Mrs. Vanderpool's house. Jennie had come over to watch Little Al and spend time with James. I arrived at Mrs. Vanderpool's at half past three and found twelve ladies assembled there, including some from Albany's most prominent colored families. They sat in the ornately decorated dining room in groups of two or three, decked out in flowery hats, smart dresses, and impeccable white gloves. I was a bit nervous since I didn't know anyone except my hostess and calmed myself by repeating one of the short poems I would later perform.

"You look lovely, my dear, but then you always do. I see you have an excellent dressmaker," Mrs. Vanderpool said. "Come and have some refreshments and then I'll introduce you to the other guests."

I was glad I had taken such care in designing my outfit, as my dress was the most fashionable one there.

She led me to a large lace-covered dining table that held an antique silver tea service, gold-trimmed china cups and platters, and fancy linen napkins. The serving dishes were laden with an assortment of rich fruitcakes, ginger cupcakes, ham and tongue sandwiches, mincemeat puffs, scones, lemon curd sponge, petite éclairs, and Scotch bread. It all looked so delicious that I hardly knew what to choose.

After having my tea and cake, Mrs. Vanderpool presented me to her daughter, Inez, a lovely, shy young woman who looked out of place among the older women. She had recently started teaching in an Albany public school and was one of the few colored women to do so. Then Mrs. Vanderpool escorted me around the room and introduced me as the "exciting new recitalist in town." The last three women we approached were engaged in animated conversation, which seemed to be dominated by a heavyset, elegantly dressed matron.

Mrs. Vanderpool interrupted her. "Mrs. Olivier, allow me to present Mrs. Johnson. She's the talented young woman I've been telling you about."

"How do you do, Mrs. Johnson?" Mrs. Olivier said, smiling but barely parting her lips.

Next Mrs. Vanderpool introduced me to the two women who had been hanging on Mrs. Olivier's every word. They also gave me icy smiles.

"Mrs. Olivier is one of our most outstanding citizens," Mrs. Vanderpool explained. "Her family has been in Albany for generations and she's the daughter of the late Christopher Henry. Surely, you've heard of him; he was the most prosperous colored Albanian in the late 1800s."

I looked blank.

"Edna," Mrs. Vanderpool said, addressing Mrs. Olivier, "please tell Mrs. Johnson about your father. She's obviously not acquainted with Albany history."

Embarrassed, I sat down to listen.

"My father, Christopher Henry, was a great Albanian and the best-known Negro of his era, even though his father had been born a slave. He pulled himself up and became the owner of two leading hotels. I grew up in Arbor Hill when only well-to-do families resided there. Why, Mother even took me on tour to Europe for six months to celebrate my twentieth birthday. We sailed first class on the SS Republic, from New York to Liverpool. Unfortunately, Father passed away in 1883, hardly a year after we had returned. He was at the height of his career and left a large estate, including hotels and several properties in Arbor Hill."

"I'm sorry about your father's untimely demise," I said. "He sounds like a truly accomplished gentleman."

Mrs. Olivier adjusted her pincer glasses. "Thank you, my dear."

"Mrs. Olivier, what countries did you visit in Europe?"

"Mother and I toured England, France, and Italy, seeing all the cultural sites of interest, and I must say that we were treated decently everywhere we went. Europeans are much more civilized than Americans."

"By the bye, where are you from, my dear?" Mrs. Olivier asked.

"Brooklyn, New York."

"Well, I'm glad you're not one of those Negroes who are starting to migrate here from the south. They seem coarse and ignorant and don't know how to speak properly."

"I guess they haven't been given a chance to learn," I replied.

Al had often told me about how colored people were terrorized and oppressed in the south and I could see how they would want to run away from there.

"They just have to get out of the gutter and pull themselves up by their bootstraps, just like my father did."

Although I disagreed with her harsh judgment of the new arrivals from the south, I smiled and timidly nodded my head. The fragrance of her expensive perfume was making me dizzy.

"All the ladies in this room take pride in being proper native Albanian," she said. "Some of us even trace our lineage back to the days of the Dutch settlement."

*But you were enslaved then.*

"Mrs. Simpson, the lady over there in the green dress, is an established music teacher. Mrs. Lewis, the lady sitting to her left, is married to the head bookkeeper at Olden's print shop. Mrs. Brown, the woman in the grey lace outfit, sitting next to Inez Vanderpool, is the wife of the first colored postman in Albany, and our hostess, Mrs. Vanderpool, is related to Stephen Myers, the most important leader of the Underground Railroad in Albany. They say that he assisted thousands of runaways to reach Canada and points west in the 1850s. Your church, Israel AME, served as a station on the Underground Railroad, and they say that Harriet Tubman once slept there in the basement."

I opened my eyes wide. "Harriet Tubman slept there? She was the Moses of our people!"

Mrs. Olivier yawned. "That's right. So you see, we have worked hard to progress and become accepted by Albany's white society and it hasn't been easy. We've met with prejudice, but that hasn't stopped us, and we don't want these new migrants to ruin things!"

My head began to spin so I asked Mrs. Olivier to excuse me and started toward the tea table. Then I spotted Inez Vanderpool sitting with Mrs. Brown and Mrs. Epps and joined them.

"You and Mrs. Olivier seemed to be in deep conversation," Mrs. Brown said.

"She was telling me about the struggles and progress of colored people in Albany."

"She does carry on, doesn't she?" Mrs. Brown said, raising her eyebrows. Then she smiled and waved at Mrs. Olivier.

"Is Mrs. Olivier married?" I asked.

"She was. Her parents never thought any colored man was good enough for her, so she remained a spinster until they passed on. Then she met and married Mr. Olivier, who nearly went through her inheritance before he ran off to Boston with a young floozy. Mrs. Olivier and her husband never had any children, so she's all alone now, poor thing."

"What a shame," Inez Vanderpool said. Mrs. Epps clucked her tongue in agreement.

"Inez, how do you like teaching," I asked.

"Oh, it's quite a challenge. The white children in my class never had a colored teacher before and don't know what to make of me. I can handle them, but it's their parents who give me trouble."

"I suppose they can't believe that any colored woman is good enough to teach their children."

"That's right and some of those same parents can barely read and write."

"Are there any colored children in your class?"

"Just a few."

While Inez was describing her experiences in the classroom, Mrs. Brown interrupted and asked me about my background. I said that I was brought up in Weeksville, Brooklyn, and had graduated High School there and that my father owned a plumbing business. I also explained that I had moved to Albany when I got married.

"And what exactly does your husband do?" Mrs. Brown asked.

"He works at the Capitol."

"I wasn't aware that there were any colored men working in the Capitol."

"Coloreds working in the Capitol," Mrs. Epps said. "That's real progress."

I didn't want to tell them that Al worked in the boiler room, so I quickly stood up and went to refill my cup. Just as I reached the tea table, Mrs. Vanderpool called me to the front.

"Ladies, this afternoon, we have the privilege of participating in a distinguished cultural event. Mrs. Evelyn Ashton Johnson will honor us with a poetry reading. Please give her a warm welcome."

The sound of restrained applause echoed through the room. Instead of a reading, I rendered a dramatic performance. First, I enacted "*Dreams,*" a short poem by the celebrated Negro poet, Paul Laurence Dunbar.

*What dreams we have and how they fly*

*Like rosy clouds across the sky . . .*

I followed the Dunbar piece with six verses of the tragic love poem "*Annabel Lee*" by Edgar Allen Poe, and then concluded the program with Longfellow's, "*The Day is Done.*". When I finished, the ladies applauded wildly and flooded me with compliments.

"My dear, I had no idea you were so talented," Mrs. Olivier remarked as she approached. "I'd love to have you at one of my soirees."

"You made the poems come alive," Inez Vanderpool said. "I wish you could perform for my class."

I basked in the glow of their praises and invited Inez Vanderpool to take tea with me on the following Saturday. After that, I thanked my hostess, made my excuses, and bade them all a good evening.

Dusk was fast approaching, but I decided to walk home through the tree-lined streets of Arbor Hill instead of waiting for the trolley. The setting sun casts weak shadows of leafy branches onto the sidewalks. Soon the leaves would turn from gold to crimson and then drift gently to the ground. I had enjoyed being in the limelight, and still jubilant, I almost skipped all the way home.

But then my guardian spirit spoke: *You gave a wonderful performance, but why did you deny your husband?*

*What do you mean?*

*You let them think he was an office worker.*

*Well, those busybodies will soon find out that he's just a stoker.*

I continued to walk, trying to sort out mixed emotions, but the dancing lilt had gone out of my step. *Was I wrong for wanting to be creative and admired? But why did I hide my husband's occupation?*

Al was resting in the parlor when I reached home. His eyes lit up as I swept into the room and breathlessly described the admiration and praise I had garnered from Mrs. Vanderpool and her upper crust friends. I ran over and kissed him.

*Evie*, I thought, *you silly goose. Denying this precious man. Lord knows I wouldn't change places with any of those society women for all the chocolates in the world.*

# CHAPTER 23

## *Albert – 1914*

I had been working in the Capitol's boiler room for nearly five years and was still struggling to take care of my growing family. Evie and I had two children by then, Little Al, a smart little rascal, who was four, and our daughter, Susie, who was just one, and sweet as a honeybee. Jennie's son, James, who was fourteen, was still living with us, although his mother sometimes took him on the weekends. Evie had her hands full taking care of the house and two small children, but James was a big help, especially with keeping track of Little Al, who was always getting into mischief. I don't know how she managed to look pretty and unruffled whenever I came home from work, but it was one of the things I loved most about her.

Shortly after Little Al was born, I began painting houses and flats on the weekends. I still had the stash Farfar had left me, but I wanted to save it for something big. Soon, I had more work than I could handle but limited it to two Saturdays a month because I was tired most of the time. We usually knocked off work in the boiler room around noon on Saturdays, but Irish allowed me to leave a couple of hours early when I had a painting job.

By that time, I had two assistant stokers, Tom Tuttle, who had worked in the boiler room about five years, and Phineas Middleton, who Irish had recently hired. Of the two, Tom was the more intelligent. He was a tall, broad-shouldered, dark-brown skinned young man with sharp features and a handsome clean-shaven face. Phineas was a big old country boy, short and muscular. He had a large flat nose that dominated his peanut colored face, a scrawny mustache, and bushy eyebrows. Lumbering from side to side as he walked, he reminded me of a big brown bear, but he sure could shovel some coal.

One August morning we arrived at work at six thirty and began stoking the boiler. Irish hadn't turned up yet; most times he didn't show up on Mondays until eight or nine, especially when he had imbibed too much over the weekend. After we tended the boiler, we took a short break and started shooting the breeze.

"Mr. J," Tom said, "Tell Phineas about your travels when you were a sailor."

Tom and Phineas, both called me Mr. J, although I had repeatedly told them to call me Al.

"Well, I visited lots of countries in Asia, Africa, Europe and North and South America, but I never got to see Australia. When our ship docked in Sydney, the colored seamen were ordered to stay on board because the Australians weren't letting any blacks into their country."

"That's a shame," Phineas said.

"Didn't they have black people there?" Tom asked.

"Yeah, they had the Aborigines, the people that were there before the Europeans came. White Australians mistreated them and drove them off their traditional lands. I suppose the government was afraid to let us enter their country because they didn't want us to give their blacks any foreign ideas! However, a few of us sneaked off the boat one night and struck up a conversation with a colored man who was cleaning up the docks. He seemed glad to meet us and began to relate what the government was doing to his people. Before we could tell him about our situation in America, we were discovered by a border guard and marched back to the ship at gunpoint."

Phineas scrunched up his face. "Well, that's one country I'll never gets to see."

"Man, there's a lot of places you'll never see," Tom said.

"Sucker, you doesn't know where I might turn up."

"Okay, guys, give it a rest," I said. "It's almost nine thirty, we'd best get back to work."

Just then, Irish staggered in, looking red-eyed and haggard. "Everything alright here?"

"Yeah, boss," Tom replied.

"I'd best be upstairs to check on that dumb janitor." One of the janitors was a Polish guy named Borys, and Irish was always baiting him. In fact, he often made belittling jokes about Albany's ethnic groups: the Dutch, Germans, Jews, Poles, Italians, and Negroes. All except the Irish. Two days later, Irish came in late again, waving the Albany Times. It was August 5, 1914.

"Would you look at this unholy mess," he said.

I snatched the paper and quickly read out the headlines: "Austria-Hungary attacks Serbia! Germany declares war on Russia and France! Germany invades neutral Belgium! Britain declares war on Germany!"

Irish shook his head and grimaced.

"Whew, sounds like chaos," I said. "You worried about England?"

"Hell No! Damn the bloody British. It's Ireland I'm concerned about. I got plenty of folks there."

"The paper says they don't expect the war to last long. Maybe those countries are just blowing off steam."

I handed the paper to Tom, who scrutinized the editorial.

"Are we going to war?" Phineas asked.

"President Wilson has declared neutrality," Tom replied.

"What that mean?"

"That means America is staying the hell out of it."

"I'm sure glad of that!" Phineas said.

Tom, Irish and I nodded in agreement.

When I reached home that evening, Evie was waiting at the door, wringing her hands. "Did you see the headlines today?"

"Yes, I read Irish's paper."

"What do you think?"

"I think I need to wash up, then we can talk. Say, it's awfully quiet in here. Where're the kids?"

"They're in the backyard with James. I'll call them up in a minute."

I quickly bathed, put on my pajamas and robe, and joined Evie in the kitchen. "How'd you find out about the war? I thought you only read the women's pages."

"I usually don't bother with the news, but Mrs. Jones knocked on our door this morning and when I opened it, there was Mrs. Schmidt, peeking out from behind her. After greeting me, they asked to see our newspaper."

"Mrs. Schmidt, the German woman?"

"Yes, I invited them into the kitchen and when I handed them today's paper, Mrs. Jones said she didn't have her glasses and Mrs. Schmidt said she couldn't read English, so I read them the front page. When I finished, Mrs. Schmidt cried out, 'Ach Mein Gott! Will war come here, will it spread here?'

"She made such a commotion that Mrs. Jones and I became alarmed and I decided to ask you about it when you came home."

"Evie, all I know is what I read in the Albany Times. The Europeans are fighting each other, and President Wilson said that America's staying out of it."

"So there's no need to worry?"

"Honey, don't trouble your pretty little head. Now dish up the dinner while I'll go and call the kids."

After a few weeks, the news of the European war became a mere curiosity, drifting in and out of my consciousness. Like most American laborers, white or colored, I had more important things on my mind, like feeding my family. Little did I foresee the brutal impact this war, the so-called Great War, would have on our lives.

# CHAPTER 24

# *Albert*

~⊙ ⊙~

On my way home from the Capital one evening, I ran into Caliph Thompson, who was coming from his job at a downtown tailor shop.

"Al, I'm glad I ran into you. The Colored Benevolent League is holding its annual Harvest Dance on the first Saturday in October and I'd like you and the missus to attend."

"Caliph, I don't know if my wife would enjoy that sort of thing."

"Of course she would. It's sure to be an elegant evening and everyone, including Albany's colored socialites, will be there, dressed to the gills."

"Let me talk to her. I'll let you know."

At first, I started to turn down his invitation, because we really couldn't afford it. But then I thought that Evie deserved a night out. She agreed and immediately began shopping for the fabric to make a fashionable new gown. I bought a fancy white dress shirt to wear with my good blue suit. In order to pay for the evening, I had to tap into my emergency fund, the money Farfar had left me, but I felt it was well worth it.

Everything was arranged for our special evening. Susie would stay with our landlady and James would look after Little Al. On the day of the dance, I came home from work early and took a nap. After a late lunch, James and I took charge of the children while Evie primped and fancied up. About six o'clock that evening, I took Susie downstairs to Mrs. Jones. Then I dressed and sat in the parlor while I waited for Evie. When Little Al came in, he asked about his mother and I told him she was getting ready to go out.

"I go out too," he said.

"You stay with James. Daddy is taking Momma out dancing."

He frowned. "What about my story?" Evie always told him a bed-time story.

"Momma will tell you a story tomorrow night."

"No story?" he asked on the verge of tears.

"Okay, Daddy will tell you one, a short one." I don't know why I said that. I collected stories and knew hundreds of them but not one for a four-year-old boy.

*Maybe I'll try a song.*

"Son, when we were little, my brothers and I used to sing about John Henry, the steel-driving man. Would you like to hear it?"

"Yes, Daddy."

*When John Henry was a little baby*

*A sitting on his papa's knee*

*He picked up a hammer and a little piece of steel*

*Said, "Hammer's gonna be the death of me," Lord, Lord.*

*"Hammer's gonna be the death of me."*

That's all I could remember, so I began to hum.

"Sing it again, Daddy."

Next, I told him the legend of John Henry, that he had worked for C&O Railway, drilling holes into rocks to blast a tunnel through a West Virginia mountain, and how there was a contest to see if he or a new drill-machine could bore the holes faster.

"When John Henry beat the machine, the other workers cheered, but then he fell down dead."

"Why was he dead, Daddy?"

"Well son, he had worked so hard that his poor heart gave out." *Perhaps this was not the right story for a four-year-old.*

He stood there for a moment with his mouth open and then asked me the strangest question. "Are you going to die, too, Daddy?"

"Why do you say that?"

"Momma says you work too hard."

"Don't worry son, I'm not going to die anytime soon."

His face lit up with relief.

I laughed to myself. *At least not until I escort your Momma to the Harvest Dance.*

Evie emerged from our bedroom at half past seven looking incredibly beautiful in a gold gown with a matching shawl, dangling gold earrings, and long white gloves. A white gardenia adorned her upswept hair and her eyes were radiant with gold dust. Or was it just the excitement of the moment? I breathed in the sweet fragrance of her jasmine toilet water and was reminded of the day when we first met. She was still my dream come true, and I hoped I was still her Prince Charming.

The Harvest Dance was held downtown in a large fraternal hall, which had been decorated with gold leaves, pumpkins, and gourds. Guest tables, covered with white linen and ornamented with orange, gold, and burgundy silk flowers, surrounded the dance floor on three sides and a mirrored ball swung from the ceiling, reflecting shards of light in all directions. The band-stand, occupied by the eight-piece Swinging Gents of New York City, was set up in front of the dance floor and the bar, which served cider and beer, was located on a sidewall. The crowd was jubilant and the ladies, fat and slim, young and old, were decked out in their finery. Their escorts were equally elegant in tailored dark-blue suits or evening attire. I imagined that many of these men were laborers or butlers and their wives may have been maids, but they had saved all year to attend this social event in style. Even among these folks, Evie stood out and many heads turned as she entered the hall and gracefully strolled to our front row table.

We were seated with three other couples including my friend Caliph Thompson and his wife. The band started off the evening by playing the familiar standards: "Let Me Call You Sweetheart" and "I Wonder and Who's Kissing Her Now." When Evie and I got up to dance, she hummed softly in my ear as we glided over the floor. Then the Swinging Gents picked up the tempo with Scott Joplin's "Maple Leaf Rag," an old favorite, and his more recent piece, the "Fig Leaf Rag." Couples jumped up and danced the two-step or even the silly Turkey Trot. Evie begged off saying that she wasn't good at fast dancing, so we watched the dancers from our table.

"Evie, don't tell me you never learned to do the two-step or are you simply trying to act refined?"

"Well, my dear husband, if you took me dancing more often you could teach me!"

Then Evie spied Inez Vanderpool doing a lively foxtrot with a handsome young man. A short while later, we strolled over to greet, Mr. and Mrs. Vanderpool, who were sitting with several of their upper-crust friends. Mrs. Vanderpool was fashionably dressed in a royal-blue gown and Mr. Vanderpool was wearing a black evening coat. Evie presented me to them although we had seen each other several times before at church.

"My, what an attractive couple you make," Mrs. Vanderpool gushed and turned to her husband. "Don't they, dear?"

"Yes, they do," he replied, looking us up and down.

I felt like a zoo animal being inspected by its caretaker, but for Evie's sake, I wore a smile during our conversation. Just as we turned to leave, Inez ran over with her dance partner and introduced us. His name was Calvin and from the way he looked at Inez, he seemed to be quite fond of her. Evie complimented them on their elegant dancing and said that she'd love to learn the foxtrot. While we stood there talking, I glanced over my shoulder and caught Mrs. Vanderpool glaring at us.

The evening progressed smoothly, and Evie said that she was glad we came. And so was I. We had been there over an hour when the Swinging Gents really began to rock. They played a fast rag and all the young couples got up to dance. Suddenly, one fellow broke loose from his partner and started doing the Shimmy. He shook his shoulders, then his hips, rapidly rotating them left, right, forward, and backward, without moving his feet an inch. The other couples moved off the dance floor and watched as he shimmied up, down, and around.

Evie placed her hand over her mouth and chuckled. "Al, what in heaven's name is that?"

"It's a new dance called the Shimmy."

She raised her eyebrows. "My goodness gracious!"

After the breathtaking Shimmy, the band's attractive female vocalist took the stage and belted out an old blues tune: "You've Been A Good Old Wagon, But You Done Broke Down." The women at our table glanced at their escorts and giggled.

"I hope you won't be telling me that anytime soon," I whispered.

Evie blushed. "Don't be ridiculous."

Later, that evening, I went to the bar to replenish our drinks and had to wait in line for a few minutes. As I was returning, I noticed a fellow pestering Evie. He was tipsy and insisting that she dance with him.

"Ahh, come on and dance, pretty lady," he said.

"I'm sorry, sir, I don't wish to dance."

Placing the drinks on the table, I sat down and gave him a warning look.

"Come on now, let's trip de-light fantastic."

"You'd better move on, Buddy. She told you she doesn't want to dance!"

"Listen here, you can't tell me what to do. I'm gonna dance with this pretty lady."

"Al, just ignore him," Evie whispered, patting my clenched fist.

The women at our table cringed when he touched Evie's arm. But I saw red and knocked that fool senseless. He lay there, unmoving, sprawled on the edge of the dance floor, red spittle running down the side of his cheek.

"What's happening over there?" one fellow shouted.

"It's a fight," another man yelled.

"He's dead," a woman at a nearby table screamed.

Caliph rushed over from the bar. "This guy's been troublesome all evening. I saw him staggering and drinking from a flask about an hour ago."

The man stirred and tried to raise himself. "You gone and punched me. Why'd you have to do that?"

Caliph and I lifted him up, steered him toward the exit, and shoved him out the door. When I returned to the table, Evie looked pale.

"What's the matter honey? That fellow wasn't hurt badly."

"Let's go home," she said. "Right now!"

"But the dance isn't over yet."

"Albert, stay if you like. I'm going home!" Evie stood up, bade all at our table good night, and marched toward the door. I had to hurry to catch up with her. We donned our coats and went outside where I hailed a carriage. Once we were seated, I tried to explain, but she cut me off.

"You humiliated me tonight. I can never show my face again in decent company."

"Evie, I'm sorry but . . ."

"Why did you have to fight him? What will the Vanderpools think?"

*I don't give a rat's ass about the Vanderpools.*

"Listen, I couldn't stand by while that fellow . . ."

"You acted like a common hooligan!"

Her words cut me to the bone. So now I was a common hooligan. It was no use trying to tell her my side of it, so I simply stared out the window until the carriage came to a halt on First Street.

# CHAPTER 25

## *Albert*

❧⟋⟍❧

Two weeks after the botched Harvest Dance, I decided to take Evie to Brooklyn for her mother's birthday, which would be coming up in early November. Secretly, I hoped this would make up for the embarrassment I had caused her.

I didn't want to tap into my emergency fund, so on Monday evening, I hurried to the Nightline to ask if the restaurant manager could get us free passage. He promised to let me know. A few days later, I received a note saying that Evie and the children could travel by stateroom if I would wait tables on the way down. I quickly agreed. Evie seemed happy about the upcoming trip but expressed concern about James.

"We'd better send James to Jennie's that weekend."

"No need. He's going with us."

"But what will we tell Mother and Father?"

"They already know we took in a boy."

"Are you sure they won't find out Jennie's secret?"

"Honey, let me handle it."

"All right, if you insist!"

On Friday afternoon, I knocked off work at three, rushed home, bathed, and escorted the family downtown to Steamboat Landing where we would catch the ferry. While Evie, Susie, and Little Al were strolling about the pier,

James, looking both excited and apprehensive, slipped up beside me. This would be his first trip on the Nightline.

"Uncle, are we going to visit my grandparents?"

"Yes, you're going to meet them at last." *Little Al must have told him they live in Weeksville. Keeping secrets is like storing water in a leaky bucket.*

"Won't Mother be cross? When I asked her about my grandparents, she said I'd meet them when I got older."

"Let me worry about that, son."

A minute later, the whistle blew and it was time to board. James and I carried the luggage, including a picnic basket filled with fried chicken, hard-boiled eggs, and sandwiches, up two flights of stairs to the first-class state-room the restaurant manager had provided. Evie and the children followed close behind. It was a carpeted room with a gold quilt-covered double bed, a fold-up cot, an oak dressing table, a large gold-framed mirror, two red uphol-stered armchairs, and a shiny glass chandelier.

"Oh my, this is so lovely," Evie said as she gazed around the room.

Then I changed into my uniform and went straight to the dining hall where I waited tables until the dinner service was over. I returned to the stateroom around eleven and found everyone fast asleep: James and Little Al on the cot and Evie and Susie on the double bed. I lay down next to Evie and passed out.

At four thirty the next morning one of the waiters tapped on the door. Still exhausted, I jumped up and got ready to work the breakfast shift. Later that morning, Evie, the children, James, and I, dressed in knitted caps and smart wool jackets, disembarked from the Nightline, looking very much like a middle-class family, and caught a taxi to Brooklyn. Fortunately, my tips just about covered the fare.

Forty-five minutes later, the taxi pulled up in front of the Ashton house, where we were greeted with hugs, kisses, and handshakes. A beaming Mrs. Ashton led Evie and the children into the parlor while Mr. Ashton, James and I parked the suitcases in the hall. When we entered the room, I knew it was time for introductions.

"Mama and Papa Ashton, I'd like you to meet James, our adopted son."

James glanced at me, Evie smiled nervously, and Mrs. Ashton embraced him.

Mr. Ashton shook his hand. "Welcome to the family, James. We're so glad to meet you."

"Thank you, sir. It's nice meeting you and Mrs. Ashton, too."

Then we headed into the dining room where we feasted on hot grits, biscuits, baked ham, scrambled eggs, stewed apples, and tea.

"This taste wonderful," I said. "Where'd you get the grits? We can hardly find them in Albany."

"A friend of mine went to South Carolina and brought back a sack," Mrs. Ashton said. "You can take some home with you."

I noticed that Evie seemed tense throughout the meal and imagined she might be afraid that Little Al or even James would spill the beans.

After breakfast, we meandered back to the parlor. Evie and her mother took a seat on the couch with the two children sitting between them, and Mr. Ashton sat in his armchair. James drifted to the corner whatnot and examined the collection of rare seashells, holding the largest one to his ear to hear the sea. I approached the ancient African mask and paid a silent tribute to our ancestors, and then took a seat near the couch.

"Evie, how's Jennie doing?" Mrs. Ashton asked. "I haven't heard from her in a while."

"She's fine. I saw her last week. I don't know why she hasn't written."

"Grandma," Little Al said, "Aunt Jennie brought me and James a big bag of peppermints when she came over."

"You boys have a very nice auntie."

"She's not James's auntie..."

"Little Al," Evie said, "Go outside and play. James, you go with him."

Little Al sucked his teeth.

"Let them stay," I said. "They don't often get a chance to visit your parents."

Evie sighed and looked cross. "All right."

Then Mr. Ashton asked James to help him carry the suitcases upstairs. When they returned, they were conversing about James's favorite subject.

"So you like to play baseball?"

"Yes, sir. I play with my pals after school. I hope to make the team at Albany High School next year."

"Well, if you come down and visit us this summer, I'll take you to a Lincoln Giants game."

"I'd really like that, sir. They're one of the best Negro League teams."

"Can I come too, Grandpa?" Little Al asked.

"It's up to your mother."

Mrs. Ashton turned to her husband. "Dear, why don't you take the children for a stroll?"

He nodded and asked, "Who wants a tour of Weeksville?"

The boys immediately threw on their coats, but Susie clung to her mother.

Right after they left, Mrs. Ashton came over and placed her hand on my shoulder. "Thank you, Albert."

I scratched my head and laughed. "What did I do this time?"

"That's Jennie's boy, isn't it?"

Just then I thought of something Ma used to say: *the truth will out.*

"Yes, ma'am, James is Jennie's son."

"This is a precious gift you've given us. We've been wanting to meet him for a long time."

No one asked, "How'd you know," but I was relieved and felt a heavy burden lifted off my shoulders.

Evie set Susie on the floor, and grasped her mother's hands. "Mother, I'm so sorry I couldn't tell you."

"Don't worry, dear. Everything's fine now."

A half hour later, I lay down in Evie's bed and slept soundly until I felt a pair of little fingers pinching my neck.

"Get up, Daddy. Dinner's ready," Little Al said.

"Dinner? I just ate breakfast."

I glanced at my watch. It was six o'clock, so I got out of bed and went to the dining room. After dinner, we celebrated Mrs. Ashton's birthday with a delicious pound cake Evie had baked. That night, as we lay in bed together, Evie recounted the conversation she had with her mother.

"Mother told me how she guessed the truth about James. She said that Jennie had stayed up in Troy after completing high school. And when Mother wrote to ask why she hadn't returned home, Jennie replied that she had gotten a job. After a year and a half, Jennie finally came to visit but seemed nervous and distracted."

"Do you remember that?" I asked.

"Yes, although I was quite young then. Mother added that she and Father were astonished when they heard we had taken in a nine-year-old boy shortly after we were married. And she asked herself, '*Who is this boy? Where does he come from?*' Then when she saw James for the first time today her suspicions were confirmed. She said that he's the spitting image of his grandfather."

On Sunday afternoon, Mr. Ashton asked James to join him in the tool shed. Little Al started to go with them, but I stopped him. I had a hunch that Mr. Ashton wanted to speak to James alone. They had been out there for a half an hour when Mr. Ashton called Little Al and me to the shed. There, he unlocked an old sea chest full of coins, collected from all over the world, and gave a generous handful to each boy.

James and I took the ferry to Albany that evening, leaving Evie, Little Al, and Susie behind to visit for the week. Once the journey was underway, we hiked up the stairs and stretched out on comfortable deck chairs, where we would spend the night.

"Visiting the old folks wasn't so bad, was it?"

"It was wonderful, Uncle."

"What did Mr. Ashton have to say?"

"He told me to call him Grandpa, and that he was delighted to meet me. He said that sometimes families keep secrets when they really didn't need to and it's usually best to get everything out in the open. Then he said to give Mother his warm regards."

Well, the cat was out of the bag and lo and below the sky didn't fall. But someone needed to tell that to Jennie.

# CHAPTER 26

## *Evie*

A cool wind thrashed me that Saturday afternoon as I walked along Pearl Street. I suppose it was a harbinger of the winter to come. Shivering, I wrapped my brown wool cape around me and hurried along the crowded downtown streets.

Upon entering the White Rose Tearoom, I was escorted to a small window table. The room smelled of freshly baked bread and was crowded with shoppers–drinking, eating, and conversing. Jennie was a bit late and as I waited, I thought about how I would tell her that Mother and Father knew her secret. When she arrived, smartly attired in a gray wool suit and a knitted lavender shawl and hat, she looked like a breath of fresh air. Jennie and I always made a point of dressing stylishly whenever we ventured downtown.

"That's a lovely outfit, Jennie. Is it new?"

"No, a friend of Cousin Mattie made the suit last spring. It's nice, but she doesn't sew as elegantly as you do."

"I wish I still had time to sew for you like I used to. What about your shawl and hat?"

"These were a gift from a friend."

"A special friend?"

"Yes. You've never met him."

The waitress brought our tea and scones and set them on the table.

Jennie spread a warm scone with jam and butter and bit into it. "Um, these are scrumptious. Aren't you having any?"

"Maybe later."

Jennie glanced approvingly at the white lace curtains and the blue and white-checkered tablecloths. "Sister dear, what's so important that you tore yourself away from your precious husband?"

"I wanted to talk to you privately."

"Is Al mistreating you?"

"Of course not. Al is good to me, except that he doesn't allow me to use my sewing skills to earn money–sometimes I do it secretly. He just wants me to care for the children and look beautiful."

Jennie chucked her tongue. "Just like a man. He doesn't appreciate your talents."

"Another thing–he disparages my psychic powers. Sometimes I get so frustrated."

"He doesn't want you to do anything he can't control. Stand up to him."

"I suppose I should."

"There's something else, Jennie."

"Go ahead, out with it."

"Al and I went to visit Mother on her birthday two weeks ago."

"Her birthday? Oh Lord, I forgot."

"They asked about you."

"I hope they don't think I'm neglecting them. I've been so busy of late."

"And they got to meet James."

Jennie's face grew pale. "You took James?"

"Al insisted. He told Mother and Father that James was our adopted son. Little Al almost spilled the beans, but I shushed him up and sent him and James outside with Father."

"Thank goodness."

"But then Mother suddenly asked if James was your boy."

"Oh my God, Evie!

"Al replied, 'Yes, he's Jennie's boy.' "

Cupping her hand over her mouth, she let out a soft cry, but then glanced over her shoulder to make sure no one was watching.

"Now they know." Her eyes brimmed with tears. "Will they ever forgive me for keeping him a secret?"

I placed my hands on her clenched fists. "I'm sure they already have. They were overjoyed to meet him."

"But how will I ever face them?"

"Write a letter and explain what happened. Mother and Father will respond to that."

She glanced at the ceiling and then at me. "I'll write them today."

We ordered more tea and scones, but her face grew anxious again.

"How did James react?"

"He was delighted to make their acquaintance."

"Oh Evie, I shouldn't have kept him away from them all this time."

I touched her cheek. "Dear, we can't undo the past. Let's look toward the future."

After a while, Jennie began telling me about her special friend, Peter Cooper.

"Where did you meet him?"

"At St. Thomas Episcopal Church in Troy. He sat next to me at the potluck dinner and we began to talk."

"You mean the white church?"

"A few colored people attend there, too."

"Mostly the snooty ones."

Ignoring my remark, she continued, "After that, I would often see him at Sunday mass. One day after church, he asked if he could walk me home. I said it was a free country and he could walk my way if he wanted to. Finally, one Sunday I invited him over for dinner at Cousin Mattie's, and we've been seeing each other ever since."

From what she told me, they were rather close, and I thought it was high time that Al and I got a good look at him.

We had just finished dinner on Tuesday evening when I decided to broach the subject with Al. "Jennie told me that she's seeing someone."

"Is it serious?"

"I think so. We should have them over for dinner, so we can meet him."

"That's fine with me. When?"

"What about the Sunday after next?"

He nodded.

"Al."

"Yes?"

"There's something I should tell you about Peter, that's his name."

"Sounds like a decent name to me."

"That's not it!"

"Well, stop beating about the bush. What's the matter with him? Does the man have two heads?" He laughed.

"No. It's just that Peter is . . . he's white."

"Who? What?"

"I said Peter is a white man."

"A white man! Why does she always have to go off the deep end?"

"Jennie's heart was broken years ago. Now if Peter makes her happy . . ."

"I hope she knows what she's doing."

"Should I invite them or not?"

"Yes, invite them, by all means."

I fetched my stationery and wrote Jennie a note inviting her and Peter to dinner.

A week later I spoke to Al about the approaching visit. "Jennie and Peter will be coming for dinner in a few days. What should we cook?"

"What were you thinking of?"

"What about a roast duck?"

"I'm not going to break the bank just because Jennie's boyfriend is coming to dinner!"

"I thought it would be nice to have something special."

Al thought for a moment. "How about I buy a piece of pork on Saturday. Then we can have roast pork, sweet potatoes, succotash, and steamed cabbage with ham hocks."

"Sounds delicious, dear, and I'll make my favorite bread pudding."

"You sure that's not too much work for you, honey?"

I detected a hint of sarcasm in his voice, so I offered to make my stewed tomatoes as well.

The anticipated day arrived. The bread pudding was cooling on the kitchen table and the pork roast and sweet potatoes were baking in the oven. Later, we would put the vegetables on the stove to simmer. When we were nearly finished cooking, Al asked if Peter knew about James.

"Honestly, I don't know, but she must have told him."

"I hope so, Evie, because I don't intend to cover up for her any longer."

# CHAPTER 27

## *Evie*

At half past one, Jennie and Peter arrived, bearing gifts–imported chocolates and a bunch of orange chrysanthemums for me, and a bottle of Old Charter whiskey for Al. Jovial introductions were made and hearty handshakes exchanged. Peter was a tall, thin, intelligent-looking man, with brown hair and slightly sallow skin. A pair of round metal-rimmed eyeglasses was perched on his nose and he reminded me of Ichabod Crane, the schoolteacher in the *Legend of Sleepy Hollow*. Jennie looked divine in a long pink dress, adorned with glass beads, and a purple velvet cape. Her face glowed with happiness and her rose-water perfume gently wafted through the air.

We showed them into the parlor where the two men became engaged in a spirited conversation about politics while we all sipped hot apple cider. Peter said that he worked as an accountant for the state government but also had private clients. After a while, I fetched the children from the bedroom where they had been playing.

"Peter, these are our children, James, Little Al and Susie."

Both boys shook his hand, but Susie backed away and clung to my legs.

As they stared at this strange white man, Jennie asked, "Aren't you going to greet your Aunt Jennie?"

They ran over and hugged her.

Jennie herded the children into the kitchen. "Come and have your lunch while the men talk. If you're good, I'll give you some of those chocolates Uncle Peter brought your mother."

After they had eaten, I put Susie in her crib for a nap and the boys went back to their room. Then Jennie and I dished the hot food into covered serving bowls and placed them on the dining table, which was spread with a blue linen cloth that matched my blue and white china.

"Peter seems very nice, Jennie."

"He's sweet and not a bit prejudiced. We have such interesting conversations. You know I can't abide an ignorant man."

"Al and I discuss the news every evening, when he's not too tired."

Jennie arranged the flowers in a vase and set it on the table. "I hope Peter and Al get along."

"I'm sure they will. By now, Al's probably telling him a funny story."

Leaving Jennie in the dining room, I went to call the men to dinner but stopped short near the parlor door when I heard them conversing.

"Peter, are you from around these parts?"

"No. I was brought up in Maine; my grandparents were Quaker farmers there. And after attending college in Massachusetts, I came to Albany and found work at the Capitol."

"I work at the Capitol, too. In the boiler room."

"So Jennie told me."

"How long have you been seeing Jennie?"

"About six months."

"That long? And just what are your intentions toward her?"

I froze on the spot, listening.

"I'm very fond of her."

"I fell in love with Evie the first day we met and asked for her hand three months later. Of course, everyone is different."

"My life has certainly changed since I met Jennie. In fact, I don't know what I'd do without her."

"Sounds like love to me. But you'd best be sure of your feelings. You don't want to hurt her, do you?"

"Hurt Jennie? Never!"

A moment of silence passed between them, a silence that seemed to be born of uncertainty. I held my breath and inched closer to the parlor door.

Then, Peter said, "Come to think of it, I do believe I love Jennie and want to do right by her."

"That might even mean breaking up with her if you're not absolutely sure you can endure the stigma you'd face as a mixed-race couple. Many people in Albany will ostracize you and there are places in this country where you could face arrest for cohabitating with a colored woman."

"You're right, Al. Jennie and I will have to give our relationship some serious thought."

Stunned, I tiptoed away from the parlor door but stopped just outside the dining room. *Why did Al have to be so blunt with Peter? Is he trying to scare him off?*

Then I heard Al say, "Okay Evie, you can come in now."

I took a deep breath and called out, "Dinner is ready."

The meal proceeded without a hitch and even though Peter seemed a little distracted, he piled his plate high with meat and vegetables.

"This is delicious, Mrs. Evie. You and your sister are both excellent cooks."

"Thank you, Peter."

I glanced over and saw Al suppressing a grin as he dished up a second helping of roast pork.

After a while, the men started conversing about politics. "Al, what do you think about the new procedure in New York to elect our U.S. senators?" Peter asked.

"It's good. Electing the senators by popular vote is more democratic than having them chosen by the state legislature."

"It would really be more democratic," Jennie said, "if women were allowed to vote."

Peter winced. "You'll have to convince the men of that."

Clearing my throat, I gently tapped the table with a fork. "Women should have the vote!"

Al laughed. "I wasn't aware that you and Jennie were suffragettes."

Jennie rolled her eyes. "It's no laughing matter, Al!"

As our guests were preparing to leave that evening, I brought in James and the children to say goodbye and Peter gave each of them a shiny silver dollar. Al and I escorted Jennie and her suitor downstairs and as we waved goodbye, I wondered where their romance would lead.

A week and a half later, I received a note from Jennie, saying she hadn't heard from Peter in over a week. She explained that after they left our house, she told Peter about James and he seemed to take it in stride. She also mentioned that Peter told her he needed time to think about something Al had pointed out. When I questioned Al, he said that whatever I overheard at the parlor door was all I was going to hear from him. So I wrote and told her I didn't know what they talked about.

Another week passed–without a word from Jennie–and I became worried. One evening, after Al and I had gone to bed, we heard a loud banging on the outside door. Al jumped up and stomped down the stairs. As I slipped on my robe, I wondered who could be calling at that hour of the night.

It was Jennie and she was carrying a suitcase. "Sorry to come so late, but I had to go home after work to freshen up and fetch my bag."

I led her to a seat in the parlor. "Are you going somewhere?"

"I plan to catch the Dayline Ferry tomorrow morning. I've asked for a week off at the factory, and I'm going home to Mother and Father."

"They'll be happy to see you."

"I hope so. Of course, they don't know anything about Peter, and I don't know if I should tell them."

A question–I dared not ask–must have been written on my face.

"No," she said. "I haven't heard from him and it's nearly three weeks now."

"Jennie, I'm so sorry."

"I guess it's over."

"At least, he could have had the common decency to make a clean break of it," I said, "rather than disappearing into the woodwork."

Al shook his head. "I can't believe he's acting this way. He seemed very concerned about your feelings."

"Talk is cheap," I said.

Al cleared his throat. "Jennie, I suggested that he think carefully about the problems you would face as a mixed-race couple. But if he really loves you, he will have to make an honest woman of you. In my book that means marriage."

Jennie sighed and shrugged. "I suppose facing society's contempt would be too much for him or maybe he didn't want to take on the responsibility of James."

"It's not about James," Al said. "I told him we wanted to keep James right here with us."

I gasped. "You told him about James!"

"Well, somehow it just came out."

Jennie began to weep.

I put my arm around her. "Peter's actions show he's not worthy of you."

My words were true, but they rang hollow in the face of a broken heart. Jennie spent the night and left early the next morning for the sanctuary of Weeksville. Three days after Jennie departed, there was another knock on the front door. This time we were at the kitchen table and had just finished dinner.

James jumped up and raced down the stairs. "I'll get it, Auntie."

"Who in the world can that be?" I asked.

Al raised his eyebrows. "This place is more popular than Sam's Barbeque on the Fourth of July."

James returned. "Uncle, someone at the door is asking for you."

"Who is it?"

"Uncle Peter."

"He has some nerve showing up here!" I said.

"James, show Uncle Peter into the parlor."

I puffed out my jaws.

"Look, Evie. We need to find out what's going on."

Al went into the parlor. I left the dirty dishes in the sink, hurriedly put Susie to bed, and told James to read Little Al a story. Then I marched, uninvited, into the room and planted myself in the lady's armchair, silently daring anyone to object.

Peter, who was on the couch, stood up and greeted me. "Good evening, Mrs. Evelyn. I'm sorry for calling unannounced."

Frowning, I gripped the arms of my chair. "Good evening."

The room went dead quiet.

Peter spoke again. "I was just explaining to Al why I haven't been in touch with Jennie lately."

"Three weeks!"

"Yes, it's been three weeks, hasn't it?"

I waited.

"After my conversation with Al, I realized I had some serious decisions to make so I went to visit my grandmother who lives on a small farm in Maine with my sister and brother-in-law. She brought me up after my parents died and we've always been close. She's a wise woman and I treasure her advice. I guess I should have told Jennie I was going out of town, but I planned to write her once I got there."

He adjusted his glasses. "A few days after I arrived, there was an unexpected snowstorm, and we were snowed in for a week. During that time, I caught a chill while trying to clear the snow and was confined to bed for another week. Poor Granny, old and frail as she is, nursed me back to health, and as soon as I felt well enough to travel, I returned to Albany to look for Jennie. She wasn't at work nor was she at Cousin Mattie's and Miss Mattie wouldn't say where she had gone. So I decided to throw myself on your mercy. I need to see her so we can settle matters between us."

"She went to visit her parents a few days ago," Al said. "She should still be there."

"I know this is an imposition, but could you please give me their address."

"I doubt Jennie wants to see you," I said, "after all you . . ."

"Evie, let Jennie decide that."

Al gave him the address and Peter stood up. "I've imposed on your good nature long enough. Thank you both. I leave for New York tomorrow morning on the eight o'clock train."

"Is that all you've got to say?" I asked.

"Yes, ma'am, except that I'm sorry for hurting Jennie."

Al walked him downstairs and returned to the parlor. "Well, that's that."

"That's what? Didn't he tell you what he was going to say to Jennie?"

"Nope, and I didn't ask!"

I glared at my husband. "Aren't you even interested?"

"Sweetheart, just let it be. We'll hear the end of this story soon enough."

## CHAPTER 28
# *Albert – 1916*

∽᯼ ᯼∾

On a brisk December day, I happened to stroll by the New York Central Railroad station and noticed a large poster on the outside wall. It immediately piqued my interest, so I stopped and studied it.

RECRUITS WANTED FOR THE COLORED REGIMENT

NEW YORK 15th NATIONAL GUARD

Inquire at Lafayette Theater, 132nd St. & 7th Ave., Harlem, NYC

I remembered reading about this regiment some time ago in the *Age*, a respected Negro newspaper. The story was that Gov. Whitman had appointed Colonel Hayward, a white army officer with distinguished service in the Spanish-American War, to organize a new colored National Guard regiment and that Harlem folks were pretty excited about it. However, some in the community were incensed because the Governor had bypassed Captain Fillmore, a colored officer who had been urging New York governors and legislators to establish the regiment for years. Others were quoted as saying that they would wait and see what this Colonel Hayward would accomplish.

I was still staring at the poster, imagining the possibilities it presented, when an old, gray-bearded colored fellow carrying a shovel trudged toward me over the snow-covered road.

"Thinking about joining up?" he asked.

"No, too old. "

"Don't look that old to me."

He looked around, and when he saw no one was watching, he pulled out a flask and took a swig. "Have some? It'll warm you up."

"No thanks, sir."

"Wish I was a young man; I'd join up in a heartbeat. Wouldn't have to shovel snow no more."

"I guess so. But I've got a wife and children to support." *To tell the truth, I wish I didn't have to shovel coal anymore.*

"Wife and kids? Well, that's a different kettle of fish." Tightening a scarf around his wrinkled neck, he lifted his brown wool cap, nodded, and slowly walked back to the station, shovel in hand.

A few months later, on a bitterly cold February morning, Tom, Phineas, and I were feeding the Capitol's hungry steam boiler when Irish entered.

"Listen here, guys, a lieutenant from Governor Whitman's office asked if I had any colored men on my staff, and I told him about you all. He's recruiting for a colored National Guard unit and wants to talk to you right after work."

Phineas scratched his armpit. "I ain't interested in being no guardsman."

"Hold on!" Irish said. "He just wants to talk to you."

"I think we should go and hear what the lieutenant has to say," I said.

Irish snickered. "The lieutenant's looking for young men, Al."

"I'm not fixing to join up, I'm just curious."

"Me, too," Tom said. "I'd like to hear the lieutenant out."

"Well, if you all is going, I might as well tag along too," Phineas said.

Irish nodded. "That settles it. I'll take you to his office later."

Phineas rested his shovel against the wall. "Listen up, boss. We better stop work early to wash up. I don't want to meet the Loo-ten-ant with coal dust on my face."

"Okay, knock off at 4:30."

At five o'clock that evening, Irish led us through a series of back passages into a part of the Capitol I had never seen before.

"Wow, ain't this something," Phineas said.

"This is the famous Great Western staircase," Irish explained. "Took fourteen years to build and cost over a million bucks."

"Jeez, I can't even imagine that much money!" Tom said.

The sight of the enormous granite staircase, with soaring arches and elaborately carved columns that shot upward toward the sky, took my breath away. It was dusk, and the soft glow of the electric lights mounted on the columns mingled with the rose-gray natural light streaming through a huge skylight.

*These are the corridors of power*, I thought. *A world away from the hellhole we're laboring in.*

When we reached Lieutenant Spencer's office, Irish knocked on the door. We gingerly entered the room, and I took note of the many framed diplomas and military certificates displayed on the walls. The Lieutenant was standing behind a large desk that held several orderly piles of documents. Smiling generously, he strode toward us with outstretched hands. Irish made the introductions and left. Lieutenant Spencer was an amiable-looking, smartly dressed, stocky man of medium height in his early forties. His square-shaped face sported long sideburns and a neatly trimmed mustache that nearly covered his upper lip. He pointed to three cushioned chairs near the desk and invited us to take a seat. Stealthily checking my fingernails and noticing that they still bore traces of coal dust, I balled up my hands into fists.

"Gentlemen, thank you for coming. As you may know, last year the Governor asked Colonel Hayward and me to organize the New York 15th, a colored National Guard regiment. The governor felt that the great Negro population of New York ought to be given an opportunity to shine in the National Guard field.

"Have you all heard about the New York 15th?"

Tom and Phineas shrugged. I replied that I had read about it and had recently seen a recruitment poster. He looked pleased and went on to claim that the regiment had the overwhelming support of New York City's Negro community.

"Volunteering to serve in the 15th will be a service to your country and your people, and if you work hard, there's a good chance for advancement to the rank of sergeant. Colonel Hayward has promised that no color line will be drawn in this unit. If a man qualifies to be a non-commissioned officer or even a commissioned one, he'll be promoted. We already have some fine Negro commissioned officers and are looking for more. Lieutenant James Reese Europe is one of them."

"Who?" Tom asked.

"James Reese Europe is a famous bandleader," I said. "He accompanies and writes music for Irene and Vernon Castle, the café society ballroom dancers."

Lieutenant Spencer nodded. "Captain Charles Fillmore and Spottswood Poles have also come on board."

"Spottswood Poles! The crack center fielder for Harlem's Lincoln Giants baseball team?" Tom asked.

Phineas's mouth fell open. "I can't believe old Spottswood joined up."

"He sure has," Lieutenant Spencer said, smiling.

"How many mens you got in the regiment now?" Phineas asked.

"I'd say about nine hundred. We need at least thirteen hundred to fill out the regiment during peacetime, but for wartime, we'd need at least two thousand men."

"Wow, that's a lot," Phineas said. "What happens if we join up and the country go to war?"

"Once the regiment reaches its wartime strength, it'll be mustered into the regular army."

Phineas rubbed his chin. "What that mean?"

"It means you'll become a soldier in the U.S. Army," I said.

"That's right," Spencer added, "but remember that all the members of the regiment will serve together in the same army unit."

The lieutenant's office grew quiet.

After a moment or so, he asked, "Well, what do you think?"

Tom and Phineas told him they were interested and would let him know soon.

"Al, you sound like you were in the service before."

"Yes, sir. I served four years in the Navy and was honorably discharged."

"What about trying the army this time? You'd make a darn good soldier!"

"Sounds tempting, but I have a wife and three kids to support and another one is on the way."

"Whew, I see your point. Say, you seem to know a lot about the regiment. Do you think you could recruit for us around Albany?"

"I'd be proud to do that, sir."

"Thanks, Al. Just let me know when you get a group together and I can meet with them."

We shook hands with the Lieutenant and left. Then the three of us hurried over to the Dockside Tavern, the rough waterfront bar where longshoremen and ice haulers hung out.

Before becoming a stoker, Phineas was an ice hauler, cutting hundred-pound blocks of ice from the frozen Hudson River in the winter and hauling them into storage shacks. In the spring, the ice would be cut into smaller chunks and sold to customers to cool their iceboxes. He said it was a tough job and most times you only worked part of the year. As we entered the tavern, two ice haulers ran up and grabbed Phineas and they grappled together like three wrestling bears.

"Phineas, you SOB, where you been?" one of them asked.

"Didn't you hear? I over at the Capitol, in the boiler room."

"I'll be damned. How's it?"

"Well, I be hauling coal instead of ice. Instead of shivering, I be sweating."

"Hell, you can't win for losing," the other ice hauler said.

"Don't get me wrong. It's all right. I works year-round and gets a week vacation, too!"

Phineas's buddies looked at him in awe. "Vacation? Can you beat that?"

We sat down at a table and as we waited for our drinks, I looked around the dimly lit, smoke-filled room and spotted a bunch of colored men who appeared to have recently come up from the south. I heard that most of them were living in shacks along the waterfront and that ice hauling was the only job they could get.

"Tom," I asked, "what do you think of the Lieutenant?"

He downed his mug of beer. "He seems like a pretty decent chap."

"He just want us to join up," Phineas said. "Course, he going to be nice."

"Not necessarily," I said. "I've come across plenty of men that were arrogant, even though they were asking you for a favor. But you're right about one thing, Phineas, the Lieutenant needs to recruit more colored men."

"Al, do you think we should sign up?" Tom asked.

"I don't know. It could be a smart move for an ambitious young guy."

Phineas wiped the foam from his lips. "I don't want to be no soldier."

"Look here," I said, "you need to make up your own minds. I wish this regiment had been around in 1900 when I joined the service. While I was in the Navy, I spent four damn years in a ship's boiler room, shoveling coal. Other than being a kitchen boy, that's all they would allow us to do."

Tom wrinkled his forehead. "Do you think it's a good deal?"

I shrugged. "If this country goes to war, they might even draft men, like they did in the Civil War."

Tom sipped his second mug of beer. "Gee, I hope not."

"Al," Phineas asked," was you alive during the Civil War?"

"Don't be a damn fool," Tom said.

I laughed and shook my head. "Anyway, it might be better to sign up now rather than be drafted later."

"I suppose so," Tom muttered.

"Are you really going to recruit for them, Mr. J?" Phineas asked.

"Didn't I say I would?"

"Are they going to pay you?"

"No. I'm volunteering."

Just then, a plump, shapely Negro waitress emerged from the kitchen carrying a tray of steaming hot cabbage, potatoes, and beef brisket. As the delicious aromas wafted through the air, my stomach began to growl, and I heard the smacking of lips throughout the room. After a few minutes, the waitress switched over to our table.

She looked me in the eye and winked. "Hi there, handsome, would you like a plate?"

"No thanks, ma'am. Smells mighty good, but my wife's expecting me home."

I gulped down my beer and took my leave.

"Sorry I'm late, honey. Had a meeting after work."

"I was worried. I thought you might have gone to see a girlfriend."

"Don't be silly. You're the only woman in the world for me." I kissed her cheek. "Tom, Phineas and I met with Lieutenant Spencer, who told us about the new colored National Guard."

"The one in Harlem?"

"Yeah. They need men, so they're recruiting here in Albany."

"Al, you're not thinking of joining up?"

"No. Maybe Tom and Phineas will."

"That's good, but why did you go to the meeting?"

"I was curious. Lieutenant Spencer wants me to recruit for the regiment."

"I hope you didn't agree. You're already so busy with your extra jobs, I hardly get to see you anymore."

"Don't worry, dear. It won't take up much time."

Waving her hand in dismissal, she told me to come and eat. And yes, it was the same leftover food I had cooked on Sunday.

I decided the most efficient way to handle the recruitment was to set up an initial meeting where men could ask questions and get information. The next Sunday I spoke to Pastor Henry about holding it at the church. He agreed and we set a date. Pastor encouraged several young men from the congregation to attend and I asked Tom and Phineas to invite the ice haulers and the other men working on the waterfront. During the next few weeks, I visited railroad terminals and spoke to colored porters. I went to places where young men worked or hung out and invited them. Most of them seemed enthusiastic about the regiment. I imagine they were looking for any opportunity to advance and a glimmer of hope for the future. There just didn't seem to be any decent work for colored men in Albany.

About thirty-five men, including Tom and Phineas, showed up at an evening meeting in mid-March. After downing sweetened hot tea and eating warm buttered biscuits, which the church sisters provided, the men listened as I told them about the 15th regiment. There was quite a lively discussion of the pros and cons. The question of whether America would enter the European war was foremost on everyone's mind.

"Why should we fight for America, if it comes to that, when America doesn't treat us right?" one chap asked.

"Listen, brothers. If we're going to further our just cause," another fellow said, "we must perform the duties of citizenship which include fighting for our country."

A young man no older than twenty stood up. "I don't wanna fight no Germans. The Germans never did nothing to me and even if they did, I forgives them."

Everyone laughed.

Then someone in the crowd shouted, "Men, we should give this country another chance and show that we're patriotic for the sake of our race."

"Look, we've already fought for this country, from the Boston massacre down to the battle of Carrizal, Mexico, and what have we gotten out of it?" a fellow about my age asked.

Finally, after all the views had been aired, I asked those who wanted to learn more about the regiment to meet with Lieutenant Spencer at the Albany Armory. The next week, twenty-five men showed up to hear the lieutenant speak, and out of these, eighteen signed up for the regiment, including, can you believe it, Phineas Middleton. A few days later, the recruits traveled down to New York City to report to the regimental office. Tom was not one of them; he said he had fallen in love and didn't want to leave his sweetheart. I was disappointed that, in spite of all the hard work, only eighteen men volunteered, but Lieutenant Spencer seemed pleased.

I had done my bit for the cause, so I should have felt relaxed, but I was worried about the future. To make matters worse, I sprained my wrist on the job and was in constant pain but couldn't take off from work because we needed the money. I had little hope of finding a factory job and the job I currently held was slowly killing me. I was already thirty-seven years old. Would I be able to haul coal in ten or even five years? If not, how would I support my family? And how would I ever send my boy to college? Every time I thought of it, I broke out in a cold sweat. Things looked bleak. War seemed imminent.

Suddenly, an outlandish thought began to play on the edges of my consciousness: *If I go to war, they'll have to give me a better job when I return. But how can I leave my darling, Evie? How would she get along without me?*

These questions haunted me night and day. When Evie said I looked troubled and asked what the matter was, I couldn't tell her the truth.

On April 2, 1917, the unholy mess hit the fan. President Wilson, who won the election on the slogan, "he kept us out of the war," outlined the case for it to the country, and four days later, Congress declared war on Germany. I heard that the 15th regiment was struggling to reach its wartime strength of two thousand men.

The day after the war declaration, Lieutenant Spencer sent for me. "I realize you spent a great deal of time and effort recruiting, and I hate to ask you to do more, but our country's at war and we're desperate to increase our enrollment."

I let out a low whistle. "Sir, I don't know what else I can do, but I'll try. Come to think of it, several of the married men who wanted to enlist, didn't, because they had families to support."

"Al, this is the Great War that's raging now, and America is going to need millions of men to defeat Germany, Austria-Hungary, and Turkey. I hear rumors that Congress will soon be instituting a draft."

"A draft!"

"You don't have to worry—you're way past the draft age. I think the limits are twenty-one through thirty. How old did you say your children were?"

"There's our nephew, James, who's nearly seventeen, Little Al, who's six and a half, and Susie, who's three. And another baby's due any day now."

"Wow, that quite a gaggle."

He leaned toward me and whispered, "We simply can't leave soldiers' families at the mercy of charity. Governor Whitman says the War Department has recommended that Congress give an allowance to soldiers' wives and children. They're even talking about life insurance for servicemen. It hasn't passed it yet, but something will be done!"

"I certainly hope so."

This conversation with Lieutenant Spencer put a bee in my bonnet, but I had no time to act on it. I was busy recruiting more men for the regiment, training the new assistant stoker Irish had hired to replace Phineas, painting apartments on Saturdays, and trying to spend more time with my wife.

Eleven days after America's declaration of war, Theresa May Johnson, our third child, was born. This time Jennie, who had quit her job at the Peabody Collar factory, stayed with us to help out. Almost every evening, her husband Peter would come over after work. Yes, they had tied the knot nearly two years ago. Evie and I had stood up for them, and Canon Tucker of the St. Thomas Episcopal Church had reluctantly married the interracial couple. They seemed very happy although they were still encountering stares and clucks from folks whenever they walked together in town. One evening after dinner, I confided my fears to Peter.

"Don't worry, Al. If you join the service, I'll help Evie and the children while you're away."

"Thanks, Peter, but it's my responsibility."

"You and Evie have been taking care of James for years. Jennie and I wanted to do our part, but we didn't know how to broach the subject."

"James is like a son to me."

"I know. But you'd be doing us a favor if you let us contribute to his upkeep."

"Let me think on it."

"Okay, we'll talk again, soon."

After mulling over my conversations with Lieutenant Spencer and Peter, the outlandish thought that had been haunting me didn't seem so outlandish anymore: *if I fight in this war, they'll have to give me a better job when I return.*

Was I going mad to think of leaving my family? Then an unsettling debate began to rage in my mind.

*I could send most of my army pay to Evie.*

*It wouldn't be nearly enough!*

*Peter said he would help.*

*Would it be right to accept his money?*

*The Lieutenant said the army would give the families an allowance.*

*Would it be sufficient?*

Then I remembered the inheritance from Farfar, stashed away in the bottom of the toolbox. Although we had used a good deal of it for family emergencies over the years, enough remained to support Evie for a few months.

The mind-bending debate started again.

*What if I get killed?*

*The Lieutenant said that Evie would receive insurance.*

*Evie would be left alone, and I wouldn't see my children grow up. No amount of insurance could replace that.*

*But what will happen if I stay and someday can't support my family?*

*Will Evie grow to despise me? Lord knows I couldn't bear that.*

This torturous, head-splitting deliberation continued for several days. Time was running out. I needed to make a decision. As I sat in the parlor late one night belaboring my situation, my eyes fell on the tattered Bible Ma had given me when I left home years ago. I grasped the Bible and knelt down.

"Dear Lord, I admit you haven't heard from me lately and I'm sorry about that. But I really need your help." When I finished explaining my predicament to God, I said, "Lord, it's in your hands, now. Amen."

After praying, I lay down, fell fast asleep, and began to dream. I was naked, except for a white towel, tied around my waist. It was dark as I lurched along a mountain trail toward a shadowy crossroad, my bare feet stumbling on the rocky ground. I froze in terror as I looked ahead, for the road on the right led to a pitch-black tunnel and the one on the left to a steep, up-winding path, veiled in smoky mist. But when I looked again I saw a tiny flame ahead and heard a voice whispering, "Walk to the end of the light."

I awoke early the next morning, and strangely enough, I knew what path to take and felt completely at ease.

## CHAPTER 29

# *Evie – 1917*

I'll never forget the day Tessie turned two weeks old. Al hadn't been his usual self for some time. He seemed troubled and lost in thought. That afternoon he came home early from work, humming and carrying a lovely bunch of daffodils. I was delighted. The flowers reminded me of a charming Wadsworth's poem, where the lonely poet encounters "a host of golden daffodils."

I arranged the flowers in my blue glass vase and placed it on the dining table. James set the table with the special china, and we all sat down to eat the delicious meal Jennie had prepared. The occasion seemed remarkably festive and I was overcome with joy at the restoration of my husband's good humor. After we had eaten, Al asked Jennie and Peter to excuse us because he had something important to discuss with me. It was already eight-thirty in the evening, so Jennie bathed Susie and tucked her into bed, James and Little Al went to put on their nightclothes, and Peter retired to the parlor.

Al led me into our bedroom where Tessie was fast asleep and shut the door. Sitting down beside me on the bed, he cradled my hand in his. "Honey, you know I love you dearly and would do anything in the world for you and the children."

"Yes, dear, but what's all this about?"

"There's no easy way to say it."

"What's troubling you?"

"Evie, I'm going to join the army."

I jumped up and opened my mouth to speak, but no words came out.

Finally, I found my voice. "Join the army? Have you gone mad? What about me and the children?"

"Please, hear me out."

My whole world came crashing down. I wanted to cry and pull out my hair. I wanted to run away. I thought: *What can he possibly say to explain such foolishness?*

"Evie, I've dug coal for three years in the mines, shoveled it for four in the Navy, and now I'm working it again at the Capitol. Keep in mind, I was injured on the job a few weeks ago. I'm not as strong as I used to be, and I can't do this strenuous job forever. What will happen when I can no longer work as a stoker? How will this family survive? How will Little Al get an education? On the other hand, if I serve this country in wartime, they will have to give me a better job when I return."

Tears ran down my cheeks. "How do you know that?"

"I believe it and I'm betting our future on it."

"But how will we carry on while you're gone?"

"I'll send you my army paycheck every month. Peter will contribute to James's upkeep, and as soon as Congress passes the new law the army will provide you with an allowance. That should bring your income up to at least what I'm earning now. And if you're ever short on money, I have some put aside you can draw on."

"You're only thinking about the money!" I stamped my foot. "I need you here. What am I going to do without my husband to take care of me? What are the children to do?"

"It won't be easy for any of us. Leaving you is the last thing in the world I want to do, but it's a sacrifice we have to make to win a better future."

"I can't raise these children by myself. I just can't."

I covered my face, frantically thinking of what I could say to make him change his mind. He placed his arm on my shoulder, but I shook it off.

"Evie, I've been the head of this family since we got married eight years ago, guiding and making decisions for it, and you've been a wonderful wife. Maybe I should've let you have more of a say, but I thought I knew best. Even so, I sense there's a deep well of strength within you. You can do this, I know you can."

"I can't and I won't. I knew when you started recruiting for that darn regiment, no good would come of it."

"Evie!"

"It's true, isn't it? Now they want to take you away from me."

"It's not like that. I'm telling you if I stay on this job much longer, I'll turn to stone and ash."

"Oh, my God!"

The image of my passionate, flesh and blood husband turning to stone and ash terrified me. Shuddering, I collapsed on his strong shoulders and sobbed bitterly. For the next few days, I walked around in a daze and prayed to wake up from this nightmare. Finally, I pulled myself together and faced the reality that Al would soon be leaving for the army.

Shortly before he departed, Al escorted James to the market and showed him where to buy the sacks of potatoes and flour each month, and he taught Little Al how to clean the mantles and change the wicks of the oil lamps.

The next day, he handed me four envelopes. "This should be enough for your expenses for the next few months, even for your chocolates. But I don't know if they'll be available during wartime."

*They'd better be!* I thought.

"When you get my army pay and the government allowance, and Peter's money, put it away for when you need it."

He led me into the hall and showed me his secret cash hoard in the bottom drawer of the tool chest. I'd known about it for years, but I didn't tell him that.

"The money in there is for emergencies, only emergencies. We'll need it when I return home from the war."

"I'll try to be frugal."

That evening, Al called James and the children into the parlor just before bedtime. He was in his gentleman's armchair, and they clustered around him on the green and yellow flowered carpet. I took a seat at the far end of the couch, cradling little Tessie in my arms. Then he told them he would be leaving in two days and going overseas to fight in the Great War to make a better life for us all.

"Boys, I'm depending on you to help Mommy while I'm gone."

"I will, Uncle."

"Yes, Daddy."

Susie stood up and scampered over to him. "What should I do, Daddy?"

"Oh, you can help Mommy dust the furniture."

"Daddy, are you going overseas to kill the Germans?" Little Al asked.

"He ain't goin' there to kiss 'em," James replied.

"Boys, boys, don't worry about killing Germans. Just hold down the home front."

"You can depend on us, Uncle."

Al gathered Susie in his arms and leaned toward the boys. "I'm sure you'll be well behaved and obedient to Mommy."

Looking as though he finally understood that his father was going to that faraway place called overseas, Little Al answered, "Yes, Daddy."

And James nodded. "We promise, Uncle."

Then Al said that he would write as often as he could and come right home after the war was won. No one mentioned that my dear heart could be killed or wounded in this so-called Great War. We dared not even think it.

On the morning of May 15, 1917, my Al left home. He was headed to Union Station where he would meet the eight men he had recently recruited, and they would ride the train to the Peekskill army camp. When I asked Al why he was joining the regular army instead of the 15th National Guard, he said that he wanted to start collecting full army pay immediately and that he and the other men would transfer to the 15th as soon as it was mustered into the army. Lieutenant Spencer had promised to make sure the transfers went through quickly.

Susie and I stood at the outside door squinting in the early morning sun, waving our goodbyes and holding back our tears as he walked away. The night before, he had held me in his arms and told me how much he loved me. He said that not an hour would pass by without him thinking of me. In the morning, I rose early and placed my photo and the solid gold cross my parents had given me in his jacket pocket. Then I cooked him a hearty breakfast: bacon, fried potatoes, scrambled eggs, hot biscuits, and tea. He was pleasantly surprised, but I couldn't let my husband go off to war on an empty stomach.

Wearing a gray fedora with the front brim snapped down, a tan sports jacket, and neatly pressed gray pants, Al–broad of shoulder, tall, and straight of back–strode down First Street. James carried his suitcase and Little Al held his hand as they escorted him to the distant corner where he would catch the trolley. Halfway down the block, he turned around and blew me a kiss.

# PART TWO

# CHAPTER 30

## *Albert – 1917*

I was in the field practicing morning maneuvers with my platoon when the drill sergeant ordered me to the camp office. It was the last week of July and I had been at the Peekskill Camp since mid-May. When I arrived at the camp office, I found the eight recruits from Albany waiting for me. We were directed to the duty officer who informed us that the 15th New York National Guard regiment had been mustered into the army and our transfers had come through.

As he handed us our orders, the officer said, "Soldiers, pack your gear and report to your new regiment in Camp Whitman by this afternoon."

I ran back to the tent and stashed Evie's gold cross and photo in my pocket, stuffing the rest of my gear into a knapsack. Then the nine of us marched to town, caught the train to Poughkeepsie, and hiked from there to Camp Whitman.

We arrived at the camp about one in the afternoon and immediately reported to our company commanders. After being directed to my new out-fit, C Company, I rushed over, and joined the action, pitching sleeping tents and field kitchens, digging latrines, and clearing out the entire area, which was thick with vegetation. The 15th regiment was divided into three battalions, each consisting of three infantry companies and a machine-gun company. C Company was part of First Battalion. Colonel William Hayward, the commander of Regimental Headquarters, ran the whole show.

That evening, I set off on foot to explore the encampment, but I hadn't gone far when I heard a familiar voice.

"Mr. J! What the hell you doing here?"

I spun around and spied Phineas Middleton looking fit as a fiddle in his army fatigues.

"I'm called Private Johnson these days."

"Don't worry. Before the war's over, they gonna make you a general."

"Thanks for the promotion, Phineas. How are you doing?"

"Okay, I guess. But this 15th regiment ain't all it's cracked up to be."

"Is that a fact? Did you guys come up by train?"

"Yeah. You should've seen the commotion at the 125th Street Station. We marched there early this morning–the band playing, *Billy* Boy–and thousands of folk came to see us off. Soldiers leaning out train windows, grabbing they sweethearts' hands. There was tears shed, kisses blown, and promises made."

"Sounds like quite a scene. Do you have a steady girl, Phineas?"

"Nope. When the war's over, I'll find me a nice gal and settle down."

I nodded and started to walk away.

"Say, Al, what your outfit?"

"C Company."

"Shucks, I'm in Company D."

I was relieved he wasn't in C Company because he tended to complain a lot.

Camp Whitman was located on the banks of a river, and most of the colored soldiers took their daily baths there. It was a great way to cool down after working in the hot August sun. Over the next few weeks, we learned military courtesy, played war games, scaled walls, and practiced hitting targets with our newly issued Springfield rifles. Our drill sergeant, Ebenezer Green, made us clean, breakdown, and reassemble those rifles until we could do it blindfolded, and he drilled us in marching maneuvers until we could start, stop, and turn on a dime. The sergeant was a barrel-chested man, with short but powerful legs. He had a large head that seemed out of proportion to his body and a yellowish-brown face, sprinkled with freckles. He never walked except to strut or spoke except to growl, at least in front of enlisted men. One day when we were out on a ten-mile march under a burning sun, I felt my energy ebbing away and my legs about to buckle. I had to draw on my inner strength to keep up with the younger men.

The next morning at roll call, Sergeant Green strutted up and looked me dead in the eye. "Private Johnson."

"Yes, Sergeant?"

"Aren't you a bit long in the tooth for all this drilling?"

"My teeth are long, sir, but they're strong and sharply filed."

He threw me a puzzled look. Then he laughed out loud. Suddenly, the forty soldiers in line, amazed to hear his laughter, shifted their eyes toward him.

"Private Johnson."

"Yes, Sergeant!"

"You're okay."

"Thank you, Sergeant."

"But that doesn't mean I won't kick your ass if you cross me. Remember, I got eyes in the back of my head."

"Very good, Sergeant."

He turned toward the line of soldiers, who were gaping at him. "What the fuck are you jokers staring at?" Eighty nervous eyes swung forward.

"Platoon, double-time march," he said, and we doubled-timed around the camp until he ordered us to halt.

At the end of the day, I collapsed on my bunk and fell dead asleep before I could pen a note to Evie. She must have wondered why I wasn't writing as often as I had promised.

I had just finished dinner one evening when I ran into Phineas Middleton again, outside the mess tent. It had been almost a week since I last saw him.

"Hey there, Mr. J. Been looking all over for you."

"Haven't I told you to call me Private Johnson or even Al?"

"Okay, okay."

"So what's up?"

"This place is full of cooties, and they driving me nuts."

"You're not the only one. I'm having to delouse my uniform every day."

Strolling along the gravel path that encircled the camp, we dished the dirt about army life.

"I wish I could get out of this dump," he said. "It's a damn jungle here, and I can't take it anymore."

"Private Middleton, are you telling me you can't cut the mustard?"

"I can't see the point of it. The army don't give two hoots about us Negroes. All the mens been griping."

"Damn it, Phineas, nobody said this trip would be easy. You signed up for the ride and you'd better see it through! Lice or no lice."

Setting his fists on his hips, he cocked his head to one side. "To tell the truth, Mr. J, I got a good mind to go A-W-O-L."

*This fool's out of control!*

I became alarmed at his crazy talk. He was an Albany recruit, and I feared he'd give our group a bad name. Glancing over my shoulder, I spied Sergeant Green walking about fifty feet behind us and hoped he hadn't heard Phineas's outburst. Grabbing him by the arm, I steered him into the woods and stopped when we reached a small clearing. It was dusk, and the mosquitoes were biting in full force. Phineas was begging for trouble, trouble that could spread to the other men.

"You'd better get a grip, soldier. This country's at war!"

"What that to me?"

"You can either do the time in the field or in the brig. And believe me, that's real hard time."

While I was castigating him, I saw the muscles of his jaw and neck tighten; this boy was strong as an ox and I knew he could flatten me. We stood there in the moonlight, glaring at each other, but after a short while, he sucked his teeth, swatted the mosquitoes, and spit into the bushes. I doubt if he had ever thought about doing time in the brig.

"Okay, Mr. J, I'll tough it out."

"Good. You'll do alright."

As for him calling me "Mr. J" again, well, I just let it pass.

A few nights later, I lay in my bunk, tossing and turning. It had been over four months since I last saw my Evie, and I was feeling lonesome. I took out her photo and I stared at her loveliness in the dim light of the barracks. Pressing it to my lips, I closed my eyes, envisioned her soft body, recalled her sweet rose-water scent, and drifted off to sleep. When I awoke the next morning, I couldn't find the photo. I stripped the bunk, shook out the sheets, and searched the floor, but it was nowhere to be seen. I was in a panic. Evie's photo meant the world to me, and I was prepared to wake up every last soldier to see who had taken it. Just then I noticed Private Simon Curtis entering the tent with something in his hand.

"What's that you got?" I asked.

"A sweet, darling girl," he said, planting a kiss on it.

Sprinting across several beds and waking up the occupants, I snatched it.

"Damn it. This is my wife you're kissing."

"Sorry Pops. When I got up this morning to go to the john, I saw her on the floor, so I picked her up. She looked so pretty I decided to keep her."

I grabbed him by the neck. *This joker took my Evie to the latrine.*

I was about to throttle him when my buddy, Teddy Wilson, awakened by the commotion, grabbed my shoulder. "Let him go, Al. Private Curtis didn't mean any harm. He's a country bumpkin–still wet behind the ears."

I released my hand from Curtis's throat. He coughed and gasped for breath.

"Sorry I choked you, Private, but don't ever touch this photo again."

By this time, nearly everyone in the tent was grumbling about the disturbance and one soldier yelled, "What the hell's going on?"

"Not a thing," I said, "go on back to sleep." But then the bugle sounded reveille, and they all had to scramble out of bed.

After evening roll call, Teddy Wilson and I ambled into the barracks. He was about my height, slightly over six feet, dark-skinned, and strikingly handsome. His short black hair was slicked back exposing a sharp widow's peak, which made him look intelligent. And that he was. Teddy usually scrutinized the newspapers for stories and editorials concerning our people or politics, and he and I often engaged in spirited debates. I heard that he had even attended Fisk University.

"What got you so worked up this morning, Al? You're usually cool, calm and collected."

"I usually am, but when it comes to my Evie, all bets are off."

# CHAPTER 31

## *Evie*

Sunlight streamed through the bedroom windows, birds chirped their melodies with abandon, and the branches of the crab-apple tree swayed in the breeze. That morning promised a lovely spring day, but what was spring to me? Now that Al was gone, it seemed winter, bitter winter.

The morning before that morning I watched my husband walk away to war and felt abandoned and afraid. During the night, I piled the bed high with quilts and nestled beneath them, trying to find a safe hiding place, imagining I could stay there until this wretched war was over. After a while, I was awoken by a frantic cry–Tessie, hungry for her morning feeding. As I nursed my baby, desperate thoughts plagued me.

*What if he doesn't return?*

*What if I never see or hold him again?*

*What if his battle-ravaged body is buried in a strange* land?

*Oh, why did he have to leave me?*

I trembled and tried to change the conversation, as I rocked my helpless child.

*Little Tessie, your daddy will come home.*

The next few weeks dragged by in an endless procession of dreary days. Every evening the children would kneel at their bedside and pray for their father, and after they had gone to sleep, I would lie down and read and reread his letters. I would close my eyes and recall his face, his smell, and his touch and cry bitterly.

*This bird in the gilded cage must fly on her own.*

Late one evening, as I sat in the parlor, staring into the lantern light and wondering how to snap out of my despair, Little Al tiptoed in. "Why aren't you asleep?"

"I was sleeping, Mommy, but an angel in white woke me up."

"Boy, you'd better get right back to bed."

"But the angel sent you a message."

I was losing patience and my face became distorted with anger. "Well, what is it?"

He stood there, on the verge of tears, but stubbornly held his ground. "She said . . ."

"Go ahead."

"The angel said to tell you that Daddy will come home safely."

Wiping the tears from his eyes with his pajama sleeve, he turned and slowly trudged away. "Good night, Mommy."

"Good night, son."

Just then my guardian spirit showed up. *"Evie! It's time to stop grieving and take care of this family."*

*"But Al's gone, and I don't know if I'll ever see him again."*

*"Trust that you will. The angel's message is a good omen."*

At that moment, an unexpected feeling of relief flooded over me and I thought: *Al will be all right. The angel said so.*

I ran into Little Al's room, and finding him in bed, I kissed him on the forehead. "Thank you, dear."

"Mommy," he murmured, opening his eyes, "can you tell me a story tomorrow night?"

"Yes, dear. I certainly will."

I returned to the shadowy parlor and began to look deep within.

*All my life I've been accustomed to someone guiding me; first, my parents, then, Jennie, and finally, Albert. And here I am, adrift with only my own wits to depend on. I'm responsible for this family now, and I must stretch and grow and search for that untapped resource Al saw in me. I'll pull myself together and be a good mother, even if my heart is aching.*

The following morning, I woke up bright and early and tidied up the apartment. Then I baked a tray of raisin scones and scrambled a few eggs for the children. When I inspected the cupboard, I discovered that my store of vegetables and staples had run low, so after breakfast, I set out for the market with James and Little Al, leaving Susie and baby Tessie with Mrs. Jones.

The market was teeming with Saturday shoppers looking for the freshest produce. But all we could find were a few heads of cabbage, a bunch of carrots, a sack of potatoes, a bag of onions and a few green tomatoes. Next, we were off to the grocery and I was surprised at what I saw. Posted on the walls were large colorful signs from the newly created US Food Administration entreating shoppers to conserve food. There were signs promoting "wheat-less Mondays" and "meat-less Tuesdays." Another sign urged shoppers to eat oatmeal and cornmeal porridge, instead of wheat, and to use rye and barley flour for baking. When I inquired about it, James explained that the government needed the wheat to feed the soldiers and the starving European allies.

"Save the wheat for the fighters," Little Al chanted. "Didn't you know that, Mommy?"

Reluctantly, I removed one of the two sacks of wheat flour from the shopping basket and replaced it with a sack of barley flour, not having the slightest idea how to cook it. We had run low on sugar, so I sent James to fetch two bags from the shelves. He returned with only one.

"Auntie, my teacher said we should cut back on sugar. They need it for the troops."

I made a sour face. "We also need some here, James."

"But Auntie, suppose it was Uncle who wanted sugar for his tea."

"Okay, we'll just buy one, but you better not complain if your tea isn't sweet."

"I won't, Auntie."

Little Al pulled on my hand. "And I'll just put a bit of sugar in my cereal if it helps my daddy."

"That's nice, dear.

"Oh, James, run and get two large jars of grape jam or is that also rationed?"

James scratched his head. "Gee, Auntie, I don't think so. My teacher didn't mention anything about jam."

When we went to pay for the groceries, I greeted Mr. Kelly, the store proprietor, who was standing behind the counter.

Leaning toward me, he whispered, "Mrs. Johnson, I saved two imported chocolate bars for you. They're the last ones we have in stock."

"Oh, thank you. And by the way, do you have any of those peppermints I like so much?"

"Sorry, ma'am, we're all out."

With our purchases loaded on the red wagon that once belonged to Mrs. Jones's nephew, we trudged to the butcher shop where I bought a piece of pork and then returned home. I unpacked the groceries and set aside a small chunk of butter, a cup of sugar, two cups of flour, half-dozen eggs, and a few potatoes and onions and took them down to Mrs. Jones who didn't get out much.

About three o'clock that afternoon, I heard a knock on the front door. To my surprise, it was Inez Vanderpool carrying a container of fresh strawberries. We had gotten to be good friends since I performed at her mother's tea party.

"I'm sorry to drop by unannounced, Mrs. Evie, but I heard that Mr. Johnson joined the army and I was wondering how you were getting along."

"I was under the weather for a while, but I'm doing better now."

"Glad to hear that. And Mr. Johnson?"

"He's doing basic training in Peekskill. Can you imagine a man his age marching up and down? Anyway, I received a letter from him the other day, saying he's fine, except for missing me. I'm glad his unit hasn't gone overseas yet."

"That's where the awful fighting is. Are the children all right?"

"Yes. Tessie's in her crib and the rest have gone downstairs to play. Let's have a cup of tea while it's quiet."

"You sure it's no trouble?"

"Not a bit."

We sat at the kitchen table sipping tea and munching sugared strawberries and the raisin scones I had baked earlier.

"Thanks for these luscious strawberries, Inez."

"I thought you'd like them."

"I'd better put a few aside for the children before I finish them." I giggled and stuffed another strawberry into my mouth.

Inez wiped the crumbs from her lips. "These scones are delicious."

"I can't imagine what they'll taste like with barley flour."

"Neither can I! And I can't get used to drinking tea with only one teaspoon of sugar."

"One teaspoon! I usually take three or four. With my sweet tooth and these children to feed, I'm afraid I'll run out of sugar before month's end, but I've come up with an emergency plan."

Inez raised her eyebrows. "An emergency plan?"

"When I was in the market today, I bought two large jars of grape jam. If I run out of sugar, I'll put jam in our tea."

We chuckled, and I refilled her cup.

"By the way, Inez, how's your young man?"

"Calvin's fine. He had to register for the draft last week and he wants us to get engaged before they call him up. However, Mother insists that I break off with him."

"Good heavens! Why?"

"Remember, I told you that he owns a shoe and boot shop, which is doing rather well. Mother says that when he's drafted, he'll lose it and have nothing to offer me when he comes home."

"What does your father say?"

She shook her head. "He always agrees with Mother."

*Mrs. Vanderpool has forgotten what it's like to be in love*, I thought.

"Maybe Calvin can sell the shop and open another when the war is over."

"That's what I thought! I told Mother I could save part of my salary, meager as it is, and help him buy a business when he returns. She became livid and said, 'What would people think? A man is supposed to provide for you!'

"Oh, Evie, what should I do?"

I stretched my arm across the table and stroked her hands. "Do you really love him?"

"Desperately."

"Then tell your mother you won't break up with him, but promise her that you'll wait until he comes home and gets back on his feet before you get married."

"That's brilliant. And I'll write him every day while he's gone."

Days and weeks passed. Life returned to normal, as normal as it could be with a husband away at war. James resumed practicing baseball. Little Albert went back to playing tag with his friends, and Susie followed me around the house, dusting all the furniture she could reach. As for me, I was learning to take on the full responsibility of the household. I was growing. I was stretching my wings. But one thing that hadn't changed was my aversion to cooking. One evening, after a meal of canned tomato soup, and saltine crackers with cheese, Little Al said he was going to write and tell his father how much he missed his good tasting stew. I realized then I'd have to make a better effort at feeding my children. Thanks to my husband's judicious planning, I had enough money to get by, unlike so many women who were forced to take factory jobs in order to feed their families. I was shocked to hear that some women, even colored ladies, were doing men's work at the munitions plants!

In early July, I received an alarming letter from Father. Mother was ill, the doctor said it was heart trouble. A few days later, Jennie and I caught the early-morning train to New York City, taking baby Tessie with us. Cousin Mattie came over to watch the other children. When we reached home, we found that Mother was still trying to cook and take care of the house but was constantly getting short of breath. Every so often, she would have to hold on to the furniture to keep from falling. Father was trying to help, but he was clumsy in the kitchen. Besides, Mother was left alone on weekdays when he went to work.

I assessed the situation and decided to take Mother home with me, so I could nurse her back to health. At least, she could get some rest there. Jennie and I were in the dining room having a mid-afternoon snack when I shared my plan. Mother was resting in the parlor.

Jennie jumped up. "You always want to be in charge."

"What on earth do you mean?"

"Your plate's already full. Mother would be better off staying with Peter and me. She needs proper nutrition and you don't like to cook."

"Don't worry. I'll take care of her and cook her nourishing meals, too."

"Cheese and crackers?"

Mother must have heard us arguing because she came into the room. "Jennie, I think I'll stay with Evie. With Al gone, she could use my help. Besides, I'd like to get to know my grandchildren better."

Jennie glared at me but sat back down. "Alright, Mother, have it your way."

Mother put her arm around Jennie's shoulder. "I hope you'll come to visit us often."

"I'll try, but I have a husband to take care of."

"And a fine one he is, my dear."

It was settled. All that remained was to break the news to Father when he returned from work. We broached the subject after dinner as he sat in the parlor smoking his pipe.

"Girls, I've been trying to hire someone to look after your mother, but she insisted she didn't want any strangers in the house."

"Father," Jennie said, "you know how private Mother is."

"Well then, perhaps it's best you take her with you."

I ran over, took his hand in mine, and kissed his cheek.

Three days later, Father escorted us to Grand Central Station where we would catch the train to Albany. This would be the first time they would be separated since they were married and they tenderly hugged and kissed each other goodbye.

After the train pulled out, Mother murmured, "Oh Lordy, will I ever see him again?"

A chill ran through me.

"Of course you will," I said, gently patting her clenched hands.

"And he'll be alright?"

"He'll be fine," Jennie replied.

Mother smiled and seemed reassured. Even so, a melancholy air settled on us as we thought of Father, standing alone on the platform. When we disembarked in Albany, Peter was waiting with a taxi that would carry us home to First Street.

# CHAPTER 32

## *Albert*

⟡

After a few weeks at Camp Whitman, the 15th regiment broke camp and was split up to guard various sites around the state while the War Department decided where to send it for combat training. C Company was dispatched to New Jersey to protect the railroad tracks. It was tiresome and sometimes dangerous work. One Sunday in late August, I took the Hoboken Ferry to New York and caught a trolley to Brooklyn to visit Mr. Ashton. I wanted him to understand why I had left the family and joined the service. Since Mrs. Ashton was away in Albany, he was glad for the company. We cooked a mess of sausage and potatoes, ate dinner, and then parked ourselves on the front porch.

"How's Mother Ashton?"

"She's enjoying her visit. Here tell, Little Al is really something. She said he keeps asking her about her long red hair, and James waits on her hand and foot."

I smiled at the good news.

"And your business, how's it going?"

"Pretty well. It seems that everyone who can afford it wants indoor plumbing."

We sat there for a while without speaking.

Mr. Ashton cleared his throat. "How are things in the army, Al? I was surprised to hear you joined up."

"Sir, I only enlisted to give us a better chance for the future. We have young children to raise, and I can't do stoker's work much longer. I need a better job."

He nodded. "Thought it was something like that."

I had finally cleared the air with Mr. Ashton and felt relieved.

After a moment, he began relating recent events that had taken place while I was in training.

"You must have heard about the calamity in East St. Louis during July."

"No, sir. We were pretty much cut off from any news while in the camps."

"Well, one hundred and twenty-five colored men, women and children were slain in a race riot there early last month. A witness reported in the *New York Age* that he saw white people massacre helpless Negroes in downtown East St. Louis, where a black skin was a death warrant."

I gasped. "Good Lord Almighty!"

"They even pulled their victims off streetcars and murdered them. They say the police didn't interfere with the carnage and some of them joined in."

He went on to relate how roving mobs lynched colored men and burnt down colored peoples' houses and businesses, leaving six thousand souls homeless. The riot went on for a day and a night before it was spent of its fury.

"Those blasted racists," I said.

I shook my head trying to dispel the horrific images of lynched men hanging from lampposts, mothers beat to death in front of their children, terrified children smashed with clubs, and people running to escape the fire, only to be attacked by the white mob. Suppose it had been Evie and my children at the mercy of that bloodthirsty rabble? As I sorted out what had taken place, my blood began to boil, and I was angry, angry at America for letting it happen, over and over again. Tears stung my eyes. Here we were trying to make the world safe for democracy while our people were being slaughtered. I began to think I had made a terrible mistake leaving Evie to fight in this war, but like Phineas, I was trapped so I had to make the best of it.

Soon after my visit to Mr. Ashton, a rumor spread that the 15th regiment would be going to Camp Wadsworth in Spartanburg, South Carolina. We sorely needed additional training before we shipped overseas, but not in racist South Carolina. After dinner one evening, my buddies and I were lounging outside the sleeping tent discussing the situation when Private Teddy Wilson approached, holding the *New York Times*.

"Did you see this shit, man?"

"What's going on?" I asked.

"The Mayor of Spartanburg says that colored soldiers aren't welcome in his town, especially northern Negroes who expect to be treated like white men. He says they'll treat all colored soldiers exactly like they treat their resident Negroes."

"And you all know what that means," I responded.

"The Mayor warns we'll be knocked down if we go into their soda joints, and that they don't allow Negroes to drink from the same glass a white man may later use."

Lyle Thomas, a tall, lean, squinty-eyed mate, flared his nostrils and sucked his teeth. "Shucks, I'd like to take a piss in their white-assed drinking glasses."

"We haven't even gotten there," I said, "and they're already planning a lynching party."

Lyle Thomas snapped his fingers. "We'll be going there peaceful like, but if those rednecks want a fight, what the hell, we'll give them one."

Lucky Lewis, who was barely eighteen, slightly chubby, and the youngest member of our crew, bit his thumbnail. "You'll heard about those Negro soldiers in the 24th infantry that got so fed up with mistreatment in Houston that they shot up the town the other day?"

"Now they're all in the brig," I said, "facing a court martial and maybe a firing squad."

Lyle gritted his yellowish teeth. "At least they got to knock off a few crackers."

"Hold on, guys," drawled cool-headed Cephas Jackson. "Nothing's come down from the War Office yet, and rumor has it that Captain Ham Fish wrote his buddy, Franklin Roosevelt, at the Navy Department, asking that we be dispatched to France for training."

"Yeah, they must ship us right to France," I said. "We signed up to fight the Germans, not the South Carolina rednecks."

# CHAPTER 33

## *Albert*

∽☙ ❧∼

Before I could say, Jack Robinson, we were on a train headed for Camp Wadsworth, Spartanburg. Defiant but wary, we recalled the Mayor's hostile words, quoted in the *New York Times*. According to that article, Spartanburg was a mill town of 25,000 people, deeply rooted in Jim Crow. The local Negroes, mainly sharecroppers and farm laborers, were poor and downtrodden. The town leaders had pleaded for an army base to be built near Spartanburg because of the economic benefit it would bring, but they hadn't counted on northern Negro troops being stationed there.

As the train approached the outskirts of town, I spied vast fields of snow-white cotton. It was a familiar scene. I was raised in the south, ran away to sea at seventeen, traveled the world in ships, crossed America in trains, settled down in Albany and now, at the age of thirty-seven, I was headed back to where I started from. I was apprehensive; I had witnessed the violence of southern white men. I knew how deep their hatred ran. I knew the length and breadth of their fears. We disembarked in Spartanburg and spotted the welcoming committees: small groups of scowling white men giving us the evil eye and mouthing the word "nigger." We knew they weren't crazy enough to attack two thousand armed black soldiers, so we paid them no attention and marched the few miles to Camp Wadsworth.

The two-thousand-acre camp resembled an enormous canvas city and was jammed with thirty-five thousand white troops of the New York 27th division. Six weeks before we left the north, our men had watched from the sidelines as New York City gave the 27th division a huge send-off. Throngs of cheering people lined the streets of Fifth Avenue, waving flags and banners. The 15th regiment was given no such farewell.

Our regiment was allotted a block of land on which we pitched two hundred and fifty, eight-man tents in neat rows. A wooden mess shack, with electric lighting, stood at the head of each row and a bathhouse and a latrine were located at the foot. From day one, we started preparing for overseas combat by learning warfare strategies as well as French. Along with the other soldiers stationed there, we began digging a vast network of trenches in which we would receive our training. The red clay soil was heavy, the ground rough, and the campsite hilly. Digging was hard work. However, we lightened the load by singing to the ragtime music of our regimental band, conducted by Lieutenant James Reese Europe. I was confident that once the trench system was completed, the 15th would be thoroughly trained and ready to face the bloody Germans.

One day when we were knee-deep in dirt and dead tired from digging a nine-foot trench, Lyle Thomas wiped his sweaty brow and asked, "Are we digging all the way to hell, man?"

"No," I said, "but if you don't dig deep enough when you reach the front, you'll find your ass in heaven!"

Although we worked like the devil during the day, we had nothing to do at night, except play cards, or write letters. Cephas Jackson, a fine-featured, soft-spoken mate, said he wanted to be an artist and went around sketching soldiers from our company. He produced an excellent likeness of me, which I sent off to Evie. When they saw his work, some white soldiers from the New York 27th asked him to draw them also. I thought Cephas was a fine artist but doubted whether a colored man could make a living at it.

Bored with camp life, many colored soldiers were drawn to the bright, shop-lined town square in Spartanburg. There they got a taste of southern hospitality. Some were assaulted and called derogatory names and others were not allowed to buy anything in the shops. I decided to stay away from town as much as possible and advised young Lucky Lewis to do the same.

"Don't think this uniform will protect you. A lot of folks down here would rather have German soldiers parading through their streets. Some would even offer them a cool glass of lemonade."

Another reason I stayed clear of the town was that transportation was nearly nonexistent. To get there, we would have to walk three and a half miles along the ominous Snake Road.

A few days after our arrival, Cephas Jackson recounted an incident that happened in town. "Me and a soldier from D Company and three white soldiers from the New York 27th were walking along, laughing and joking when a gang of four young hoodlums attacked, snarling curses, 'You fucking niggers, go back to where you comes from and the same goes for you nigger lovers.'

"I didn't want no trouble so I ignored them, but one of our white buddies yelled, 'You ignorant peckerwoods! Why aren't you in the army defending your country?' The hoodlums started throwing rocks and the fight began: the white soldiers against the white southern boys. Us black soldiers stood aside fearing we'd be blamed, but I was ready to jump in if need be. In less than a minute, the military police arrived and ended the fight, sending the gang on their way with a stern warning."

Colonel Hayward must have gotten wind of the many racial incidents that were occurring because he called the entire 15th regiment together. We assembled on a large field and Hayward climbed on a bathhouse roof so he could be heard. I remember parts of that speech as clearly as if it was yesterday.

"Men, I urge you to refuse to meet the white citizens of Spartanburg on the plane of prejudice and brutality and to act with restraint even in the face of physical abuse. If violence occurs, make sure that none of it is done by our side."

*That's a hell of a lot to ask,* I thought.

"This is an opportunity to win the respect of the whole world," he said, "with advances in the elimination of prejudice to follow. You are camped in a region hostile to colored people, and I'm depending on you to break the ice in this country for your race. We are about to win this regiment's greatest victory!"

*Our greatest victory should be against the Germans, not other Americans.*

The Colonel paused and looked down from his rooftop perch. We enlisted men waited with rapt attention. "Men of the 15th, I am asking each of you to lift up your right hand and swear to refrain from violence of any kind . . . under any conditions."

The crowd was dead quiet. No one moved an inch. But then I felt my right hand rising on its own. And when I glanced around I saw a sea of two thousand hands stretched toward the sky. At that moment, a thunderous cheer rose up for the Colonel: "Hip-hip hurrah."

The day after Colonel Hayward's speech, Lieutenant James Europe announced that our band would be playing in the town square that evening. Lyle Thomas and I decided to attend, and we set out along Snake Road, taking Lucky Lewis with us. Upon our arrival, we spotted a large group of colored people gathered across the street from the town square. We strolled over and introduced ourselves and waited for the music to begin.

Soon afterwards, I spotted Colonel Hayward and his officers moving through the square wearing raincoats that concealed their small arms and realized he must have had a contingency plan in case of trouble.

"Lucky," I whispered, "if the shit hits the fan, beat it back to the base."

"I got my running shoes on, and don't worry, I got your back."

"Thanks. I appreciate that."

"I ain't running nowhere," Lyle Thomas said, snapping his fingers.

"Didn't you promise the Colonel not to resort to violence?"

He rolled his eyes. "Okay, I'll run, too—if it come to that."

The fifty-five-piece Negro orchestra, which included eighteen of the finest reed instrumentalists from Puerto Rico, mounted the platform, and the stunned crowd started grumbling. They must have been expecting an all-white band. But when James Reese Europe's crew started playing ragtime, the music overtook the malice in the white folks' hearts, and they began swaying to the beat and stomping their feet.

The colored people standing with us were also shocked by the band's dusky complexion. Bursting with pride, old folks clapped, young men and women danced, and wide-eyed children laughed in amazement. One young lady snatched Lucky Lewis and spun him around until he was breathless. Then Noble Sissle, the band's soloist, enthralled everyone with a captivating ballad. As the song goes, "there was peace in the valley," but in this case, it only lasted for an evening. The soldiers of the 15th regiment had rejected violence, but that didn't mean the town folks did. Each day there were more and more provocations. Our men became outraged when they learned that Captain Napoleon Marshall, Harvard graduate and member of the New York bar, was thrown off a bus in town after paying his fare, yet the men kept to their word. Then, a few days after the concert, a major incident occurred.

# CHAPTER 34

## *Albert*

~⊙〇~

As we headed toward the mess tent that morning, a soldier from D Company raced up to us. Phineas ran close behind him.

The soldier waved his arms. "Did you all hear? Two of our mens gone missing. They never returned last night after going to town."

"What the devil happened," I asked.

"They buddies think the mens been lynched or arrested."

"Lynched! Oh my God," Lucky Lewis said.

"Maybe by the town police," Phineas added.

"Did anyone witness this?" I asked.

Lyle Thomas flared his nostrils. "These rednecks need to be taught a lesson!"

"But what about the promise we made to the colonel?" Cephas Jackson asked.

"That didn't include tolerating a lynching," Teddy Wilson said.

The soldier from D Company grimaced. "We ain't takin' this shit lyin' down!"

I raised my hands. "Hold it, guys, we can't go on wild rumors. We have to bring this to the Colonel."

"What the hell you think he's going to do?" Lyle Thomas asked. "He told us to overlook what they do to us."

---

184

Phineas puffed out his chest. "This is one thing we ain't going to overlook!"

They were all riled up, and it was no use reasoning with them. Lyle, Teddy, Phineas and the soldier from D Company left to round up more men. When their number reached fifty, they lined up in front of the bathhouse and began the three-mile march down Snake Road.

"Should I go with them?" Lucky Lewis asked.

"No! You stay here with Cephas."

I was worried about the explosive situation and about the men themselves, especially when I thought of the colored soldiers in Houston who had rebelled and were now serving long prison sentences, so I went in search of Sergeant Peters, the Colonel's aide. However, it took me a nearly an hour to find him.

From what I later learned from Sergeant Peters, he confronted Colonel Hayward with the news, and they both jumped into a car and sped into town, where they found the detachment of fifty soldiers. The leaders of the detachment told Hayward that they had delegated two soldiers to go to the police station to find out what happened to the missing men. Next, they said that if their suspicions proved true, they were prepared to retaliate. Hayward and Peters rushed to the police station and found the two delegated soldiers there. The police claimed there had been no disturbance in town that night and swore they had never seen or arrested the missing soldiers. While Hayward checked the police blotter, Peters and the delegated soldiers searched the cells and yard. No trace of the men was found. Hayward, Peters and the two soldiers rushed back to the waiting detachment and reported what they had seen. After hearing Colonel Hayward's plan to organize a search party, the fifty-man detachment marched back to camp. When they arrived, they found that the two missing men had turned up; they had gotten lost on the way back to camp and had slept overnight in a field.

During the next few days, the drill sergeants took us on marches of ten miles or more and worked us hard, until we were too exhausted to think about the bigots in town. Tensions seemed to lessen when the colored community invited our men to their churches, and a few white businessmen arranged for entertainment at the camp. On Sunday, a group of eight soldiers, including

Teddy Wilson, Lucky Lewis, and myself, traveled to town to attend an afternoon church service where James Europe and Noble Sissle were going to perform. The church was a simple wooden building with pews on both sides of a long middle aisle leading to the altar. On the wall behind the altar hung a large wooden cross. I don't know how many people usually attended these services, but that one was packed with folks: sharecroppers, blacksmiths, maids, and washerwomen, all dressed in their finest outfits, which for some were a clean pair of farmer jeans. A few worshipers looked as if they may have been teachers or businessmen. I had planned to sit in the back row, but as we entered the sanctuary, two female ushers hurried over and escorted us to the front pew. All eyes were watching as we squeezed in beside Lieutenant Europe and Private Sissle. After we were seated, Reverend Portlock, the dignified, middle-aged minister, read selections from the Old and New Testaments. A pretty woman in her twenties, wearing a wide straw hat adorned with fruit and flowers, was sitting across the aisle, and nudging three young children to stay awake. Amused, I nodded at her and she returned a smile. An elderly gentleman, seated in the pew behind us, leaned forward and whispered that the lady was Mrs. Portlock, the pastor's wife.

After preaching a sermon of hellfire and brimstone, Reverend Portlock asked our group to stand. "Brothers and Sisters, we're blessed to have Lieutenant James Reese Europe, conductor of the finest regimental band in the United States Army, Private Noble Sissle, the soloist, and these brave soldiers from the New York 15th regiment worshipping with us today."

The congregation applauded and an old, crackly voice cried out, "God bless our boys, Pastor."

Then Reverend Portlock fixed his righteous gaze on us. "I want you men to know that as long as you're in Spartanburg, this is your church. You're always welcome here."

"Thank you, Pastor," we responded.

"Church, we are in for a spiritual treat! Lieutenant Europe and Private Sissle have agreed to perform for us."

Murmurs of excitement ran through the congregation as James Europe took his seat at the piano. His nimble fingers flew over the keyboard producing a soul-stirring version of the familiar spiritual, "Swing Low Sweet Chariot." Starting with a slow, deliberate pace, he gradually increased the tempo and pitch until the music cascaded over the audience like a mighty cleansing river, *coming for to carry me home*, mending wounded hearts and soothing the all broken places of the soul. Hands clapped, feet tapped, and bodies swayed. Next Noble Sissle, accompanied by Europe, took center stage, singing the well-loved hymns, "Amazing Grace" and "It Is Well With My Soul." His passionate delivery planted seeds of redemption in the garden of our beleaguered spirits and brought tears to nearly every eye, including mine. The music ended, and the sanctuary became still. Then thunderous cries of "Amen" and "Hallelujah" reverberated throughout the room.

After the service, Reverend and Mrs. Portlock led us into the hall, a smaller building adjoining the church, and introduced us to the leaders of Spartanburg's colored community, educators, ministers, and business people. The hall was jammed packed with church members, all enjoying a tasty repast of pound cake and lemonade.

It was dusk when we broke away from the good folks of Spartanburg and headed downtown. As we passed through the quiet streets, Lieutenant James Europe expounded on his plans to establish a Negro orchestra after the war that would tour the whole country. I told him I was looking forward to it.

The next evening, I ran into Sergeant Earnest Peters and was shocked to learn that Colonel Hayward had secretly traveled to Washington to meet with Secretary of War Baker about the explosive situation brewing in Spartanburg. Two days later, we received instructions to break camp and proceed to Camp Mills, Long Island to await travel orders for France. We had been in Spartanburg for all of two weeks. To me, it was an eternity. As we moved down the road toward the special trains that would carry us to Long Island, we proudly marched through a wall of white men: soldiers from the New York 27th division, who serenaded us with the popular George Cohan tune, "Over There."

*Over there, over there*

*Send the word; send the word over there*

*That the Yanks are coming*

*The drums are rum-tumming everywhere . . .*

I was sorry to be leaving the brave men of the 27th, sorry that our regiment hadn't gotten to train in the new trench system it had helped to build, but Lord knows, I was delighted to get the hell out of Spartanburg.

In Camp Mills, we ran into trouble again, this time from an Alabama regiment that was billeted near us. They had put up signs stating, "This side for coloreds" and "This side for whites." Needless to say, we tore them down. The fighting got so bad that we were ordered to turn in our ammo, but the Alabamians were allowed to keep theirs. When Captain Ham Fish heard a rumor that the Alabama rebels were going to stage a sneak attack on us, he sent Sergeant Ebenezer Green to borrow ammo from another regiment and ordered us to fight back if attacked. That night, we lined up in the rear of the barracks, loaded guns in hand, and waited in the dark. If the Alabamians burst in, we would mow them down.

"Al," Lucky Lewis whispered, "Do you think we'll survive this fight?"

"Sure we will. You heard Captain Fish. 'Don't give an inch!' "

"I hope those racist bastards turn up soon," Lyle Thomas said. "I can't wait to give them a dose of they own medicine."

I understood just how he felt. Bitter anger had congealed in my gut and I was developing a taste for Alabama blood. All of a sudden, we heard footsteps approaching and I tightened my finger on the trigger of my trusty Springfield rifle.

# CHAPTER 35

## *Evie*

Al had been gone for five months, but it seemed much longer. With an ailing mother and four children to look after, I had no time to dress up and look pretty, like I used to when he was here. I had no time to read poetry, design crafts, or even sew outfits for my little girls. The children tried to help: James made the fire in the coal stove, swept the floors, and washed the dinner dishes. Little Al dried them and took out the garbage. The boys vied to pamper Mother, bringing her a glass of water, or steadying her as she moved about the flat. Susie followed her around, dusting every chair she sat in.

The only break in my routine was attending Mrs. Jones's weekly tea parties. One afternoon, while enjoying spicy gossip with Mrs. Jones, Mrs. Schmidt, and Mrs. MacHennessy, I got up to replenish Mrs. Jones's teacup.

"Looks like you'll be getting a letter soon, Mrs. Jones."

"What makes you think so?"

"It's in the pattern of the leaves."

"I hope it's from my nephew in New York City. I haven't heard from him in quite a spell."

"You read tea leaves?" Mrs. Schmidt asked.

"I used to, but my husband discouraged it. I'm out of practice these days."

Mrs. Jones raised an eyebrow. "Once a seer, always a seer."

*I had abandoned my psychic practice years ago, but I still pined for the uplift it gave me. Why couldn't Al be more understanding about it?*

All at once, Mrs. Schmidt and Mrs. MacHennessy began badgering me to read their leaves and looked disappointed when I begged off.

Mrs. Jones smiled, but her eyes pleaded. "My dear, couldn't you do it as a favor to me? Just this one time."

"All right, I'll try."

The two women brightened and leaned forward in their chairs.

*They think it's a game I can do willy-nilly*, I thought.

I picked up their teacups, drained off the remaining liquid, and inspected the pattern of the leaves. Familiar images formed in my mind, but I wasn't certain what they meant. When I told the women what their patterns suggested, they seemed delighted.

Mrs. Schmidt was my German neighbor who lived next door with her husband and two young sons. Mr. Schmidt worked at the General Electric plant in Schenectady, the plant where Al had inquired about a job some time ago, but they weren't hiring coloreds. If Al had landed that job, he wouldn't have had to leave home. Mrs. MacHennessy also lived on the block. She and her husband had emigrated from Ireland about ten years ago. They had four children, ranging in age from one to fourteen. Mrs. Jones once told me that Mrs. MacHennessy would often have to borrow potatoes from her at month's end, although Mr. MacHennessy earned good wages at a munitions factory.

While the tea party was winding down, Mrs. Schmidt fidgeted in her seat. "Mrs. Johnson, much more I want to find out."

Mrs. MacHennessy nodded. "And I'd like to know how my family in Ireland are faring."

"Ladies, as I said, I'm out of touch with all that. Besides I can only reveal what the tea leaves show."

"We want to hear what you see in cup," Mrs. Schmidt said.

"I'd like to help you, but I couldn't possibly spare the time. I'm swamped with housework and I have my ailing mother to care for."

*These ladies have husbands with good jobs to fall back on. I'm here alone with no one to help me, except the children.*

Mrs. Schmidt slumped. "I understand."

Mrs. MacHennessy clasped her hands. "I know it's not easy for you."

I began to sympathize with these immigrant women. It was wartime, and each of them was anxious to find out about their relatives in Europe. A minute later, Mrs. MacHennessy whispered something to Mrs. Schmidt and Mrs. Schmidt nodded.

"Mrs. Johnson," Mrs. MacHennessy said, "if you read for us, we could pay a little, and do housework, or help with your mother."

I was shocked by their offer, but then I thought: *This might be my only chance to recoup my skills. If I read for them, I can always stop before Al returns.*

"Ladies, I suppose I can fit you in once or twice a week, if you assist with the washing and ironing."

"It seems like a fair exchange to me," Mrs. Jones said, and they all agreed.

For the next several nights, I sat alone in the parlor, closed my eyes, and gradually tried to revive my psychic powers and after two weeks, I called each lady in for a sitting. They were pleased with the sessions and the readings went on for quite a while. With the help of these women, who did much of the laundry, and Jennie, who began visiting Mother more frequently, I carved out precious time for myself.

Little Al seemed fascinated by Mother's red hair and kept pestering her about it. In response, she simply smiled. One November evening, when we were huddled around a blazing coal stove in the parlor, Mother asked, "Albert, would you like to hear the story of my red hair?"

I stopped my knitting. James closed his book and Little Al and Susie ran and sat at her feet.

"My grandfather was a slave in the state of Maryland who ran away to Canada on the Underground Railroad. Boys, do you know where Canada is?"

"It's up north, Grandma," James answered.

"And have you heard of the Underground Railroad?"

"Is it a train?" Little Al asked.

James doubled over with laughter. "No, silly. It's a secret route that runaway slaves took to freedom."

"That's right," Mother said. "They followed the North Star and stayed in safe houses along the way. Once they reached Canada they would be free." She took a deep breath and rested for a moment.

"When my grandfather reached Ontario, Canada, he found work on a farm and met my grandmother, who was a bondservant there. They say her bright red hair attracted him. Grandmother had been born across the ocean in Ireland, but when she was a young lass, the potato crop failed and people were starving, so her parents sent her overseas to work in Canada. She would have to labor seven years for the farmer who had paid her passage. A year and a half after my grandfather arrived at the farm, my grandmother completed her seven-year term and she and my grandfather got married, left the farm and moved east to the city of Ottawa. There they had a child, a little girl with blazing red hair. She was my mother."

The children gasped and drew closer to her.

"My mother grew up and moved to upstate New York, where she fell in love with my father, an Iroquois Indian. When they decided to marry, the tribe expelled him because the elders wanted him to choose a wife from their people. So my parents trekked all the way down to Long Island where my father found work in a shipyard and my mother became a dressmaker. That's where I was born and like my mother and grandmother, I had bright red hair."

Susie and James clapped, but Little Al scratched his head. "Grandma, why doesn't Momma have long red hair?"

Mother laughed. "She took after her father."

I became annoyed by Little Al's fixation on Mother's hair and gave him a withering look.

He dashed over and hugged me. "Momma, your African hair is nice, too."

Mother's health was failing, but she perked up whenever Father visited. While we awaited his arrival on a Saturday morning, she said, "Evie, I'm so pale. Put a dot of pink on my cheeks."

I applied the rouge, James held up a mirror and Little Al and Susie watched.

"That's too much! I don't want to look like a harlot."

"What's a harlot, Grandma?" Little Al asked.

"Never you mind," I said. "Mother, you look fine. What about a touch of red on your lips?"

"Evie, you know I don't color my lips! What would my church sisters say?"

When Father arrived, Mother blossomed like a morning glory opening to the sun and they were like a young couple again. I watched them, hoping that Al and I would be that much in love when we reached their age.

Before he left on Monday morning, Father took me aside. "She's looking better than the last time I saw her. Do you think she'll be coming home soon?"

"Maybe . . . in a little while."

"Good. I'll be back in two weeks."

I escorted Father to the front porch and kissed him goodbye. As he descended the stairs, I had a chilling premonition: *Mother may never return to Weeksville.*

# CHAPTER 36

## *Albert*

꒰ ꒱

"**S**tand down, men. Stand down." The gravelly voice of Sergeant Ebenezer Green rang out in the quiet night and Captain Ham Fish stepped inside. "Men, the battle has been averted. I confronted the officers of the Alabama regiment and told them our soldiers would shoot to kill if attacked. They said they were rounding up the ringleaders of the planned assault and had put the rest of their men under lockdown."

Relieved, I lay down with my rifle at my side and wondered how many wars we'd have to fight before we reached the battlefield.

Two days later, the 15th regiment moved to new quarters in New York City where we were confined for nearly two weeks. When the bugle sounded reveille on November 11, we jumped out of bed and marched to the pier. There we took a ferry to Hoboken and boarded the USS Pocahontas, a dull, gray German passenger boat that had been detained in New York at the outbreak of the war. Although it had been refitted, it still looked shabby. This would be our home for the next few weeks. In the evening, we gathered at the ship's rail and watched as the Pocahontas steamed into the lower bay and joined a convoy of troopships sailing to France. My buddies and I huddled together as the cold wind buffeted our faces.

"We're finally on our way!" Cephas Jackson said.

"You think this old tub will make it?" Teddy Wilson asked. "Never learned to swim."

"Hey," I said. "The army didn't bring us all this way to drown us."

However, my confidence was short lived. One hundred miles out to sea the piston broke, and the ship had to be tugged back to port, while the rest of the convoy sailed on. Then the regiment was sent to Camp Merritt, New Jersey, but several soldiers went AWOL.

Shortly before we boarded the ship again, the army gave us forms to complete. One of the officers explained that Congress had passed a new law: our spouses would get half our pay plus an allotment from the government. We could also purchase inexpensive life insurance in case the worst happened. A few soldiers complained that their salaries were too small to give anybody half of it, even their wives. I signed up for both the allotment and the life insurance.

After we boarded the Pocahontas for the second time, a fire erupted in the boiler room, and to make matters worse, we were compelled to stay on board for ten days while they revamped the ship. On December 12th, we stood shoulder to shoulder on deck, our caps pulled down, collars turned up, and hands stuffed deep in our pockets. Snow, sleet, and wind pummeled our bodies, as we set out once more. It was dark and for safety sake, lights were not permitted on deck, not even a lighted cigarette. Again, we watched as the shoreline receded. Again, we joined a convoy of troop ships. For better or worse, we were finally on our way. As we sailed out to sea, some prayed for safe passage, some said the ship was cursed, and others swore that saboteurs and spies were aboard. Now that we were headed for the Western Front we questioned whether we were ready to face the battle-hardened Germans.

"Do you think we'll get additional training in France?" Teddy asked.

"We'd better," I replied. "White troops train for at least six months."

Lyle Thomas whistled. "All we got was two weeks of drill and a haircut!"

Lucky Lewis punched the air. "Ready or not, here we come! Those Germans better watch out!"

After a while, I staggered below to my berth and fell fast asleep. I was dreaming of Evie, looking into her lovely eyes and stroking her soft skin, when the ship jolted violently. Men jumped out of their bunks, fast as jack-rabbits, donned life jackets, and ran for the deck.

"Al, let's go!" Cephas yelled.

Even though the distress signal was blasting, I took a few seconds to fully awake for I didn't want to leave the dream. By the time I hit the floor, everyone was gone, and I couldn't find my life jacket. *I'll be damned. This ship may sink, and I don't have a jacket.*

I frantically searched the area and located one on the far side of the room. Then I ran back to get my shoes, but my size elevens were missing. Some joker must have worn them because he left his size nines behind. Carrying the shoes, I bolted up the stairs, struggling to put on the life jacket. The deck floor was icy cold, so I squeezed my feet into the too-small shoes, as best I could.

Just then, I spied a sailor rushing by. "What the hell's happening, mate?"

"See that tanker over there?"

Through the darkness, I could just make out an immense black shape.

"Its lines became entangled with ours, and it slammed into our ship."

"Yeah, I felt that!"

"Captain's already sent sailors down to cut the ropes and put bumpers between the two vessels."

By the time I pushed my way to the rail, the crew had lowered a sailor down to inspect the damage. When they pulled him up, he stretched out his arms and shouted, "Big hole." Next, he reached up with one arm and added, "Above waterline."

I sighed in relief. At least, we wouldn't drown, not yet. Colonel Hayward insisted on repairing the ship at sea and negotiated with the Convoy Commander for the other ships to wait for us until dusk. Otherwise, we'd have to turn back again. Hanging over the ship's side in slings and working in the freezing cold, our men and the ship's crew joined forces to patch the gaping hole with iron plates. I held my breath as I watched. By a stroke of luck, the work was completed just before dusk, and we were on our way. Everyone had something to say about the ill-fated journey. The superstitious blamed the jinx, the suspicious faulted the spies, and the naysayers said we'd never make landfall.

Cephas Jackson joined me at the rail as the darkness rolled in. "I've prayed about this, Al, and I've a strong feeling we'll go all the way this time."

"I hope so."

"And the sooner we get to France and enter the fray, the sooner this terrible war will be over."

"Lord knows."

I'm not one who likes to complain, but by all accounts, it was a miserable journey. We were sailing on a gray ship, on a gray ocean, under a gray sky, and it seemed as if a spirit of grayness was permeating our very beings. For many, this was their first time on the high seas and they quickly learned the agony of seasickness as the ship tossed and rolled. The worst part was the unending nights. So as not to be a target for German U-boats, all lights were turned off at 4:30 in the afternoon and kept off until 7:30 in the morning. Thus, our days were compressed into nine-hour intervals and then it was pitch black except for the little blue running lights in the passageways leading to the toilets. There we were, a bunch of guys with time on our hands and nothing to do but stare into the darkness. One afternoon, as we sat in the mess hall, we grumbled about the dreaded nights.

"How are we going to get through this," Teddy Wilson asked.

Lucky Lewis grinned. "We could sing."

Lyle Thomas shook his head. "Hell no."

"Al," Cephas said, "I hear you used to tell interesting tales to the stokers."

"Phineas has a big mouth."

"All joking aside, what about entertaining us with a story tonight?" Teddy asked.

Others joined the chorus demanding a tale. So I agreed but insisted that each of them tell a story, too. During the next ten nights, groups of men huddled around me, as I described my travels over the seven seas and my trip across America. I narrated Cousin Sister's amazing chronicle of love, pain, and healing during and after slavery, and Mr. Ashton's harrowing tale of escape from Madagascar. Each time, after I finished, other soldiers would have their say.

Lucky Lewis talked about his pa being killed by a falling crate on the docks. "I'll never forget the day when the dock workers carried Pa's crushed body home in a wagon. I was ten years old and couldn't believe he was dead until we laid him in the grave." He also described how his mother wept when she realized he would be going off to war, despite President Wilson's promise to keep America out of it.

Cephas Jackson shared his dreams of becoming a painter. "I plan to study art in Paris after the war. They call it the City of Lights."

"I never heard of no Negro painter," Lyle Thomas said, waving his hand.

"What about Henry Tanner the famous colored artist? His work hangs in museums and galleries all over Paris."

"I'll be damned," Lyle said. "Maybe we'll all go to Paris."

I was impressed that Cephas had the whole thing worked out. He was a man who refused to let America crush his dream – even if he had to go to Paris to claim it.

One night, Lyle Thomas spoke about his father, who owned a barber-shop in Harlem. "My old man and me was always arguing. He didn't like me coming home late at night. He tried to teach me barbering, but I had higher dreams than that. I wanted to be a performer like the famous Bert Williams."

"You ever seen Bert Williams on stage?" Lucky Lewis asked.

"No. But I once saw him at the bar in Marshall's Hotel where all the colored musicians be hanging out. He was looking sharp!"

As I listened to their stories, I got to know these men who would soon be fighting alongside me on the battlefield.

We had been at sea for thirteen days when we ran headlong into Christmas. I spent the morning on deck, imagining I was at home with Evie and the children. Despite the cold, clusters of soldiers gathered in the open air, conversing quietly to ward off loneliness. I paced back and forth and then joined a group of my buddies at the rail. As we looked out over the unforgiving ocean, a heavy gloom settled on us. All was quiet except for the sound of waves lapping against the ship's hull.

"Do you think we'll ever get to France?" a young soldier asked.

Teddy Wilson scanned the horizon. "This is the danger zone. Anything could happen."

"Heck," Lyle Thomas said, "it would really be a bitch if the Germans torpedoed us on Christmas Day!"

"Guys, we survived the Spartanburg racists and the Alabama bigots," Cephas Jackson said. "And now by the grace of God, we'll land safely in France."

Lyle sucked his teeth. "You sure about that, Preacher Boy?"

Just then Lucky Lewis cried out, "It's Christmas. Let's celebrate." And he began to sing.

*Silent night, holy night,*

*All is calm, all is bright . . .*

His strong, crystal clear voice rang out against the wind, sweeping away sadness and fear as his warm breath formed misty clouds in the frigid air. It could have been the memory of Christmases past or the hope of those to come, or simply his precious song, but something sent chills up and down my spine. As Lucky crooned the last verse of Silent Night, Sergeant Ebenezer Green joined the group.

He puffed on his cigar and exhaled the foul-smelling smoke. "Well done, Private Lewis. I hope you can fight as well as you can sing."

"Thanks, Sarge," Lucky said. "And a Merry Christmas to you."

A few minutes later, we all trooped down to the mess hall where a small miracle awaited: roast turkey with all the trimmings.

On the morning of December 27th, a lookout shouted, "Land ahoy." My buddies and I raced to the rail and spotted a rocky coastline ahead.

Phineas Middleton stared wide-eyed at the coast. "When I gets off this lousy bucket, I'll kiss the ground."

The ship entered a channel, about a mile wide, guarded on both sides by snow-capped cliffs. After we had sailed for a time, the channel opened into a magnificent bay filled with strange looking French sailboats. On the north side of the bay lay the Port of Brest, with a beautiful cathedral and quaint houses sitting high on a hill. It was lovelier than I could have imagined. We disembarked from the Pocahontas on a snowy, blustery New Year's Day, amid blaring sirens.

Hundreds of French soldiers and townspeople had congregated on the pier, joyfully shouting, *"Yankees noirs, Yankees noirs!"*

*They're welcoming us as black Americans. Do you hear that Spartanburg?*

I took a deep breath of French air and like Phineas, I was overjoyed to be on solid ground. The regimental band assembled on the pier and began to play *La Marseillaise*, the beloved French national anthem, while spectators stood at rapt attention. After performing a few numbers, the band fell in behind the troops and we marched up the hill to the railroad station.

The train whistle blasted, and we were on our way. No one told us where we were going, but nearly everyone claimed we were headed to the Front.

# CHAPTER 37

## *Evie*

One frosty afternoon in early December 1917, Jennie and I went Christmas shopping. It had been ages since I felt this free, and I planned to enjoy myself even though I didn't have much money to spend. The first place we visited was Whitney's Department store, which was packed with customers, all seeking the perfect gift. As I scanned the main floor, I noticed that the elegant European fashions that used to inspire my designs were missing from the racks. In fact, the shelves looked fairly sparse, and I despaired of finding anything I could afford. Jennie and I decided to visit the children's department, so we rang for the elevator. When the door opened we were astonished to see a middle-aged Negro man operating the lift. We stepped inside.

"Are you ladies going to the employment office?" he asked, raising an eyebrow. "I don't think there are any openings left."

"We're going to the children's department," Jennie said, in a frigid tone.

"Sorry, ma'am. That's on the second floor."

Even in that department, I couldn't find any inexpensive toys, so I bought practical gifts: undershirts and long johns for James and Little Al, red wool mittens and a muffler for Susie, and a pink bunting for Tessie. Later that week, I would go to the confectionary shop and purchase candy canes for their Christmas stockings. After shopping, Jennie and I went to the store's dining room and there we received a second shock: an attractive colored waitress showed us to a table and took our order. I had heard that colored people had been hired at factories in Troy and Schenectady, but this was different. This was Whitney's.

There were only a few customers in the elegant dining room, with its gray patterned walls, sparkling chandeliers, and spotless white tablecloths, so we didn't have to wait long for our order. When the waitress brought the toasted cheese sandwiches, carrot and beet salad, and tea, she smiled, and I returned the favor.

"Sister dear," I asked, "did it take a war to get colored people hired here?"

"Apparently so. This war's shaking up the world, even in Albany."

"I wish my Al could've stayed at home instead of traipsing all over Europe."

"I'm sure he could've gotten factory work once the war began," Jennie said. "He should have tried the munitions plants."

"But what would have happened when the war was over? They'd probably give those jobs to returning servicemen and he'd be out in the cold."

"You're right. Either way, he'd lose." Jennie took my hand in hers. "How are you faring, my dear?"

"I'm terrified. I hope he doesn't try to be a hero! Suppose he's killed in action. Suppose he's not himself when he returns. War changes people." My eyes brimmed with tears as Jennie squeezed my hand.

"If anything happens to Al, you can depend on Peter and me."

I snatched my hand away. "I don't want your charity! I just want my husband back!"

*It was easy for her to talk, Peter was safe and sound at home.* I took a deep breath and tried to calm my racing heart.

"Jennie, I'm sorry."

She nodded and signaled the waitress to bring the check. "Let's go home."

On the following Saturday afternoon, I bundled up Tessie and Susie and took them for a stroll in the bright winter sun. It had snowed lightly the day before and as we walked along, Susie planted boot prints on the sidewalk. On the way home, I ran into Mrs. Schmidt.

"Mrs. Johnson, you know I good American," she said grabbing my arm. "My son, he good American, too!"

"Yes, he's a fine boy." Her son, Karl, a tall, blond boy about sixteen years old, was James's classmate at Albany High School. I got to know him when he helped James plant a victory garden for Mrs. Jones last summer. Mrs. Schmidt started trembling and breathing heavily.

"What in the world's the matter?"

"They try to beat him. They, they . . ."

"Come up to my place and we can chat."

Lifting Tessie out of the carriage, and taking Susie by the hand, I led Mrs. Schmidt up the stairs. She sat down at the kitchen table and after I made her a strong cup of tea, she spoke.

"This morning, Karl and my little one, Günther, went to dry goods store and were walking home through park when Günther ran ahead. Karl called to him in German. A group of men rush over and ask Karl if he was German. He say, 'Yes.' Then they rough him up, call him a Hun, and say they don't allow German to be spoke in America. Günther runs back and starts kicking them. They push him on ground. They shake Karl hard and ask if his parents buy Liberty Bonds to support war. He said he didn't know. They call him a slacker and say they will come after him and parents if they don't buy bonds."

I gasped. "Oh, my God!"

"Now both Karl and Günther afraid to leave house and my husband has no money to buy Liberty Bond. Günther even say he want to change his name to George, after President George Washington."

"What they did is terrible! It's all because of this darn war." We sat at the table for a few minutes and sipped our tea.

"Mrs. Schmidt, maybe the boys should stay out of that park and only speak German at home. Some of these people are fanatics. They've banned teaching German in schools, removed German books from libraries, and stopped orchestras from playing German music, even Beethoven! What's even sillier is that they want to change the name of sauerkraut to Liberty cabbage."

"Mrs. Johnson, I very afraid for Karl...if men find him again, they may hurt him bad."

I shook my head and thought for a moment. "Wait here. I'll be right back." I went to the bedroom where James was amusing Little Al with Cracker Jacks baseball cards and told him what had happened to Karl. A few weeks ago, a bank had awarded a blue Liberty Bond button to Peter when he purchased a hundred-dollar bond, and Peter had given it to James.

"James, do you think Karl can borrow your Liberty button?"

"Auntie, it's my only war souvenir."

"Dear, I'm sure he'll be careful with it."

I could tell he didn't want to part with the button, but he finally agreed. A minute later, we entered the kitchen where Mrs. Schmidt sat wringing her hands.

"Good afternoon, Mrs. Schmidt."

"Good afternoon, James."

He removed the blue button from his pocket and placed it in her hand. "If Karl wears this whenever he goes out, they'll leave him alone."

"Thank you very much. He'll return it after war's over."

She placed the blue button in her purse. "But won't you need it, James?"

"No, ma'am, I don't believe I look German."

"Ha, ha," she chuckled, and then took her leave.

It was Christmas Eve when Father arrived bearing an armload of toys and gifts, including a lovely pink and violet shawl for Mother. The next morning, Mother and Father watched as the wide-eyed children opened their gifts and searched their stockings for treats. She was wrapped in her new shawl and propped up in Al's parlor chair. Father sat close by. I was sure he noticed that Mother was getting weaker, but they both put on a brave face. After the gifts had been opened and the treats eaten, Mother went in for a nap. When Jennie, Peter, and Cousin Mattie arrived that afternoon, the family gathered for Christmas lunch and Father fervently prayed for Al and his men at the Front.

I was fast asleep that morning in early January when I heard a voice crying, "Mommy, Mommy get up." I woke up in a daze and saw Little Al and Susie standing at my bedside with frightened expressions on their faces.

"For Heaven's sake, what's the matter?"

"Susie and I tried to wake Grandma, but she wouldn't open her eyes."

I jumped out of bed and raced into Mother's room. Cradling her limp body, I repeatedly called, "Mother, Mother," but there was no response. When I realized she was no longer breathing and had no pulse, I began to weep. After a minute or so, I noticed Little Al, Susie and James standing in the doorway. Tears were streaming down their faces.

"Children, Granny has passed away and gone to be with God."

Mother's passing was a shock to everyone even though she had been ill for some time. Peter and Cousin Mattie sent a telegram to Father and made the funeral arrangements. Jennie and I braided Mother's hair, dressed her in her favorite green suit, and laid her in an open casket draped with the pink and violet Christmas shawl.

I explained once again to Little Al and Susie that Grandma had gone to heaven, but when Little Al kept sneaking into the parlor to touch her red hair and whisper her name, I wondered just how much he understood about death. James took Mother's passing very hard, nevertheless, he helped to take care of the younger children. When Father returned to Albany, accompanied by two of Mother's closest friends, he was still in a state of shock. He had last seen Mother on New Year's Day. Upon his arrival, he went straight to the parlor to say farewell, his eyes overflowing with tears.

A steady stream of visitors, including family, friends, church members, and neighbors, dropped by to pay condolences the afternoon before the funeral. After Mother was buried, Father remained with us for three days, but then said he had to get back to his business. I knew he'd be lonely without Mother, so I promised to visit him as soon as I could.

That night as I lay in bed, I prayed. "Lord, you've taken my mother. Please spare my husband."

## CHAPTER 38

# *Albert — 1918*

The words, "*Chevaux* 8, *Hommes* 40," painted on the outside of the train, meant that each car could hold eight horses or forty men. There were no horses riding that day, but there were well over forty men jammed into our car.

Sergeant Ebenezer Green squatted next to me for most of the journey, warming his hands with his breath and rubbing them together. "Damn, this train is colder than a witch's tit!"

"You can say that again," I replied, wiggling my cold stiff toes. Despite my discomfort, I had to laugh. It was a long time since I heard that expression. After many hours on the frigid train with nowhere to sit except a pile of straw, we arrived at our destination.

As we disembarked and stretched our aching limbs, Teddy Wilson whispered, "Where the hell are we?"

"No idea," I said.

Lyle Thomas eyed the scene. "It's damn quiet. I don't even hear gunfire."

We were near a town, a town with a bad smell and dismal gray buildings. It was evening and freezing cold. We marched onto a large field and were greeted by a group of Negro soldiers.

"Welcome to *Saint-Nazaire*," one soldier said as he handed me a cup of steaming hot coffee. "Name's Private Jim Butts, but my friends call me Big Jim." Big Jim was thick-necked and muscular.

"Thanks for the java, Big Jim. It really hits the spot. I don't mean to be rude, but where in the hell is *Saint-Nazaire*? Are we anywhere near the front?"

"Nah. Was you expecting to be?"

"We're the New York 15th, a combat unit."

He made a mocking face. "Well, I wishes you good luck getting there, but I doubts the General's going to let you all fight. He thinks Negroes has strong backs but weak minds. We guys are part of the labor division, unloading ships, constructing warehouses and . . ."

Before Big Jim could say another word, Sergeant Green ordered the Company into the run-down wooden barracks. As I entered, I was nearly overcome by the stench of mold and rotting animal carcasses.

The next morning, right after roll call, Lieutenant Spencer addressed First Battalion. "Men, I know you're disappointed at not being sent to the front right away, but General Pershing has a very important job for you to do here. The army needs to expand the port to accommodate the ships that will be carrying American troops and war supplies. You'll help develop the port and build the warehouses. Do your job well and I'm sure our regiment will soon be sent to the front."

His words hit me like a ton of bricks. We had been recruited as a combat force and were being shanghaied into this labor division. I wanted to yell: *This is not what we were promised*. But I knew he didn't call the shots and was just as subject to General Pershing's whims as we were.

When he finished speaking, there was a loud collective groan from the men. Then we drifted into small groups.

"This is a real bitch. We're going to be common laborers," Teddy Wilson said.

Cephas Jackson shook his head. "I could've done this kind of work at home and get paid better."

"I bragged to my friends I was going to help whip the Germans," Lucky Lewis said.

Lyle Thomas balled up his fists. "I've got a good mind to run the hell away!"

"I'm as angry as you are," I said, "but there's nowhere to run, nothing we can do, except to follow Pershing's orders and wait and see what happens."

So after cursing the General and otherwise letting off steam, the men of the 15th resolved to follow orders. First Battalion was assigned to lay five kilometers of railroad track from the port to storehouses in the nearby town of *Montoir*. Second and Third battalions were commissioned to build docks and hospitals and to construct a large dam. The weather was cold and rainy, the worksites muddy, and the work backbreaking. Some of the men caught the flu and were hospitalized. Some died. The only solace in that miserable camp was our band and its upbeat music. Early in the morning, the band would play on the field as we trudged to our worksites, and it would play again at the end of the day when we returned. One morning in mid-February, there was no music to be heard, just the whistle of a bitter wind.

"What happened to the band?" Cephas asked as we marched to work.

"Not a clue," Teddy said.

Later that day, we were shocked to learn that General Pershing had ordered our band to perform at the opening of a new entertainment and rest center for American troops at the famous mountain resort, Aix Baths, hundreds of kilometers away. They had left by train early that morning. This was the last straw, and our morale plummeted even further. After supper, my buddies and I gathered around a campfire to keep warm.

"Do you think our dear friend, the General, will invite us to the Baths?" Lyle Thomas asked, flaring his nostrils.

"No colored soldier is ever going to visit that resort," Cephas Jackson said, "and there ain't nothing to do here for enjoyment."

Bored senseless by camp life, I walked down to the docks one evening to watch the stevedores unload a cargo ship and spotted Big Jim sitting on a log, sipping a cup of java.

"How you doing, man?" I asked.

"Dog-tired. We be at it for over twelve hours and we still ain't done."

"Holy Mackerel!"

Big Jim arched an eyebrow. "Has the General ordered you to the Front yet?"

"Hell no! And he had the god-awful nerve to send our band away to play at a resort!"

He shook his head. "Al, think you can get a pass on Sunday? I know a nice little café where we can drown our sorrows."

"Sounds good. I'll try."

Big Jim said that he would have no problem getting a pass since his labor crew had unloaded five tons of cargo in record time that week and the lieutenant-in-charge was delighted.

On Sunday afternoon, Big Jim and I snaked through the narrow streets and back alleys of *Saint-Nazaire* and finally arrived at a barn-like structure. Inside was a rustic café with wooden tables and chairs. The place still smelled of horses and cows, its former occupants. There was a potbellied stove in the center of the room and a wooden bar on the left wall. Jacques, the middle-aged café owner, was standing behind the counter serving wine and a pretty young girl about eighteen was filling small baskets with chunks of bread and cheese. After greeting Jacques in French, Big Jim introduced me, saying I was part of a colored combat unit waiting to go to the front.

"Welcome *Monsieur*," Jacques said, smiling and pumping my hand.

On our way to a table, Big Jim whispered that Jacques had lost his eldest son in the war and his two younger sons were presently at the front. When we sat down, the young girl took our orders: coffee and wine for us both. Then a wiry old Frenchman in a tattered blue suit and a black beret started playing the harmonica and put a tin cup for donations on a nearby table.

There were twenty-five to thirty soldiers in the café. Four heavily made-up women in their mid-thirties were walking around and conversing with them and according to Big Jim, they were probably drumming up business for the bordellos in town. Another woman, younger and prettier than the rest, started dancing and singing to the harmonica music. The mood was festive.

"This is some crowd," I said.

"All the stevedores comes here when they can. They feels comfortable with Jacques."

"Do they all have passes?"

"Can elephants fly?"

"What about the MPs? Do they ever raid the joint?"

"Jacques has a spotter watching out for them."

He pointed to a soldier sipping a glass of wine and peeking through a small window. "If MPs come, he'll be able to see them when they make the turn up the road a piece."

We downed our wine and ordered another round, leaving the coffee untouched.

"So Al, what's going on at home? Been gone for almost a year."

"I hear that good-paying factory jobs have opened up to coloreds but lynching and race rioting are still rampant. And President Wilson hasn't uttered a word against it."

"What you expect? Wilson's a cracker, ain't he?"

"Yeah, and a damn hypocrite too! He kicked most of the coloreds out of government jobs and installed segregation on those who were left. With all his hogwash about making the world safe for democracy. Hell, isn't America part of the world?"

Big Jim sucked his teeth and shrugged.

"What brought you to *Saint-Nazaire*, Big Jim?"

"I was working the docks in Newport News and a contractor come 'round saying he looking for an experienced crew to work for the army in France. It sounded pretty good, so I volunteered."

"Newport News. I'll be darned. Virginia's my home state, too."

"Actually, I was born and bred in Mississippi. Finished seventh grade there. The school was just a shack, but Teacher Brown did all she could. Know what? When the Lord made Mississippi, he made a bad miss-take. There sure is some ignorant and mean white folks down there."

"So you just wanted to get away?"

"I had to run from Mississippi. Run for my life. Had a job hauling cotton at the warehouse. Saw how they cheated colored farmers on their cotton weights and the farmers too scared to say a thing. I was thinking about hooking up with my sweet gal and leaving when the white snake she worked for raped her. When I found her in the woods, she was bruised and battered, and nearly out of her mind. I picked her up and carried her home to her ma. Two days later, I caught that snake going through the woods and beat him bad, broke some bones. He pleaded for his life. I'll tell you he won't rape nobody else again. But I had to make tracks because I knew the Klan be after me. I had to leave my sweet gal and run. So I went to Newport News and changed my name, just in case they came a-looking."

*Damn them!* I thought.

"Ever hear from your sweet gal again?"

"Wrote Pastor Williams to let her know where I was. He sent me a letter saying she's moving up north to her cousin in Ohio, and if I still wanted her, I should look for her up there."

"Do you love her, Big Jim?"

"Lord knows I do. You know what? I'm going to write her tonight and tell her I still wants her if she still wants me. My sweet gal and me can start a new life together in Ohio."

I went to the backyard toilet and when I returned, I said, "I see the army is working you stevedores hard."

"Man, you don't knows the half of it. Many times, we work sixteen hours a day, stopping shortly for rest and chow. They treat us like beasts of burdens, lifting, hauling, struggling, rain or shine. Why we didn't even get rubber boots or work gloves 'til shortly before you arrived. Plenty guys already caught pneumonia."

"It's a damn shame."

"But the worst part is they gives us no respect. Without our sweat and toil, no soldier would have rations to eat, uniforms to wear, and even bullets to shoot—nothing to fight the Germans with. Yet, they keeps us penned up in camp most times, with only an occasional pass. White boys go to town freely. They support the hundreds of whorehouses that sprung up recently."

"Lawd a mercy!"

"It's gotten slightly better with the commander who came in recently. At least now we gets enough to eat."

I was appalled by the army's treatment of these hardworking men. Wearily, I signaled the young waitress to refill our glasses and I slumped down in my chair. All of a sudden, I felt an overpowering urge. I stood up, shouted for attention, and lifted my glass. "Gentlemen and ladies, I wish to make a toast."

Big Jim's mouth fell open. The soldiers' eyes popped wide. And the harmonica man and the ladies ran to the bar for a free glass of wine.

"I salute you stevedores and all the men in the labor battalion for the excellent job you're doing under difficult circumstances. You're the backbone of the war effort and are truly a credit to your country and especially to your race."

The soldiers rose as one, and clinking their glasses, they downed the wine and said, "Here, here, Brother. You talking truth."

Big Jim shook my hand. "Thank you, Al. We sure does appreciate that."

Just then, the spotter whistled loudly, warning that MPs were approaching, and nearly everyone, including the five women and the harmonica man, scurried out the back door. Big Jim returned our wine glasses to the bar while I scribbled a few French words on a slip of paper. Meanwhile, Jacques and the young waitress stayed behind the counter.

Two MPs burst in, shouting, "Nobody move!" The older of the two had a deeply lined ruddy face and a paunchy belly while the younger one was thin and pink pimply-faced. Scowling, they surveyed the scene and seeing that most of their prey had escaped, they stomped over to our table. Immediately, we pulled out our passes and handed them to the older MP, who tossed them on the floor.

"What you guys drinking?" the younger MP said.

"Coffee," I replied, sipping from my cup.

"What these boys drinking?" he asked Jacques.

"They're drinking café."

"Then what the hell you doing here?" the older MP asked, saliva spraying from his mouth.

"Learning French," I said. The younger MP moved closer, twirling his nightstick dangerously close to my head.

"This one's a smart ass," the older MP said. "Whoever heard of a nigger learning French? I've a good mind to run you boys in."

"Sergeant, if you arrest me, please contact Colonel William Hayward, Commander of the New York 15th regiment, and inform him that Private Albert Johnson was detained for learning French."

With his eyes glued on the two MPs, Big Jim inched his chair away from the table. His nostrils widened. His eyes narrowed. And his neck and jaw expanded like a snake. "We got passes and we ain't breaking no laws!"

*There's no way I'm leaving here with these MPs,* I thought. *I might wind up stone cold dead, in a ditch.*

The older MP began to curse, but getting no response, he turned to the young girl behind the counter. "What you doing here? Are you a prostitute?"

"She's my daughter, you bastard!" Jacques said.

"Where's the other boys that was drinking here," the younger MP asked.

"*Cherchez dans tes culs,*" Jacques spat out.

"Speak English," the older MP said, but Jacques remained silent. The younger MP glanced warily at Big Jim, who was positioned to attack and do damage.

"Let's get the hell out of here and look for them other niggers," he said, placing the nightstick under his arm. The older MP nodded and they both left.

"Whew, that was a close call," I said.

"Don't worry, Al. I was ready for them."

"Well, I hope they don't catch the soldiers that ran away."

"They won't. Those guys will take the back streets and alleys to the camp." He winked slyly. "In fact, some might even take a detour at a bordello."

Jacques brought out two glasses of wine and a basket of bread and cheese, garnished with a few precious slices of salami. "My friends, this is on house. Good luck at the Front, Private Al."

When he returned to the bar, I whispered to Big Jim, "What did he say to those MPs when they asked where the other soldiers were?"

"He told them to look up their asses." We had a good laugh, and after eating our tasty repast, we walked back to the camp.

During the last week of February, I received a letter from Evie, saying that her mother had passed away. I had a feeling it was coming, but I was still shattered. I thought about how much Mr. Ashton, Evie, and the children would miss her. The next Sunday I was wandering around the camp when I ran into Sergeant Earnest Peters, from Headquarters Company, and he invited me to his room to share a bottle of French wine. I settled down in a chair as he poured two cups of wine.

"Nice quarters, Peters."

"Working for Headquarters has its rewards."

I guzzled the wine. "But this camp is the pits."

"I'm sick to death of this rat hole, too." After we downed several more drinks, he pulled his chair up to mine and said he had something important to tell me, but I must keep it under wraps.

"Colonel Hayward has just left to see General Pershing to plead our case. He said he plans to tell the General that the proud 15th is rotting away here and that he doesn't want to command a regiment of ditch diggers!"

"Wow, I hope General Pershing doesn't court-martial him."

"Remember, Private, the walls have ears."

"Sarge, my lips are sealed."

When I left the sergeant's quarters and three empty wine bottles later that day, I felt a lot better. Whether it was the wine or the secret he shared, I can't say. I even began to whistle as I wobbled into the barracks and collapsed on my bunk.

The 15th regiment received orders to break camp in mid-March. As we packed our gear, Lucky Lewis asked, "Where do you think they'll send us now, Al?"

I shrugged. "I just hope we're not jumping from the frying pan into the fire."

"Can anything be worse than this!" Teddy said.

The men in the barracks looked worried, but like true soldiers everywhere, they picked up their guns, strapped on their gear, and marched toward the unknown.

# CHAPTER 39

## *Albert*

W e boarded a train and journeyed north. After we had been traveling for several hours, I glanced out the window and witnessed a spectacle that shook me to the core: vast fields of graves marked with small white crosses. I wondered about the poor souls resting there–men, who had been alive, men, who had cherished hopes and dreams, men, who had fought for home and country, men, who had loved and perhaps been loved.

*Would I end up in one of these cross-marked graves with green grass sprouting overhead?*

After a daylong journey, we disembarked from the train and began a ten-kilometer march to our destination, the Argonne, deep in France's Champagne Province. Upon our arrival, I took in the new surroundings: shell-scarred buildings and ravished meadows, the smell of smoke and gunpowder, the sound of bombs and rockets, and the faint glow of explosions in the darkening sky. French soldiers were loading horse-drawn wagons with food, supplies, and munitions, and servicing the big guns for battle. Warplanes were buzzing overhead. Here was France in the belly of the Great War.

We marched to our dismal barracks, dropped our gear on the muddy floor, and amassed on the open field.

Then Colonel Hayward, standing on a wooden platform, addressed the assemblage. "Men of the 15th, the army has renamed our unit. We are now the 369th regiment and are part of the new 93rd division." He paused as if to let it sink in and a buzz of whispers reverberated throughout the ranks.

"What's wrong with our old name?"

"I never heard of the 93rd division!"

"Man, this is crazy!"

An army division usually contained three or four regiments and 10,000 to 15,000 men. We were one regiment, with only 2,000 soldiers.

"Sir, where's the rest of the 93rd division?" a soldier shouted from the rear.

The colonel called us to order, again. "Men, I know you've been anxious to reach the Western Front. Well, we've finally made it. We're going to be a real combat unit, however, we won't be fighting as part of General Pershing's American Expeditionary Forces."

We remained frozen as expressions of puzzlement crept onto our faces.

Colonel Hayward continued. "The general has assigned all four regiments in the 93rd division to the French army. From this point on, our regiment—the 369th—will be part of the 16th division of the 8th Corps of the 4th French Army, commanded by General Henri Gouraud. The remaining three regiments in the 93rd will serve with other French army units. Soldiers, get a good night's sleep. You start your field training early tomorrow morning."

Astonished, I stumbled into my tent, trying to make sense of it all. For once my buddies were speechless, as they looked at each other, shaking their heads in disbelief.

After a few minutes, Teddy Wilson asked, "What the hell's going on, Al? Have you ever heard of anything like this?"

"I don't know any more than you!"

"Are we still part of the American army?" Lucky Lewis asked, his voice quivering.

"Sure," I responded. "The General has loaned us to the French."

Lyle Thomas snorted. "Humph. Like you loan your stinky socks to a friend."

"Look," I said, "we're confused and disgusted, but at least we're at the Front. Let's see what the French army has in store for us."

Cephas tightened his lips into a grimace. "I hope they don't use us as cannon fodder!"

A chorus of murmurs agreed.

"That makes no sense," I said, "they need good fighting men, not dead ones." Exhausted, I stretched out on a bunk, wrapped myself in a blanket, and yawned. "I'm off to sleep and suggest you do the same."

The next morning our regiment began the grueling preparations to become an effective combat unit. Our French training officer welcomed us, explaining that the Germans outnumbered them and had pushed the French line back sixty kilometers. He also told us that General Pershing was delaying the deployment of the American forces, saying they weren't ready yet.

"Neither are we," I whispered to a soldier standing near.

Each platoon of about 25 men was assigned a French interpreter who translated everything the training officer said. French enlisted men demonstrated their fighting techniques using gestures and facial expressions. Everything was new: French principles of combat, French maps, French weapons and gas masks, and much more. My head was spinning with the unfamiliar material. There was no time for joking around, although Lyle Thomas managed to get off a few quips, accompanied by the usual snapping of fingers.

On the evening of our third day, I ran into Sergeant Ebenezer Green outside the mess tent. We had just finished a tasty supper of hearty French soup, crusty bread, and wine.

"How you doing, soldier?" he asked.

"Besides being bushed, I'm not sure. We're in a foreign army trying to learn a lifetime of information in three short weeks and we can't even speak the language. I wonder if I can do it, Sarge."

"You ain't alone, Private, I'm struggling to learn all I need to know in the non-com officers' training."

He was a master sergeant, I was a lowly private, but it seemed as if we were in the same boat. We ambled over to a bombed-out farmhouse and sat down on the low brick wall, and I decided to confide in him. "Sarge, my buddies and I feel demoralized and abandoned by the American army."

"It's not only you, Private. This whole development has shocked the regiment's officers, even Colonel Hayward. As far as I know, we're the first American regiment to serve under a foreign flag."

Sarge Green rolled his eyes and looked around to see if anyone was near. "I hear that Colonel Hayward complained to a French officer that the American general had put the black orphan in a basket and left it on the French army's doorstep! The story goes that the French officer replied, 'Velcome, leetle black babbie.' "

Despite my misgivings, I had to laugh. "Do you think we're here as shock troops?"

"The French are giving us the best training they can in the short time they have. They're getting ready for a massive German spring offensive. So they need to hold the line and they need us to hold our part of it!"

Sarge scratched his wooly head. "What's that saying about a chain?"

"It's only as strong as its weakest link," I replied.

"Yeah, that's it. They're desperately trying to keep the Germans from Paris. We're only about 200 kilometers away. As for being shock troops, shit, we all shock troops, especially French enlisted men. Last night, I shared a canteen of wine with a French sergeant named Pierre Moreau, a survivor of Verdun.

"Pierre told me that they lost four hundred thousand young Frenchmen in Verdun and the Boche lost almost as many."

"The Boche?"

"That's their nickname for the Germans. It means cabbage head. They also call them Huns. Getting back to Verdun, soldiers were trapped there for months on end in stinking, muddy trenches, under constant fire from the big guns. They shared their ground holes with piles of rotting, maggot infested, bodies–their fallen comrades. Many of them went crazy. It was such a slaughterhouse that a young French lieutenant wrote in his diary, 'Humanity is mad. Hell cannot be so terrible.' The diary survived, but the young lieutenant did not."

A cold shudder ran down my spine.

"Your best protection, Private, is to learn everything they got to teach you. That way, you and your buddies have a better chance of staying alive. I've been watching you. You're a born leader. Whatever you do, the rest of your mates will follow."

*A leader? With no rank or direction.* We stood up and shook hands.

"Good luck to you, Sarge."

"And to you, soldier." He smiled slightly and strode away.

When I returned to the barracks, I repeated what Sarge Green had told me, but left out the ghastly tale of Verdun. From then on, we became determined to absorb as much as we could from the training. Every evening after dinner we practiced French and learned to decipher their army maps. Teddy excelled at map reading and Cephas had a knack for languages, so they helped the rest of us.

We had been in the Argonne about a week when Lieutenant James Reese Europe and the band, fresh from their assignment at Aix Bath, rejoined us. That evening, one of the trumpeters said that the band had played in several towns and villages on their way to the resort, giving the war-weary citizens their first glorious taste of ragtime.

When Lieutenant Europe asked about the French officers, I replied, "They treat us like human beings. That's more than I can say for the Americans."

"Yeah," Lucky said. "It seems like they're doing everything they can to help us be good fighting men."

On the first day of training, we were issued French helmets, gas masks, grenades, knapsacks and Lebel rifles, which weren't as accurate as the American Springfield guns. When he heard our complaints about the Lebel, the training officer said, "Don't worry about it. The grenade is more effective in trench warfare than your rifle. It can kill or maim several enemies at a time. Thus, it's essential that you practice throwing them with deadly aim. It's just like throwing a baseball."

Yes, there were many ways of dying in this war to end all wars and one of the most terrifying was by inhaling poisonous gas. I was more afraid of gas than explosive shells, even though we always wore our gas masks around our necks. The Germans had a nasty trick of firing tear gas first, which burns your eyes, and makes you want to take off your mask. Then they would fire the deadly ones—mustard gas, which blisters your skin and forms acid in your eyes and lungs, or phosgene, which makes you cough uncontrollably as your lungs fill with body fluids. With phosgene, they say, you'd be dead in twenty-four hours or at least, wish you were.

After three weeks of intensive instruction, our training officer said that we were combat ready and would be assigned a five-kilometer sector to defend against the Germans. A few days later, General Henri Gouraud, Commander of the 4th French Army, arrived at the camp, accompanied by General d'Oiselle, commander of the 8th Army Corps, and General Le Gallais, commander of our own 16th Division. As the artillery rumbled and the sky blazed with red and orange, General Gouraud inspected the French troops and decorated several of them for bravery. After that, the General approached the 369th regiment.

I had heard a great deal about the legendary General from French soldiers who claimed he had the heart of a lion, so when I saw him up close, a bearded, frail, one-armed man, I was shocked. Then I looked into his eyes, eyes that seemed to flash with fire, and I was drawn to him. The General limped up and down, reviewing our lines, and I imagined that many of us were hoping that we would also earn a medal one day. Just then an astonishing thing happened. The three generals, led by Gouraud, marched to the 369th regiment's flag-bearer, and doffing their hats, respectfully bowed to the American flag. At that moment, I had no idea what the future held for us, but I knew we had passed our first test.

# CHAPTER 40

## *Evie*

D uring the long winter days after Mother passed away, I became despondent and longed for spring, the season of rebirth. And I longed for Al's gentle touch. Yet, when spring arrived, the melancholy lingered and I became seriously ill with the flu. Jennie came over to nurse me while Cousin Mattie looked after the children. After a two-week convalescence, I was up and about again. Fortunately, none of the children took sick, but poor Jennie was stricken with flu a few days after she returned home.

When the schools closed for summer vacation that year, Jennie, James, the children, and I took the train down to New York City to visit Father. We hadn't been back to Weeksville in quite some time and Father seemed happy to have us home again. After the children settled in, I wandered through the house, sensing Mother's spirit in each space, especially in the bedroom she had shared with Father. As I entered the kitchen where Mother and I had spent so many hours together, I suddenly experienced an overwhelming feeling of loss, but for Father's sake, I tried to hide it. Jennie and I took over the house, cooking, cleaning, and filling it with fresh-cut flowers and the sound of music. To our delight, Father had spruced up the garden–Mother's special place–with colorful plants and greenery. During our three-week stay, we felt like young girls again, singing while we worked, swinging in the grape arbor, visiting old friends, and attending church services and tea parties. James and Little Al spent their time exploring the neighborhood and making new friends.

I hadn't told James, but I planned to leave him with Father for the rest of summer. I had discussed the matter with Jennie and she agreed that James would be just what Father needed, good company. And Father could begin teaching him the plumbing trade. I broke the news to James one afternoon while in the dining room, having a snack of biscuits and lemonade.

"But Auntie, I promised some friends to coach their baseball club this summer."

"Who are they?"

"Freshmen at my high school. They want to try out for the team in September."

"I thought you'd want to stay with Father. He's so looking forward to it."

He winced. "You told him already?"

"I wanted to see if it was all right." Jennie breezed into the room and took a seat.

"Mother, I've made plans for the summer."

"This is more important," Jennie said. "Besides, it's time you started learning a trade and Father can teach you plumbing."

James frowned. "I don't want to be a plumber!"

"Well, what do you plan to do once you finish high school?" I asked.

He shrugged. "I'd like to play baseball with one of the Negro teams. That's why I practice so much."

Jennie scowled. "That's no life for you! Traipsing all over the country without a place to lay your head."

He moved to the edge of his chair. "I don't mind if it's hard as long as I can play ball."

"Let's be practical, James," I said. "You have to learn some kind of skill besides baseball and it might as well be plumbing."

Jennie's face brightened. "Someday you may be able to take over Father's prosperous business."

James looked down at the floor. "But Auntie . . ."

Just then we heard Father at the front door. "Girls, I'm home." Jennie went to the hall and beckoned him into the dining room.

"You're early today," I said.

"We finished the plumbing job around three and I thought I'd come home to spend the afternoon with you all."

"That's wonderful," Jennie said. "We were just talking about the summer arrangements."

Father went over and patted James's shoulder. "Son, I'm glad you'll be staying here this summer. I hope it fits in your plans." I became anxious and looked at Jennie who was biting her lip.

"Yes sir," James replied. "I'm okay with it."

"That settles it," I said, breathing a sigh of relief.

After returning to Albany, I felt guilty that we had pressured James to stay in Weeksville, however, three weeks later I received a letter that allayed my fears. Father wrote that James was going to work with him every day and learning plumbing. And on Sunday afternoons, he was playing baseball with a local club. Father also mentioned that they had attended a Lincoln Giants game and the team was well on its way to a winning season even though its star player, Spottswood Poles, was in France with the 369th.

*Thank goodness everything turned out all right,* I said to myself. *And James will have plenty of time to teach his schoolmates baseball when he returns home in a few weeks.*

Anyway, that's what I believed at the time.

# CHAPTER 41

## *Albert*

~~~~~

**W**e set up base camps in Auve, Hans, Maffrécourt and Moulins, small villages about eight to fifteen miles from the front. Even in these villages, we saw German airplanes flying overhead and heard the loud rumble of distant guns. The men could talk of nothing else than fighting at the front and I wondered what it would be like to meet a German face to face in battle. Like the other men, I put on a brave front, but underneath, I felt anxious and uncertain.

One evening, Lucky Lewis skipped around the barracks and boxed the air. "When those Huns see us, they're going to run."

"You sure it's not the other way around?" Teddy Wilson asked. "They say the Germans are fierce."

"Well, they ain't never come against the boys from Harlem. We'll show them who's fierce," Lyle Thomas said.

A few days later, the regiment assembled on the field and marched toward the trenches with the band playing the Star-Spangled Banner and the Marseillaise. Captain Little was in command of First Battalion since Lieutenant Spencer was away, attending a weapons training course. As we moved from the camp, we witnessed the ever-increasing signs of devastation in the surrounding countryside: rutted roads, shell-holed fields, and bombed out houses. I shuddered to think that men and women had once lived in these homes and children had played in these fields.

Early the next morning we arrived at our assigned five-kilometer sector, CR Melzicourt, which was located in the Bois d'Hauzy woods, part of the vast Argonne forest, and was bordered on the east by the Aisne River. We moved cautiously into and through the trenches, trenches that were already occupied by French enlisted men, who greeted us with swigs of wine from their canteens. I was shocked when a tall fellow with craggy features and an unkempt black beard embraced me, saying, "*Bienvenue le camarade.*"

French soldiers were called the *poilus* because of their shaggy hair and beards, but Lyle Thomas renamed them the stinky ones. After a week or two in the trenches, we began to smell just as bad. We shared everything with the *poilus* including grub and wine. The day after we arrived, I squatted down next to the *poilu* who had welcomed me. His name was Luc Girard. Speaking in French and broken English, Luc told me that he was married and had a little daughter, named Cecile. I said I had a wife, three little ones, and a nephew at home. He looked amazed that I would leave them and come overseas to fight for France. Luc told me stories of what his countrymen had endured during the first three terrible years of war. He told me about French farm women who had hitched themselves to plows to till the soil when all the horses had been taken to war. His eyes lit up when he described Paris, the jewel of Europe, and said that the French army was determined to keep the Germans from Paris at any cost.

*At any cost*, I thought. *I suppose we black Yankees are part of that reckoning.*

The *poilus* taught us the nitty-gritty of trench life and showed us around the underground city we now called home. This city consisted of three long trenches–zigzag lines, parallel to the front, one behind the other. The trench we were occupying was known as the front line. It was closest to the German lines and, therefore, the most dangerous. About eight kilometers behind the front line was the support line and eight to twelve kilometers behind it was the reserve line. High piles of sandbags and acres of barbed wire protected the trenches on all sides. There were also communication trenches that connected the front, support and reserve lines. Troops moved back and forth through these trenches and soup men delivered food and supplies. We would spend ten days at a time at the front line and then be rotated to the rest area or other positions. A region known as "no man's land" separated the French and German front lines and was marked off with thick barbed wire fences on both sides. One of the *poilus* terrified young Lucky Lewis with wild stories of French and German deserters who haunted no man's land and feasted on corpses and live bodies.

The trenches were muddy hellholes, full of greedy rats that ate everything in sight. The only way to keep them out of our food was to store it in metal canisters. One of our men, feeling the need for a protective amulet, kneaded a piece of bread into a cross and stored it in his pants pocket for safekeeping. That night after he fell asleep, the rats gnawed a hole in his pocket to get to the cross. The worst of it was feeling their clammy feet crawl over my face while I tried to rest. The trenches were also full of lice that laid their eggs wherever there was hair. They got so bad that I shaved my head, but it didn't help much because they migrated south. Then I understood why the *poilus* were always scratching their beards, heads, and crotches. When we were off duty, we stayed in underground areas within the trenches called dugouts, which contained sleeping bunks. They were also infested with vermin. Adding to the discomfort of trench life was the white powder that coated everything. We tasted, swallowed and breathed its acrid fumes. One morning as I was returning from watch duty, I spotted Lyle, Lucky and Cephas talking with Luc, so I joined them.

"What the hell is this white stuff?" Lyle asked as he wiped it off his hands.

"Smoke from German exploding shells," Luc said.

Lucky Lewis looked around. "Lord, now all your brown faces done turned white."

The white stuff was bad, but the constant noise was worse. It was driving me crazy and the only way I could calm down was to imagine I was at home, sitting in our quiet parlor with Evie. Five days after our arrival, our French comrades pulled out, and CR Melzicourt was turned over to the 369th. Like Luc and the other *poilus*, we were determined to defend it at any cost.

Despite the ever-present danger, trench life became tedious after a while. Watching. Waiting. And eating the same tasteless grub. I thought we'd be fighting man to man, but we hardly ever saw the enemy. In this war, it was man against machine. All the attacks were done at night or just before dawn. We arose before daybreak, took our positions at the trench wall and watched the enemy lines. If there was no suspicious movement by sunrise, we stood down and had breakfast. At dusk, we checked out the enemy lines again. At nightfall, the trenches came alive with activity. I was on the squad that repaired holes in the barbwire. Others dug underground tunnels or delivered vital materials to the front line. The most dangerous activities were performed by small groups of trained men who ventured into no man's land on secret missions.

During the next few weeks, we held the line against a terrific German bombardment, ducking into dugouts when it got too bad, and we successfully turned back their raiding parties. Then the spring rains came and made our lives even more miserable. We spent hours bailing out the trenches. Everything was damp and stank of mold. My boots were constantly wet, my uniform and underwear clung to me, and my face was covered with sticky mud even the rain couldn't wash off. The tedium of trench warfare combined with the constant rain got to the men and they started squabbling.

"Did they bring us here to wait–while our asses rot?" Lyle asked.

"Somebody's got to do it," Lucky said, "else the Huns will overrun the line."

"Shit, I haven't seen a German close up yet," Lyle responded.

"You'll probably run when you do," Teddy said.

"Fuck you!" Lyle snarled.

I frowned at them. "We're here to hold the line and that's what we'll do." They grumbled, but to my surprise, they quieted down. I secretly shared my buddies' frustration and wondered if anyone at home knew or even cared that we were mired in this cesspool.

Then something happened that put the 369th regiment on the front pages of Albany's newspapers, as well as the *New York Age*. It started in mid-May when First Battalion moved back to the front line after resting in a nearby village. On the evening of May 13, Lieutenant Pratt assigned Corporal London and four privates to a listening post in no man's land to watch for suspicious activity by the Germans. The listening post was merely a narrow hole in the ground, surrounded by barbed wire. Privates Henry Johnson and Needham Roberts from C Company took the first watch while Corporal London and the two remaining privates went to sleep in a nearby ditch. Lieutenant Pratt and eight other privates, including me, hunkered down in a dugout close to the French lines. Suddenly, I was awakened by the sound of gunshots and grenade blasts. I jumped up, grabbed my weapons, and along with the others, followed Lieutenant Pratt out into the night. As we crawled through the dark, I suddenly heard someone yell, "corporal of guard" and then there were blood-curdling screams, more gunshots and explosions, and the sound of running. We moved quickly but cautiously toward the listening post, about thirty meters away. It could've been a trap.

"Where the hell is Corporal London?" Lieutenant Pratt whispered.

"Maybe he's down," one of the privates said.

When we reached the listening post, I saw Needham Roberts sprawled on the ground and didn't know if he was dead or alive. Henry Johnson was also on the ground, muttering and trying to crawl, and holding a bloody bolo knife. Meanwhile, Corporal London with the two other privates rushed over from the ditch and said that a German raiding party had cut them off. Teddy and I jumped into the hole, lifted up Roberts, whose uniform was soaked with blood, and placed him on a stretcher. We put Johnson on the other stretcher and helped transport the two men back to the dressing station behind the French lines, where medics tried to stop the profuse bleeding. I was no doctor, but I knew they were in bad shape and I had a personal stake in Henry Johnson because he was my homeboy from Albany. Teddy and I stayed with the wounded men until an ambulance arrived to take them to the base hospital, eight kilometers away.

Just before daybreak the next morning, Captain Little and Lieutenant Pratt proceeded to the listening post to investigate what had happened the night before. Privates Cephas Jackson, Sammy Woods, and I were assigned to guard them against snipers. What we found was incredible: numerous bloody footprints, blood-filled holes in the ground, chunks of flesh impaled on barbed wire, and a stash of wire cutters abandoned by the enemy. We followed the trail of blood to the Aisle River where the retreating Germans had crossed to the other side. After surveying the scene, Captain Little said it looked like Privates Johnson and Roberts had held off twenty-four Germans and killed or wounded more than a few. Shortly after we returned to base, Colonel Hayward arrived in a mule-driven wagon accompanied by three American war correspondents. When these reporters learned about the heroic feats of Privates Johnson and Roberts, they went about interviewing everyone, and I heard that they visited the hospital a few days later to question the injured men.

The 369th regiment continued to hold the line against the Germans through the rest of May, despite the enemy's fierce bombardments. Early one morning, Teddy and I woke up in the dugout, which reeked of mildew, sweat, and farted gas.

"How'd you sleep?" Teddy asked, yawning.

"Man, I slept like a log. I was so tired that even the lice forgot to bite."

He laughed. "Ain't that something?"

"What about you, Teddy?"

"Me? I was so tired that the rats thought I was dead and went to fetch the undertaker."

"You're a real card, man. We better wake up the rest of the guys, it's almost dawn."

A short while after the failed German incursion, Sergeant Ebenezer Green asked me and several other soldiers to join a raiding party into German territory. I agreed, figuring it was time to pay back the Huns for what they did to Johnson and Roberts, both of whom, it was said, could be crippled for life. Thirty of us crowded into a reserve trench while Sergeant Green explained the mission: gather intelligence, take prisoners, and demoralize those German bastards. Then we studied the enemy positions from photos that had been taken by French surveillance planes, and we rehearsed for the raid.

The next evening, we gathered again, and Sergeant Green announced, "Men, we're going over the top tonight. Leave all personal belongings behind and remove anything that would identify your unit. Now change quickly into these French uniforms and soft caps, but don't wear your helmets. They make too much noise."

"Helmets are our only protection," one soldier whispered.

"They could also be our death warrant if the Germans hear us coming," I said.

"If this raid is successful," Sergeant Green added, "it'll buoy up the fighting spirit of our men."

I didn't want to part with Evie's photo, but I obeyed for the sake of the mission. Nevertheless, I couldn't venture into enemy territory unprotected, so I tucked Evie's gold cross inside my boot. Removing our water bottles, we fastened razor-sharp knives, clubs, grenades, and wire cutters to our belts. The idea was to move stealthily, take the enemy by surprise and get the hell out before the German reserves could react. It was a dangerous mission.

I took my final gulp of water and went to relieve myself, squeezing out the last drop of pee. There were no toilets in no man's land. And even if there was, the enemy could hear you pissing a mile away and that would be your last long one. Later that night, we worked our way through the communication trenches to the jumping-off point. Then we crawled on the muddy ground to an opening in the French barbed wire and entered the dreaded no man's land. The ground stank of mildew and dead animals and biting flies swarmed around our heads. Crawling still, we moved toward the German lines, passing shell holes, burnt trees, and shrapnel. Just then we had a stroke of good luck. One of the guards at a German listening post was sneaking a puff, and we saw the glow of his cigarette in the dark. Drawing near, we cut the barbed wire around the listening post and waited anxiously. There was no response. Sarge Green slipped up behind the smoking Hun and clubbed, gagged and bound him. Meanwhile, Teddy circled behind the second German guard.

When this guard heard the thump of the club, he whispered, "*Heinrich, was ist das,*" and Teddy finished him off.

We slithered to a hole in the German barbed wire that had been cut the night before by our soldiers and crawled through one by one until we were all on the other side. German territory! A wave of fear cascaded through my body. Moving quickly, but noiselessly, we made our way to the German front-line trench. Once there, we cut through more barbwire, spread out, and at sarge's signal, bombarded the sleeping soldiers with grenades. It was their last sleep. Immediately, our men ran back to the German fence carrying the surviving guard. It would only be a matter of minutes before the German reinforcements would arrive at the destroyed trench and come after us in full force. After snaking through the hole in the fence, we began making a mad dash through no man's land toward the French line when machine gun fire started strafing the whole area. I jumped into a shell hole and after a few seconds, Sarge Green fell in beside me. I lay there shivering and praying, face down in the dirt, as German bullets whizzed overhead.

Finally, the firing let up, so I whispered to Sarge, "Let's run for it."

He didn't answer. I then noticed a wet stickiness on my side. Sarge Green had been hit. It was too dangerous to stay there because the Germans would soon be searching the area and I couldn't abandon him in no man's land.

"Hold on, Sarge, I'll get you out of here."

Somehow, I picked him up and carried him to the hole in the French barbwire, thinking: *if this man dies, what will happen to the rest of us.* Teddy and another soldier were waiting there and pulled us through. As I collapsed on the ground, they lifted sarge on to a stretcher and rushed him to a medic.

# CHAPTER 42

## *Albert*

❧

I don't know exactly when Sergeant Green died, but they told me he was gone by the time they reached the dressing station. As the *poilus* claimed: He had earned a wooden cross.

The tough, gruff, invincible Sergeant Ebenezer Green, of the 369th regiment, U.S. Army, was buried in the Maffrécourt churchyard cemetery in a section called Sergeant's Hill. Grim-faced soldiers, black Americans and white Frenchmen, gathered around his grave as the American flag fluttered in the wind. The chaplain offered a stirring invocation for this brave soldier, and the band played taps. Shortly after that, I received a field promotion to the rank of sergeant. I hadn't sought it, but I was determined to give my best to the regiment and set a good example for my men, especially now that Sergeant Green was gone.

Soon after my promotion, the U.S. Army started shipping hundreds of untrained draftees into the regiment as replacements, soldiers that had no inkling of the 369th's proud history, and C Company had to take its share. As I set about training these men, I drew on the lessons I had learned from Sergeant Green and from our French training officer. Everyone had something to say about the new recruits.

"What the hell's wrong with these new soldiers?" Cephas Jackson asked, shaking his head.

"They was plucked right out of the cotton fields!" Lyle Thomas said.

Teddy Wilson grimaced. "These sad-assed recruits don't know anything and don't want to know anything."

"Yeah, every time the Germans turn up the heat," Cephas added, "these guys sneak back to the safety of the villages. They claim to be 'catching the train.' "

"Sarge, they're making our regiment look bad," Lucky Lewis said.

"I know. I told these recruits I'll work with them night and day to whip them into shape, but I'll shoot anyone I catch sneaking off!"

Lyle Thomas cackled and snapped his fingers. "And that will be their last train ride!"

The recruits kept arriving, and I did my best to train them, but it seemed like it was never enough. It looked as if the American army was trying to sabotage the progress the 369th regiment had made.

When our rotation at the front came to an end, we moved to a rest area in Hans. On the second day of our ten-day rest tour, I sat in an outdoor café, leisurely sipping a cup of coffee. Earlier that morning, I had the luxury of a hot shower and had changed into a crisp, clean uniform. As I lingered in the café and watched the pretty young ladies stroll by, I began to feel human again. After a while, I got up and meandered through the village, noticing that, despite the obvious signs of war, some of the residents were still tending their gardens. I caught sight of an elderly man working in his and stopped to chat over the fence. He picked a bunch of ripened green beans, rinsed them off, and handed them to me. I couldn't remember the last time I had eaten fresh vegetables and these were delicious. I continued to stroll through town until I spotted a brewing ruckus a fair distance ahead. Two colored soldiers were brawling while others were gathered around them. When I came closer, I recognized Phineas Middleton, that son of a gun! The other guy was Bobby Brown, one of the new recruits. Stopping at the edge of the crowd, I waited to see where this would go.

"What you say, soldier?" Bobby Brown asked, curling his lip.

"I asked what cotton patch they snatched you from?" Phineas replied.

"Who you think you is, you overgrown booger bear?"

Phineas spat through his teeth. "Cotton Boy, I'm a real soldier. Not like you and your gang who keep sneaking off when the going gets rough."

"We catch the train 'cause we have no quarrel here."

"Be careful, boy. Your train's a-gonna crash."

"Who gonna crash it?"

The two men circled each other.

Suddenly, Bobby Brown pulled out a switchblade. "Where I comes from, we knows how to fix jackasses like you."

With his fists raised, Phineas continued to dance around Bobby, who was shifting the knife from hand to hand.

Bobby Brown snorted and glanced at the crowd. "See, this sucker's scared now."

I knew it was time to intervene, so I stepped between the crowd and the combatants. "Put the weapon down, Private Brown!"

"Sergeant Johnson, this chump is . . ."

"Put the damn knife down!" I gripped the handle of my revolver. He dropped the knife, and I picked it up.

"Private Brown, empty your pockets and spread eagle on the ground. Now the rest of you, get the hell out of here." The crowd began dispersing.

"Private Brown, get up and walk ahead of me."

As we walked away, I called back, "Private Middleton, I'll deal with you later." I led Bobby Brown to a nearby side street, where we stood facing each other.

"You're in deep shit, Private. Threatening a fellow soldier, keeping an unauthorized weapon, and so on."

"Aw, Sergeant, I wasn't really going to cut him. Please don't put me in the brig. I'm a claustropho."

"Then why did you pull a knife?"

"That man was disrespecting me."

I poked my fingers into his chest. "Soldier, respect has to be earned!"

It made no sense locking this boy up, not in the middle of a war zone, so I placed him under field arrest. For the remainder of the rest tour, he had to report outside my tent an hour before sunrise every morning and stand at attention until I dismissed him after sundown. I would also discipline him with drills and push-ups. By the time I finished with Private Bobby Brown, he would think twice before pulling a knife on anyone except a lousy German.

The day after the knife-pulling incident, I chastised Phineas Middleton about his provocative actions. "We don't have time for this crap. The next time, I'll put you under arrest, too."

"Sorry, Sergeant Johnson," he said, hanging his head.

On our last evening in Hans, I marched Bobby Brown to a wooded area and ordered him to sit down on a log. I sat opposite him. "What's eating you, Private?"

"Sergeant, from what I understands, you mens in the 369th volunteered to come here. I be drafted. White folks been lynching us, cheating us, and keeping us under they heel in Georgia since our people was freed and now they sends us off to die like rats in this country so that other white mens could be free. I don't buy it!"

"Private, most of us joined this regiment, on the chance it would improve our lives and the lives of our people. The army and the politicians expected us to fail. Wanted us to fail, so that the lies they spread about us–that we are inferior to white men–would be proved true. I'm glad the U.S. Army turned us over to the French. It was a blessing in disguise. We have proven our mettle. We have come up strong on the battlefield and earned the respect and admiration of the French people."

Bobby Brown squirmed on his log seat.

"Private, I know you don't want to be here, but I'm not going to let you put another soldier's life in danger by not doing your duty. Tomorrow when we go back to the trenches, you will carry out your assignments, protect fellow soldiers, and kill Germans. Otherwise, I'll put you under the jail."

"Yes, Sergeant."

"Private Brown, you're dismissed." He eased up, saluted, and scurried away. The next morning, we would return to the front where I would keep a close watch on Private Bobby Brown from the state of Georgia.

Back in the trenches, the news was not good. Rumor had it that the Germans had broken through the Allied defensive lines at several places. Even though those locations were a good distance away, I had a hunch that the Huns would attack us next. One night, shortly after our return from Hans, my buddies and I gathered in a dugout to blow off steam.

"Sarge Al, when do you think the Germans will attack?" Cephas asked.

"I doubt if even General Gouraud knows that."

"Well, I hope they come soon," Teddy Wilson said. "I'm sick and tired of waiting like a sitting duck."

"Better a sitting duck than a dead bird," Lyle Thomas said.

"All we can do is to wait and stay ready," I responded.

Lucky Lewis danced around. "I'm ready, willing and able! We'll push those cabbage heads all the way back to Berlin."

Soon our resolve was put to the test. In June, the Germans pumped up the pressure with an intensive bombing campaign. We had experienced shelling before and, in a way, had gotten used to it. However, this time, the shelling was constant and overwhelming. As tons of ammunition hit the ground, mud flew everywhere and covered everything. Smoke, dust, fire, and noise were the order of the day. The explosions came like fast falling rain and the ground shook like jelly. On and on it went, hour after hour, day after day. I didn't know how long we could take it. Finally, Private Sammy Woods ran out of the dugout waving his arms and lay down on the trench floor, screaming incoherently. He would have been blown to bits if it weren't for two soldiers who dashed out and dragged him to safety.

To make matters worse, the Germans flooded the air with the dreaded mustard gas, delivered in yellow-marked shells. Even with our masks on, any exposed skin would be blistered. Soup men, who transported our meals to the frontline, frequently couldn't reach us, so we were hungry. Some soldiers fell ill, while others became shell-shocked. Horses and mules, our lifeline of transportation, were shot, blown up, or drowned in the mud. Amidst the chaos of shells whirling overhead, explosions and fires on all sides, and the specter of noxious gas everywhere, fear crept in and took hold. It was like the fear of God when you've committed a mortal sin, but worse than that. At least, God is forgiving and merciful, but the shells were not forgiving nor did the gas show any mercy. This fear was overwhelming, paralyzing, piss making, jaw clenching, bone chilling, and heart stopping.

The sky was lit with the colors of death. The earth was quivering, and we had nowhere to run. Then I remembered that God is still God, so I knelt in the mud and through chattering teeth, I prayed.

# CHAPTER 43

## *Evie*

Little Al entered the third grade on the Monday following Labor Day and James started his senior year at Albany High School. I was proud as they both marched off that morning, smartly dressed in their new school outfits.

That afternoon when James returned from school, he burst into the kitchen where I was preparing a snack and commenced to tell me about his day. As I placed a glass of milk and a cheese sandwich on the table before him, I suddenly remembered he had received a letter–a rare occurrence–and went to fetch it.

"This came in the mail this morning." He scrutinized the envelope, front and back, tore it open, and finally read the letter.

"Well, what did your mother say?"

He exhaled loudly.

"Go ahead."

"She wants me to come and stay with her for a few weeks. I could go to school from there."

*How dare she,* I thought. *Without even consulting me?*

James bit his lip. "Think I should go, Auntie?"

"She'd like to spend more time with you."

"But how will you get along without me?"

"It won't be easy, but we'll manage. You can take the trolley to your mother's after school tomorrow." I hugged him, and he seemed relieved that I had made the decision for him.

Just then Little Al rushed in and I placed his snack on the table. He plopped down and grabbed the sandwich.

"James is leaving tomorrow to stay with his mother for a while."

"That ain't fair. He's been away all summer."

"Don't use ain't," I said.

"Who's going to help me with my homework?"

"I will."

He screwed up his face, bit into the bread and gulped the milk. A coating of white covered his upper lip. "Momma, can I go with him?"

"Aunt Jennie only asked for James."

James playfully punched Little Al's shoulder. "Don't worry, kid, I'll be back in a wink. Then I'll teach you more baseball tricks."

"Yeah," Little Al said, scowling. They finished their snack and ran down to the backyard to see Susie.

The next day, I was in the dining room stitching a dress for Tessie when James entered, carrying his uncle's tattered valise.

"I'm going now."

I fetched my purse and handed him fifty cents.

"Thank you, Auntie, for all you've done for me. I know I promised Uncle to look after you, but I'd like to get to know my mother better."

"We'll be fine. It's only for a short while."

As I escorted James to the door, Little Al and Susie ran to meet us. We stood together, each of us saying a special goodbye. Then he kissed me on the cheek, hugged Susie, and shook Little Al's hand, promising to return soon. Smiling, he bounded down the stairs and went out the front door. At that moment, I felt a deep sense of foreboding and I began to tremble.

Inez Vanderpool dropped by two days later to tell me about her new students. We went into the kitchen and while we chatted, I made a pot of tea.

"Most came in well-scrubbed and eager to learn, but some of the colored children, whose parents had recently migrated from the South, appeared to be tired and even hungry. It was hard for them to concentrate."

"Oh, my."

"I plan to help these children as much as I can, even if I have to bring in some bread for them to eat."

"I could bake a tray scones for them, perhaps once a week."

Inez grasped my hand. "Oh, Evie, you're too generous." I poured the tea and placed a platter of Social Tea biscuits on the table.

"By the way, Inez, how's your young man?"

Her shoulders slumped. "I haven't heard from Calvin for some time. I pray he's all right. His unit is stationed close to Boston."

"He's probably busy. You'll get a letter soon."

"Look at me, feeling sorry for myself and I didn't even inquire about Mr. Johnson."

"It's Sergeant Johnson nowadays, he received a promotion. I hope that doesn't put him in more danger."

"I'm praying that the war will be over soon, so we can get on with our lives. The newspapers say that the Germans are losing, but they refuse to give up. Like cornered animals, they're vicious and very dangerous."

I threw up my hands. "Good Heavens, Inez! Please change the subject. I'm already worried to death about Al."

"Sorry. Didn't mean to upset you."

After Inez left, I hurried into my bedroom, closed the door, and ate two Hershey's chocolate bars to calm my nerves. They weren't nearly as good as the Belgium chocolate I used to buy, but one had to make sacrifices in wartime.

One evening, several days after Inez's visit, I was in the parlor idly flipping through the newspaper when a small article caught my eye. It was about an outbreak of grippe or influenza among the soldiers stationed close to Boston. I had come down with flu during April, and it hadn't been pleasant, but this article said that a few Negro soldiers at the camp had died. One of the white officers claimed that this was because Negroes had weaker constitutions than whites. To me, that was pure hogwash. Then I recalled that Inez's young man, Calvin, was stationed near Boston, but I decided not to tell her about the outbreak because I didn't want to alarm her. Anyway, it was probably nothing. Newspaper reporters like to exaggerate things.

It wasn't a week later when I saw a larger article on page two of the newspaper which reported that many more soldiers–both colored and white–had contracted influenza, several had died, and the Boston army base was under strict quarantine. The military doctor said that this flu strain seemed to affect the young and the strong, but he predicted it would not spread to the civilian population.

My first thoughts were of Calvin. *Does he have the flu? Is that why he hasn't written Inez?* I took several deep breaths, trying to quell my fears. *Should I tell Inez? But what could she do except to worry?*

After this, I no longer skimmed the paper but searched each page for news of the grippe. Two days later I saw a headline at the bottom of page one: *Influenza Hits Boston.* The outbreak had spread from the army camp to the general population. Now ordinary people in Boston were getting sick and dying: mothers, fathers, and children.

*Children, oh my Lord, not children, too.*

Dropping the paper, I ran to Tessie's crib, lifted her up, and hugged her. Next, I hurried over to where Little Al and Susie were sleeping and felt their foreheads. Normal temperatures. Thank God. I returned to the parlor, slumped down in the chair, but I couldn't read another word because I was terrified.

A few minutes later, I tried to calm myself. *Boston is miles and miles away,* I reasoned. *I don't believe those nasty flu germs can travel that far. They'd die along the way!*

After those reassuring thoughts, I relaxed a bit, but that night I tossed and turned in my sleep.

# CHAPTER 44

## *Albert*

Despite all the hardships we endured that June of 1918, the men of the 369th regiment stood their ground against the Germans and held the line in CR Melzicourt, the sector we had occupied since coming to the front. On July 1st, a French unit relieved us, and we moved to an encampment near the village of Maffrécourt. Upon our arrival, Captain Little warned that the Germans would probably mount a major offensive on the night of July Fourth and that our unit would lead the counterattack.

"Wow. Lead the counterattack!" Lucky Lewis said. "That's an honor!"

Lyle Thomas sucked his teeth. "I'll pass on that damn honor."

However, most of the men were ready to push forward and get the war over with. Even though we were near a village, this was not a rest tour. Each night, we marched to our fighting positions at the second line and were hunkered down by 10:30 p.m. We watched and waited expectantly and when there was no attack by daybreak, we returned to the barracks.

July Fourth arrived, and we observed the holiday by playing baseball. That night as we marched to our defensive positions, I recalled the vast fields of white crosses I had seen and thought that if the Huns attacked, many of us would die before the morning.

"Think they'll come tonight, Sarge?" Cephas asked.

"Good chance. They think we'll all be drunk celebrating the holiday."

"Well, this is it. We'll finally get to fight them man to man."

"Yep, the Germans know it's do or die for them, so it's going to be brutal."

He touched my arm. "Good luck, my friend."

"Same to you, soldier." We took up our positions and waited, but the Germans never showed.

Three days later, General Gourand sent a letter that was read to the entire French 4th Army. He warned that we might be attacked at any moment, adding that the bombardment would be terrible and the assault fierce. In the letter he declared: *In your breast beat the brave and strong hearts of free men. Nobody will look back; nobody will fall back one step. Everybody will have only one thought–kill, kill many until they have had enough of it. And it is why your General tells you: that assault, you will break it, and it will be a beautiful day.*

*Gouraud, General Commanding the 4th Army*

After hearing the General's words, I wanted to beat the Germans single-handedly just to please him. I thought about how colored people in America had been enslaved and were still struggling for equality. There in France, on that battlefield, I was a free man, equal to all other free men, helping the French preserve their liberty.

Night after night we remained on high alert and waited for the attack, which still didn't come, and after continuous readiness and false alarms, the men grew weary in body and spirit.

"What the hell are the Huns waiting for?" Cephas asked, after another uneventful night in the trenches.

"Maybe for hell to freeze over," Lyle responded.

"They'll try to attack when we least expect it," Lucky Lewis said, "but we'll be ready. Won't we, fellas?"

"I guess so," Lyle muttered as he rolled his eyes.

On July 14th, Bastille Day, the French army command gave bottles of champagne to all the troops. Luc and some of the *poilus* who had welcomed us when we first arrived at the front dropped by our barracks to celebrate. They had been on a rest tour and would be returning to the front that night. After filling everyone's cup to the brim, we offered toasts.

"*Vive la France,*" Luc said.

"To the great General Gourand," another French soldier exclaimed.

"To the *poilus,* the heart and soul of the French army," Teddy added. We clicked the cups and downed the wine.

Lucky Lewis licked his plump lips. "This is the bestest champagne I ever tasted."

"It's the only champagne you ever tasted," Lyle Thomas said, with a wink.

That night, all hell broke loose. The German big guns thundered at midnight, thumping the combined Allied positions over an eighty-kilometer front. The French 4th Army artillery answered, and the battle of Champagne-Marne began! For the next six or seven hours, the shellfire was terrible as the night sky lit up bright as day, masking the moon, and all we could do was to take cover in the trenches. We knew that the fierce bombardment was only a lead-up to the hundreds of thousands of German troops who would be crossing the Marne River in a few hours and attacking the French front lines. We were in the second line, so we wouldn't bear the direct brunt of the attack.

"This looks like the big one," Lyle Thomas shouted, looking up from the trench floor.

"Keep your damn head down or you'll lose it," Teddy Wilson answered.

In the morning, rumors of the battle were flying like chicken feathers in a slaughterhouse. All we knew was that the front line directly ahead of us had held, and no Germans had gotten through. At 8:00 a.m., our battalion marched five kilometers west to Camp Bravard, where we met up with the rest of our regiment and awaited orders for a counterattack. At the same time, we learned that the 369th regiment was being transferred from the 16th division to the 161st division. At Camp Bravard, we grouped behind a steep hill that protected us from the ongoing artillery fire, and some of the men, exhausted from the night's battle, stretched out in the sun to doze.

A few hours after lunch, an aide from General Gouraud brought news of the battle that quickly spread through the encampment: most of the German troops failed to break through the French front line, and those who broke through were stopped by French troops before they reached the second line.

As a result, there were isolated pockets of enemy troops biting into the French lines. Our mission was to reclaim those enemy controlled areas. On July 18th, we continued marching westward to our new front-line positions where we would support the troops of the 161st division. That night, the road on which we traveled was clogged with men and supply trucks and there was little room for us to maneuver. It was a deathtrap because the narrow road offered no protection, and the German artillery could bombard us at any moment. Just past midnight, a squadron of enemy planes passed overhead.

"I hope they've already dropped their load," young Lucky Lewis said as we wove our way through the congestion. We were walking single file and he was just ahead of me.

"I think they must have. They're taking no interest in us."

"Won't they notify the gunners that we're here?"

"Yeah, but the Germans can't fire until their planes are out of harm's way."

"Sergeant Al, we'd best hurry."

We finally reached our destination about two in the morning and were led into the safety of the trenches. Just then, we heard a terrific explosion. The Germans were shelling the road we had just traveled. It was another narrow escape. The next morning, we occupied our attacking positions in the Vilquin sector. Our orders were to dislodge a pocket of German troops who had broken through the French lines and were entrenched in an area in front of the enemy high ground. The Germans on the high ground would be throwing everything they had at us to protect their men. When the whistle blew, all the troops, except for C Company, went over the top and raced toward the enemy lines.

C Company, however, had orders to reinforce a French battalion under attack in a section called Christoferie. Marching that night under constant fire, we moved in small groups through communications trenches to our new fighting location. Suddenly, there was an explosion, and I was violently knocked to the ground. When I came to early the next morning, I was flat on my back in a dugout.

Teddy was patting my face with water. "Al, you okay?"

"What the hell?" I said as I wiped grit from my eyes.

Through a haze, I saw four soldiers staring down at me.

"What happened?" I asked.

"Last night, the communication trench was hit by a shell," Lieutenant West said, "and you were closest to the impact."

"Was anybody hurt?"

"We were all knocked down and bruised," Teddy said. "You were covered with dirt. We dug you out and carried you here."

I had a splitting headache, and when I tried to sit up, the room began to spin.

"Rest, Sergeant," Lieutenant West ordered as he pushed me down. "By the way, it was a direct hit on the trench."

"A direct hit? Jeez, I'm lucky to be alive. In fact, we're all damn lucky." I reached into my shirt pocket for Evie's gold cross. *It's still here. Thank God.*

"We were saved by the sharp bend in the trench," the lieutenant said. "It must have absorbed most of the impact."

*We were saved by Evie's cross*, I thought, and I gripped it tightly. That afternoon, still groggy, I took my position at the trench wall, with my rifle in one hand and the cross in the other.

Three days later, we pulled out of Christoferie and rejoined the rest of the regiment in Vilquin where our boys had just driven out the Germans. When I ran into Phineas, he told me that our troops had decimated the enemy in the counterattack. Nevertheless, fifty-one of our men had been wounded, one having his left foot blown off, and twenty had been killed.

"Louie Crawford, my main man in D Company, was hit by a damn shell," Phineas moaned, "and there ain't enough left to bury him."

I placed my hand on his shoulder and tried to comfort him. Afterward, he related what he and his fellow soldiers had encountered as they fought their way through a bloody no man's land: cadavers with guts hanging out, brown and white arms and legs detached from their bodies, and lonely heads of young Germans, clean-shaven and mostly blonde. Even Phineas seemed shaken when recalling this grisly scene.

Our new position at Vilquin was fraught with danger. Although the Germans had been dislodged from that location, there was still a constant threat from German sharpshooters on the high ground. Men were warned never to leave the trenches for any reason and those who went out, did so at their peril. Our trenches were frequently shelled and sometimes when you least expected it, German sharpshooters would rake the entire area with machine-gun fire. Casualties were mounting, and it got so bad that we had to spend most of our days holed up in dark, smelly dugouts. Even crawling to the pit-in-the-ground toilet was a challenge. Most of the men in my patrol tried to hold their water until dark, but an unfortunate few were pressed to make that dangerous journey in daylight.

At night, teams went out to repair the trenches, rebuild the parapets, and replace the barbed-wire entanglements. It was hazardous work even in the dark. The only amusement we had was when a group of Moroccan soldiers who occupied nearby trenches dodged the sniper bullets and paid us a visit. We taught them how to throw dice and won most of their money. They didn't drink alcohol because of their religion, but Heaven knows they took to gambling like ducks take to water.

# CHAPTER 45

## *Albert*

⁓⦿⦿⦿⁓

In mid-August, a French unit took over our positions in the hated Vilquin sector, and our regiment went on rest leave. I was so happy to leave Vilquin that I would have gladly accepted a ticket to hell, as long as it was round-trip. First Battalion was billeted in Hans, where once again I enjoyed hot showers and a clean, deloused uniform. Compared to Vilquin, Hans was paradise.

The day after we reached the camp, a buzz of excitement spread through the barracks like wildfire. A U.S. Army mail shipment had arrived in the village. After lunch, we assembled in front of the barracks while an army clerk handed each lucky recipient a precious envelope. Letters were our life-lines, our lifelines to home, our lifelines to sanity. They anchored us. They reminded us that there was someplace beyond the madhouse in which we existed, a madhouse of scattered body parts, death, and dying.

Even if the news from home was commonplace and trivial, the letter was still cherished. It was a good-luck charm—at least we thought so. It kept the bullets from striking, the shrapnel from wounding, and the gas from blinding. The letter may have come from a dear wife or sweetheart. Hopefully, it wasn't a "Dear John" letter. That could never protect anyone. While we were still gathered outside the barracks, a soldier from North Carolina tore open his letter and read it.

"Lordie be, would you all listen to this. It's from my Ma."

*My Dear Son,*

*I hopes and prays you're all right and not in the hands of those dev-ilish Germans. Folks in town are saying they're torturing and blinding colored soldiers just out of plain meanness. Everyone in church is going on about it, including Pastor Killens. Son, please write soon 'cause I'm real worried.*

*May the Good Lord keep and protects you.*

*Your loving Ma*

"Tell Ma not to fret," I said. "The Huns have to catch us first and so far, they haven't captured anyone in the 369th." The North Carolina soldier smiled as he gave me a thumbs-up sign.

That day I was fortunate enough to receive two letters, one from Evie and, to my surprise, one from Little Al. I read them hastily and then sprinted over to the baseball field where C Company was playing K Company. I'd read them again in the evening. After the game, Teddy and I went for a stroll around the village. We had over an hour to kill before dinner call.

"You pitched a damn good game today," I said.

"Thanks, Al, but we still lost."

"Hey, you win some, you lose some. See you got a letter. Hope it's good news."

"Mighty good news," he said patting his shirt pocket.

"Someone special?"

"It's from Amanda, my girl in Philadelphia."

"Didn't know you had a girl. You've been keeping mighty quiet about her." We stopped and leaned against a fence on the outskirts of Hans and Teddy lit a cigarette.

"So tell me about this Amanda of yours."

"You know I studied at Fisk University in Nashville but had to leave school the year before graduation."

"You said you had to go to work to support your younger brother and sister."

"They were living with my aunt in Harlem, but when she got injured on her job, she couldn't work for a while, so I returned to New York and found a job as a messenger."

"Was your brother in school?"

"My brother and sister were in high school and I wanted to give them a chance for a good education. They've both graduated by now."

"That was the best thing you could have done for them."

*I wish Pa had let me finish eighth grade and sent me on to high school. It would have made a hell of a difference in my life.* A well of bitterness filled my gut, but I tried to shake off.

"Amanda and I were in the same English class at Fisk," Teddy said. "One day, I introduced myself and when she smiled at me, a burst of sunshine lit up my life. At first, we talked about our schoolwork, but as we got to know each other, we also shared our dreams. We fell in love and I planned to ask her father for her hand as soon as I graduated and landed a teaching position.

"After I left school, she continued her studies and received her degree. Now she's back in Philadelphia, living with her parents and working as a schoolteacher. When I visited her, her parents were polite but cold. I suppose they thought I wasn't good enough for their daughter."

He put out his cigarette on the fence post and tossed it into the grass. "The last time I saw her, she said that her parents wanted her to marry a well-to-do suitor, but she told them she was in love with me. During that visit, her father took me aside and said if I really loved Amanda, I would do what's best for her and give her up. I've been pondering his words ever since.

"When I wrote her last month, I released her from our vows and explained that we couldn't get married anytime soon."

"How did she react?"

He touched his shirt pocket again. "She said she'll wait for me, no matter long it takes."

"You're a good man, Teddy, and you've got yourself a good woman!"

"Quite honestly Al, I'd be lost without her."

We started walking again and came to a wooden bench on the edge of a meadow filled with violet wildflowers. Taking a seat, I faced the sun, letting its warmth ease my tensions. Teddy seemed happy about Amanda's letter, but I suspected it was a happiness tempered by anxiety.

"Teddy, have you made any plans for the future?"

"Plans? I may not survive this war."

"I may not either, but I intend to. And after the war, I plan to return home, put my arms around Evie, and find a better job."

"Well, if you put it like that, I'd like to finish up my year at Fisk and get a high school teaching position in science, so Amanda and I can be married."

I nodded. "That's a plan, a good plan."

His shoulders sagged. "I've been saving my army pay but don't have nearly enough money for school." He lit up another cigarette, took a deep drag, and blew out the smoke.

"Did you have any special advisors at Fisk?"

"Let me think . . . Dean Braithwaite. He was disappointed when I had to leave."

"Write the Dean. Explain your situation and see what he comes up with."

"I'll do it! I'll write to him tonight."

We stood up, stretched out our stiff frames, and hurried back to camp, arriving just in time for dinner.

That evening, I sat on my bunk and slowly reread the precious letters from home. Teddy was composing a dispatch to Dean Braithwaite and Cephas was drawing stark war scenes in his copybook. I once asked Cephas if he had a girl back home and he replied that art was his woman and his life. Then, I noticed Lyle Thomas playing solitaire and wondered why he seldom, if ever, received any mail.

"No news from home today?" I asked.

COAL, WAR & LOVE

"Naw. Those guys I used to hang with never answered my letters."

"Have you written to your father?"

"I already told you that my Pa and I had a falling out!"

"You should let him know you're okay."

"I doubt he wants to hear from me."

"Man, you're in the danger zone! He's bound to be worried."

Lyle raised his eyebrows. "Think so? Maybe I'll drop him a line."

I resumed reading my letters, but Lyle interrupted me. "Hey, how's that little boy of yours."

"Come and hear what he wrote."

*Dear Daddy,*

*How are you? I am fine. So is Mommy, James, Susie and baby Tessie. I help Mommy around the house and take out the trash. We miss the stew you cook on Sundays. I pray every night for God to bring you home soon.*

*Your son, Albert*

"Jeez, what a smart kid," Lyle said. "He's a chip off the old block."

"He's smarter than his old man," I replied. "I want him to get a good education. I want him to go to college."

"College? What you say? I barely made it out of eighth grade."

"I didn't even get that far. My pa didn't allow it. But I want my boy to go to college!"

We finished our ten-day rest tour in Hans and started out on a long trek to Camp Owens, where we spent two weeks drilling and practicing maneuvers. During this time, wild rumors flooded the camp: it was said that the 369th regiment would be merging with the American Expeditionary Forces in the Allies' final push against the Germans. We were Americans, and we had proven to be tough and audacious fighters. So most of us believed the rumors.

# CHAPTER 46

## *Evie*

~⊙ ℮~

It was the end of September when the flu arrived in Albany. When I heard about it, a rush of terror gripped my heart, and I wondered how to keep my children safe. A few days later, I received an unexpected letter from Father.

*My Dear Evie,*

*I don't mean to alarm you, but we've had an outbreak of flu here in New York City. Don't worry. I'm fine. Incoming travelers have been examined at the railway station, and those with flu symptoms have been quarantined. Police are arresting anyone who spits in the streets or coughs or sneezes without using a handkerchief, and city health officials are trying all means to keep the outbreak under control.*

*How are things in Albany? I hope it doesn't spread up there. I ran into Dr. Grange early this morning, the new doctor in the neighborhood that graduated from Meharry Medical School. He was on his way to do rounds at the hospital and said he had treated patients for sixteen hours the previous day. He looked pretty darn tired. I asked if I should close down my business for a while, but he said I probably wouldn't get the flu since I had it before and it's mainly striking young adults. I'll advise my young workers to stay home for a few days. Maybe it's a blessing in disguise that you and Jennie had the flu last spring.*

*When I asked his advice about keeping the children safe, he counseled that all of you, particularly James, should stay out of crowds, and more importantly, to stay away from anyone coughing or sneezing. He also suggested disinfecting all household items with iodine solution and washing the children's hands with carbolic soap. Please let me know how you're faring. I can come up to Albany if you need me.*

*Yours truly,*

*Father*

"Oh Father," I cried aloud, "it's here, the beast is already at the gate." Then I decided I would keep my children away from other people. I would take Little Al out of school. James was staying with Jennie and Peter, so I wrote Jennie, telling her to keep him at home until the flu season was over. The next morning, I gave the letter to Charlie, the Irish mailman.

Little Al was unhappy about staying home, and I wondered how to explain the situation without frightening him to death.

"Momma, I want to go to school."

"Honey, there are bad germs going around. You may get sick there."

"I'll be careful. I won't catch them."

"No, you can't go until the grippe goes away."

"But none of my classmates are sick. I want to play with them!"

"Albert, if you don't listen, I'll write your father and he'll give you a spanking when he comes home. Now go play in the backyard."

He sucked his teeth, slammed the kitchen door, and stomped down the back stairs. Susie was already there, playing with her doll.

I slumped on the kitchen chair. *They should be safe in the backyard,* I thought, *as long as no other children come over.* Just then, I heard Tessie crying so I went to see about her.

Later that afternoon, I glanced out the back window and saw Tony Blonski, Little Al's classmate, hanging over the backyard gate. He was carrying his book bag and must have been on his way home from school. Little Al, stood on the other side, laughing and talking. I ran downstairs and told Tony that Little Al was not allowed to have company.

"Can I come back tomorrow, Mrs. Johnson?"

"No, I'll let you know when Al can play with you. Now go on home."

He gave me a funny look and slowly walked away.

"Bye, Tony," Little Al said.

"Bye, Al." Little Al went and sat on the garden swing. I followed him.

"Didn't I tell you not to play with other kids until the grippe goes away?"

"We wasn't playing, we was just talking."

I reached down and pulled his ear.

"Ow! That hurts."

"I don't want you around any other children, not talking or laughing or playing. You could get very sick and even pass the flu on to your sisters. Do you understand?"

"Yeah."

"Yes, Mother," I said.

"Yes, Mother," he repeated.

Susie, who must have sensed the tension between two people she loved, came over and hugged me. "I love you, Mommy."

"Thank you, dear. I love you, too." As I plodded up the stairs to the kitchen, I thought: *How long must I keep them isolated like this?*

Four days after I received Father's letter, I went to the front porch to wait for Charley, while Little Al and Susie were in the backyard, watching Tessie. I was hoping to get a letter from Al and to hear from Jennie. I lingered on the porch for several minutes and was getting ready to go inside when I saw him walking toward the house, carrying his mail pouch and wearing a white facemask. I ran down the steps to meet him.

"Morning, Mrs. Johnson, I got mail for you," he mumbled through the mask.

I stared at him.

"Oh, this," he said. "The post office ordered all mailmen to wear masks to help stop the grippe from spreading."

The very mention of the grippe made me shiver.

"But Charley, is it that bad here?"

"Listen to this Mrs. Johnson. Yesterday after I delivered your mail, I went on to the MacHennessys, the Irish family down the block. You know them, don't you?"

"Yes, I know Mrs. MacHennessy quite well."

"I had a package for them from Sears and Roebuck. I knocked on their door, but no one answered. It seemed a bit strange, so I walked to the back of the house and looked through the window. You can't imagine what I saw."

"What?"

"Three kids sprawled on a mattress, not even moving. I ran to the corner to get Officer Robbie and brought him back to the house. He tried to rouse the kids by banging on the window, but there was no response. I left him there because I had to deliver the rest of the mail. When I saw Robbie this morning, he told me that he raced to the police station to report the situation and they sent an ambulance and a public health nurse to the house. Robbie broke in, and he and the nurse found the whole family, mother, father, and three children, in bed, dreadfully ill with the grippe. The ambulance carried them all to the hospital."

I gasped. "Heavenly days! But what about little Fiona, the baby girl?"

"Jesus, Mary, Joseph," he intoned, closing his eyes. "The baby, poor thing, was dead in the crib."

"Good Lord!" As I uttered a brief prayer for little Fiona, I felt my knees buckling and nearly fell to the ground.

Charley steadied me and helped me up to the porch. "Are you all right, Mrs. Johnson?"

"I'm okay now. It's just the shock of it."

"Oh, I almost forgot your letter."

"Thank you, Charley."

Stuffing the letter in my pocket, I entered the hall, sat on the bottom step, and prayed again. *Dear Lord, please help me protect my children.* After a short while, I stood up and knocked on Mrs. Jones's door. It was quiet inside, so I knocked again, more loudly than before.

*Could she be down with flu? Oh, my God, is the beast in my house?*

I banged on the door and yelled, "Mrs. Jones, Mrs. Jones." Then I heard a small voice.

"Hold your horses, I'm coming." A surge of relief ran through me.

"Oh, it's you, Evie. What in the world's the matter?"

"I'm sorry dear, but when you didn't answer I thought you might be ill."

Mrs. Jones looked bewildered but invited me in. As we sat at the kitchen table, I told her about the deadly flu outbreak in Albany and what had happened to the MacHennessys, and poor little Fiona.

She shivered and pulled her robe tightly about her. "Holy Heaven protect us!" Glancing around the kitchen, she asked, "Can it come through the walls?"

"No, no. They say it's transmitted by a cough or a sneeze. I suggest you stay indoors."

"Don't worry, Evie. I have no plans to go anywhere!"

"But you should open your windows. It's a bit musty in here."

She got up and cracked the back window.

"I'm keeping the kids home until this blows over. I have plenty of potatoes and cabbage in the larder if you need some."

"Thank you, Evie. I'll let you know. Will the milkman still make deliveries?"

"I think so, but I'm sure he'll be wearing a mask. In fact, I'm going upstairs now to make us facemasks."

"Will I need one if I don't go out? I don't want to put you to any trouble."

"Just use it when you answer the door." I left Mrs. Jones pondering this new turn of events and brought the children up for lunch.

After putting Tessie in her crib for a nap, I went into the dining room and sewed six face masks, making them extra thick by encasing white quilting between layers of white cotton fabric. Then Little Al, Susie, and I spent the rest of the day washing down the whole apartment, including the furniture, floors, doorknobs, and walls with hot soapy iodine water to get rid of any lurking germs. It had been a terrible morning, but somehow, I felt a bit more in control by the afternoon.

That evening I reached into my pocket for a *handkerchief* and found a letter. *Oh, my goodness, I nearly forgot it. Maybe it's from Jennie, maybe James is coming home. I really need him now.*

It wasn't from Jennie. It was from overseas. What a blessing to hear from Al when my spirits were so low! I carefully opened the envelope and removed a stained piece of ivory stationary. Holding it up to my face, I tried to catch a whiff of Al, but all I could smell was the dirt of the trench. At last, I stretched out on the bed and began to read it.

> *My Dearest Evie,*
>
> *I'm writing to you during a break in the shelling. It's dark in the dugout and I barely have enough light to see. Our makeshift can-lamp is sputtering, and we don't have any more fuel, so I'll be quick.*
>
> *I just want to let you know that I'm well and I pray that you and the children are the same. Tell Little Al to ask the Good Lord to end this blasted war soon (excuse my language). Evie, please continue to pray for my men and me and give my regards to your father.*
>
> *I remain your devoted and loving husband,*
>
> *Albert*
>
> *PS. Write my ma and pa and tell them I'm* okay.

I hugged the letter to my heart, mouthing the words, "He's *all right.* Thank you, Lord."

Later that week, Inez knocked on our door. As we sat at the kitchen table, I told her my fears about the flu outbreak.

"Evie, most of my students are still attending class. Don't you think that the Mayor would have closed the schools if the outbreak was that bad? That poor family down the block could just be an isolated incident. You should let Albert return to school."

"Perhaps I'm being overcautious, but better safe than sorry."

Inez rolled her eyes.

"Guess what? I found out why I haven't heard from Calvin."

"What happened?"

"One day last week, I saw our mailman and told him that I had been expecting a letter from my fiancé in Boston and was it possible it had gotten lost in the mail. He said he remembered delivering a few letters addressed to me from Boston. They were in light blue envelopes. I ran home and confronted my mother, and she confessed that she had hidden them. There were three letters in light blue envelopes, just as the postman said. The last one was postmarked three weeks ago. I was furious with Mother and went to the post office the next day and asked them to hold all my correspondence there."

"My stars! What did Calvin say?"

"That he was well and wanted to know why I wasn't writing. I nearly cried when he asked if I had changed my mind about marrying him. I wrote back immediately and told him what had happened and that, of course, I still wanted to marry him. That was three days ago, and I haven't heard back yet."

"Be patient, Inez. He might be out on field maneuvers."

"Evie, you're such a good friend. I don't know what I'd do without you!" We drank our tea and she left.

*Was she right about my being too cautious with the children? But what about the MacHennessys and their poor baby? No, I don't believe it was just happenstance.*

# CHAPTER 47

## *Evie*

❧

On October 8–I'll never forget the day–Charley rang the bell and delivered a printed notice from the mayor of Albany. As I stood on the front porch reading it, my legs turned to jelly. Mayor Watt announced that there was an epidemic of Spanish influenza in the city and that all schools, theatres, dance halls, and most public places would be closed to halt the spread of the disease. An advisory from the United States Public Health Service was printed on the bottom of the page. It read:

> **Influenza** *is spread by droplets sprayed from Nose and Throat*
>
> *Cover each COUGH and SNEEZE with a handkerchief*
>
> *Walk to work, if possible*
>
> *Do not spit on floor or sidewalk*
>
> *Do not use common drinking cups or towels*
>
> *If taken ill, go to bed and send for a doctor*

So I was right after all, but that was no consolation. Three days later, three hundred and thirty-two new cases were reported in the newspaper. And the city's chief health administrator announced that for the first time in anyone's memory, churches would be closed on Sundays and public wakes and funerals would be banned until further notice. Only the saloons would remain open.

*Who could be so foolish,* I thought, *to frequent a tavern when death is stalking? Well, if those drunkards get sick and die, it's their own darn fault!*

My daily life in Albany nearly came to a standstill and the newspaper was my only lifeline to the outside world. Every morning after breakfast, I reviewed Little Al's schoolwork with him. The newspapers printed lessons for each grade because teachers had no idea when classes would begin again. I kept a pot of hot water simmering on the coal stove and set a basin of water and a bar of carbolic soap on the kitchen table. Every two hours or so, I herded Tessie, Little Al, and Susie into the kitchen and washed their hands. Little Al balked, claiming I was washing his skin off. I kept up the routine of wiping down the house with disinfectant, and after the milkman, paperboy, and the mailman left, I scrubbed the front porch. A day after the Mayor's proclamation, I heard from Jennie. She apologized for not writing sooner and asked how we were weathering the crisis. She also said that they were doing well. I was annoyed because she didn't seem to be that concerned about the children and me.

During the next few weeks, confusion turned to chaos. The newspapers reported that the number of new flu cases was rising sharply, and thirty to forty people were dying each day. Everyone was vulnerable, from the chairman of Standard Oil to the factory worker at General Electric. Because of the war in Europe, there was a shortage of doctors and nurses and those who were on hand were horribly overworked. Hospitals overflowed with patients and the city set up makeshift infirmaries in any available space, even in the parks.

One afternoon, I heard the squeaking of wheels and ran to the front window. Passing by was a long line of funeral carts that must have been on the way to the cemetery. Both fear and compassion took hold of me. Those poor souls wouldn't even get a decent burial. I had read that coffins containing the dead were stacked three high at Dorchester Funeral Home on Broad Street and at Graceland cemetery because most of the gravediggers had come down with flu.

I don't know why I continued reading the newspaper, but I couldn't stop. Each day there were more and more dreadful stories. A laborer couldn't get medical attention for his wife and three children who had the flu, so he cut their throats, saying, "I will cure them." It was simply horrific. They say that desperate times call for desperate measures, and times were certainly desperate then. Doctors had no medicine to cure the flu, so people turned to home remedies, hanging bags of garlic around their necks, or swallowing lumps of sugar laced with turpentine. Others flocked to drugstores to buy patent medicines, which flew off the shelves. I couldn't imagine what else to do to protect my children, so I kept them at home, gave them cod liver oil to drink, and continued washing their hands.

Sometime in the middle of this, I ran out of food and we were reduced to eating dry barley pancakes for supper. Mrs. Jones's cupboard was also bare. I would have to go shopping soon or my children would go hungry. I put on my mask and cotton gloves and steeled myself for the outside journey.

"Don't go, Mommy, you'll catch the grippe," Little Al said, crying and tugging at my hand.

"I'll be fine, honey. I'm wearing my mask and gloves." Leaving the children with Mrs. Jones, who was also terrified at the prospect of my venturing out, I uttered a short prayer, stepped onto the front porch, descended the stairs, and walked to Kelly's grocery store.

It was only a few blocks away, but it seemed like a thousand miles. As I approached the store, I saw several people standing on the sidewalk, well apart from one another. All were wearing masks. Among them was my German neighbor, Mrs. Schmidt, who seemed ill at ease when she spotted me. She waved, and I nodded. The other people glanced at me suspiciously, but I ignored them. At the store's entrance, I noticed a handwritten sign on the door: *Leave Your List And We Will Fill It.* I fished in my purse for pen and paper and hastily wrote down what I needed, throwing in a few scarce items like sugar and butter as well. While we were waiting, a young woman coughed or perhaps just cleared her throat, but everyone jumped and moved far away from her. After a few minutes, Mr. Kelly threw open the door and his helper, a redheaded boy about fifteen, placed a bag of groceries and a bill on the step. Both were wearing white masks and gloves. A balding middle-aged man rushed toward them, examined the bill, handed Mr. Kelly the money, and picked up the bag. And so it went until my turn came.

"I'm sorry about all this Mrs. Johnson," Mr. Kelly said through his mask.

"I understand why prudence is necessary under these circumstances, Mr. Kelly. After all, if you got sick and closed the store, what would we do?" I paid the bill and picked up the two heavy bags.

"Can you carry these by yourself?" he asked.

"Yes. I'm stronger than I look."

I struggled down the block with the packages and when I reached home, I was pleasantly surprised to find sugar, butter, three chocolate bars and a small package of peppermints, among the other groceries. I hadn't expected those goodies, but I suppose Mr. Kelly was willing to indulge me since I was a very good customer. Suddenly, I had an urge to do something extravagant. I sliced a piece of bread, spread it thick with butter and jam, and slowly bit into it. After relishing this treat, I carried a share of the provisions down to Mrs. Jones and fetched the children.

That evening, after the children had gone to bed, someone knocked on the downstairs door. It was Inez, wearing a mask and carrying a small suitcase. I was shocked because it was rather late to be calling. Besides, during her last visit, I suggested that she not call again until the epidemic was over. When we sat down at the kitchen table, I noticed that her eyes looked red and puffy.

"Inez, whatever is the matter?"

She removed the mask and propped up her head with her hand. "I was supposed to meet Calvin at the train station this afternoon about two. He has a three-day pass. I waited, but he wasn't on the train. I stayed there all afternoon into the evening. He never showed up! What could have happened? Oh God, I don't know what to do."

I reached across the table and took her hand. "You poor dear. I'm sure he's fine, the flu season is over in Boston. You'll probably get a letter tomorrow or the next day explaining it all."

When I rose from the table to make a pot of tea, I spotted her suitcase again. "Were you going somewhere?"

She sighed. "We were going to New York City for three days. They say the flu epidemic has run its course there, too."

My eyes grew wide. "Just the two of you, alone?"

"We wanted to be together before his unit shipped overseas."

I couldn't believe what I was hearing. Inez Vanderpool was risking her virtue on a three-day pass. I placed the cups, spoons, and a bowl of sugar on the table and poured the tea. "Oh, my goodness, Inez. How could Calvin ask you to do such a thing? You could be ruined in decent society."

She looked down and twisted her hands together.

*This war is changing us,* I thought. *It's turned everything upside down. Hundreds of thousands have already been slaughtered, families are being destroyed, and men are being blown apart or crippled for life. And now with this flu epidemic, no one is safe. Can I fault Inez for wanting to be with the man she loves, if only for a few days? However, the world will blame her.*

Finally, Inez broke the silence. "I might as well confess. We planned to be secretly married in New York."

"Was that wise? Anything could have happened."

Her face took on a puzzled expression. "What do you mean?"

"Well, you might have become, um . . . with child."

"After only three days?"

"It only takes one night, dear. If it happened, you'd have to give up your job. And remember you promised your mother you would wait to marry."

"My mother!" Inez shot upwards in the chair. "She didn't keep her part of the bargain, so I'm not keeping mine."

"But you're still living under her roof. I don't think you and Calvin thought out this plan. The war should be over soon, and you can get properly married then."

"I suppose you're right, Evie." She took a deep breath and stood up. "I'd better get home now."

"Get some sleep, Inez. Things will look better in the morning."

As I showed her out, I thought: *I hope things do get better in the morning, not only for Inez, but also for my children, and for my husband in the danger zone.*

It was Halloween, the last day of October, but no one wore costumes, ate candy, or enjoyed merriment that day. I was washing the dinner dishes when Little Al ran in and said that someone was knocking on the outside door. Wiping my hands on the dishtowel, I put on my mask and cotton gloves and went down to answer it.

*Oh dear, I bet it's Inez again, with more hullaballoo about Calvin. I'm getting sick and tired of it.*

As I opened the door, a cold gust of wind blew in, chilling me to the bone. A strange man was on the porch, a man in Western Union garb, a man holding a telegram.

"Mrs. Evelyn Johnson?"

"Yes, that's me."

Wobbling, I reached out, grasped the telegram, and hugged it to my breast. *Good Lord,* I prayed, *please let my Albert be alive.*

# CHAPTER 48

## *Albert*

❧ ❧

The men of First Battalion stood shoulder to shoulder on a hillside in Champaign, listening intently while Major Little spoke about the impending battle. He warned that the fighting would be worse than anything we'd seen so far and that many of us could die. He said that one million Allied troops, stretched along an L-shaped battle line, would be going over the top: the French 4th Army in Champaign, the Americans to the east in the Argonne Forest, and the British in the northwest. Our dream of merging with the American troops had come to naught, and our regiment was still part of the French 4th Army. Together with French and Moroccan units, we would play a small but crucial role in the Allied advance against the Germans.

Major Little paused for a moment and then announced, "Men, tomorrow, September 26, 1918, is D-day, the launch of the great Allied fall offensive we have all been waiting for."

As I stood there listening to the Major, my mind began to wander. A week after our regiment had returned to Hans from Camp Owens, we were ordered to break camp again. In the middle of the night, we were loaded into a *camion* train, which wasn't a train at all. It was a convoy of one hundred and fifty canvas-covered trucks driven by Senegalese drivers. I was surprised that these African drivers were speaking French until someone said they were from the French colonies. Our driver, Demba, was a tall, handsome young man with an intricate pattern of scars on both sides of his dark-brown cheeks.

Lyle Thomas seemed fascinated by these scars and whispered that Demba probably got them in a fight.

"Those marks are cut into your face when you're a child," Teddy said. "They identify your tribe."

"I'm glad I'm not part of that tribe," Lyle said.

After driving for half the night, the convoy stopped for a rest break, and we stood around the truck chatting with the driver. He seemed just as amazed to meet colored American soldiers, as we were to meet him.

"How'd you find yourself here, all the way from Africa?" Teddy asked. The driver replied in French, and Cephas, who understood it better than the rest of us, translated.

"It was no accident, my friends. The French came to our village looking for young men to fight in their army. There were no volunteers, so they began conscripting us. Many boys in my age group ran away to other villages and even to neighboring countries. I started out with a group of them one morning but returned that evening to say farewell to my mother. Alas, I was caught, along with some other village boys. At daybreak the next morning, they marched us out of the village, along a narrow dirt road that ran through a dense forest. In my fright, I stumbled, and when I looked ahead, I saw my mother and the other village women stepping out from behind the trees. On the opposite side of the road was my father, the chief, with the village men. A Wolof-speaking African soldier warned them to return to their compounds and pointed his gun at them. Yet, the villagers stood like stones. A French soldier fired a warning shot, but the villagers still did not move. We captives were prodded forward at gunpoint. As I marched past my mother, close enough to touch, I saw that her face was set like a wooden mask. And my father, also grimacing and pressing a shield and spear to his chest, stood silently–powerless against the iron guns. After we had passed the villagers, a deep-throated moaning began. I was afraid to look back, but I still remember the sound of my mother and the village women wailing as if I was already dead."

Demba breathed deeply and stared into the darkness. "When we had completed a half-day march, I spotted a hyena in the bushes, an unlucky sign, and I also believed, although walking and breathing, I was a dead man. My soul would wander aimlessly because no burial rituals would be done for me: no washing of my body and wrapping it in white cloth, and no handing out kola nuts to the mourners."

As the Senegalese driver continued to weave the threads of his tale like a tapestry, we became spellbound.

"After three days," he said, "we reached the white man's compound. Many young men from other villages and tribes were there in the fenced-in coral. The soldier-chief wrote our names in a book and tied a metal tag around each of our necks and gave us blankets to sleep on and food to eat. Then he told us we were going over the big sea to help the French people fight the evil Germans. When the boat arrived, we were led into it, and no man was allowed to remain behind."

Lucky Lewis grimaced. "It sounds like what the white man did to our people when they brought them to America as slaves."

The Senegalese driver had more to say. "When we reached France, my countrymen were used as shock troops and many fell in combat or died from the cold. Several of us younger ones who had attended school in the colony and could speak French were taught to drive and repair transport trucks. That's how I became a driver, and I've been here for over three years."

A worried look clouded Lucky Lewis's face. "What'll you do when the war's over?"

Demba smiled. "I'll return to my village. My family will be astonished that I'm alive. Perhaps they'll slaughter a cow and hold a celebration."

My buddies and I looked at each other in amazement. This was an ugly side of the French we didn't know about. Just as we were about to flood him with questions, we got the signal to board, so the conversation ended. But in my heart of hearts, I hoped that he would survive the war and get to see his family in Senegal again.

We drove all night to our new positions near the battlefield. As I said good-bye to Demba, our eyes locked in an embrace, and a deep well of understanding sprang up between us. I knew I would never forget him.

So there we were on a hillside in Champagne listening to Major Little drone on about the Allied offensive. First Battalion would be held in reserve while Second and Third Battalions, along with the Moroccan and French units, would go over the top in the early morning. The Moroccans were fierce warriors, who gave no quarter and took no prisoners! I liked and respected them. They would be in the first wave of the attack, and I imagined them climbing out of the trenches with sharp knives held between their teeth and running toward the enemy lines like a pack of wolves.

While waiting in the reserve area, we studied pencil-drawn maps indicating the battle plan. Major Little explained that our first objective was to take the town of Séchault. Our troops would have to cross the Dormoise River, just north of us, capture the German high ground called Bellevue Signal, which was a series of steep hills and ridges, and then pass through a valley to Séchault. It wouldn't be easy. After we had taken Séchault, we were then to proceed one and a half kilometers through Les Petits Rosiers, a small dense forest, to the town of Challerange where there was a strategic German railroad junction. The ultimate objective was to destroy that railroad line which supplied equipment and fresh troops to the German army.

At eleven o'clock that night the Allied big guns spoke forcefully, announcing the start of the battle of Meuse-Argonne, and the German artillery retorted. We listened from our protected reserve trenches as the bombardment and counter-bombardment went on for six hours and shells whizzed above our heads. The night sky flashed red and yellow and the earth shook under the constant barrage. At daybreak, a soldier brought word that the Moroccan and French troops, along with Second and Third battalion, had gone over the top and were already fighting their way through enemy lines. We would soon have our turn. Instinctively, I patted my pocket that contained Evie's gold cross and photo and nibbled on chocolate from my ration bag filled with sardines, hardtack, and hard-boiled eggs. In the late afternoon, I spotted Lucky Lewis leaning against the trench wall, staring at a small photo in the fading light.

"It's my mom," he said.

"How's she?"

"Okay, I guess. Wrote her a note telling her I love her—just in case I don't make it."

"Don't worry, Private. You'll make it home fine."

"Just in case I don't, Sarge, promise you'll visit her. I'm her only son."

He put the photo in his pocket. "She's right there on West 134th Street, in Harlem."

"Okay. Now let's try and get some sleep."

The next day, Colonel Haywood ordered First Battalion onto the battlefield. Moving over a devastated countryside, we slowly advanced to the deserted trenches on the south side of the Dormoise River. As we moved ahead, the French artillery moved with us. A team of four strong horses pulled each big gun and three soldiers pushed from the rear of each wheel, while the team driver cracked his whip and cursed. The horses strained to move their enormous loads through the thick mud over a ground filled with shell holes, trenches, and barbed-wire entanglements. We had just settled down in the trenches when we heard a loud commotion at river's edge. Peering over the parapets, we saw the men of Second Battalion struggling to cross the Dormoise River, single file, on a frail, narrow footbridge. Most of the troops had already crossed and were taking cover behind a steep hill. The Germans, perched on the high ground, Bellevue Signal, were shelling the soldiers on the footbridge with many of the shells landing in the water, and drenching the men. It was almost comical until the Germans started shelling our trenches and we had to quickly take cover.

An hour later, we came out of hiding and crept downstream one by one toward a stone bridge that also spanned the river. Once across the bridge, we climbed a steep hill and deployed on an adjacent plain, taking cover when the enemy bombarded us. After the attack, we advanced, keeping well behind Second Battalion, which was trying to drive the Germans off Bellevue Signal. Soon, news came that the Germans had pulled back, but had left several machine gunners there. We sheltered in nearby trenches but couldn't move ahead, so Cephas and three other soldiers volunteered to take out the gunners. Leaving before sunrise, they were to work their way around the hills and ridges and sneak up behind the enemy. I began to worry when they hadn't returned by nightfall and asked permission from a reluctant Lieutenant West to mount a search. Carrying stretchers and extra canteens, Teddy, Lyle, and I set out way before dawn and traveling by moonlight, we followed the paths we thought the men had taken. Before long, we found the first man, shot dead through the chest, and after an hour, we found two other lifeless bodies. I felt pretty sure that Cephas was also gone, but we kept searching, keeping low to the ground, moving from bush to bush.

"It's getting light," I whispered. "Another half an hour, we'll have to go back."

Just as we were about to turn around, I heard a groan from a shell hole about thirty feet away.

"Be careful, Sarge, it could be a trap," Teddy said.

"You guys stay here behind these bushes. If I get hit, leave me, and make your way back to our lines."

As I crawled to the shell hole, I caught sight of a dead French soldier stretched across the opening. A few seconds later, I heard another groan. I rolled the dead man over and discovered a soldier pinned beneath him.

"Cephas."

"Sarge," he moaned softly. "Thank God."

He was alive but barely conscious. We lifted him out of the shell hole and carefully carried him back to our line. He had been shot in his right arm and shoulder. While we waited for the stretcher-bearers to take him to the field hospital, I dressed his wounds. He said he was hungry, so Teddy boiled water and added bouillon cubes and hardtack to make a mush. That was all we had.

"Sarge, I shot a German gunner," Cephas muttered, "but when I went after the other one, he let me have it and I tumbled into a shell hole. A French soldier found me and tried to help, but he was shot dead and fell on top of me.

"Couldn't move after that. I was hungry, thirsty and trapped, so I reached around the dead man with my good arm and grabbed his canteen of coffee."

Just before he was carried away to the field hospital, I stuffed the last of my chocolate rations into Cephas's pocket.

"You think I'll still be able to paint?" he asked.

"Sure, you will," I replied, "and you'll become the most famous Negro artist in Paris."

While awaiting orders to move out, Teddy, Lyle and I went to sleep in the trenches. That afternoon, we observed endless streams of injured men being carried back through the lines to the field hospital and realized that Second and Third Battalions had suffered heavy casualties. I wondered how the medics were handling the situation and questioned one of the stretcher-bearers.

"How're things back at the hospital?"

"Terrible. Doctors' aprons soaked in blood and the dead stacked up like sacks of flour." The stretcher-bearer and his partner were rushing back to no man's land to pick up more of the wounded.

I leaped out of the trench and shouted, "And the living?"

He turned. "Docs and medics are working fast as they can, but many poor souls are bleeding to death before they can help them."

Shivering as the horrific scene flashed before my eyes, I imagined Cephas, writhing in pain.

Before dawn the next morning, we received orders to lead the assault on Séchault one kilometer away. The other battalions had done their part, now it was our turn. After Séchault lay the town of Challerange and the railroad, the German lifeline. Under heavy sniper fire, we made our way up to Bellevue Signal and wiped out the remaining Germans gunners. Then we descended a steep hill, thick with undergrowth, and spread out over an open field. Snaking along on hands and knees, we advanced toward the southern edge of Séchault. The place was chock-full of snipers that gave us a hot welcome.

Séchault was a small town with stone and brick buildings neatly laid out along straight streets and avenues. It sat in the middle of a large plain and was surrounded by a series of drainage ditches that we would later use as trenches. Our first task was to take out the 77-millimeter German field gun that had been firing at us. After accomplishing that, our soldiers ran from house to house, ridding the place of snipers by throwing grenades through open doors and windows.

There were other snipers hidden on the plains north of town that would rake the streets with bullets as we attempted to cross. It was during such a crossing that young Lucky Lewis was shot down in the middle of the road. Dodging the bullets, Lyle Thomas ran back and dragged him into the brick house where I had taken cover. Lucky had been hit in his side and left leg, and I tried to stop the bleeding.

"Sarge Al," he whimpered, "remember your promise, about Ma."

"Shut up, boy. You'll make it. I won't allow you to die." I gave him water from my canteen and we stayed by his side for some time.

Evening was approaching when Lieutenant West ran in, "The town's clean. We're moving into the ditches."

"This boy's seriously wounded, sir."

"There's nothing you can do for him. The stretcher-bearers will be coming later to take the injured to the field hospital."

"Yes, sir, give me a moment, please."

"Don't be long."

"Go on now, Lyle. I'll follow you in a jiffy," I said. Lyle's eyes were moist with tears. This was our boy on the ground, our Lucky mascot.

He squatted down and touched Lucky's face. "Bye, soldier. Stay strong."

"Bye, Lyle and thanks."

"Be careful," I said as he slipped out the door. "The Germans are still dropping shells out there." I knelt at Lucky's side.

"Sarge, I'm scared," he moaned.

"I know, son. I am, too."

I removed Evie's gold cross from my pocket. "Hold on to this, boy. Help is on the way."

"Thanks, Sarge," he said as he tightened his hand around the cross.

After laying my canteen on the ground next to him, I tied white gauze to the doorknob to alert the medics. Then I ran down the street, praying,

*Lord, many have died in this war to end wars, but could you please spare this one young boy.*

By the time I caught up with C Company, they were holed up for the night in a ditch, and I had regained my hard-as-nails composure.

"How's the boy?" Teddy asked.

"I hope the medics get there soon." A gloomy spirit settled on us and we became quiet.

After a while, Bobby Brown asked, "Think we'll get any chow tonight, Sarge?"

"I doubt it."

We hadn't eaten for more than eighteen hours.

"Wasn't it Napoleon that said, 'An army marches on its stomach'?" Teddy asked.

Before I chanced a reply, Lyle Thomas said, "Yeah, but it retreats on its ass."

*Good Old Lyle. We could always depend on him for a laugh, even in the worst of times.*

Bobby Brown gritted his teeth. "I'm so hungry I could eat a bear."

"Have you ever met up with one?" Teddy asked.

"No, but I sure could eat one."

"What makes you think the bear won't eat you?" Lyle asked.

"If he do, God bless him, at least I won't be hungry no more!"

I had no idea when we'd get our next meal, so I tried to think of something else. Closing my eyes, I imagined this town before the war, with men bustling up and down the streets and women strolling to market to shop for fresh produce. I bet I could have gotten a nice mug of beer and some tasty sausages in the tavern.

A little while later, I was summoned to Battalion Headquarters, a dark building near the outskirts of town. The Major and his officers were there, cutting large loaves of bread into hunks and distributing them to the platoon leaders. He said that a sergeant had discovered a hidden stockpile of loaves earlier that evening. As Teddy and I carried these rations back to my famished squad, I thought: *I wish I had a mug of hot coffee to go with this bread.*

Even though I was bone tired, I slept fitfully that night, worrying about Lucky. Besides, we were exposed, undermanned, and afraid of a German counterattack. The next morning, I awoke before dawn and learned that Second and Third Battalion had turned up at our lines during the night with only half of their men present and accounted for. Doctor Stevens and his team of medics had also arrived and were already transporting the many wounded to a dressing station. I found one of the stretcher-bearers and told him where to locate Lucky. The expected enemy counterattack didn't materialize, but instead, we were hit with a terrific shell bombardment that lasted several hours. When the shelling ceased, we marched over the northern plains toward Les Petits Rosiers woods. We would have to traverse these woods to reach the town of Challerange and the German railroad.

It was about one o'clock in the afternoon when we finally entered the woods. We expected the French artillery to knock out the German defenses, but no such support came. The woods were dark and scary with a Hun hiding behind every tree. They shot at us with impunity from concrete pillboxes and many of our men fell wounded, including Lyle Thomas, who was hit in the leg. We dragged him behind a tree for shelter and tried to keep moving forward, but we couldn't advance without exposing ourselves to gunfire. This was turning out to be a real duck-shoot, and we were the sitting ducks. So many men were injured or worse that after two hours, Major Little pulled us out and even as we retreated, a German shell hit D Company. Gathering up the dead and wounded, we crept back three hundred meters and took cover in the trenches facing the woods, fearing the next day's killing encounter.

"What the hell happened to our French artillery cover?" Teddy asked.

"All I knows is if we goes back in these woods again without the big guns, we be history," Bobby Brown declared.

"We already history, we be a memory! We be dead," Lyle Thomas said, just before the medics arrived to carry him and the other wounded to the dressing station in town.

That night in the trenches, we were thirsty, hungry, exhausted, and afraid. Kenny Davis, a soldier in our platoon, dozed off and when he awoke, dashed up and down, screaming that his momma was calling. Two of his buddies restrained him and said that Kenny's mother had died several years ago.

After that, everyone grew quiet, each of us seemingly lost in his own thoughts. I looked up and beheld the blue-black sky, aglow with radiant stars. *Would this be the last time I'd ever see it?* I thought about my life and the things I would change if I could. It was then I decided to let go of all the old bitterness I held against Pa and to release the jealous resentment I felt toward my brother, Grant. I became ashamed that I'd let it cause a rift between us. Slumping down in the ditch, I asked: *Lord, what can I do to make it right?* A voice in my head urged me to count my blessings. Instinctively, I reached into my shirt pocket, and searched for Evie's gold cross, but instead found only her photo! So I took it in hand and pressed it to my lips.

*Evie, the angel of my life! That I would love her was inevitable, that she would love me in return was a miracle. Will I ever see her again? Hold her again? If the worst happens, will she find a good man to care for her and the children? But, my God, I can't bear to think of that now.*

# CHAPTER 49

## *Evie*

❧⟞⟌ Ꮬ⟍❧

**T**hey say that God doesn't give you more than you can bear. But does God know my shoulders aren't that broad? Does God care that I'm at my break-ing point?

The telegram I received on Halloween read:

*James very ill with grippe. Don't come, you have children to think of. Doing everything possible. Peter*

Early the next morning, I left the children with Mrs. Jones, and headed to Jennie's house, wearing my mask and gloves and praying that James would still be alive when I arrived. As I rushed down the tree-lined block to catch the trolley, I imagined the worst that could happen and trembled with dread. I was taking a chance, but I had to see him.

The trolley conductor, who was also donning a mask and gloves, cast me a wary glance as I boarded and proceeded to the backbench. Sitting alone, I tried to remember happier times when we were all together, but the present nightmare kept intruding. After we had gone a short distance, a man in the front seat started coughing, so I jumped off the trolley, and lifting my skirt, ran the remaining ten blocks to Jennie's. I knocked frantically on the door, and after a moment she appeared. Her tear-stained face registered shock and dismay when she saw me, breathless and disheveled.

"Oh my God, Evie, why did you come? It's too dangerous."

"I had to see him, Jennie. How could this happen?"

She led me into the parlor where Peter, seated in an armchair, was bracing his head with his hand and looked as if he hadn't slept for days. As I approached, he stood up, took my gloved hands in his, and uttered a few consolatory words.

We walked over to Jennie, who was standing near the parlor door, and I repeated the question. "How could this happen?"

She clenched her hands as if to pray. "After the schools had been closed for a while, James begged me to let him go to the park and play baseball. When the newspaper said the worst of the flu was over, I let him go and everything seemed to be all right. Then three days ago he came home sick."

She closed her eyes. "Oh, Evie, I'm so sorry."

"Has the doctor been here?"

"He was here yesterday," Peter said, "but there was nothing he could do."

"The doctor advised us to order James a coffin." Jennie sobbed as she fell into Peter's arms.

*How could the doctor be that cruel?* I thought.

After a while, Jennie regained her composure and showed me into James's room, which smelled of carbolic acid and human sickness. When I saw him lying there, limp and lifeless, my blood turned to ice water, but I willed myself not to cry. His face was flushed, and white foam coated his cracked lips.

I wanted to run and take him in my arms but remained at the foot of the bed with Peter and Jennie.

"James dear," I called, "it's me, Auntie." He didn't respond.

"How long has he been like this?" I asked, my voice cracking.

"Since yesterday morning," Jennie replied.

"What about the hospital?"

"No room," Peter said. "A public health nurse came by early this morning, but she just tried to make him comfortable."

Again, I called him.

He opened his eyes. "Auntie." Then his voice faded.

"Yes dear, it's me. Don't be afraid . . . you'll get better soon."

As tears of helplessness flowed down our cheeks, Jennie, Peter, and I knelt to pray. Prayer was all we had. After the last amen, I remained on my knees for a moment, trying to shore up faith and courage, trying to believe that a miracle was possible. When I arose, I went to James and took his hand in mine. I touched his forehead and felt its fevered warmth through my glove. I asked Jennie for a cold cloth and gently patted his face and arms. A few minutes passed.

"James, Auntie has to leave now. Your Uncle and I love you very much, and Little Al can't wait for you to get better."

He opened his eyes, tried to smile, and closed them again.

I turned to Jennie. "Keep patting him down with a cold cloth and try to break the fever. And Peter, let me know if there's any change."

"Of course, we will," he said.

When I reached home, I went directly upstairs, stripped off my clothes and placed them in the wash bucket with hot water, iodine, and carbolic soap. Then I scrubbed my body from head to toe, got dressed in fresh clothes, and went down to Mrs. Jones's apartment.

While the children were eating a snack, Mrs. Jones pulled me aside. "How is he, Evie?"

I shook my head. "I don't know if he'll make it."

"I'm sure he will," she said, hugging my shoulders. "God can't be that cruel."

# CHAPTER 50

## *Albert*

D og-tired and completely drained, I drifted off to sleep in the trench near the dreaded woods. Sometime later, I was abruptly awakened by a group of French soldiers who had just arrived. A young *poilu* climbed into the trench and hunkered down beside me on the muddy ground.

"What the hell's going on?" I asked.

"*Nous vous soulager,*" he mumbled. I thought he said their unit was going to relieve us, but it sounded too good to be true.

"What you say?"

"*Nous vous soulager,*" he repeated.

An incredible wave of relief surged through me. These French troops would be entering the woods in the morning, instead of us. The young soldier asked if I had anything to eat. I told him we hadn't eaten for thirty hours. But then, I remembered I had saved a piece of bread to eat later. When I removed the squashed, linty bread from my pocket and handed it to him, he gobbled it down and went right off to sleep. I tried to fall asleep, too, but suddenly felt guilty. If this young boy, this slightly bearded *poilu*, goes into those devilish woods tomorrow, he will surely die!

At five thirty the next morning, I was awakened by gun thunder. The French artillery had finally arrived and was shelling the woods, destroying the cement pillboxes and chasing the German snipers out of hiding. I took off my dew-dampened shirt and hung it on the trench wall. The young *poilu* was already awake, checking his weapons and getting ready for the upcoming battle. At seven o'clock all the troops were served a hearty breakfast from a mess wagon which had arrived earlier that morning. Then, wishing our French comrades good-bye and good luck, we watched as they marched off with full bellies, toward the Petits Rosiers woods. There they would finish the job we had started.

The 369th moved back into Séchault and I received permission from Lieutenant West to search for Lucky Lewis and Lyle Thomas in the dressing station. As I entered the makeshift hospital, I encountered a pitiful sight: about two hundred injured men lying on the floors of two enormous rooms. Some were groaning while others were asleep or unconscious. The air was thick with the smell of sweat, piss, pus, and carbolic acid. As I moved through the wounded warriors looking for Lucky, I carefully stepped around them, nodding a greeting of encouragement to each man who was awake. When I reached the far side of the room, I spied Lyle Thomas, his bandaged leg in a splint.

"How you doing, soldier?" He opened his eyes and gave a sign of recognition. "Don't know, Sarge. They can't operate until I get to the real hospital."

"Try and hold on. They'll have you out of here soon."

I entered the second room but didn't find Lucky there either, so I made my way to the door. Outside, I spoke to a stretcher-bearer who said that Lucky must have been carried back through the lines to the hospital.

For the next two weeks, we were constantly on the move, by foot, train and truck, sleeping anywhere we could lay our weary heads, and by the time we arrived at the defensive trenches deep in the Vosges Mountains, I was completely worn out. The mountains are in Alsace, an area that both the French and the Germans claimed as their own. There, we were expected to hold the line against the Germans who occupied trenches on the other side of a no man's land. They took to shelling us twice a day, once in the morning and once at night. In fact, it became routine until one evening a shell killed five of our men. One of them was Leon Bibbs, a brave, young soldier from New Jersey.

As I knelt close to him, blood gushing from his chest, he moaned, "Why now? War's almost over."

His question tormented me but had no answer. *Why does one man die and the other one live?*

After I had been in the mountains several days, I began to feel invigorated as I inhaled the crisp air and took in the breathtaking landscapes: gently rounded summits, shimmering lakes, thick pine forest, thundering waterfalls, deep valleys, and grassy meadows. No wonder the Germans and French had fought over this place for centuries.

We had been hearing rumors about an armistice since mid-October when we first arrived in the mountains, but we knew that the battle wouldn't be over until the warring parties accepted the terms. So we defended our ground and waited for this terrible war to end. On November 11, 1918, Lieutenant West passed the word that the armistice had been signed at daybreak in a railroad car in the Compiègne Forest, and hostilities would be stopped along the entire Western Front at eleven o'clock that morning. At the designated hour, church bells rang joyously throughout the Vosges. Then the mountainside grew strangely quiet, and I imagined I heard birdsong and the rippling of brooks. The battle had been won. There were no shells screaming overhead, no machine guns firing, no grenades exploding—only the quiet of a peace being born. As the impact of the peace dawned on us, we became jubilant. We laughed, cried, shouted, hugged, and danced. And at last, we gave thanks to the Almighty. The German soldiers cheered loudly while the church bells rang. Many of them ventured into no man's land and came close to our lines. They looked battle-worn, homesick, and war-weary. And so did we! I guess they were tired of getting shot in the ass, bombed to smithereens, maimed, killed and left to die on foreign battlefields. And so were we!

That evening Teddy and I made a fire in front of the trench, warming ourselves against the autumn chill. Other soldiers gathered in small groups and did the same.

"Would you look at those fireworks the Germans are shooting off?" Teddy remarked.

"They're celebrating the end of the war. They've been singing the whole afternoon. I can't make out the lyrics, but the melodies sound haunting and bittersweet," I replied.

"To me, they sound hopeful, even though their army was defeated, and they don't know what the future has in store."

"We colored soldiers don't know what the future holds for us either, Teddy, even though we helped win the war."

"That's exactly what I was thinking, Al."

As we watched the German fireworks light up the dark blue sky, I thought about the comrades we had lost, comrades buried deep in French soil, comrades who would never return home.

After a spell, Teddy spoke again. "Gee, I'm sorry our wounded buddies are not here to celebrate. Have you heard anything about them?"

"Cephas and Lyle are recuperating in the hospital. I asked Major Little's aide to make inquiries about Lucky two weeks ago, but I haven't heard back yet."

"It's hard to get any news up here, except for military orders. Even our mail hasn't come through."

During the first few days following the armistice, our camp became swamped with prisoners of war, refugees, and interned French citizens, released by the Germans. They were hungry as well as cold and raggedy, and we had to feed them as best we could. Later that same week, Major Little's aide sent for me.

"Sergeant Johnson, I put out feelers about Private Lucky Lewis and the report I received was that he died in hospital. I'm very sorry. He was a good soldier."

"He certainly was. Thank you, sir." Squaring my shoulders, I saluted and walked back through the trench. When I reached the dugout, I plopped down on a bunk and questioned God.

*Why did he have to die? He had barely lived. What was it he whispered to me one day in the trenches? He said he had never even loved a woman.* I had seen so much of death and destruction that I had almost become indifferent to it, yet I was shaken by the death of this boy. However, there was no time to mourn. The very next day we received orders to move out and occupy the Alsace towns bordering the Rhine River.

As the regiment marched southeastward down the mountain paths into the valleys, we passed through bustling towns where crowds of celebrating residents, dressed in colorful alpine costumes, welcomed us with French flags, flower-strewn streets, and banners that read, "*Viva La République.*" In one village, young ladies ran over and kissed our stubbly cheeks. First Battalion settled in two adjacent towns, where Major Little became the military governor. Second and Third battalions were located in nearby villages.

Early one morning Major Little, accompanied by soldiers from First Battalion, set out for the Rhine River, the strategic waterway that separates France from Germany. The Major detailed that the 369th regiment would be the first of the Allied forces to reach the Rhine, and we were elated that we would arrive there well before the American Expeditionary Forces. As we approached the river, we saw the last of the defeated Germans crossing to the opposite bank on a ferryboat. Others were already on the German side, watching us warily. Upon reaching the river, we put down our rifles and sent up a thunderous cheer. Bobby Brown ran into the water, drenching his boots and trousers. We all followed suit, scooping up river water, splashing each other, and washing our hands and faces—relishing the sweet taste of victory.

On December 9, the 369th regiment departed the Rhine River valley, handing over the administration of the towns to the French army. We traveled down the narrow mountain road in a *camion* train, while truckloads of French troops moved up toward the Rhine. There, they would cross the river and occupy Germany. When our *camion* train stopped briefly, I ran up and down to see if Demba was, by chance, one of our drivers. But he wasn't, and I gave up hope of ever seeing him again. At the base of the mountain, we pulled over to allow a French caravan to pass. I was standing on the embankment when I heard a familiar voice.

"Albert, mon ami!" There he was, driving a troop-filled truck, headed toward the Rhine.

Waving furiously, I ran alongside his truck, shouting, "Go well, my friend. Journey safely to your village in Senegal."

He threw back his head and laughed, his white teeth flashing against his dark brown skin. "*Merci beaucoup*, Albert."

Our *camion* train continued to journey south for many miles and when it reached a fork in the road, it turned westward. From then on, all I could think of was Evie and home.

# CHAPTER 51

## *Evie*

I was fast asleep when the doorbell rang at six that morning. It was the day after I had gone to Jennie's house. In a daze, I scurried out of bed, slipped on my dressing gown, and stumbled down the stairs. When I opened the door and saw Peter, I screamed and collapsed on the doorstep.

He must have carried me up the stairs and sent Little Al to borrow Mrs. Jones's smelling salts for when I came to, I saw my sleepy-eyed child with tears cascading down his plump cheeks. I lay there as he questioned Peter.

"Uncle, why did James have to die?"

"I don't know, my boy. He's with the Lord now."

Little Al screwed up his small face. "Was it because he loved baseball?"

"What do you mean?"

"Maybe he loved baseball more than God, and God was jealous."

"No, Little Al, that's not why he died! Even we adults don't have all the answers. We just have to trust God and accept His will."

"Yes, Uncle," he said. But his face was still distorted with grief. Peter took Little Al in his arms, pressed him close, and held him there as if he wished to soak up his pain.

With Peter's help, I sat up on the side of the bed and taking a deep breath to steady myself, I hugged Little Al tenderly. "I know how you're feeling, son, but Uncle Peter spoke truly. You can't fight with God. You still have a big brother. He's in a different place now, but he's watching over you. Remember his laughter, his kindness, his friendship, and always continue to love him."

Little Al nodded, wiping his wet cheeks with his pajama sleeves, and then toddled back to his room.

After a moment, I turned to Peter. "How's Jennie doing?"

"She's grieving."

"Wait for me. I'll go to her."

When I was ready, I asked Mrs. Jones to stay with the children.

Peter and Jennie's house was as quiet as a tomb, except for the ticking of the grandfather's clock. Signaling Peter to stay behind, I immediately went to their darkened bedroom and found Jennie curled up on a rose-colored quilt, shrouded in a long black dress.

I tapped her shoulder. "Jennie, I'm here."

She opened her eyes. "Oh, Evie, he's gone. James is gone."

"Peter told me."

"What are we going to do without him?"

I helped her sit up and sat down beside her. She reached out to hold me, and I enfolded her in my arms—two bleeding hearts entangled together. Neither of us spoke for a while.

"We have to go on, Jennie, despite the pain. James would have wanted it that way."

"Why couldn't I have died instead of him?"

"The Lord took James. We can't change that."

"But I gave him away to you and Al."

"You shared him with us. I can't tell you what a blessing he's been."

"You were a better mother to him than I was," she moaned.

"You did your best and he loved you very much—and Peter, too."

Burying her head in her hands, she wept uncontrollably. "It's all my fault! I thought the flu had passed, and when he begged to go out, I let him."

"Don't torture yourself, Jennie. You did what you thought was right." I squeezed her shoulder and pulled her closer.

Rivers of tears flowed down our grief-stricken faces while we desperately clung to each other. I was empty and there was nothing else I could give her. When I looked up and saw Peter in the doorway, his face an ashen white, I beckoned to him to come and hold his wife. Then I left and returned home. The next day the newspapers reported that the Spanish flu, or grippe, was rapidly disappearing from the city and life in Albany was returning to normal, however, it was too late for James and I was brokenhearted.

Father traveled up to Albany and together with Cousin Mattie took charge of the funeral arrangements. He was a pillar of strength, but I knew he would mourn this loss just as much as we did. On the seventh day of November, my nephew, my sweet boy, was laid to rest in Graceland Cemetery, as grieving family, friends, teachers, and schoolmates gathered around. His short obituary read:

*James Sullivan, born May 30, 1900, passed away November 2, 1918. He was a senior at Albany High School and an outstanding pitcher on the school's team. James loved baseball and enjoyed spending time with his family. He will be greatly missed by his mother and stepfather, Jennie and Peter Cooper; aunt and uncle, Evelyn and Albert Johnson, and their children, Albert, Jr., Susie, and Tessie; grandfather, James Ashton; and cousin, Mattie Pierce.*

*Rest in peace beloved child; May the Lord bless your immortal soul.*

November 11, 1918 should have been a most festive day. Church bells clanged. Flags fluttered. Thousands of beaming men, women, and children paraded and danced through the streets of downtown Albany. It was an enormous celebration, a magnificent party, and a thanks-giving rite. The Great War was over. The Germans defeated. The armistice signed, and the peace assured. Husbands, brothers, fathers, sons, and lovers would soon be returning home.

My guardian spirit roused me that morning and compelled me to go. Wearing a black dress and veil, I joined the others in their festive march. As

I walked along staidly, without smile or frown, women nodded, and men doffed their hats, believing I was a war widow. Inez, also garbed in black, walked beside me, supporting my arm. We proceeded slowly through the jam-packed streets while others made way for us amid the jousting crowd.

I whispered to Inez, "Have you heard anything from Calvin?"

She opened her black purse and retrieved a blue envelope. "I received this from him yesterday. He said he was sorry he couldn't meet me as planned, but all leaves were canceled. His regiment was shipping out and the army didn't allow them to contact anyone until they reached France. I'm so relieved."

"I'm happy for you, my dear."

"I told Mother I plan to marry Calvin just as soon as he's discharged, whether she consents or not."

"What did she say?"

"She was about to put up a fuss when Father finally stood up and took my side. So it's all settled." Inez and I continued to stroll amid the revelers for three-quarters of an hour and then returned home to the children.

As I sat alone in our lantern-lit parlor that evening, I thanked the Lord that Al was out of danger and would be coming home soon. But then I thought of poor James. *How will I ever tell Al?*

# CHAPTER 52

## *Albert*

❦

F ive days after leaving the Rhine River Valley, our regiment arrived on the Plains of Münchhausen in the Alsace region of France. We took our place among the thousands of French soldiers assembled on the perimeter of an enormous square.

It was a mild December day and the sun was shining brightly on the field. We stood at ease, facing the center of the square, quietly conversing with one another, and wondering what the day would bring. I had a feeling that something momentous was about to happen. Suddenly, a chorus of trumpets sounded, and we snapped to attention.

As I stood there, I thought about the men we had lost. Half of our original regiment was dead or wounded. *Most likely, we are about to experience some sort of pageantry, but can pageantry wash away the horrors, waste, and degradation of this war? Can it ease the pain of comrades lost or maimed? Can it bring Lucky back to life, or enable Cephas to paint again?*

Then a group of horsemen in brightly colored military uniforms galloped toward the assembly. The leader, riding a cream-colored stallion, and wearing crimson breeches, a light blue greatcoat, and a redcap embellished with gold oak leaves, was General Lebouc, Commander of the 161st Division. I saw the General and his officers guiding their prancing steeds to the center of the square. There they dismounted, and word was passed around that all units to be decorated should approach the General. From the 369th regiment, Colonel Hayward, holding the American flag, Major Little, carrying the regimental colors, and Colonel Pickering stepped forward. General Lebouc praised the heroic achievements of the 369th in the taking of Séchault and pinned the *Croix de Guerre,* France's highest military award, on the flags. Then he kissed each officer on both cheeks. After all the deserving regiments had been honored, the whole assemblage paraded around the square, including strutting foot soldiers, trotting mounted cavalry and rumbling artillery. It was an amazing spectacle. That afternoon, we hiked fifteen kilometers back to our barracks, tired, but proud that our efforts and sacrifices had been recognized and would go down in history as a credit to our race. Two days later we received notice that the 369th regiment had been released from the French army.

*Well, I guess that makes us American again.*

We continued our journey southwestward and on December 20th, set up camp on the outskirts of Belfort. For the next few days, I scoured the town for souvenirs for Evie and the children but had no luck. Then the day before Christmas Eve, I walked into a small, dimly lit store and encountered Madame Adélaide, an attractive, middle-aged shopkeeper.

She greeted me warmly. "*Bienvenue*, Welcome, *Yankee noir.*"

"*Salut*, Madame."

We began a lively conversation in mixed French and English about the blossoming peace, and about life in America.

Finally, she asked, "You from Har-lem?"

"No, I'm from Albany, but most of our men are from Harlem."

"So what can I do for you, Sergeant?"

"I need to find presents for my wife and children." She seemed a bit confused, so I showed her Evie's photo.

"Oh la, la, she's beautiful," she said, waving her hands.

"*Merci.*"

"And lucky, too."

"Why do you say that?"

"A fine looking gentleman, like you, is in love with her and is returning home safely from the war. Many will never come back." A note of sadness crept into her voice.

Turning up the lantern wick, she went to the back of the shop, brought out several items, and laid them on the counter. One that immediately caught my eye was a large hand-stitched scarf of pink silk, trimmed in lace, with red appliquéd roses blooming at the corners.

"It's lovely, isn't it?" she asked.

"It's perfect! But I doubt I can afford it." I fingered the softness of the silk.

"I give you good price. This once belonged to another beautiful lady who sold it to buy food. And I was saving it for a special person."

Madame Adélaide also helped me pick out keepsakes for the children: an Eiffel Tower locket for Susie, a harlequin doll for Tessie, a postcard book of Paris for Little Al, and for James, playing cards depicting paintings from the Louvre. As she wrapped my purchases, she told me what the townspeople had endured during the war. Nearly all the men had joined the French army, including her husband and son. Her husband died in battle three years ago, and her son was still in the army. After the Germans bombarded the town, she closed the shop and worked on the farms. She reopened it the day after the armistice was signed.

Thanking Madame Adélaide for her kindness, I reached over the counter to pay her. To my surprise, she gently placed her hand on mine and for a moment, our eyes locked. Then I looked away, breaking the spell, grabbed the packages and headed straight for the door.

As I left, she called, "*Merci*, my dear Sergeant. Come back if there's anything else you need."

I never returned to Madame Adélaide's shop, but I was grateful for her generosity. As I strolled back to the base, my arms filled with gifts, I began to feel the Christmas spirit. On Christmas Eve morning our long-delayed mail finally arrived. I was overjoyed when I found a letter and a holiday package from Evie. Placing the package on my bunk with the intention of opening it on Christmas day, I headed out of the barracks to find a private spot to relish her letter. Just then, I ran into Teddy.

"Hey Al, I received a letter from Dean Braithwaite today saying they're going to offer me a full scholarship at Fisk and a part-time job on campus."

"That's great."

"I also heard from Amanda. She said her parents have had a change of heart about me since they read the glowing reports of our regiment in the *Philadelphia Tribune*."

After he left, I darted behind the barracks and eagerly opened Evie's letter, postmarked November 15. She had written it over a month ago.

*My Dearest Husband,*

*I don't know how to tell you this, but our James has passed away. He caught the Spanish flu while staying with Jennie and Peter and died on November 2nd . . .*

I read the first few lines again and again. *Oh, my God, James is dead. I should have been there to protect him.* Tears streamed down my face and an unbearable pain immobilized me. Several moments later, I made my way into the surrounding countryside of barren farmlands and deserted woods. As I staggered through the cold woods, wandering from leafless tree to leafless tree, I thought about a boy, a boy who entered my life nine years ago, holding a cardboard suitcase and a worn-out baseball mitt. A boy who made fire in the coal stove for his auntie. A boy who took his little cousin under his wing. A boy with hope in his eyes and forgiveness in his heart. When I thought about this boy, this boy who loved baseball, I rolled up the pain and buried it deep within. *When I get home, Evie and I will mourn this child of ours together.* The graying skies of dusk caught me unaware, so I picked up the pace and hurried back to the barracks.

On Christmas day, the men did their best to be jolly. I told no one about James's death, not even Teddy, and pretended all was well, wishing my comrades, "Merry Christmas," joining them for a special Christmas supper, and handing out the cookies Evie had sent. Quite frankly, I didn't think I could bear anyone's sympathy just then. Immediately after finishing our meal, we heard strains of familiar music and rushed out of the mess hall into the adjoining barnyard. Lieutenant James Reese Europe and the band had just returned from a performance in a nearby town. Their music had lifted the spirits of battle-weary citizens all over France. That afternoon, soldiers and townsfolk crowded into the large barnyard and swayed to the music. When baritone Noble Sissle mounted the makeshift platform and sweetly crooned, "Joan of Arc, They Are Calling You," an enormous wave of sorrow engulfed me. So I slipped away to the empty barracks and escaped into the land of Nod.

The day after New Year's, we boarded a train for Le Mans, the enormous American forwarding camp where we prepared to return to civilian life. After spending a week there, our regiment was summoned to the port of Brest, which signaled that we'd be shipping out soon. We'd be going home! When we arrived in Brest, we expected to be treated as heroes, but Brest soon shattered our illusions. A few minutes after we detrained, Private Bennie Nelson of First Battalion made his way to the latrine but got lost on his way back to C Company. He approached an MP to ask for directions, but the SOB knocked him on the head with a baton and placed him under arrest. When our unit heard about it, we surrounded the MP, intending to thrash him, but Captain McClinton persuaded us to disperse. I was seething with anger, but I didn't want to do anything to delay our departure.

After Private Bennie Nelson rejoined C Company, First Battalion set out on a march to Camp Pontanezen, where the entire regiment would be quartered until we shipped home. We trekked five kilometers through the countryside and paused on a hill to take a breather. Just then, two MPs on horseback rode down the hill, coming to an abrupt halt in front of Major Little, who was standing at the rear of the column. Bobby Brown, Teddy Wilson, and I were close enough to overhear their heated exchange.

"Major, will you tell those soldiers up the line to stop the disturbance," one of the MPs said.

"What are you talking about, Corporal?" Major Little asked.

"There's a lot of niggers up front yelling, 'Who won the war?' " the other MPs said. The Major ordered the MPs to dismount, stand at attention, and address him as a superior officer. They refused, saying that they didn't have to answer to him. Meanwhile, our men up the line continued to chant, "Who won the war?"

"Are you going to stop that ruckus?" the first MP asked.

"There is no ruckus. These men have been chanting this all through France whenever they met French or American troops. And the other troops would respond: 'We all won the war.' You people in this town are the first to act as if you don't like our men. Now I advise you to go about your business!"

As they galloped down the road toward Brest, one of the MPs yelled, "This'll get you two months." We had no idea what he meant and at the time we didn't care. When the news of the altercation traveled through the ranks, the men grumbled that the whole regiment had been insulted, but Captain McClinton warned them again to keep their cool.

"My God, did you all hear how those MPs disrespected Major Little?" Private Bobby Brown said. "Hell, I wanted to slap the white off their faces and just imagine, those suckers ain't fought a lick in this war."

"To tell the truth," Teddy Wilson said, "I hate them even worse than I hate the Germans!"

I nodded. "I thought we were in France, but it sure feels like America."

Because of the altercation with the MPs, our departure from Brest was delayed for three miserable weeks. Finally, we were assigned to the SS Stockholm that would set sail on January 31, 1919. After we boarded the ship, Teddy and I stood at the railing watching the pier. The long-awaited departure was bittersweet because Lyle, Cephas, and Lucky, were not going home with us. Then I noticed a medic pushing a wheelchair up the gangplank. From a distance, the occupant looked familiar and when he got closer, I recognized him.

"I'll be damned if it's not Lyle Thomas."

Teddy cocked his head. "A bad penny usually turns up."

When he spotted us, Lyle grinned. "Gentlemen, we meet again."

"Anyone here from C Company?" the medic asked, as he wheeled Lyle onto the deck.

"That's us."

"We're sending this boy home and he'll need help. Are you men up to that?"

"Absolutely."

Handing us Lyle's duffle bag and crutch, the medic went to sign off with Captain McClinton and we started to push the wheelchair across the deck.

"Hold on," Lyle said as he stood up and walked toward the rail. "I let him push me 'cause I was enjoying the ride."

Teddy laughed. "You can't keep a good man down."

Lyle snapped his fingers.

Once the journey was underway and we sailed into the open sea, I thanked the Lord for life and limb. As I opened my eyes and glimpsed the retreating coastline, I whispered, *Farewell, dear France, I'll never forget you. You taught us the art of combat. You treated us as equals. You danced to our music. You shared your bread and wine. You honored our valor and kissed both our cheeks.*

## CHAPTER 53

# *Evie – 1919*

It had been three months since my beloved James passed away and a pervasive sadness had descended on my spirit. Susie and Little Al did their best to cheer me up although they had also suffered loss. Then during the second week of February, I received welcome news from Father. The 369th troop ship had landed in New York and the city would honor the regiment with a victory parade on February 17. When Father suggested that Little Al and I attend the festivities, I frantically began preparing for the journey.

Leaving Susie and Tessie with Mrs. Jones, we took the train to New York City, and Father met us at Grand Central Station, which was jammed with soldiers and sailors of all stripes. I was excited because the next day I would see my husband whom I hadn't set eyes on for two years. We spent the night with Father and rose early the next morning.

"Evie, the parade will start on 61st and Fifth," Father said, "and when it reaches 110th, it'll go up Lenox Avenue. We're headed up to Harlem."

"Little Al, hurry up and get dressed," Father said. "I want to get a good spot."

"Me, too," Little Al replied.

When we arrived at 125th Street, we found a large crowd assembled, and with Father in the lead, we pushed our way to the curb. It was a great spot for surveying all that was going on. People were hanging out the windows. Grown-ups and children lined the streets waving small American flags.

Everyone was talking, smiling, and laughing with one another, and nearly everyone wore white badges that read, "Welcome home, the fighting 15th."

"Grandpa, who's the fighting 15th?" Little Al asked when a young man handed him a badge.

"That was the name of the 369th regiment before they left for France."

I glanced around and saw a sad-faced young woman wearing a black armband. Perhaps she had lost a husband, a brother, or even a sweetheart in the war. My heart cried out to her and I thanked my lucky stars that Al had survived. As I was standing there, a plump, middle-aged lady in a blue coat and a large purple hat propelled her way toward me through the crowd. She was holding the hand of a pretty young girl, wearing a red plaid coat and bonnet.

"Lovely day for a parade," she said. "Is someone you know marching?"

"My husband, Sergeant Albert Johnson. I'm Mrs. Evelyn Johnson." The lady introduced herself, and in turn, I presented her to Father and Little Al.

"My son's in the parade, too," the lady said. "Praise the Lord, he's alive and well and has come home from the war. This is his daughter, Caroline. She lives with me in Harlem."

I smiled at Caroline.

"Say hello to Mrs. Johnson," she said, tugging her granddaughter's arm.

Sour-faced Caroline said a reluctant hello. Little Al grinned at her, but when her grandmother looked away, she stuck out her tongue.

"I'm surprised to see so many children at the parade," I said.

"Most schools in Harlem have closed for the day so the children could attend. This is history!"

I nodded in agreement. The lady and I continued to chat until she spotted a friend in the crowd and went to greet her.

After several minutes, a thickset elderly gentleman in a black top hat and a long black coat worked his way to the curb and stood next to Little Al. "Is your poppa in the parade, boy?"

"Yes, sir. He's a war hero!"

"What you say! Few years past, I knowed them when they was marching up and down Seventh Avenue, with broomsticks instead of rifles. My, my, times has changed."

"Haven't they?" Father interjected. "You can't fight the Germans with broomsticks."

The man and Father both laughed and shook hands.

"Alphonso Magee, a citizen of Harlem."

"James Ashton, from Brooklyn, and this is my daughter, Mrs. Johnson."

Mr. Magee lifted his top hat, exposing a shiny baldhead.

I returned his greeting with a cautious smile.

"Mr. Ashton, these boys done good! I'm so proud of them," Mr. Magee said.

Father glanced over his shoulder at the young woman wearing the black armband. "And some made the supreme sacrifice. They say that over two hundred men died and more than eight hundred were seriously wounded."

"I'll be darned!" Mr. Magee said.

"Well, things should get better for colored people because of what these men achieved."

"Amen to that."

"Mr. Ashton, what's the other name for the 369th?" Mr. Magee asked. "I forget."

"The Germans christened them the Harlem Hellfighters."

"Harlem Hellfighters. That's right. I remembers it now."

"The newspapers reported that the regiment endured a hundred and ninety-one days at the front, more than any other American unit. They never lost a foot of ground and none were ever taken prisoner, even though the Germans tried their darndest to capture them."

"Is that a fact?" Mr. Magee said, "and those vicious Huns had the nerve to call our boys bloodthirsty SOBs."

Upon hearing his crude language, I raised my eyebrows and gave Mr. Magee a withering look. He tipped his hat, grinned sheepishly, and apologized. Then he backed away and faded into the crowd. I stepped off the sidewalk and looked down the block. There was no sign of the parade. Little Al stood on tiptoes and studied the empty street. After a while, he got restless, so Father told him to sit on the curb.

"Mother," Little Al asked, gazing at the sky, "do you think James is watching the parade from heaven?"

I choked up and couldn't answer.

"I'm sure he is," Father said.

Just then, we heard music and the loud tramping of a thousand boots. Little Al jumped up and peered down the road.

"Look. They's a-coming. They's a-coming," a woman yelled from a third-floor fire escape. Heads popped out the windows. More people scrambled onto the fire escapes, and crowds packed the rooftops–all looking toward the music. A moment later, the band came into view: musicians with blazing trumpets, horns, and drums.

"Grandpa, who is that white man marching in front?" Little Al asked as he strained to see the approaching spectacle.

"It's Colonel Hayward, commander of the 369th regiment, and walking behind him are his officers."

The band played on, their bouncy music filling the air. Following the band were the soldiers, spread out across the roadway in long columns that had no end. The marching soldiers came nearer. They stood tall: their heads facing forward, their glossy boots stepping up and down, their helmets and rifles glistening in the sun.

*Thousands of men,* I thought. *How will I ever see my Albert?*

"Mother, do you see him yet? Do you see him yet?"

"Not yet. He'll be marching with First Battalion."

"And Grandpa, who's that colored man in the open car?"

"Oh, it's Sergeant Henry Johnson, the war hero from Albany."

"Isn't he's the one who received that French medal for bravery?" I asked.

"Yes, the Cross of War," Father said. "And he was the first American to earn one!"

"A colored man!" I clapped my hands. "My goodness. The U.S. Army must have been furious."

Sergeant Henry Johnson grinned and waved his helmet back and forth while the crowd roared. As the endless stream of soldiers tramped by, people shouted, "Hooray," and waved their flags. I scanned each column as it passed, but Al was nowhere to be seen. Then the band began to play "Here Comes Your Daddy Now." Spectators on both sides of the street were swaying and dancing. Flowers, thrown from the rooftops, rained down on the marchers.

A lady held a pink blanket-wrapped toddler over her head. "Look-a-here! Jimmy! It's your little girl." All the women were calling to their sweethearts, husbands, sons, and brothers. Suddenly, they broke loose from the crowd and ran toward the marching men. The soldiers smiled but kept pressing forward, so the laughing, singing women, and their children joined the parade, even though the police tried to chase them away.

"Mother, how will I ever see my father now?" Little Al asked, his eyes filling with tears.

Grabbing my son's hand, I pulled him closer and prayed that we'd somehow spot Albert among the crush of bodies.

"Evie, isn't that him?" Father shouted, pointing down the street to a tall bronze figure.

"I think it is."

The bronze figure came closer.

"Yes! That's him! That's my Albert."

Father grabbed Little Al's other hand and the three of us ran to my husband.

"Albert," I called out, my voice trembling with excitement.

"Daddy," Little Al hollered.

Looking surprised, Sergeant Albert Johnson mouthed, "Oh, my God," and broke into a broad grin. But like the other soldiers, he continued marching straight ahead so Little Al, Father, and I strutted beside him.

The entire entourage paraded past the uptown reviewing stand at 135th Street where Governor Al Smith and the other big shots were waiting. At 145th Street, the marching men entered the subway. Father said they were headed downtown to the 34th Street Armory for a luncheon in their honor.

Before my Al disappeared into the underground, he turned and said, "Evie, I love you," and I felt as if I was hearing it for the first time. Then Father led us through the jubilant crowd to a small diner a few blocks away, where we enjoyed hot tea and a sandwich before heading to Brooklyn.

As we knelt by his bedside that night, Little Al prayed, "Thank you Lord for bringing my daddy home from the war."

I was also grateful, but I wondered how long it would be before he really came home and held me in his arms.

# CHAPTER 54

## *Albert*

A week after the victory parade in Harlem, I was honorably discharged from the army, and given a sixty-dollar bonus, plus a seven-dollar travel allowance. I was also issued red chevrons to be sewn on the left sleeves of my army coat and uniform, which indicated I was now a civilian. It felt strange to be on my own with no orders to give or take. No saluting and saying, "Yes, sir" or "No, sir." I was happy to be going home, but I knew I would miss my buddies.

Before I returned to Albany, I had to visit Lucky's mother in Harlem. It would be a difficult task. Perhaps she would blame me for being alive while her son was dead. Perhaps she would think I should have done more to protect him. Nevertheless, it had to be done. I planned to call on Mrs. Lewis after she returned from work, about seven that evening. Later, I would spend the night at Mr. Ashton's in Brooklyn and leave the next morning for Albany.

The train from the Long Island army camp dropped me at Grand Central Station about three in the afternoon, and with four hours to kill I traveled up to Harlem, found a tavern, had a few drinks, and thought about the future. I still couldn't get over the shock of seeing Evie, Mr. Ashton, and my boy at the parade.

I arrived at Lucky's apartment on 134th Street at half past seven, hoping Mrs. Lewis would be at home.

She answered the door after I knocked twice and once I introduced myself, she greeted me warmly. "Come right in Sergeant Johnson. Lucky's letters are full of you and I'm glad you've come. He admires you so much."

I felt a slight twinge. *I hope and pray the army has informed her of Lucky's death.*

"Well, ma'am, he told me a lot about you and his sisters and how much he loved you all. He was a brave soldier."

She gave me an odd look and asked if I would like a cup of tea. She was what we called such women in the South, soft and pleasingly plump. Her graying hair was parted in the middle and neatly rolled into chignon buns on both sides of her head.

A few minutes later, she returned from the kitchen, carrying a teapot and a plateful of lima beans, ham hocks and buttered biscuits that she placed on a small table in the corner of the room. "I thought you might be hungry and these were nice and warm on the stove."

I protested that I didn't want to trouble her, but I devoured every bit of it.

She watched me as I ate, smiling all the while.

*This is a courageous woman*, I thought.

After I finished eating, we took a seat on her worn but comfortable maroon couch and I thought I'd better get back to the business at hand. "Ma'am, Lucky asked me to visit you when I returned to the states. I'm sorry for what happened to him. He was like a younger brother to me."

"Well, thanks for calling, Sergeant Johnson. I was upset to hear he had been wounded, but I believe he's healing nicely. Do you have any idea when he'll be returning home?"

*Oh my God, she doesn't know. Damn the army!* I'd have to tell her the bad news before I left that evening and hoped someone else was at home with her.

"Mrs. Lewis, I'd like to meet Lucky's sisters."

"Peggy's at work, but I'll go and fetch Dorothy."

A lovely young girl with a cinnamon-colored complexion and dark bobbed hair bounced into the parlor and took a seat facing her mother and me. After we were introduced, she began reminiscing about her younger brother, Lucky, and how much she missed him. I cringed as she went on talking about him as if he was alive and getting better.

Glancing at my watch, I thought: *It's late. I'm just going to have to break the news to them. But how?*

I took a deep breath and turned to Mrs. Lewis. "Ma'am, when Lucky was badly wounded, he asked me to visit you in case he didn't make it . . ." I grew quiet, trying to find a way to soften the blow.

Dorothy spoke up. "It was nice of you to come anyway, Sergeant. He'll be glad when we tell him we got to meet you. In fact, we received a letter from him just the other day."

"The other day?" I stammered. "Can I see it?" Dorothy sprang up and ran to fetch the letter.

*Oh my God, is it a letter from the grave?*

"So what were you saying about Lucky, Sergeant Johnson?" Mrs. Lewis asked.

"Nothing important, ma'am. I just need to see that letter."

Dorothy returned to the parlor. "Here it is."

I felt strange perusing their personal correspondence, but there was something I had to check. Major Little's aide had informed me in November 1918 that Lucky had died of his wounds. But this letter was dated January 31, 1919, more than two months later. I gasped and wiped my brow with a handkerchief.

Mrs. Lewis looked concerned and placed her hand on mine. "Are you alright, Sergeant Johnson?"

"I'm fine. Just fine." The report of Lucky's death must have been a case of mistaken identity and that damn army never informed the battalion of the error. When I realized Lucky was alive and mending, I was overjoyed.

"The letter says he's recuperating in a recovery center near Paris," Dorothy said, "and he'll come home as soon as he's better."

"If you ladies don't mind, I'll copy down Lucky's address, so I can write him, and I'll leave my particulars with you."

"Oh, he'd love to hear from you," Mrs. Lewis said.

After a few minutes, I stood up. "I'd best be going now. It was a real pleasure meeting you folks."

Dorothy fetched my coat and accompanied her mother and me to the front door.

"Sergeant," Mrs. Lewis said, "we very much enjoyed your visit. Please give our warm regards to Mrs. Johnson and the children."

Echoing the sentiment, Dorothy extended her small hand. I bowed and kissed it. Mrs. Lewis looked shocked, but Dorothy, covering her mouth, tried to suppress a giggle.

"Something I picked up in France," I said, and then I took my leave.

# CHAPTER 55

## *Evie*

L ittle Al and his friends were sledding in the snow that afternoon. Susie and I were in the kitchen baking scones, and Tessie was nearby, playing with her doll.

Suddenly, Little Al ran in. "Momma, Momma, Daddy's home. I'm going down the street to meet him!"

"Oh, my God, I look a fright."

Leaving Tessie with Susie, I hurried into the bedroom, brushed my hair, splashed on Essence of Roses cologne, and powdered my cheeks with rouge. There was no time to change, so I wrapped my flowered green shawl about my shoulders and went down to the porch. Before long, he appeared at the foot of the stairs and we stood there for a second gazing at each other. Then he bounded up the steps, taking two at a time, and swept me into his arms. It was freezing cold, but when he kissed me, I felt a rush of incredible warmth.

"Welcome home, my darling," I whispered.

"I've been dreaming of this moment," he said, "ever since I went away."

As Little Al and his friend, Tony Blonski, lugged his army duffle bag up the stairs, I heard giggling.

"Momma, my friends saw you kiss Daddy," Little Al said.

"Well, they've had their show for the day. Let's go inside." Taking my husband by the hand, I led him into the warm kitchen. Little Al followed.

Susie was waiting near the kitchen door. "Daddy," she cried, reaching out to him.

He picked her up and kissed her. "Susie! My, how you've grown."

Then he saw Tessie sitting on the floor and squatted down beside her. "So this is the newest member of the family. Hello there, sweetie." He held out his hand, but Tessie pouted and drew away,

I ran over and touched his shoulder. "Tessie, this is Dada. Can you say 'hello, Dada'?" She scrambled up, grabbed my leg and frowned.

Al laughed. "Look, she was only a month old when I left, so she doesn't know me."

"Well, I'm sure she'll get to know you soon, dear."

I made a pot of tea, buttered the warm scones, and sliced the cheddar cheese and ham. Then our family, grateful that the Lord had brought husband and father home, gathered around the table in that welcoming kitchen and gave thanks.

After the children had been put to bed that evening, Al and I cuddled up on the couch and exchanged stories of what had taken place while he was away. We laughed at the humorous tales but avoided the heart-wrenching ones, like the passing of our beloved James or the losses and horrors of war. Later that night, he took me in his arms and I prayed he would never let me go. I trembled as he showered my body with kisses and told me how much he loved me. After we made love, we fell asleep holding each other, but I was awakened in the middle of the night by a piercing cry.

"Wounded men are screaming, 'help me, mate,' but we couldn't stop, we couldn't stop to help them."

I shook Al gently, and he became quiet, but his face was wet with perspiration. At that moment I realized that the Great War had not been left behind.

The next morning, Al roamed from room to room, as if searching for something he'd lost, and then settled down in his gentleman's armchair to read the newspaper. Susie and Little Al followed him into the parlor and leaned against his chair, trying to get his attention. I was on the couch with Tessie on my lap.

"Daddy, I can jump rope, jump to a hundred," Susie said.

"No, you can't," Little Al said.

"Yes, I can. Well, almost a hundred."

"Daddy, you should see me throw a baseball. Straight, just like James."

At the mention of James's name, I felt a twinge in my chest and saw a sadness creep into Al's eyes. He left the room, and soon returned holding four packages wrapped in brown paper. "Thanks, Little Al and Susie, for taking care of the home front while I was away. I'm proud of you," he said, as he handed each one a package.

After opening their gifts, the children threw on their coats and ran outside to show the treasured souvenirs to their friends. Al pecked me on the cheek and gave me a gift, too. Inside was an exquisite pink silk scarf bordered with fine lace and red roses.

"Oh my, this is so lovely! Where did you ever find it in war-torn France?"

"A big-hearted lady sold it to me."

Then returning to his armchair, he removed a colorful harlequin doll from the last package and held it out to Tessie. She tiptoed across the rug, snatched the doll, and dashed away.

Carrying her back to her father, I said, "Tessie, this is Dada. Remember I showed you his picture." I pointed to Al's photo on the lamp table.

"Dada," she chirped.

"Yes, sweetie, this is Dada," I repeated. I gingerly placed Tessie on Al's lap and was delighted when she rested her head on his shoulder.

Suddenly, Al grimaced. "This kid bit me!" He quickly handed her back to me.

"Tessie, that's not nice," I said.

He rubbed his neck. "Leave her be, honey. We'll get to know each other in time."

A few days later, Al and I bundled up against the cold and took Tessie for a stroll around the neighborhood. The day was sunny, and the sky was clear as we pushed her stroller through a thin layer of snow. When we returned,

Mrs. Jones invited us in for hot tea and crumpets. We chatted a while and Al thanked her for being such a good friend while he was away.

As we were about to leave, Mrs. Jones rushed into her bedroom and brought out a basket of neatly ironed clothes. "Evie, Mrs. Schmidt left this for you."

In the excitement of Al's return, I had forgotten all about my arrangement with Mrs. Schmidt. I had stopped reading tea leaves when the Spanish influenza threatened Albany but took it up again in January. In turn, Mrs. Schmidt resumed doing my laundry. Mrs. MacHennessey didn't participate because she was still mourning the death of Fiona, her baby girl.

Al carried the basket upstairs and I followed holding Tessie. After putting her in bed for a nap, I entered our bedroom where Al was waiting.

"What's all this about, Evie? Why is Mrs. Schmidt doing your laundry?"

I hesitated, but I decided to make a clean breast of it and recounted the whole story.

"I don't like you telling fortunes for the neighbors. If you need help with the laundry, we can hire someone—once I get a better job."

"It's only for one or two women."

"Whatever the number, I don't like it."

"It's not only about the laundry! These women urged me to read their tea leaves because they needed something exciting and bright in their lives. Something to look forward to. And I agreed because I enjoyed helping them. What's wrong with that?"

Al walked to the window and glanced out. His hands were clenched as he turned toward me. "Has anything else been going on that you need to tell me about?"

A lump formed in my throat. "Yes, I've been taking care of this family since you went away. I had to take up the slack although I was ill prepared for it. When the flu struck, I was terrified, but I kept our children safe from harm—except for James, who was at Jennie's. So I had a Great War of my own, here—with the Spanish flu!"

"I see . . . so now you want to be head of the family."

"You're the head! But if reading tea leaves gives me pleasure, why are you trying to take that away?"

Al shook his head and stalked from the room.

*What gives me the courage to defy to my husband? But now that I've done it, there's no turning back.*

He was quiet all through dinner, and Little Al, sensing something was amiss, looked back and forth between us. Later that evening, as I sat in the kitchen staring at an open book of poetry, he called me into the parlor.

"Evie, I don't want this to come between us. If you still want to read tea leaves for the women, go ahead. It's entirely up to you."

I breathed a sigh of relief. "Thank you, dear."

We were having dinner on the following Saturday when I noticed Little Al playing with his food. "Eat your dinner. It's getting cold."

"I'm not hungry, Mommy."

"They'll be no dessert for you, young man."

He screwed up his face. "Daddy, when are you going to cook that stew you use to make?"

Al chuckled. "Let's see. Maybe tomorrow if your mother doesn't mind."

"Not in the least," I said.

"Evie, do we have a chicken?"

"Yes, I bought one this morning. Also, potatoes, carrots, onions and dried peas."

The next morning, Al got up early and cooked a chicken stew before going to church.

When the aroma of the simmering stew wafted through the house, Little Al ran into the kitchen. "Umm. Sure smells good, Daddy."

"The stew's for dinner," I said. "There's oatmeal and toast for breakfast."

Following church services, Al suggested that we go to Graceland Cemetery to visit James's grave. I wasn't sure it was a good idea because he was still having terrible nightmares about the war. Besides, it was the middle of March and the weather was chilly. Nevertheless, I agreed.

At the cemetery, I led Al and the children along a gravel pathway that separated neat rows of graves, stopping only when we reached a small, nondescript tombstone. Al knelt and ran his fingers over the frosty letters: JAMES SULLIVAN. I remained on the side of the grave, holding Tessie's hand, while Little Al and Susie stood at its foot.

Suddenly, Al grasped the tombstone and tried to shake it from the ground. "Oh, my God, why did this boy have to die?"

Little Al cried out, "Daddy, what's wrong?" Susie looked frightened.

*My poor husband never had a chance to mourn,* I thought.

After a moment, Al stood up. "Evie, we shouldn't have brought them here, not when the pain is so raw."

I reached out and took his cold hand in mine, my eyes brimming with tears.

"Daddy," Little Al said.

"Yes, son?"

"James is all right. He's in heaven, isn't he?"

"Yes, son. James is in heaven. He's with the Lord.

"Honey, let's take the children home and have dinner. We'll come back in May or June when the weather is warmer. We can bring flowers and a picnic basket and invite Jennie and Peter to come along."

"Sounds wonderful, dear."

Al lifted Tessie, who this time offered no protest, and we walked out of the graveyard.

That night after we'd gone to bed, Al and I, wrapped in each other's arms, wept quietly over the loss of James.

# CHAPTER 56

## *Albert*

Evie was waiting in the doorway the day I returned from the Great War. She was the vision I had dreamt about, awake and asleep, for the past two years. That night as I buried myself in her embrace and breathed in her essence, I thought I had died and gone to heaven. Little did I know that the hell of war would haunt my dreams for some time to come.

Coming home felt strange, even though I treasured being there. I had to get to know the house again and yet I remembered every inch of it: the bedroom with its bright blue quilt and curtains and the kitchen with its green and red linoleum. I wandered from room to room getting my bearings and went into the parlor to make peace with my gentleman's armchair. The luxury of this existence, the tranquility, the security, the cleanliness–compared to the foulness and perils of the trenches–was almost too much for me, but I tried to settle down. During my absence, Evie had changed. She was more outspoken and more adamant about getting her way and I supposed I would get used to it.

I had been home about two weeks when I decided to look for work. Much to my surprise, Evie had been frugal while I was away and hadn't needed to spend our savings. Moreover, I still had most of my sixty-dollar discharge bonus so that gave me a little leeway. That Monday morning, I rose early and put on my neatly pressed uniform, with the war medals and red chevrons attached. I had made a list of prospective employers and my first stop would be Governor Smith's office. When I shared my plan with Evie over breakfast, she seemed dubious.

"Have you made an appointment, dear?"

"Nope. I'm just going to pop in and ask to see him."

A worried look crossed her face. "Well, don't be disappointed if he can't meet with you. Governor Smith just took office in January and I imagine he's very busy."

"Evie, let me handle this!" She looked hurt, and I was sorry I had snapped at her.

"Alright, dear. You know best."

Carrying the morning newspaper and an army discharge booklet, I hurried down the block toward the trolley. Even in my haste, I couldn't help but notice the black-draped door of a house across the street and wondered if the war had claimed another victim. Halfway down the block, I caught sight of Mr. Kaminski on his porch. As I walked by, he smiled and tipped his hat. I nodded in return. Although we had been neighbors for several years, he had never smiled at me before. Maybe it was the uniform.

I arrived at the governor's office at 9:30 a.m., prepared to wait all day if need be. As I approached the reception desk, I glanced around the waiting room, tastefully furnished with couches and chairs. The prim, middle-aged receptionist appeared startled when she saw me.

"Good morning, ma'am, I'm here to see Governor Smith."

She adjusted her horn-rimmed glasses. "Do you have an appointment, soldier?"

"No, ma'am, but I believe the Governor will want to see me."

"The Governor has a busy schedule today!"

"Yes, ma'am. I don't mind waiting." She stiffened her shoulders and shuffled the papers on the desk. I waited for her to take down my name.

But instead, she inquired, "What exactly is your business with the Governor?"

"It's a military matter . . . concerning the Great War."

"Alright. I'll tell him you're here."

"Thank you. By the way, I'm Sergeant Albert Johnson of the 369th regiment."

After scribbling it on a pad, she blurted out, "Take a seat, Sergeant."

I settled down in a comfortable chair and read the army-issued booklet, "Where Do We Go From Here?" One of the things it stressed was that veterans should continue paying their life insurance premiums, which they were entitled to keep for five years. It was an inexpensive way for me to protect Evie and the children.

There were three other men in the waiting room, all civilians, and each was called in to see the Governor according to his turn. About one o'clock, the Governor came out and spoke to the receptionist.

Then, glancing around the room, he said, "Hello there, soldier. Are you waiting for me?"

I stood up. "Yes sir, I'm . . ."

"He's Sergeant Johnson, from the 369th regiment. He doesn't have an appointment, so I told him you probably couldn't see him."

"Well, Sergeant," the governor said, "I'm on my way out. Can you come back this afternoon?"

"Certainly, sir."

"Miss Perrywinkle, put Sergeant Johnson down for three o'clock."

"Yes, sir."

I left the office intending to get coffee and a sandwich but then decided to look up my old boss, Irish. He seemed surprised yet pleased to see me. We sat in his cramped office and caught up over mugs of steaming hot tea, his favorite drink besides whiskey.

"How you been, Al?"

"Pretty good."

"Missed you here. Hard to get good workers these days who understand the big boiler."

"Can't truthfully say I missed the big boiler."

We both laughed.

"So how'd the army treat you?"

"The less said about that the better, but once we reached the front, our regiment became part of the French army."

"Good. I'm glad it wasn't the British. With those buggers, you might not have gotten back alive. How was it over there, anyway?"

"Terrible. Pure hell." I went on and described the reality of the war and the price both soldiers and civilians paid.

"I'll be damned!" he said as I finished.

"So how come you weren't drafted?" I asked. "You don't have any kids."

"Got a deferment because of my indispensable position at the Capitol."

We laughed again and then he led me into the boiler room. The heat and smell were awful, and its soot-covered walls began to close in on me. *God help me if I have to come back here to work.*

Two men, one about my age and the other somewhat younger, were feeding the boiler but stopped when they saw me. Their white faces and hands were grimy with coal dust. When Irish introduced us, they nodded but didn't crack a smile. Then Irish and I returned to his office.

"I suppose you're looking for your old job back."

"I don't think I can do that work anymore."

"Nonsense, you look strong as a bull. I'll try to make a place for you here. After all, you fought for your country." He refilled our tea mugs and passed me a plate of soda crackers.

"I'd prefer a factory job. It's less strenuous and the pay is better."

"In that case, go and see my cousin at General Electric. He's a foreman there."

I nodded. "Say, have you seen Phineas? He was recently discharged."

"Not yet. He'll be looking for work, too. Gee, I can only hire one of you."

"And what about Tom Tuttle?"

"Drafted the summer after you joined up." Irish scratched his head. "But that's all I knows."

By then, it was nearly three o'clock, so I got up to leave. As I walked toward the door, Irish said, "Al, let me know if you're coming back. To tell the truth this place ain't been the same since you left with all your stories and jokes."

"I'll be in touch, Irish."

At three thirty Miss Perrywinkle showed me into the Governor's office. He looked up from his large oak desk and smiled. "Welcome, Sergeant Johnson. So you're from the 369th. I reviewed your parade a few weeks ago with Governor Whitman. Very impressive!"

"Thank you, sir." I sat down and quickly took in the scene. It was an imposing office with dark green carpeting and gold-hued wallpaper. An over-sized map of New York State hung on the wall behind him and two splendid Hudson River landscapes were mounted on the adjoining walls. I was surprised to see a German officer's helmet perched on the side of the desk.

"Sergeant, were you aware that it was Governor Whitman who established your regiment as the New York 15th four years ago?"

"Yes, sir. I recruited about thirty volunteers for the 15th at the request of Lieutenant Spencer, the governor's military attaché."

"Excellent. Governor Whitman told me how proud he is of the regiment, and especially of Albany's Henry Johnson–being the first American war hero. His name was splashed all over the newspapers. Did you know him?"

"He was my mate in C Company. The night we came under attack, Privates Johnson and Roberts saved many lives while inflicting major damage on the German raiders."

The Governor raised his eyebrows and leaned over his desk toward me. "Now tell me honestly, how was it over there?"

I moved to the edge of my seat. "Pretty bad, sir. Much worse than I had ever imagined."

And for the next hour and a quarter, I recounted what we soldiers witnessed and experienced during the Great War: the unspeakable carnage, the widespread destruction, the inconsolable sorrow, and the heroic triumphs. He listened intently, hanging on my every word, and even waved away Miss Perrywinkle when she entered the office to deliver a message.

I shifted back in my chair. "That's about the size of it, Governor."

He stared at the German officer's helmet. "Now, Sergeant, what can I do for you?"

"Sir, I need a job to support my family of five. Before I joined up, I worked in the Capitol's boiler room, but I'm not a spring chicken and can't do that work much longer."

"How old are you?"

"Thirty-nine, sir."

"So you were about thirty-seven when you volunteered and had a wife and three children?"

"Our baby was only two months old. Also had a nephew who died of flu while I was away."

He looked amazed. "And what sort of education do you have?"

"Didn't have much formal schooling, Governor. But I educated myself through travel abroad, while in the Navy, and by my journeys across America after I was honorably discharged."

He drummed his fingers on the desk. "Well, Sergeant, I can't promise anything, but I'll see what I can do."

"Thank you, sir." After that, he instructed me to leave my address and military particulars with Miss Perrywinkle and said that he'd be in touch by the end of the week. Walking toward the trolley, I struggled to contain my rising expectations. *This was just an interview. Nothing was promised.*

Governor Smith was a newly elected Democrat, and many of New York's darker skinned citizens were waiting to see if his policies would bring about improvements in their beleaguered lives. I was optimistic. But to tell the truth, I would have almost been willing to work for the Devil if he offered me a way out of the coal. When I reached home, Evie greeted me with a kiss.

"Got to see the Governor, honey, and asked him for a job." Her eyes snapped wide open. "He said he'd let me know."

She threw up her hands. "Thank the Lord."

"Evie, don't go getting your hopes up."

I went out early the next morning to explore additional job prospects and on my way home, I took a trolley to the block where Tom Tuttle lived. There, I encountered an elderly woman and inquired about the Tuttle family. Lifting her cane, she pointed to a brick house across the street—a house with black crepe on the door. Hoping against hope, I rang the doorbell and Tom's sister, a pretty young woman, invited me in and confirmed my fears. Tom Tuttle had perished in the Great War.

Over the next several days, I visited many of the factories in Troy and Schenectady. Most times the supervisors turned me down flat, but Irish's cousin said he would let me know if anything came up. Nearly two weeks had passed, and I still hadn't heard from Governor Smith.

As I lay in bed on one evening, I muttered, "At least he could have let me know, one way or the other."

Evie snuggled beside me. "Don't worry, dear. Something good will happen soon. My guardian spirit said so."

"Forget that nonsense! Did she tell you where I should look for a job?"

"No dear, not yet."

"Humph!"

"Albert, I have an idea," she whispered in my ear.

"Let's hear it."

"Remember how you used to paint houses on the weekends before you went into the army?"

"Yeah."

"You could start your own business. I'll draw up some signs and you and Little Al can post them."

"Evie, that's all right to earn extra money, but I have five mouths to feed. I need a steady job."

"Okay. It was just an idea." We lay there awhile, nestled under the heavy quilt.

"Honey," I said, "put the signs together. I might as well try to make a few bucks until a real job comes along." I kissed her, secretly hoping her guardian spirit's prediction would come true.

On Saturday afternoon, Little Al and I posted twenty of Evie's signs around Arbor Hill and on Monday I received an inquiry from a neighbor and rushed over to his house.

"Could you do it as soon as possible, Mr. Johnson? My wife wants our place brightened up now that the war's over."

"Sure. I can do it next Saturday."

I went out again on Tuesday morning, still searching for a steady job, and when I returned that evening, I headed straight for the parlor and plopped down in my armchair. *If nothing turns up soon, I'll have to go back to the coal.*

Dismayed and dead tired, I pretended to be asleep when Little Al and Susie entered the room.

"Daddy's sleeping," Little Al whispered. They tiptoed out but returned a few minutes later.

"Daddy, here's a letter for you," Susie said. I opened my eyes as she handed me a long white envelope, marked with the Governor's crest.

"Thank you, Sweetie."

"Aren't you going to read it?" Little Al asked.

"Yeah, in a little while." By this time, I expected a rejection and didn't want to face it on an empty stomach.

Just then, Evie called us to the table: hot buttered biscuits, beef stew, and a tasty vanilla pudding. After dinner, I retreated to my armchair and tore open the white envelope that was burning a hole in my pocket.

# CHAPTER 57

## *Albert*

❧ ❧

The next morning, I arrived at the Lieutenant Governor's office at ten past nine and was ushered in to see him at nine thirty. He was at his desk perusing a stack of documents but stood up as I entered.

"Good morning, Sergeant Johnson."

"Good morning, sir."

After offering me a seat, he sat down. "Governor Smith asked me to see what we can do for you, if anything."

"Yes, sir." I shifted back and forth in the chair, waiting for the hatchet to drop.

"Well, the only thing that might fit the bill is a messenger's job. By the way, how's your reading?"

"Quite good, sir." I opened my newspaper and began to read the editorial column out loud. Fortunately, it expressed a favorable opinion of the Governor.

"That's fine," he said.

"Would you like a sample of my writing, sir?"

"That won't be necessary. So far, we've been using messengers from the Capitol pool, but the governor thinks that his office should have a special courier, a conscientious, discreet, and trustworthy person. Someone who can get to know the legislators."

He raised his eyebrows and scrutinized me. "Do you think you fit the bill?"

"Yes, sir."

"Well, after reviewing your fine military record, so do I. Are you interested in the position, Sergeant?"

"Most assuredly, sir!" We both stood up.

"Good. Miss Perrywinkle will escort you to the personnel office to fill out the paperwork. They'll give you the particulars of salary and vacation time. Can you start work next Monday?"

"Yes. Sir, will I be wearing a uniform?"

"You'll wear a suit. But your army uniform will do until you can buy one." He came out from behind his desk and shook my hand.

I left and went in search of Miss Perrywinkle. As I strode down the hall, I thought: *I've been tied to the coal for much of my life. I've breathed it, tasted it, dug, lifted and hauled it. It's been a second skin and it's even seeped into my pores. Now it seems I'm going to be free of it–for good, I hope.*

"Congratulations, Sergeant Johnson," Miss Perrywinkle said.

"Thank you, ma'am."

"You'll be the governor's courier, but you'll also be expected to do whatever is needed around the office."

"I'll be glad to do whatever I can."

"Do you mind if I call you Al?"

"Just call me Sergeant Al."

After completing the business at the personnel office, I rushed down to the boiler room and broke the good news to Irish.

"You really got a job with Governor Al Smith?" he asked.

"Yup."

"Wow. I voted for him."

It wasn't surprising. Like Irish, Al Smith was a Catholic, one of the first to become a governor and, to boot, he was against Prohibition!

"Al, how the devil did you pull it off?"

"Lady Luck was with me," I said, smiling from ear to ear.

"Must have been the luck of the Irish!"

"Could have been." I took leave of Irish and strolled to the tailor shop on Front Street where my friend, Caliph Thompson, worked. I hadn't seen him since returning to Albany.

"Welcome home, hero!" he said, as he glanced at my medals. "I heard you were back."

"I'm no hero. Just another fighting man."

"You guys done good, damn good. So what can we do for you?"

I told him about the new job and explained I needed a conservative brown suit. I already owned a blue one. After he took my measurements, I picked out the material, a fine but costly wool serge. The shop owner, Mr. Fineman, who had been eavesdropping on the conversation, said he'd give me a discount since I was a veteran and a friend of Caliph.

After leaving the shop, I walked several blocks to a confectionery on Broadway and purchased a large box of chocolates for Evie and a bag of red cinnamon candy for the children. Finally, I began my journey home, happy as a jaybird. At my new job, I would earn nearly twice my old salary, wear a suit, and have a week's paid vacation. I couldn't believe my good fortune. Shortly after dinner that evening, I asked Evie for a few sheets of her stationery. Then I retreated to the quiet of the parlor and wrote a letter to Pa telling him and Ma about my new job and one to my brother Grant, apologizing for the way I had treated him.

I received my first full paycheck from New York State at the end of the April. I had settled into the job and knew the names and positions of most of the legislators, Republicans and Democrats. To celebrate, Evie invited several friends to dinner on a Saturday evening. There were Jennie and Peter, Mr. Ashton who traveled up from Brooklyn, Cousin Mattie, Mrs. Jones, Inez, and Calvin, who had just been discharged from the army. Peter brought a bottle of wine and two jugs of apple cider, Evie made a cake and pudding, Jennie baked yeast rolls, and I cooked a pork roast, white potatoes, and green beans. And we all had a jolly good time.

During the next two months, I received both good and bad news. First, I heard from Lucky, who had recently returned from France. He said he was happy to be home but complained that his injury had left him with a slight limp. He needed work and was looking for an apprenticeship. I answered immediately.

*Dear Lucky,*

*I'm glad that you've recovered and have finally come home. Don't be disturbed by your small handicap. Think of General Gouraud who achieved so much despite his many injuries. It would be good to get trained in a skill. Ever thought about plumbing? My father-in-law's business is thriving these days, with so many people wanting indoor plumbing. I'm sure he could use your help. I'll drop him a line and see.*

*Your buddy,*

*Al*

Mr. Ashton replied he'd be glad to give Lucky a try and, soon after that, Lucky landed the job. It wouldn't pay much at first, but he'd be getting valuable training.

On the heels of that good news, I received a crushing blow. On the evening of May 9, I opened the newspaper and couldn't believe what I saw: Herbert White, a drummer in the Harlem Hellfighters band, stabbed Lieutenant James Reese Europe, the celebrated bandleader and composer. I dropped the paper, told Evie I was going out and ran to the railroad station to see if any of the porters were around. They usually had copies of the *New York Age*, and I was sure it would have more details of the story. When I found Deek Williams, he was sitting on a bench, staring at the front page of the *Age* and slowly shaking his graying head. I eased down beside him.

"Ain't this some shit, Al? One of our leaders struck down by one of our own. You knew him, didn't you?"

"Yes. James Europe was a musical genius and a man of great vision. He had big dreams for Negro music and won over all of France playing music that was birthed and inspired by colored people. Ragtime! And a new kind of music they haven't even named yet."

Deek took out his handkerchief and blew his nose. "Well, you can't blame the white man for this."

"No, I guess you can't."

Deek sighed. "The newspaper says that the band played in New York to glowing reviews and moved on to Boston. That crazy Herbert fellow was acting strangely during rehearsals, and James Europe reprimanded him. Well, you know the rest. That jackass knifed him in the neck, and an hour or so later, Lieutenant James Reese Europe was dead."

I grimaced and clenched my fists. "Great God Almighty. A good man cut down in his prime!"

"It's a crying shame," Deek said. "I suppose you knew the other fella, too."

"Herbert White came out of a South Carolina orphanage without a pot to piss in and James Europe gave him his big chance. That's gratitude for you. I've a mind to go down to New York and throttle that boy with my bare hands."

Deek grabbed my wrist. "Take it easy, Al. Police already got him under arrest."

I took a deep breath. "All I can say is America has lost one of its greatest musicians and as you pointed out, our race has lost a leader."

Deek handed me the newspaper. "Guess you'll want to keep this."

"Thanks, Deek. I'd like to show it to my son." I stood up and so did he. "I'd better get going. Maybe we can have a drink together soon."

"Sure, Al. Make it before that damn Prohibition kicks in."

"Yeah. That'll be a bitch."

"No. It'll be a crime!"

About two weeks later, I heard from Teddy Wilson. He shared the good news that he and Amanda were officially engaged. He also said that he had written an account of our regiment's achievements for *The Philadelphia Tribune*, the city's oldest Negro newspaper, and they had given him a temporary job until he returns to Fisk in the fall. I was happy for Teddy. With his intelligence and drive, and Amanda at his side, he would go far, despite the obstacles he would face as a colored man in America.

One fine Sunday afternoon in June, Evie and I took the children to Washington Park, a spacious place with a big lake, swings, fountains, promenades, bike paths, and lovely flowerbeds. The streets bordering the park sported expensive mansions occupied by what they called the quality or high society. After entering, Evie and I sat on a bench and the children ran off to play nearby. As was her habit, Evie began to read a small volume of poetry. I lounged next to her, savoring the warmth of the afternoon sun and the sweet aroma of spring blossoms. When a white, well-to-do passerby gave me a disdaining look, I answered by tipping my Panama hat. He responded with a nervous smile.

*What a lucky guy I am,* I thought. *A beautiful wife, three bright and spirited children, and a steady job with a decent salary. And what a miracle to hear my children's laughter again! Oh, James, how we miss you.* I had escaped the Great War with life and limb intact although I could still hear the heartbreaking cries of wounded and dying comrades in my dreams.

And I kept wondering about Cephas and Lyle. *Lord knows I did my best to keep them safe during the war. Now it's up to them.*

Evie closed her book and inched toward me. "Kitty cat got your tongue?"

"I was thinking about Cephas and Lyle. I haven't heard from them." Just then, an image of Cephas, lying in a shell hole, his artist arm shattered by a sniper's bullets, flashed across my mind and I shuddered.

Evie rested her head on my shoulder. "Dear, why don't you drop them a line?"

"Maybe I'll do that." The children skipped over and said they were thirsty, so I led them down a brick path to a nearby water fountain.

That evening, I wrote a letter to Lyle and mailed it to his father's barbershop in Harlem, and two weeks later, I received a reply. He said that he and his father had reconciled, and he was working hard in the shop, cutting hair and giving shaves, something he swore he'd never do. Using part of his sixty-dollar discharge bonus, Lyle had spruced up the shop, promoted it around Harlem, and attracted some well-heeled Seventh Avenue Negroes. I can see him now, snapping his fingers and telling everyone in earshot what a big war hero he was. My letter to Lyle netted two fish. He said that Cephas had wandered into the barbershop one Friday evening looking for work. They were both shocked to see each other. Lyle related that Cephas was renting a little room in Harlem and that he could hardly use his right arm, no less draw or paint with it. The army was giving him a tiny disability allowance, and he was eking out a living cleaning up shops after hours. Lyle said that he talked his father into hiring Cephas two nights a week.

*What a damn shame*, I thought. *I was afraid of something like this. The man has talent. The man had big dreams.* After reading Lyle's letter, I wrote to Cephas in care of the barbershop and tried to encourage him not to give up on his dream, even if he has to learn to paint with his left hand. I enclosed a five-dollar bill, which I could ill afford, to buy artist supplies. I didn't hear back from him, but Lyle wrote that Cephas had received the money.

On the last Friday of July, I knocked off work a little early and dropped by Irish's office to ask if he had heard from Phineas Middleton. Irish was nowhere to be seen, but to my surprise, Phineas was there, sprawled on a chair.

"Phineas! I'll be damned!"

"Al. Oh, my God. So good to see you." He ran over and bear-hugged me.

"Welcome back, soldier. I guess you heard I'm with the Governor now."

"Yeah. I was planning to come and visit you."

"That office is too busy. Drop by my house, instead. So how've you been?"

"Al, I been to hell and back!"

Phineas always had a tall tale to tell, so I sat down. "No kidding. What happened?"

"Well, it's like this . . ."

Just then Irish walked in. "Al, I hired back your old friend."

"Thanks, Irish. I appreciate that." I started sparring with Irish about Albany politics, but after a few minutes, Phineas interrupted.

"We getting ready to knock off soon. How's about going to the Dockside Tavern for a drink?"

"Okay, but I can't stay long. Evie's expecting me."

We took a corner table in the tavern and placed an order. Soon a buxom, smiling waitress brought our drinks along with a plate of steaming hot fried potatoes.

"What's troubling you, Phineas?"

He threw me an exasperated look. "Remember Bobby Brown from Georgia? The one who tried to knife me?"

"I made a soldier out of that boy."

"Well, he nearly got me lynched!"

"What the hell?"

"I ran into him at camp just before we was discharged and we decided to travel to Georgia together. My cousins live in his hometown and I wanted them to see me in my uniform. When we arrived, I went to visit my folks, but later that afternoon, I hooked up with Bobby. We was a-strutting up and down Main Street, greeting folks and laughing out loud. I should've known there was trouble ahead when some of the white mens gave us dirty looks.

"One cracker yelled out, 'Whose toilets did you boys clean overseas?' Bobby answered, 'Don't know about that, but I shot a whole bunch of Huns in the ass.' Well, that must have done it. When you tell one cracker that you shot another cracker, even if that cracker is a Hun who's trying to kill the first cracker, you asking for trouble."

Phineas downed his whiskey and ordered another. I did the same.

"That night after Bobby, his girlfriend Lula, and I come home from a juke joint, a group of eight crackers showed up and burned a cross outside Lula's cabin where we was staying. The crackers yelled, 'Come on out you smart-mouthed nigger or we'll burn that claptrap down.' Hoping he could talk some sense into them, Bobby went out, but they grabbed him and put a gun upside his head. It was dark except for the fire burning on the lawn but Lula and I could see and hear everything from the window. 'Where's that other nigger soldier you was with?' one redneck asked. 'He left a long time ago,' Bobby said. The cracker ran the gun muzzle along Bobby's jaw and said, 'Nigger, we going to string you up.' "

Phineas paused to take a breath while I waited impatiently.

"Then I ordered Lula to load her shotgun. She say, 'It stay loaded, Phineas.' I took the shotgun in my hand and put the revolver I had smuggled out of the army in my belt and said, 'Lula when I gives the signal, snatch open the door and jump back.' I don't know if it was because I took them by surprise or what, but they scattered like chaff in the wind when I charged out the door shooting wildly and yelling French and German curses. The cracker holding Bobby was hit in the shoulder and Bobby dropped to the ground. I think I hit one or two others as they ran away, yelling, 'Nigger's gone amuck.'

"Bobby jumped up and ran into the house. 'They be back soon with they friends. We better cut and run.' Lula snapped, 'You ain't leaving me behind.' So the three of us made our way through the woods and the swamps of Georgia, almost eaten alive by mosquitoes, until we reached North Carolina. All we had with us was two canteens of water, and two duffle bags, packed with clothes and the guns, a few loaves of bread, some fried chicken, and a dozen peaches. I suppose the crackers torched the house when they got back, but we was long gone."

"Whew! Where's Bobby and Lula now?"

"They headed north for Chicago by rail. He got relatives up there. I hopped a train to New York. I heard from my folks down South the other day that some colored soldiers has been lynched returning home from the war. Some, right in they uniforms."

"Oh, my God!" I said, reeling from the shock that things were even worse than I thought.

"So we be lucky. It'll be a cold day in hell before I goes back to Georgia."

We finished our drinks and fried potatoes, which were cold by then, and headed out the door.

That summer of 1919 came to be known as 'red summer.' And when I learned about the widespread lynching and murders of our returning soldiers and other colored folk, I became enraged. *America,* I thought, *have you no soul?*

I was sitting in the parlor one August evening when Evie came up and put her arms around me.

"Is something wrong, dear? Is it something I've done?"

"You've been wonderful. Forgive me, if I ever forget to tell you that. I'm just disheartened about some of the things that are happening to our people."

"Al, I know you expected the war to change things. Be patient. Give it time."

"Damn it, Evie. This country's had plenty of time to right the wrongs done to us since the end of slavery. How much time do they want?"

She bit her lip and seemed on the verge of tears. "But what can we do?"

Trying to contain my fury, I left the house and wandered down the dark streets of Arbor Hill. A while later, I found myself at the Dockside Tavern where I ran into Johnny Earl, a soldier I knew from the 369th. It was near closing time and most of the patrons had already left. We greeted each other warmly and after a drink or two, I told him what was on my mind.

"I feel the same way," he said. "Colored men have fought and died for this here country and others will be invalids for the rest of their lives."

I slammed my fist on the table nearly overturning the lit candle. "And there's no public outcry against the violence. Even the President, the one who sent us into that damn war, has said or done nothing about it!" I downed another drink, but it couldn't wash away my bitterness.

Then Johnny Earl removed a folded page from his pocket and spread it out on the table. "Have you seen this piece by Dubois? It's from the *Crisis*, the NAACP magazine."

"No."

As I pulled the candle closer, Johnny Earl read the encircled lines, "We are cowards and jackasses if now that the war is over, we do not marshal every ounce of our brain and brawn to fight a sterner, longer, more unbending battle against the forces of hell in our own land."

Stunned, I eyeballed him. "These are our marching orders, soldier." He slid the page toward me, whereupon I read Dubois's final words aloud. "We return. We return from fighting. We return fighting."

The white-hot rage I felt began to fade, and although I grieved for the lost new world I had hoped for, I believed it could be possible in my son's lifetime.

"We've got to band together with our people," Johnny Earl said, "and make this land live up to its ideals."

"Yeah. We've got to. For the sake of our children."


In August 1920, Evie gave birth to Irene Elizabeth, our fourth child. To support our growing family, I took on weekend catering jobs for lobbyists who frequently held shindigs for the legislators (and their girlfriends) in Saratoga Springs, a town famous for horse racing, gambling, and bathhouses. Catering was far more lucrative than my former side jobs. In fact, I made enough to hire a kitchen man and a few waiters to help prepare and serve the refreshments. It was during prohibition and the lobbyists asked if I could get hold of some liquor. I hesitated at first, but they assured me that they would pay off the Saratoga Springs police chief. So I made arrangements to get several bottles of Canadian whiskey from my porter friends who regularly worked the trains going to Canada. They brought in the bottles, hidden under the train's dirty laundry, and delivered them to the roadhouse where the parties were held. As a precaution, I instructed my waiters to call it ice tea, serve it from pitchers, and toss it immediately if there was ever a raid. This went on without incident for quite a while until the governor got wind of it and ordered me to stop serving whiskey.

Toward the end of 1921, I received a letter postmarked from Paris. It was from Cephas. To my amazement, he had made it to France working on a tramp steamer. He explained that his arm had gradually grown stronger with use and that he was painting again. He had recently begun art studies at Académie Moderne, a school on the left bank, and was part of a small but thriving community of Negro painters, musicians, and writers, who were flocking to the beautiful City of Lights. There, they would claim their dreams. I hoped France would treat them well. I believed that she would.

# PART THREE

# CHAPTER 58
## *Evie – 1923*

The Great War changed things, some for the better, some for the worse. It changed the mood of the country, it changed people's attitudes (but not their prejudices). It changed the way they ate, the way they dressed, the way they worked, the way they danced, and the way they spent their wages. It even changed women's hemlines, which were getting shorter every year. The Great War changed people and Al and I were no exception.

Before the war, Al treated me like a Kewpie doll, all head, and no brain, and I usually went along with it because at the time I was young and madly in love. However, when he returned after being away for nearly two years, I was no longer the naive woman he had left behind. I protested when he tried to control my activities or made family decisions without my input. After a while, he began to ask my opinion about domestic matters–that is, except in the case of family finances. And even though he worked hard to provide for us, I still wanted a say in how we spent our money.

In the past, he had never allowed me to work, so I had to hide it from him, whenever I sewed for a customer. One Sunday, after church, Mrs. Vanderpool asked if I could make the bridesmaids' dresses for her friend's daughter, who was getting married in June. At first, I begged off because I didn't think I would have the time. Besides, I didn't want to cause a ruckus with Al. But when Inez explained that the bride just wanted long, flapper-style dresses without the usual frills and ruffles, I decided to take on the job. Again, I was careful not to let Al get wind of it, but one Saturday in May it all came out in the wash.

Al went out after breakfast that morning, saying he'd be back in the early afternoon. After he left, I removed the partially finished garments from my hope chest (silk dresses and small hats in a lovely shade of peach) and brought them to the dining room. I had to work fast because the wedding would take place in three weeks. I was still sewing an hour and a half later when I heard the apartment door open.

Lugging several bags of groceries, Al headed toward the kitchen but stopped short at the dining room door. "Are you making a new outfit? Your closet's already overflowing."

"No, dear, I'm sewing dresses for a wedding."

"We're invited to a wedding?"

"I'm making dresses for the bridesmaids."

"What? Don't you have enough to do around here?"

"Honey, can we talk about it later? The young ladies will be coming for a fitting on Monday."

He stormed into the kitchen to prepare a big batch of chicken salad for a political reception he would be catering in Saratoga Springs. Soon the apartment was filled with the delicious aroma of simmering chicken and celery, and I was tempted to ask him to put some of it aside for dinner. But I didn't dare.

I delivered the finished outfits to the bride's home the following week and collected my earnings. As usual, I put the money away for a rainy day. To my surprise, Al never brought up the subject again and of course, neither did I.

By the spring of the following year, I had five children to feed, clothe, and care for, including our son, Philip, who was almost a year old. I also had tons of laundry to do. A washerwoman did the sheets, towels, and blankets, and two neighbors did the ironing in exchange for their readings. But I still had lots of diapers and clothes to wash. One Saturday afternoon, there was a loud knock on the downstairs door and Al ran to answer it. To my astonishment, two husky men carried a brand-new Maytag washing machine up the stairs and into the kitchen and demonstrated how the new contraption worked.

After showing the men out, Al returned to the kitchen, grinning like a Cheshire cat. "Well dear, what do you think?"

"Thank you, darling. It's simply beautiful." I was delighted with the washing machine but at the same time worried about the expense.

"Are you sure we can afford this?"

"Don't worry. The store has a new monthly installment plan."

"But, won't you have to work extra hard to make the payments?"

"Evie, let me handle the finances. All you have to do is look beautiful and take care of the children."

Al was fond of saying that all I have to do is look beautiful and take care of the children. Didn't he realize that attending the needs of husband and children was challenging work? And did he have any idea of what it took for me to look beautiful every day?

Our life together became a series of compromises. I let him control the finances, and he allowed me to have a say in family decisions. However, one day Al crossed the line. It all started on a fateful morning in March 1925 when I fetched a letter from the mailbox. It was addressed to Mr. Albert Johnson and was from Theodore Jones, the nephew of Mrs. Jones, our land-lady who had died last November. She had been a good friend; God rest her soul. Since she passed away, Al had been sending Theodore a postal money order for the rent every month, so I was curious about the letter. I'm almost ashamed to admit it, but I steamed it open and found out that we would have to vacate our apartment in a couple of months because Theodore, who resided in New York City, was selling the house to his cousin. I was upset. Al and I had lived in the apartment for nearly sixteen years. When I recovered from the shock, I made a paste of flour and water, glued the envelope closed, and placed it on the lamp table next to Al's armchair.

That evening, I waited for Al to mention this new turn of events, but he said nothing. A few days passed, and he still didn't speak of it and I couldn't bring it up because then he would know I had opened the letter.

After a few weeks, I noticed that whenever he was reading the newspaper, he would close it when I entered the room. One day, he dozed off with the paper spread open in his lap. I tiptoed in and saw that he had been browsing the classified ads: "Homes for rent or sale."

*He's looking for a house to rent! How dare he without consulting me.*

My guardian spirit spoke up. "Your husband started this, let him finish it."

So I held my tongue.

One evening after dinner, Al asked me to join him in the parlor. First, he told me about Theodore Jones's letter and explained that he didn't say anything about it because he didn't want to worry me. Then he hit me with a bombshell. He said that he had picked out a house to buy!

I clenched my teeth. "Without me even seeing it!"

"Darling, I think you'll like it. It's similar to this one, only larger."

"I can't believe you're buying a house without consulting me."

"I haven't signed the papers yet."

Remembering the words of my guardian spirit, I said, "Well, my husband, if you've done all this without asking me, go ahead and do the rest!" I stood up and marched toward the door, but he pleaded with me to come back.

"Evie, if you don't like it, I'll tear up the contract. Just come and have a look."

I agreed to go with him on Saturday. That morning, I dressed carefully since I would be meeting the property owners, but as I emerged from the bedroom, Al complained that my smart new suit looked expensive. When we reached Lark Street, Al pointed out the house, a plain, brown, two-story dwelling on a steep hill. He rang the bell and introduced me to Mr. and Mrs. Peterson, a white couple, who seemed pleasant enough, and after a brief chat, Mrs. Peterson showed me around. Despite my misgivings, I liked the large rooms and airy kitchen, and I was delighted with the modern gas stove, which would be easier to use than our coal stove. The electric lights on the ceilings were wonderful. I pulled the switch and the room was full of daylight. I smiled and told Mrs. Peterson that she had a lovely home, however,

I quickly wiped the smile off my face when we entered the parlor where our husbands were waiting. After conversing a few minutes, we followed Mrs. Peterson down the back stairs, descending into an enchanted garden, awash with color: pink, red, orange, yellow, lavender, and purple. When I beheld the lovely flowers and lush greenery and breathed in the sweet aroma of lilacs, I couldn't help but smile.

While Al and I were strolling home, I noticed a happy, young couple, walking arm in arm, and was reminded of the time when we were first married and very much in love.

*That was many years ago*, I thought. *We're different now—life and war have changed us. But thank goodness we still love and need each other.*

We were about halfway home when Al finally spoke. "Well, dear, did you like it or not?"

"It was alright. Has the bank approved the mortgage loan? Mrs. Peterson said you've applied."

"Yes, it has." He stopped dead in his tracks and sighed heavily. "Evie, if you don't want the house, I'll go to the bank on Monday and withdraw the application."

I strolled on without a word, letting him stew in his own broth.

# CHAPTER 59
## *Albert – 1925*

❧ ❧ ❧

There're a few big decisions a man makes in his lifetime: getting married is one of them, buying a house is another. I had taken the first one sixteen years ago and was debating about taking the second. It wouldn't be easy for a colored man like me to get a mortgage, but I had excellent references and a steady job. I had been working at the governor's office since returning from the war and had become a trusted employee there.

Buying a house would be expensive, so I needed a plan. As a first step, I opened a bank account with the money I had saved from my catering jobs. Then in December of 1924, I received an unexpected windfall: a one hundred and fifty-dollar veterans' bonus from New York State! In spite of that favorable omen, I was still hesitant about buying property, so I put the idea on a back burner.

A few months later, I got a letter from Mrs. Jones's nephew saying that he planned to sell the property and that we would have to move out fairly soon. I didn't tell Evie because I wanted time to figure out what we should do next. Evie and I had five children: Albert, fifteen; Susie, twelve; Tessie, eight; Irene, five; and Philip, a cute little tyke of two. I believed it would be difficult to find a reasonably priced apartment that was large enough.

One evening, I slipped into the hall closet and counted the cash remaining in my tool chest. Two hundred and twenty bucks plus change. These funds when added to our bank account savings might be enough for a down payment, thus I decided to take the plunge and look for a house in Arbor

Hill. I said nothing of this to Evie. I was afraid if she got involved, I'd wind up spending more than I could afford.

I checked the newspapers and walked around the neighborhood after work. I looked at several properties. Some were too expensive, and others were run down. After I had been looking for two months, I heard about a house on north Lark Street and went to investigate. It was a two-story brown frame house in good condition with a delightful garden. In addition, it was a two-family residence, so we would be getting rental income that could help pay the mortgage. According to the owners, Mr. and Mrs. Peterson, the house had recently been modernized, with gas lines for the cooking stove, a coal heating furnace, and electric lights. To me, it was perfect, but would Evie like it?

After I negotiated with the Petersons to lower the price, I approached my bank for a loan. I was on pins and needles waiting for a reply, which would be mailed to me at the governor's office. Two weeks later, I got word that the bank had approved the loan. Once Mr. Peterson and I signed the papers, the house would belong to Evie and me. As would the mortgage!

I did all of this without Evie suspecting a thing, but when the Petersons asked if my wife wanted to inspect the property, I began to worry.

*How will I tell her?* I thought. *I may have gone too far this time.*

The evening after I received the bank's letter, I asked Evie to join me in the parlor, leaving Susie and Tessie to wash the dishes.

"What is it, dear?" she asked as she sat down in her lady's armchair.

"Honey, some time ago, Theodore Jones wrote and said that he was going to sell the house."

"I was afraid that might happen."

"I didn't want to trouble you, so I've been looking around for a house to buy."

A strained expression clouded her face. "You want to buy a house?"

"I've been thinking about it."

"But can we afford it? And how would we get the down payment?"

343

"I've saved some. What I really want to tell you is that I've found a house for us."

"Without me even seeing it?" she said through clenched teeth.

*She has every right to be angry,* I thought.

"Albert, I can't believe you've picked out a house without asking me first."

"I haven't signed the papers yet," I said.

"Well, my husband, if you've done all that without consulting me, go ahead and do the rest." She stood up and strode toward the door.

"Evie, please come back." Sighing, she retraced her steps and sat on the edge of her chair.

"Look, honey, if you don't like it, I'll tear up the contract. Just come and see it."

She gave me a frigid, unsmiling glance. "All right. I'll have a look at your house."

"Our house, Evie."

On Saturday, I paced up and down near the door. "Evie, we'll be late. I told the Petersons we'd be there by one."

"I'll be ready in a minute." She stepped into the hall looking splendid in a green and grey plaid suit, white blouse and a green-feathered cap.

"Mother, you look lovely," Susie said.

"Where did you get that outfit?" I asked. "It looks expensive."

"We all have our secrets, don't we, dear?"

"Little Al and Susie, watch the kids. Your mother and I are leaving."

Evie swept into the Lark Street house like a queen inspecting her realm. Mrs. Peterson escorted her through the house, while Mr. Peterson and I remained in the parlor. Once we were alone, I whispered to him that the loan had been approved and we'd be signing the papers at the bank on Wednesday. At that time, I would give him a down payment of $1,000, my life's saving, and the bank would pay him the balance of the sale.

"But don't mention anything to Mrs. Johnson," I said. "I have to square things with her first."

"Okay, but will she go for it?"

"I'm sure she will, once she's seen the house." *I hope and pray she likes it, otherwise, I'm in deep crap.*

Half an hour later, Evie and Mrs. Peterson strolled into the parlor. Mrs. Peterson said that she was taking Evie to see the garden and invited us to tag along. We descended the back stairs and entered a magical place where yellow daffodils, purple irises, pink and red roses, and lavender lilacs were in bloom.

Evie was quiet as we walked home.

"Well?" I asked. "Did you like it or not?"

"It was alright. Has the bank approved the mortgage yet?" I was startled that she knew about it.

"Ah . . . yes," I stammered. For once I didn't know what to say. Maybe the truth would help. "Evie, I'm sorry. I should have told you I wanted to buy a house, but I was afraid you'd pick out one more expensive than we could afford."

She didn't smile or utter a word.

"If you don't like it, I'll go to the bank and withdraw the application."

*It'll make me look like a damn fool*, I thought.

We continued to walk, and after several minutes arrived home. As we climbed up the front stairs, Evie said, "It's a lovely house and I'm glad we'll be staying in the neighborhood."

I sighed in relief.

From then on, even after we moved to 66 Lark Street, even when we sat in our rose-filled garden, even as she relaxed her lovely head on my shoulder, even as we sipped lemonade and entertained guests on the grassy lawn, Evie always referred to our home as Al's house. I suppose it was to remind me of how foolish I'd been. When friends asked me about the house, I told them it was my heaven on earth–but only if Evie was there to share it with me.

# CHAPTER 60

## *Evie*

**W**hen we moved into our new home on Lark Street there were drapes and curtains to sew, furnishings to buy, and rooms to paint. Once the house had been spruced up, I invited Mrs. MacHennessy and Mrs. Schmidt to drop by. They said they loved the house and the décor, but they were most impressed by the electric lights. When I showed them into the kitchen, Mrs. Schmidt ran over to the cook-stove.

"Where you put in coal?" she asked.

"It runs on gas."

She stroked it reverently. "No coal!"

"You're very lucky," Mrs. MacHennessy said, touching the cross she always wore around her neck. "Everything's nice and new."

Little Al started his freshman year at Albany High School that September and from the very first day, he complained about the three-mile walk to school. Soon, I got tired of hearing his protests and broached the subject with his father.

"Little Al's school is far away and no trolley runs there. It's awfully hard for him to get back and forth every day."

"What do you suggest?"

"Could you buy him a bicycle?"

"Evie, I've just bought and furnished this house and I'm up to my neck in debt. I don't have money for a bike. Besides, I'm trying to save for the boy's college education."

"I don't want him to get discouraged by the long hike."

"Stop babying him. When winter comes, he'll have to walk through the snow, so he might as well get used to it now."

"All right, dear."

Each morning Little Al would grumble as he set off for school, and in the afternoon, he would return panting and dragging his school bag. Then one day he came home whistling a popular ditty, "If You Knew Susie, Like I Know Susie." I smiled when I heard it.

"Mother, I met a new friend today. His name is Matt and from now on we'll be walking to school together."

"How nice. Does he live around here?"

"Not too far, he cuts off near Pine Road."

Little Al and Matt became fast friends and I was delighted that he found a buddy since there weren't any kids his age on our block. And for a while, I didn't hear him complaining about the long walk. Little Al said that he shared his college plans with Matt, but Matt replied he wanted to get a good job right after he finished high school. Then winter arrived, and the snow fell, and the temperature dropped. On one particularly cold afternoon, Little Al came home half frozen. I rushed him into the warm kitchen and gave him a cup of hot tea with honey and a few buttermilk biscuits.

"Mother, Matt said he's sick and tired of walking in the cold."

"Did he?"

"Yes. And so am I."

"I'm sure you are, dear, but don't let your father catch you talking like that. You have a goal in life and sometimes you have to make sacrifices to reach it."

He sighed. "Yes, Mother."

"And you need to tell that to Matt, too."

I became concerned and told Little Al to ask Matt over for Sunday dinner, so Al could talk to him about the importance of education. Unfortunately, he never accepted the invitation. Little Al and Matt continued their daily trek to school, despite snowstorms and freezing weather. Then one day, as if by some miracle, spring arrived and they both finished the school term with decent grades and in good spirits.

The second school year, however, was a different story. Winter came early with snow up to their backsides and temperatures crouched below zero. At least, Little Al had the woolen socks and knee-high boots his father had bought, but he said that Matt only had rubbers, so snow kept getting into his shoes. Despite the brutal weather, the boys persevered. Then one January afternoon, Little Al came home looking distraught.

"Whatever is the matter, dear?" I asked.

Dragging his feet, he trudged down the hall, dumped his book bag, and removed his boots. "Matt's dropped out!"

"Oh, no!"

"This morning he waited for me on the road and whined that it was too darn cold to walk to school and that he wasn't going anymore. Matt said that his father wants him to help out on the truck, delivering coal, and told him he was wasting his time in school because they'd never give him a good job even if he graduated. Then Matt grimaced and asked me, 'So what's the use of going, Al?' "

I shook my head. "What a shame."

"Momma, I tried to argue with him, but he wouldn't listen and ran off down the road without even saying goodbye."

Placing my hand on Little Al's shoulder, I steered him into the kitchen where a cup of hot milk was waiting. I felt bad for Matt. Without a high school diploma, he had no chance of getting the good job he had dreamed about. I felt sorry for Little Al, too. He had lost his buddy and that must have hurt. About a month later, he met Clarence Mitchell, a freshman at the school, and they became friends. Clarence was a diligent student, who loved music and played the piano brilliantly. In my opinion, he was a more suitable companion for my son than Matt ever was.

In April of that year, we received a telegram stating that Father had suddenly passed away. He had retired a few years earlier, sold his business, and was living off the proceeds. On Friday morning, Jennie and I packed up the children and took the train to our Brooklyn home. Although I was a grown woman, married with children, I still felt like Father's baby girl, and his passing nearly overwhelmed me. Jennie also seemed driven to despair, for she had never gotten over the death of her son, James. Thank goodness, neighbors, relatives, and church members stepped into the void and helped out. Al and Peter came down on Thursday evening and Father's funeral was held on Saturday morning. Al, Peter, Little Al, and Susie returned to Albany the next day, but the rest of us stayed on for two weeks. My children loved their grandpa and I knew they would miss him terribly.

My daughter, Susie, was growing into a lovely young lady. She was her father's delight and Little Al's enthusiastic cheerleader. She spent most of her spare time tidying the house and supervising her three younger siblings. Good-natured and intelligent, Susie seldom complained, except when her mischievous sisters, Tessie and Irene, rifled through her belongings.

One afternoon, Tessie scampered up to me, while I was in the kitchen. "Momma, Susie wants to be a school teacher and marry a handsome man. It says so right here in her diary."

Irene, her younger sister, was hiding behind her.

"Haven't I've told you to leave Susie's things alone?"

I slapped Tessie's hand and snatched the diary. The very next day I bought Susie a lockable journal, where she could record her heart's longings in secret. As for her wanting to be a teacher, I hoped we would have enough money to send her to teacher's college after she finishes high school.

The next few years passed quickly. The children and I were happy, my husband was content, and life was good. Then disaster struck.

# CHAPTER 61

## *Albert*

Little Al was in his first year of high school and was doing well, despite his complaints about the long trek to school.

*Today's kids are spoiled. When I was a boy, I had to walk everywhere, there was no trolley. I was lucky to hitch a ride on a horse-drawn wagon.*

One Sunday morning Little Al came into the kitchen while I was preparing a chicken stew for dinner.

"Can I help cut up the vegetables, Dad?"

"Why don't you make us some tea and toast? And while you're at it, slice a few pieces of cheese and baloney sausage."

After he prepared this simple meal–cooking was not his strong suit–Little Al and I sat down to eat, and he began to tell me about an incident that happened at school.

"Dad, I was on my way home on Friday, when an upperclassman ran up and said, 'Kid, how long you going to take to graduate?'

"I told him four years, like everybody else. He said, 'None of the colored kids finish in four years! They all get held back if they don't drop out.' "

"How'd you answer him?"

"I said I didn't know what he was talking about, but I'm going to finish in four years. He shouted, 'Oh yeah?' and I hollered back, 'Yeah, I want to go to college!' "

"You told him right, son."

"The guy smirked and said he never heard of no colored kids going to college. I said, 'Maybe you never heard of it, but I have.' "

I was proud of how Little Al handled that situation and glad I had told him about my war buddy, Teddy Wilson, who was a graduate of Fisk University.

"What do you think, Dad?"

"Pay no mind to that silly boy. There'll always be someone trying to hold you back and crush your dreams. You're going to finish high school on time and then go to college. I don't know how you're going to get there, but I want you to go."

"Yes, Dad."

*I'm saving as much as I can for my boy's schooling, but will it be enough?*

Near the end of that school year, Little Al said he wanted a summer job. So when I heard that New York State would be holding an exam for summer pages to fill in for vacationing employees, I encouraged him to take the test.

He bit his thumbnail. "I doubt they'll accept me. I'm just a freshman."

"If you really want the job, take the damn test!" I said.

I thought nothing else about the exam until one afternoon when I was sitting at my desk talking to Walter and Terry, two young newspaper reporters who covered the political scene in Albany. They sometimes tried to pump me for information about the governor, but I was tight-lipped. Usually, we just discussed interesting items in the news and they never got tired of hearing my stories about the Great War. That afternoon, we were discussing the fallout from Dr. Nicholas Butler's call for the repeal of Prohibition. A lot of temperance folks were furious with him.

"I'm with Butler," Walter said. "We need to end it."

"That's right," Terry added. "I enjoy having a drink now and then, but that doesn't make me a drunkard. Besides, it's causing violent crime to spiral out of control. Just look at the gang wars in Chicago."

Nodding in agreement, I glanced down the hall and saw Little Al skipping toward me.

"What are you doing here, son?"

He handed me a long white envelope. "Dad, this came in the mail while I was at school."

Tearing it open, I read the letter silently. "Congratulations, son. You passed the exam with flying colors!"

He broke into a grin. "Thanks, Dad."

"I'll hold on to this, for now," I said, placing it in my pocket. "See you at home."

That evening I made an announcement during dinner. "Son, I showed the letter to Mr. Mullins, the Assistant Deputy Controller, and he said he may have a summer job for you in the Capitol's mailroom. Go and see him after school tomorrow."

"A real job. Thanks, Dad."

Evie beamed. Susie clapped and said, "That's wonderful, Little Al."


Mr. Mullins hired Little Al and told him to report to Mr. Collins, the mailroom supervisor, on the Monday following July Fourth. When the big day arrived, I cooked him a good breakfast and gave him carfare and lunch money.

"I know I don't have to tell you not to mess up on this job. I vouched for you and I don't want to be embarrassed."

"Don't worry, Dad, I'll do my best."

"I know you will. It's just that a few of the boys we hired in previous summers didn't take the work seriously, causing a mess." To tell the truth, I was talking about white boys because I couldn't remember any colored boys who had ever become pages.

Several days later, Little Al and I had a leisurely chat as we rode the trolley home from work. "How's it going?"

"All right, Dad. At first, Mr. Collins complained I was too young, but I listened hard when he rattled off my duties and after I completed my assignments, he said I was okay."

"That's good."

"But Mr. Collins and his deputy, Mr. Simon, keep teasing me."

"How's that?"

"I've been getting to work early and when they find me waiting for them at the mailroom door, they always ask if I slept there. This morning Mr. Simon told Mr. Collins that I was trying to take Mr. Collins's job and Mr. Collins said, 'Fat chance!' "

I laughed. "Get used to it, boy! You're the new kid on the block, a colored kid at that."

"Okay Dad, but don't tell Mother or Susie about it."

Little Al worked hard in the mailroom that summer and I was proud when Mr. Mullins invited him to come back again the next year.

They say that the best-laid plans of mice and men often go awry. I don't know about the mice's schemes, but during Little Al's last year at Albany High School, and Susie's first year there, my plans for his higher education suddenly fell apart. What happened was this. One afternoon Little Al called me at work saying that Susie was ill and running a high fever. By then, I had installed a telephone at home. I instructed him to call the doctor immediately and told Miss Perrywinkle I was leaving. When I reached home, Little Al and the other children were gathered in the hall outside Susie's room with worried expressions etched on their faces. Susie was stretched out on her bed and Evie was sponging her down with a cold cloth. A few minutes later, the doctor arrived, and after examining her said she needed to be admitted to the hospital. He called ahead to make arrangements and Little Al rushed down the street to fetch a taxi. Evie and I escorted our daughter to the hospital, and once she was settled in the ward, left her there.

I was worried, but I had to be strong for Evie, who was nearly beside herself. During the past several years, she had lost her mother, father, and James. Now Susie was desperately ill. That evening, I went to sleep holding her in my arms, but when I awoke in the middle of the night, she was gone. Creeping into the parlor, I found her on her knees. She had fallen asleep, praying. After two and a half dreadful weeks in the hospital, my darling Susie was allowed to come home to recuperate, but the doctor said we had to be careful. Her lungs had been weakened by the illness. Evie and the children, especially Little Al, were delighted to have her back. I was too, but at the same time, I was troubled that her medical bills had nearly wiped out all my savings.

*My son will be graduating in June,* I thought. *But how will I get the money to help him through college?*

It was a chilly Sunday morning in April when I decided to have a talk with Little Al. Evie and the rest of the family were still asleep when I roused him and asked him to join me in the kitchen. I had prepared a pot of tea and warmed up the cinnamon-raisin scones Evie had baked the night before. He came in garbed in his woolen robe and slippers and plopped down at the table, stifling a yawn. Fighting back the anguish I felt about my financial situation, I told him how pleased I was that he'd be graduating on time, and with good grades.

Then I reminded him of my dream. "I want you to go to college. I don't know how you're going to get there and I can't send you because I've spent most of my savings on Susie's medical bills. But I want you to go."

"Dad, Mr. Mullins offered me a full-time job in the mailroom after I graduate. I was thinking of working there for a year to save for school."

"Okay, take a year in between, but don't get comfortable there. I want you to go to college. I never had the chance!"

He assured me he had no intention of getting stuck in the mailroom, working under Mr. Collins and Mr. Simon.

On graduation morning, Peter drove Evie, Susie, Little Al and me to the ceremony at Albany High School. I was so proud you would have thought that Little Al had climbed Mt. Everest and, in a way, he had. Jennie and Cousin Mattie stayed at the house to prepare a special lunch and watch the younger children. Little Al was one of a handful of colored students graduating that year, so we stood out among a sea of white faces. Even in this crowd of middle-class and well-dressed parents, Evie shone like a polished jewel and many heads turned as we strolled to our seats. After the ceremony, Little Al's teachers came over and shook our hands.

Later that evening when the festivities were done, our guests had departed, and the rest of the family had gone to bed, I lingered in my armchair and pondered: *This boy has done his part, but with little or no money, how in the world can I help him achieve his dream?*

## CHAPTER 62

# *Evie – 1929*

Little Al experienced his first delicious taste of freedom the summer after graduation: going about with friends, buying new clothes, dressing up, and taking lots of photos with the Brownie camera his father had given him. He was an intelligent, handsome (although somewhat short), refined young man with a decent job, and therefore quite popular with the young ladies at church.

Susie and I loved hearing about his escapades. It was as if I was young and carefree again. He and his friends went strolling around Arbor Hill, picnicking in the park, and canoeing on Lake Washington. If the weather was rainy, they might take in a talkie. *"Cocoanut"* featuring the zany Marx Brothers was one of his favorites. Often, they would drop by our home for tea and cake on Sunday afternoons, the young men sporting their smart Sunday suits, and the young ladies wearing starched dresses, straw hats, and white gloves. On those memorable occasions, Clarence Mitchell, Little Al's best friend, would entertain us by playing classical and popular tunes on our secondhand piano.

That delightful summer flew by quickly, and in the fall, Little Al enrolled in a night course at Magellan School of Accounting. When I asked why he was studying accounting, he replied, "When I finish these classes I can make extra money keeping the books for small businesses."

"That's fine, son, as long as it doesn't interfere with your college plans."

"It won't, Mother. I promise."

One Saturday afternoon in January, Little Al arrived home carrying two shopping bags. After unpacking one of them, he called me into the dining room to show off his purchases: a blue broadcloth shirt and a grey thin-striped pair of trousers.

"Thin stripes make you look taller," he said.

I sneaked a peek at the price tags. "They're very nice."

"They were on sale."

"But do you really need them? Are you saving enough for college?"

He frowned. "You're right, Mother. I should be putting more aside for college, but this is the first time I've had enough money to buy my own clothes. I want to look stylish, especially when I take out the young ladies."

"What's in that other bag, dear?"

"Oh, this?"

It was a handsome double-breasted brown wool coat, with broad shoulders and pointy wide lapels. After trying it on, he strutted up and down.

"How much was it?"

He showed me the receipt.

"Albert, this is too costly. You need to take it back."

His shoulders slumped.

"What will happen to your college plans if you haven't saved enough by August?"

"I can always work another year in the mail room."

I clutched at my heart. "Oh, my. You'll never get to college that way! What will your father say?"

"Mother, let me take care of Father!"

"Alright . . . But according to him, the economy is getting worse and they may not even have a job for you next year."

He winced. "I'll return the coat on Monday and try and save more."

"That's good."

After he gathered up his purchases and went to his room, I sat down at the dining table and thought: *My son is extravagant. And I can't blame him because I'm extravagant too. Lord knows I've always had an eye for fashion.*

But then, I worried: *Will he have enough money for college when this in-between year is over?*

# CHAPTER 63

## *Albert — 1930*

⤳⤳ ⤳⤳

In early April, I met Little Al after work and asked him to take a walk with me before going home for dinner. We strolled down Broadway following the trolley tracks.

"How's your accounting course progressing?"

"Very well, Dad. It's almost finished. The teacher said he would recommend me for a bookkeeping job if one becomes available."

"Have you given up on college?"

"Not at all, sir. I spent the last two Saturday afternoons at the library, searching through catalogs to see which schools have the best business and economics programs."

"Good. Do they offer any scholarships?"

"I haven't investigated that yet, sir."

"Well, you'd better get cracking. Time's flying and I'm sure they do these things well in advance."

"I will, Dad."

"And son, going out with friends is fine and dandy, but you need to get serious about your future. Times are hard in this country and the economy's in a mess. Governor Roosevelt seems quite concerned about it."

"Yes, Dad."

We caught the trolley the rest of the way home and arrived just in time for dinner.

Tossing and turning in bed that night, I thought: *How will this boy ever get to college? I can't take out another loan and I know he hasn't saved enough.*

Later that week, when I delivered a confidential message to the governor, he asked how my boy was doing, and I explained my predicament. He said he might be able to help and would make some inquiries. A week later, Miss Perrywinkle said that the governor wanted to see me so I rushed to his office.

After dinner that evening, I asked Little Al to come into the parlor. He seemed nervous as he entered and took a seat on the other side of the lamp table.

I leaned forward and smiled. "Son, have you ever heard of Dartmouth College?"

"Dartmouth College? Dartmouth is an exclusive white boy's school."

I nodded. "Last week I mentioned to Governor Roosevelt that you had excellent grades and wanted to attend college, but I didn't have the money to send you. He called me into his office today and said he had contacted a Dartmouth trustee, and that the trustee could probably get you a four-year working scholarship!"

Little Al's mouth fell open. "Governor Franklin D. Roosevelt?"

"Yes. I told the Governor to let me talk to you before he makes any arrangements."

Little Al gulped for air, while beads of perspiration broke out on his forehead. He removed his glasses and wiped his face. "Thanks, Dad, I'm very grateful for your help, but Dartmouth is way out of my league."

"What? It could be your ticket to college!"

"Gee, Dad, it would be bad enough being colored at Dartmouth, but being poor and colored, I just couldn't take that."

I struggled to hold my temper. *This will make me look like a damn fool.*

"Okay," I said, throwing him a look of disbelief. "I'll tell the Governor not to trouble himself any further." A heavy silence pervaded the room until I spoke again. "So what the devil are your plans, if I may ask?"

"Actually, Dad, I was thinking of attending New York University. It has the curriculum I want, and I already have a place to stay."

"Where's that?"

"Reverend Hodges has been transferred to a church in New York City. He said he has a room for me—a hall bedroom on 132nd Street, near 8th Avenue. I can rent it for five dollars a week."

I waited to hear the rest of it.

"See, Dad. I plan to attend night school and work during the day. I can also earn money keeping books for small businesses."

"Damn it, boy." I thumped the table and nearly toppled the lamp. "Don't you know that tons of people are out of work these days? And many small businesses are going under. Haven't you seen the bread lines? Your mother had to give a sack of potatoes to Mrs. MacHennessy because her husband's work hours were cut back."

"But Dad, President Hoover said that the high unemployment would only last another sixty days. By the time I get to New York, it should be over."

"Hoover's been spouting that malarkey since the stocks crashed in October, yet things keep getting worse, and he's doing nothing! We're in a depression. What kind of work do you expect to find?"

Little Al wrung his hands. "I don't know, but I've been praying to find a job down there."

Taking a deep breath, I tried to calm down. "Praying is well and good, but a realistic plan is much better. Isn't there any school in Albany that offers your program?"

"Nothing at night. Besides I'd like to get away from Albany."

I clenched my jaw, opened the newspaper, and pretended to read. *This boy's head is in the clouds. Just like his mother's*!

# CHAPTER 64

## *Evie*

Susie and I were putting away the dinner dishes when we were startled by a commotion in the parlor. A minute later, Little Al darted into the kitchen and plopped on a chair.

"Mother, I feel terrible. I've disappointed Dad."

"Would you like a cup of tea, dear?"

"Thanks. I'd love one."

Susie reached out and stroked his shoulders. "Don't worry. Things will work out for you."

I poured the tea and Susie left to get the children ready for bed.

"Mother, I want to attend NYU. I have a place to stay but don't have the money for tuition and living expenses."

I stirred four teaspoons of sugar into my tea and sipped it. He did the same and when he had finished, I lifted his cup and swirled the remains. When I saw the rainbow spreading across the leaves and heard soft music in my head, I knew a way would be made. I placed my hand on his. "My dear boy, what you have now are the pieces of a plan. Like a jigsaw puzzle, secure the pieces you know and the rest will fall into place. And I'll ask my guardian spirit to smooth the way."

Whenever I started talking about my guardian spirit, my husband's eyes glazed over. He said that it was just my imagination. Little Al sometimes appeared to think that way, too, but at that moment, he was looking for a lifeline to hold on to.

"Please, Mother, check with your guardian spirit, she might have some good ideas for me."

The next day, Little Al mailed his application to NYU, and a month later, he received an acceptance letter to their business program, which would begin in September. I was thrilled. As I predicted, the pieces were falling into place. He shared the good news with the family over dinner.

Susie beamed. "I'm so happy for you."

I glanced at my husband. "See dear, I told you he would go to college."

Al wrinkled his brow. "But how's he going to pay for it, Evie? We don't have the money!"

"Be patient, dear. It'll all fall into place."

"But will NYU be patient for the tuition? Will his landlord be patient for the rent? His stomach patient for food?"

Susie winced. I sighed, and Little Al looked upset that his joyful news had sparked a family quarrel.

Al rose and trudged across the dining room, his shoulders sagging. When he reached the door, he paused and turned. "Congratulations, son. I'd send you to that college if I could."

Little Al jumped up. "I know you would, Dad!"

I ran and took Al in my arms. "Darling, you've been a wonderful husband and father."

Later that night, as we lay in bed, I snuggled up to him and pecked him on the lips. "Honey, don't be upset. You've done all you could do for our son. You've worked yourself to the bone! Now it's up to him and the Lord."

He propped up his head on the pillow. "I just want him to get a good education and become a leader of our people. I never got the opportunity."

"I know that, dear."

He studied me for a moment and spoke again. "The other day, Deek Williams gave me a copy of *The Messenger*, a magazine he discovered in a

Harlem bookstore. It described the changes that have happened in Harlem since the Great War ended. Colored people have been reinventing themselves! And I'd like to think we veterans helped to spark that change."

I fondled his stubbly cheek. "We were very proud of you fighting men."

"Evie, there seems to be a new spirit of hope and race pride, a new self-confidence, and new demands for our rights. And colored writers, poets, artists, musicians, and leaders are expressing these ideas and have declared themselves–New Negroes! I want our son to be a part of that. And he can't do it without a college education."

"I completely agree, dear. But remember, it's his future. It has to be his dream. Give him a chance to work it out for himself."

"Okay, Evie. I suppose you're right." He wrapped me in his arms and caressed my face with his kisses. "Mrs. Johnson, have I ever told you how much I love you?"

"Yes, dear, but not often enough."

Little Al had been working full-time in the Capitol mailroom for a year when Mr. Mullins called him into his office. He related the encounter when he returned home from work that evening.

"Mr. Mullins asked me to work in the mailroom for another year. I said I planned to attend NYU in September."

"What did he say?" I asked.

"That Dad mentioned I might not be going to college. When I explained that everything was in place, but I needed a job in New York City, he said he would see if his friend, Mr. Tobias, had a position for me at the Port Authority. Mr. Mullins and his friend will be leaving for a hunting trip in the Adirondacks this Saturday. I'm to check back with him when he returns, the first Monday in August."

"Good heavens. I hope you thanked him."

"Now Mother, don't get excited. It's a long shot!"

"But didn't the tea leaves predict a good outcome?"

"Maybe. And please don't mention this to Dad."

From that day on, Little Al seemed tense and said he regretted not saving more for college. A week later, I was in the dining room stitching yellow and green pinafores for Tessie and Irene when he entered.

"Mother, if Mr. Mullins's friend doesn't offer me a job, I've come up with plan B."

I stopped sewing and looked up. "What in the world is that?"

"I'll take my meager savings and register for one class at NYU. If I don't find work, I'll return to Albany when the semester ends. At least, I would have tried."

Alarmed, I began imagining my son adrift in New York City with little or no money.

"Do you think that's wise, dear?"

"I'm placing myself in the hands of God. After all, he brought Father home from that terrible war."

"Well, that's true."

Once he had reached this decision, Little Al's mood brightened. He went about the house singing, "When You're Smiling," a song made popular by the famous Louie Armstrong. I enjoyed hearing him sing, even though he couldn't carry a tune, but I was a bundle of nerves about his crazy plan B and prayed that the Lord would make a better way.

Through all the uncertainty, I tried to cheer up my husband who seemed down in the dumps. Late one evening, I sat in the parlor reading a book of poetry and when I glanced up, I noticed that Al was staring at the ceiling.

"Can I get you a cup of tea and some sweet biscuits?"

He shook his head. "I guess Little Al won't be attending college this year. We only have a month left."

"Don't worry. Everything will work out fine."

"Do you know something you're not telling me?"

"It's just a feeling, dear."

"Humph! You and your second sight!" He picked up a magazine and thumbed through it. I retreated to the kitchen and consoled myself with a piece of Belgium chocolate. I didn't relish keeping secrets, but I didn't dare tell him about Little Al's plan B.

Little Al was in charge of the mailroom the three weeks that Mr. Mullins was away since Mr. Collins and Mr. Simon were also on vacation. When I asked how he was managing without them, he said that he streamlined the mail system and that everything was running like clockwork.

On the first Monday of August, I was in the garden watching the birds and listening to their songs while they splashed in the water bath. It was late afternoon and I was garbed in a pretty sea-green frock, waiting for my husband's return. Even after twenty-one years of marriage, he was still my Prince Charming.

Suddenly, I heard a voice calling from the back porch.

"Mother."

"I'm here beneath the tree."

Little Al ran down the stairs, greeting me as he approached. "You look lovely in that color."

"Thank you. Did you see Mr. Mullins today?"

"He called me into his office this morning and complimented my handling of the mailroom but didn't mention anything about Mr. Tobias or a job."

"Oh, dear. Do you think he forgot?"

Little Al shrugged and slumped down beside me on the bench. "Don't worry, Mother. I still have plan B."

"Son, go and ask Mr. Mullins about the position."

"I don't feel comfortable doing that."

"Do you want your father to speak to him?"

He jumped up. "Keep Dad out of it!"

Startled by his sharp tone, my shoulders stiffened.

"Sorry, Mother."

"It's alright, dear."

He took my arm and we ascended the back stairs and entered the kitchen. "So you're still determined to go to New York City?"

"Yes, Mother."

I took a deep breath. "Wait here. I'll be back."

A few minutes later, I returned holding a small envelope wrapped in white lace and tied with a violet ribbon. He was at the kitchen table, impatiently drumming his fingers.

I handed him the envelope. "Here's thirty-three dollars. Don't open it until you reach New York."

"I can't take this. It's your rainy-day money."

"Hush, it'll be your umbrella. It rains in New York, too."

He quickly slipped the envelope into his pocket. "Thank you, Mother, for believing in me."

Just then I heard Al coming in from work and whispered, "Don't say a thing about the rainy-day money."

A few days passed. Little Al had already reserved his hall bedroom at Reverend Hodges's apartment and had notified NYU that he would enroll. He had even started walking to work to save on carfare and had gone to Union Station to purchase a ticket to New York. On Friday, I was in the kitchen inspecting the tasty supper Susie had prepared, when he entered.

"You'll never guess what happened today, Mother."

"Just tell me."

"When I reminded Mr. Mullins I'd be resigning in three weeks, he said, 'Al, I've been so busy since I came back, I forgot to tell you that Mr. Tobias has a job for you in New York City. Regrettably, it only pays nine hundred bucks a year.'

"I told Mr. Mullins I'd take the job."

Uttering a silent prayer of gratitude, I hugged my son.

"There's more, Mother; you'd better have a seat."

*What else could there be?*

"After I agreed to take the job, Mr. Mullins said if I stayed in Albany, he'd put me in charge of the mailroom when Mr. Collins retires in October. Just imagine, he offered to make me Head of the Department! That's a big job for a colored man–and at eighteen hundred bucks a year."

I gasped and nearly tumbled from the chair. "Dear, you must tell your father the good news this evening. He's been worried sick about you."

"I'll tell him as soon as I decide. I know what Dad would choose, but this is my life and I need to make up my own mind."

# CHAPTER 65

## *Albert*

$\sim\!\!9\,c\!\!\sim$

A week after Mr. Mullins returned from vacation I stopped by his office to say hello. We had been friends even before Little Al began working in the mailroom.

He immediately rose from his desk and shook my hand. "Sergeant Al, how's it going?"

"Pretty well, sir. How was your hunting trip? Did you snag any bears?"

"Not hardly, but we did get a deer. I let my hunting partner, Mr. Tobias, keep the antlers and we divided up the venison. It was good to be away from the office and–to tell the truth–from my wife."

We both laughed.

"Al, you've got a fine boy there–smart as a whip and very efficient. He kept the mailroom in tiptop shape while I was away. Did he tell you I offered him the Head position when Mr. Collins leaves in the fall?"

I was stunned. Little Al hadn't said a word. "But what about Mr. Simon?"

"He'll keep his job as deputy, but we need some fresh blood leading that department. Anyway, my hunting partner has also offered Al . . ."

"Sorry to cut you off Mr. Mullins, but I have to hurry back to the governor's office. See you later."

"Okay, Sergeant Al."

I was upset and had to get out of there fast. I hope Mr. Mullins's offer doesn't scuttle Little Al's college plans. My first impulse was to confront my son, but then I remembered Evie's words, "It's his dream and his future, not yours," so I carried on as if nothing had happened.

The next evening, Little Al came into the parlor while I was reading. "Can I talk to you, Dad?"

"Sure." I folded the newspaper and placed it on the table. Then he told me what I already knew but added that Mr. Mullins's friend, Mr. Tobias, had offered him a job in New York City. I was flabbergasted.

"I didn't tell you about it before because I needed to make up my own mind."

"And have you?"

"Yes, Dad."

"Good." *This boy's becoming a man*, I thought.

On the Saturday preceding Labor Day, the whole family accompanied Little Al, looking smart in a brown traveling suit, to Union Station where he would catch the train for New York City. Susie was wearing a two-piece lilac outfit with shiny glass buttons, looking nearly as lovely as her mother who was attired in a robin-blue dress and shawl. Tessie and Irene were dressed in green and yellow flowered pinafores, and Phillip was sporting his favorite outfit—a dark blue sailor suit with a white cap. I gazed at my beautiful family as we stood on the platform, crowded with the holiday travelers.

*I'm a very lucky man*, I thought.

I placed my arm around Little Al's shoulder and pressed fifty hard-earned dollars in his hand. With this and his small savings, plus whatever money Evie had slipped to him, he should have more than enough to pay for his courses at NYU, buy books and meals, and pay the rent, until he collected his first salary from the Port Authority.

The train rolled in and it was time to say good-bye. Susie, my sweet rosebud, looked sad. Tessie, my rough and tumble daughter, appeared worried.

Irene, the family prima donna, was crying her eyes out. And Philip, our youngest, was scrunching up his face.

Little Al kissed his sisters' cheeks and playfully threw Philip up in the air. "Be a good boy now."

Philip snickered. "I'll have our room all to myself."

I shook Little Al's hand and told him once again how proud I was. This had been my dream even when I was deep in the muck and mire of the Great War. Dabbing her tear-filled eyes with a lace handkerchief, Evie advised him to eat properly and to stay away from fast women. She gave him a big hug and handed him a basket full of goodies, including her spice cupcakes and my fried chicken. Just then, Deek Williams showed up.

"Hey Deek, are you working today?" I asked.

"Naw. Finally got a day off. Just popped by to say so long to this fine young man of yours."

After greeting Evie, he shook hands with Little Al. "I hear you'll be staying in Harlem."

"On 132nd Street, sir."

"You'll like it there. Harlem swings."

Deek turned toward me. "Don't it, Al?"

"Absolutely!"

Evie gave me an anxious glance.

"Yeah," Deek added, "Harlem's something else!"

The train whistle blew. Little Al boarded and found a window seat. And we waved goodbye until the train pulled out of the station.

# CHAPTER 66

## *Albert*

❧⨀☙

I stood on the platform next to my beautiful wife watching the train carry off our son to college. I was so happy that my heart was about to burst. Evie was overcome with **anxiety,** and tears flowed down her cheeks, streaking her rouge.

"I'm sorry Father isn't here to witness this great day," she said.

I nodded. "This reminds me of the time I left Lexington, Virginia, traveled to Norfolk, and signed up on a merchant ship, destination unknown. I was seventeen, full of adventure, and a little scared, but determined to seek my fortune."

"Did you find it, dear?"

"Oh, yes. I found you, didn't I?"

She blushed and squeezed my hand. "Do you think he'll be alright down there in Harlem?"

"Sure he will. After all, Harlem's not another country. Besides, he's in touch with the folks at Bethel AME Church and I've given him Lyle Thomas's address as well."

We watched the retreating train until it was out of sight.

"Daddy, must we stand here all day?" Tessie asked. "I'm tired."

"Let's go," I said, taking a last glance down the deserted track. With the children in tow, Evie and I strolled arm in arm to the trolley that would carry us home to 66 Lark Street.

---

*Life's funny. Sometimes we think we know it all, but we really don't—like the time I told Little Al that planning is much better than prayer. I've come to realize that it wasn't just his hard work and strategies that got us to this point, although that was part of it. It wasn't just my connections, either. I must admit it—it was the Lord's doing, the Lord's plan! And He sure worked it well.*

# EPILOGUE

∽☯☯∽

**C**oal, War & Love is a work of fiction based on the true-life experiences of my grandparents, Sergeant Albert Sidney Johnson, Sr. and his wife Evelyn Ashton Johnson (Evie). Research for this book included personal family records and first-person interviews, as well as primary and secondary sources (historical documentation, published books, and periodicals). Some of the most informative sources were:

Harris, Stephen L. *Harlem's Hell Fighters: The African-American 369th Infantry in World War I.* Brassey's, 2003.

Little, Arthur W. *From Harlem to the Rhine: The Story of New York's Colored Volunteers.* Covici-Friede, 1936.

Nelson, Peter N. *A More Unbending Battle: The Harlem Hellfighter's Struggle for Freedom in WWI and Equality at Home.* Basic Civitas, 2009.

*Historical Note*: My father Albert Sidney Johnson, Jr. (Little Al) relocated from Albany, New York to Harlem and attended New York University, graduating in 1936 with a Bachelor of Commercial Science degree. From 1930 to 1967 he was employed by the Port Authority of New York and New Jersey, rising through the ranks to the position of Economic Analyst. Over the years, he was also an instructor at the Combination Business School and Braithwaite Business School, serving as a mentor to many Harlem students. In 1932 Albert married his sweetheart, Joella Alston (my mother), starting a family that would grow to include three daughters (Rudean, Mary Evelyn, and Laura).

The following photo essay documents the lives of my grandparents, Albert and Evelyn Johnson, and their family.

Evelyn Ashton Johnson, 66 N. Lark Street, Albany, New York, early 1930s

Albert Sidney Johnson, Sr., Miami, Florida, mid-1930s

Governor Franklin D. Roosevelt with office staff, Albany, New York,
early 1930s. Albert Sidney Johnson, Sr., back row, 3rd from left

Albert Sidney Johnson, Sr. and wife Evelyn Ashton
Johnson, Albany, New York, late 1930s

Albert Sidney Johnson, Jr. and wife Joella Alston Johnson, Wedding Day, James Vanderzee Studio, Harlem, New York, June 1932

Albert Sidney Johnson, Jr., Graduation, New York
University, New York City, May 1936

# ACKNOWLEDGMENTS

I would like to thank my son, filmmaker Thomas Allen Harris, who conceived the idea of recording family history through the eyes of my father Albert S. Johnson, Jr., and invited me to conduct the interview that inspired this book.

Many thanks to my father Albert S. Johnson, Jr., my mother Joella Johnson, uncle Philip Johnson, cousin Harold Epps, and sister Mary Evelyn Johnson, who shared their memories of my grandparents and their times.

I would also like to thank:

Sandra Black, who edited the manuscript, offered invaluable recommendations and helped to bring this book to life in many ways.

Thomas Allen Harris and Lyle Ashton Harris (my sons), for their enthusiasm, assistance, and soul-searching questions that helped to shape this book.

Laura Johnson (my sister), who critiqued several versions of the manuscript and provided continuous support and encouragement.

Ayo Reed, Henrietta Ukwu, and Luca Chibungu (my other beta readers), who offered insightful suggestions.

Tommy Gear, for his constructive counsel, support and meticulous proofreading.

The Frederick Douglass Writers Group: Grace Edwards (leader), Roberta Frazier, and Luca Chibungu, who provided many years of encouragement and good advice.

And for their various contributions: Martha Mae Jones, Joanne Robinson, family members, and friends.

# ABOUT THE AUTHOR

**B**orn and raised in New York City, Rudean Leinaeng grew up hearing family stories about her grandparents, Sergeant Albert S. Johnson, Sr. and his wife Evelyn. This book is based on their early lives together before, during, and shortly following "The Great War."

Rudean received her BA from Hunter College and an MS from New York University and was a Professor of Chemistry at Bronx Community College. During the 1970s, she and her two young sons, Thomas and Lyle, lived in Dar es Salaam, Tanzania for two years. After participating in the struggle for women's rights and racial equality as well as the anti-apartheid struggle, Rudean and her husband Pule Leinaeng, an African National Congress activist, took up residence in Bloemfontein, South Africa.

In 2002 she co-produced the acclaimed documentary film, *Twelve Disciples of Nelson Mandela*, directed by her son, award-winning filmmaker Thomas Allen Harris. She was inducted into the Hunter College Hall of Fame for her activism and leadership in 2012.

*Coal, War & Love* is Rudean's first novel.

An Invitation from Rudean:

Dear Reader,

Thanks for reading my novel. If you have a comment or question about it, I'd love to hear from you. You can get in touch with me by liking my Facebook page (Rudean Leinaeng-Author) or visiting my website at <u>www.tulipbudpress.com</u>